This book contains scenes of graphic violence, sexual abuse, physical abuse, kidnapping, homosexual relations, sexually explicit scenes, shifting, mutilation, fighting, and death.

If you are sensitive to these subjects, please consider your personal mental health before continuing.

Part 2

A Time
of
Delicate Hope

Written by Kristy Pearson

For the fighters. For the ones who never give up.

For the ladies that have been through hell, the ladies that claw and climb and fight their way out, only to come back stronger and tougher for it.

Chapter One

Lunaya

The sound of a wailing child filled the air around me, piercing the inner most corners of my ears. I couldn't move, it was like my body was concreted to the ground. Everything hurt. The intense pain burned through my veins, paralysing me. I lay helpless on the ground, dying slowly. My eyes gazing, unblinking, at the retreating legs before me. I watched on powerlessly, until they were gone from my sight, vanishing between the snow-covered trees. Helplessness consumed me and I couldn't fight it any longer. The faint cries slipped away, until only the sound of the wind was left. My heavy eyelids slowly blinked closed, and the darkness fell over me.

~

I flew upright, panting heavily, I clutched my chest and looked around the dark space. My eyes slowly adjusted, and the realisation gradually came back to me, it was just a dream. My tired eyes scanned around the dimly lit cave, the fire just barely alive with a few slow burning embers. Alyse was still asleep in her sleeping bag, curled up into a ball, close to the fire. The entrance of the cave was dark with only the pale glow of the moon light shining on the ground. I begrudgingly got up out of my sleeping bag and traipsed over to the opening of the cave. I looked out over the trees in front of me, scanning for any signs of life or danger. The ground was splattered with patches of white snow. We will need to find proper shelter soon or we will freeze to death in this cave. I shivered as an icy wind brushed against my cheeks, the weather is turning fast. I tiptoed back to the fire and placed two more logs over the embers. Stoking the fire with a stick, the flames started to engulf the new wood, and my cold skin eagerly welcomed the heat.

I lay back down, tucking myself into my worn-out sleeping bag and rested my head on my arm. I stared blankly at the flames licking at the logs, as my mind begun to replay the dream again. Red stained snow covered the ground, littered with the bodies of my pack. The air was filled with the stench of blood and gun powder. The dying howl of my Alpha ripped into my already aching heart. Dead, all of them. My entire pack, slaughtered. And it was all my fault. A tear escaped my eye, and I winced as I could once again feel the pain that day had brought me. There was only one thing that the Goddess entrusted me with, and I failed the task. I failed her, I failed myself. Above all, I failed that sweet little girl. I wanted so much to die along with my pack, it was the least that I deserved. I would have gotten my wish if it weren't for Alyse. Ahh, Alyse, my only companion. We've been together now for near on seventeen years. I still don't know if she saved me from death, or, subjected me to a lifetime of guilt and suffering at the hands of the never-ending replay of my torturous memories. Either way, I am still thankful to have her. She found my broken and bloodied body in the aftermath of the massacre and for some reason took pity on me, nursing me back to health. She says that if it weren't for the snow slowing my heart, I would have bled to death before she found me. I still don't know what compelled her to save my life, she may never tell me. I felt my body start to drift back off to sleep and I prayed to the Goddess to spare me the pain from my nightmares.

"Lunaya, wake up".

I felt my body being rocked back and forth, shaking me awake.

"Come on, you need to get up now".

I forced opened my eyes and found Alyse's green eyes looking down at me. Her chocolate brown hair was tied in a messy bun on top of her head. Her skin was spotted with dirt and grime, and she had a smudge of ash from the fire across her cheek. Living the way we do, we go for long periods of time without luxuries like showers and mirrors. We have become accustomed to it over the years and have learned ways to live on the bare necessities.

I grumbled and pushed her hands off me, sitting up and rubbing my tired eyes.

"You couldn't give me five more minutes?" I moaned.

"The sun has already been up for a while, you never sleep this late" she snapped back, she paused and looked over my face.

"Are you okay?" she asked her voice softening slightly.

"Yeah, just another sleepless night" I said stretching my arms out above my head.

"More nightmares?"

"Yep"

"The same one?"

"As always"

"Hmm" she hummed as she watched me crawl out of my sleeping bag and begin to roll it up.

"They've been coming more and more often these past few months" she said softly.

"Yeah, I know"

"Is there something bothering you?"

"Nothing new, come on we have to get moving" I said brushing of her question, I don't want to talk about it. Simple as that. Alyse already covered up the fire and had her small, tattered backpack packed and ready to go. She turned her head over her shoulder slowly and huffed heavily.

"We don't have to leave just yet you know, we still have a few more days until the snow settles" she said sheepishly, looking over at me. I groaned internally. we have already had this argument a bunch of times. I puffed out a frustrated breath,

"I've already told you, I don't want to wait until the snow sticks. We have to find the Luna Eclipse pack before we freeze to death" I grumbled.

"Ugh whatever, how do you even know they're out here" she groaned standing up and flinging her bag over her shoulder. It's true, I have only ever heard stories of Luna Eclipse, the only all-female pack in the entire world. But the legends have been told for generations. The stories of their triumphs over their enemies and their great battles and victories, they are known worldwide. Because of their female only law, they were seen as weak by many other packs. But those of them that tried to attack Luna Eclipse were wiped out. They may be all she-wolves, but they are highly skilled and trained warriors and could stand up against any male warrior. Throughout the centuries the stories of Luna Eclipse became just that, stories. Many forgot about them and they began to believe them to be nothing more than a myth, A tale of wraith like warrior women that move silently through the world, just a scary story to tell your pups at night. But I knew better, as did my ancestors.

"Will you just trust me. Have I ever led you astray?" I huffed, placing my hands on my hips and glaring at her with a raised eyebrow.

"Weeellll..." she dragged out the word with a teasing tone. I threw my rolled up sleeping bag at her head and she caught it with a giggle.

"I trust you" she chuckled, tossing it back to me.

~

The weather turned in a blink of an eye, catching us unprepared in the middle of a snowstorm. We definitely picked a bad time of year to go hiking in the Southern Alps of New Zealand. It's the middle of winter here and this part of the mountain takes a beating. I knew we wouldn't cross paths with anybody, the tourist trails don't go up this mountain. And besides, the storm would cover over any of our tracks anyway.

We huddled together and continued to stomp through the freezing snow. The storm has been raging for maybe an hour now, the snow was already knee deep and getting deeper the further we went up the mountain. My boots were soaked through, and I could feel the icy moisture in my socks. I hope we find them soon or else my toes may fall off. The wind howled past my ears, biting at my cheeks. The sound of Alyse's teeth chattering together was almost louder than the wind.

"How f-f-far did you s-s-say" she stuttered,

"It should be here" I told her, squinting into the distance. I looked around at the trees poking out of the snow, searching for the marker. I forced my eyes to open in the cutting wind and tried hard to focus. I followed the old directions perfectly.

We are near the top of the mountain, on the southern side. It has to be here. I zoned in on a peculiarly shaped tree ahead of us. After a few quick blinks, I could see clearer. That's not a tree. That's it, the stone marker, we've made it.

"There it..." I was cut off by the unmistakable sound a wolfs howl. I turned towards the sound but couldn't see the source through the blizzard. Another howl came from behind us and then another and another, until we were surrounded. I saw movement come from behind the large stone, capturing my attention, a white wolf slowly came into view as it stalked towards us. The wolf bared its teeth and growled, closing the distance between us. The wolf stood tall and proud before us, the power emanating off it was dizzying. The wolf snarled and barked loudly, Alyse and I bowed our heads in respect.

"We mean you no harm, we only ask for shelter from the storm" I called to the wolf. It was silent for a moment, but I didn't dare raise my head to look into its eyes. It finally huffed and growled and Alyse and I stood up again. The wolf glared down on us before tossing its head and growling again. More wolves begun to appear all around us. The white wolf turned and walked back the way it came. A nudge from behind me indicated we were meant to follow. Keeping Alyse under my arm, we held each other tight and stomped through the snow behind the white wolf.

After what felt like hours, which was probably only fifteen minutes, dark structures came into view. We followed the wolf into the largest structure that sat in the middle of the others. Warmth immediately embraced my frozen cheeks as we stepped through the door. I spotted a large fire pit in the middle of the circular building and started for it, pausing to eye the white wolf. It nodded its head and I dragged Alyse to the edge of the fire. We both groaned holding our hands out towards the flames, slowly turning like rotisserie chickens to feel the heat all over our freezing bodies.

I glanced quickly around the room as I turned. It looks like a main hall or something. There are a few long picnic-like tables and benches and a raised platform. On the platform is a large throne, maybe, or just the Alpha's chair. I'm not sure, but it's a huge chair carved out of white stone with furs draped over it. Eight giant wooden columns ran up to the roof, holding it up. There were three more smaller fires in the room as well. We were surrounded by roughly thirty other wolves and women, all eyeing us closely and some brandishing weapons.

The snapping of bones alerted me that the wolves surrounding us were changing form. I turned around with my back to the fire to see a tall and muscular dark haired woman, wrapped in furs. Her black hair was in long dreadlocks tied up at the back of her head. She had red tribal paint on her right cheek and over her eyes. On her bottom lip, chin, and forehead are beautiful tribal tattoos, making her look all the more intimidating.

"Why have you come" she demanded. Her voice dripping with authority.

"Alpha" I said bowing my head, Alyse mimicked my movements beside me.

"We have come seeking shelter. I am Lunaya, formerly of the Moon Light pack" I said, still in my bowed position. The woman in front of me growled and huffed.

"Lies" she snapped,

"Moon Light was wiped out years ago".

"You're right, I am the last one. I was gravely wounded in the assault on my pack and barely survived. My companion, Alyse, saved my life" I informed her as I stood up straight, pulling Alyse up with me.

"Why do you travel with this human?" she hissed, sniffing at Alyse's scent. I paused looking quickly at Alyse before I continued. I swallowed and looked back at the Alpha,

"She is not human, but a half-breed" I said cautiously. The women around us all growled at the news. I wrapped my arm around Alyse and held my other hand out to stop their approach.

"Please, she's not dangerous. She has no wolf and can't change form" I rushed out.

"Explain" the Alpha demanded of Alyse. She held up her hand and the others halted.

"My mother was a Were, my father human. They were both killed by my mother's pack when they found out about me. An elder woman, a healer, took pity on me. She stole me away and gave me to a human family to raise me. Though I didn't change form, and I don't have a wolf. At the age of sixteen my body did change. I became stronger, faster and my senses were heightened. The family that raised me threw me out and I lived alone on the streets, until I found Lunaya three years later. I stumbled upon her slaughtered pack while roaming for a new place to stay" Alyse gripped my hand as she spoke, and I gazed at her adoringly. She has become so strong and confident over the years, and I couldn't be prouder.

The Alpha stalked towards us slowly and then circled around us in calculated steps.

"A half-breed with no wolf" she muttered as she traced her finger slowly over Alyse's cheek. I bit back the growl on my lips, knowing that if I show any aggression, we'd be toast. The Alpha's eyes flicked to me quickly and she dropped her hand, taking in my strained expression.

"You are mated" she said firmly, not asking but stating the fact.

"We are" I confirmed, squeezing Alyse's hand.

"You are Omega wolves?"

"Yes"

"Interesting" she hummed quietly. She stopped and stared at us for a moment, raking her eyes over both our bodies. Her blank face was unwavering, giving no indication to her thoughts or feelings towards us. She eventually took a deep breath and turned away from us.

"You may stay until the storm breaks, we will meet and re-evaluate your positions here again then" she called, waving her hand over her shoulder. All the other women backed away and two younger looking women stepped forward, handing us dry clothes and blankets.

"This way" one of them spoke softly. She was young, just a teenager, but very beautiful. The other was just as young and just as gorgeous. They must be related. They led us out of the large round structure and scurried through the snow to a small hut directly opposite. We hurried behind them and into the smaller building. There were two single beds, a small round table with two chairs and a big fireplace that was already alight. The floor was covered in a woven mat and the walls were covered in furs. Very rustic and yet cosy and warm.

"You will sleep here, if you leave the hut before dawn you will be killed" the first girl spoke.

"I am Maya, this is my sister Trinny. One of us will be by in the morning to take you to breakfast. You are not invited guests and not yet trusted, so don't get too comfortable. Until stated otherwise by the Alpha, you are to be escorted at all times" she paused switching her gaze from me to Alyse and back again.

"Understood?" she demanded.

"Yes, of course" I answered quickly.

"Good, there are fresh towels to bathe and extra blankets" she said pointing behind me.

"Okay, thank you".

Maya nodded her head and ushered her sister out the door.

"The bathroom?" I called after her, but she didn't respond.

Once the door slammed close behind Maya and Trinny, I looked at Alyse and she let out a long, slow breath. I smiled and crouched down in front of the fire and held out my hands. There's a stack of logs next to it, so we'll be good till morning. Alyse dropped her bag and plopped down on one of the beds. I stood again and turned in a slow circle, examining the hut. On the shelf above the fireplace is a large bowl and what looks like two water jugs. At the end of each bed was a small wooden chest, that must be where the towels and blankets are. By the door is an empty bucket, why would we need a bucket? Ooooh, I get it. I let out a small chuckle as I sat down on the bed opposite Alyse. She looked at me and tilted her head. I smiled and shook my head at her. She'll figure it out eventually.

"Come on, let's get out of these cold wet clothes". I stood up and held my hand out for her. I pulled her up and left her to undress. Unzipping my jacket, I pulled it off and hung it over the back of one of the chairs and continued with the rest of my clothes. Alyse took off her boots and socks and hung her jacket on the other chair. I checked the jugs on the shelf, and they were filled with water. The large bowl had a handle and hook attached to it. I looked back at the fireplace and there are hooks to hang the bowl above the flames. Excellent, hot water. I filled the bowl and placed it in the fireplace to heat up. I turned to Alyse, and she had one of the blankets wrapped around her body as she watched me. I checked the chests at the end of the bed and indeed found the towels and blankets.

After a few minutes I wrapped a towel around my hand and pulled the hot bowl from the fire and placed it at Alyse's feet. I dipped in the towel to soak it and begun to gently wipe the dirt from Alyse's legs. I slowly moved my way to her arms, chest and neck. Her eyes bore into the top of my head as I washed her down, not once did she pull away or refuse me. I got to her face and rinsed the clothe again before continuing. I wiped the warm water over her cheek and forehead. As the dirt disappeared, her smooth pale skin started to show through. Small wrinkles were forming at the corners of her eyes, but other than that, she looked exactly the same as the day she found me.

"You didn't have to do that" she mumbled quietly.

"I wanted to, I like taking care of you".

I picked up the pile of clothes and spread them out on the bed. I handed Alyse a pair of sweatpants, a singlet top, a sweater like top and a big fluffy jumper, and a pair of socks.

"Put these on before you get too cold" I said as I placed them in her lap. I quickly washed myself down before pulling on a pair of cotton pants, a t-shirt and a zip up jacket.

Once we were washed and changed the cold didn't feel so intense anymore. I looked at the two single beds and then glanced at Alyse. This is the first time in a long time that we will be sleeping in an actual bed. I want to lay with her and hold her close, but I also want to let her get a good night's sleep.

"What's on your mind?" Alyse asked as she stood in front of me putting her hands on my hips.

"I was thinking about moving the beds together so that I can hold you while you sleep" I brushed a strand of hair from her face and tucked it behind her ear.

"I would love that" she smiled reaching up to offer my lips a soft kiss.

"You sure you don't just want to sleep comfortably tonight?"

"I am always comfortable with you Nae. And besides, it's been so long since we have shared a bed" she smiled sweetly at me and my heart fluttered.

I stared into her piercing green eyes and cupped her cheeks. What could I have possibly done to deserve this beauty? I gently kissed her waiting lips and pressed my forehead against hers. All these years together and I am still head over heels for this woman.

"I love you" I whispered softly. Alyse snaked her arms around my back and pulled herself into me tighter, resting her head in the crook of my neck.

"And I you" she said into my skin. After a minute of embracing each other, I heard her yawn, the sound drawing a yawn from me as well.

"Let's go to bed" I said, placing a kiss on her forehead.

I let her go and stepped between the two beds. Grabbing the wooden frame of the bed, I dragged it across the mat and pushed it up next to the other one. I fanned the two blankets out over the now joined beds and gestured for Alyse to hop in. She crawled in and pulled the blanket up to her chin. I decided to place another log on the fire, save me from having to wake up in a few hours to do it then. I then slid into the bed beside Alyse and pulled her into my body. She immediately wrapped her arms and legs around me and our bodies entwined like two slow climbing vines. Her soft warm cheek pressed against mine, gave me an instant feeling of calmness and safety. Within minutes Alyse's soft slow breathing told me she was asleep.

I hope the storm breaks soon. Alyse may be strong and fast, but she doesn't handle the cold quite like a full Were can. I can't bear to see her sick again, I thought she was going to die the last time. But then again, the longer the storm holds on, the longer we can stay here for. I just hope the Alpha can see enough reason to let us stay, or at least let us continue on with our lives. Alyse being a half-breed has always been a dangerous thing to announce, but this is our last chance at a pack, and it had to be told. I feel somewhat good about our chances. Something about this Alpha and the way that she studied us, it gave me a little hope.

I breathed out deeply, an issue for tomorrow, I guess. I closed my eyes and in no time, I slipped off into my own slumber.

Lunaya

A soft knock on the door quickly drew me from my sleep. I lurched off the bed and took a defensive stance facing the door. Another knock, harder this time, then followed by a voice,

"Are you awake? It's Maya". She banged on the door again, her knocks getting harder and louder.

"Yes, we're awake" I answered quickly. I leaned down and shook Alyse to wake her up.

"Breakfast is being served, you must come now" her voice called through the door.

"We won't be a moment" I called back. I sat on the edge of the bed and pulled my boots on, the heat of the fire had basically dried them out. Alyse sat up next to me and pulled her boots on quickly too. I stood up and grabbed her jacket, holding it out to help her put it on. I then pulled my own jacket on and turned to look at Alyse. She nodded at me and I opened the door. Maya stood by the door with a sour look on her face.

"I better not have missed out on the hash browns" she grumbled looking over us. She stomped off towards the large hut and we followed closely behind.

It was still snowing but the wind had all but gone now. This could be bad, especially if the Alpha deems the weather now calm enough to send us back out in it. Thick layers of snow clung to the roof of the large hut and all the huts surrounding it. I took in as much of the little village that I could before we walked through the door. It was quiet outside, no people. They must all be inside out of the snow. Smaller huts, similar to the one Alyse and I are in, are littered around the area. I counted only fourteen, but I can't see the whole area, so I assume there's more. The large main hut stood in the middle of everything.

As we entered the building, I was taken aback by the number of women inside. There must have been roughly two hundred, maybe a little less. They were all seated on the long tables eating their food and chatting. All eyes turned to us as they noticed our arrival and an eerie quiet consumed the hall. Some looked curious, others just straight up murderous. I reached for Alyse's hand and pulled her closer to me. We came to a stop at the far back wall of the hut and the women all slowly returned to their plates and conversations.

"Here" Maya snapped, pushing a plate into my stomach. I passed it to Alyse and took the next one she held out. She walked to a long table set up like a buffet. Large bowls and trays lined the table, most of which were almost empty now. I piled some scrambled eggs on my plate and put some on Alyse's too. I took a strip of ham and a cooked tomato and again gave the same to Alyse. I looked down at the end of the table and saw Maya with a hash brown hanging out of her mouth and three more on her plate. I smirked a little, managing to hold in the giggle.

"They're good, ay?" I asked her, she looked at me and a slight flush covered her cheeks. She swallowed and smiled awkwardly,

"Uh yeah, they're my favourite" she mumbled before walking away.

I looked out over the hall and eyed a small space at the end of one of the tables. I headed over to it with Alyse behind me. As I went to sit down, a black-haired woman lifted her lip and growled. I paused for a second, gaging her mood. I sniffed at her subtlety, she's anxious and maybe a little fearful.

"Can we sit here?" I asked softly. She lifted her head slightly and looked at me out of the corner of her eye. She nodded her head and then turned her body away from us. I nodded to

Alyse to sit and she did. We enthusiastically ate our food. It's been so long since we had a meal like this. Our food is usually foraged and cooked over an open fire, if not eaten raw. This is definitely a welcome change.

"Excuse me" a firm and husky voice pulled us from the last of our breakfast. I spun around and looked up at the woman. She had smooth caramel skin with dark eyes and short dark hair. Like the Alpha, she too had a tribal tattoo on her chin. Only this woman was twice the size, huge. For a she-wolf, she is massive, and it was almost all muscle.

"Alpha wishes for you to join her" the woman told us, not asking but telling us.

I nodded my head at the woman and quickly turned back to my plate to shove the last few bites into my mouth in one go. Alyse and I both stood up and followed the woman to the other side of the room. The Alpha sat at a table with a group of other strong, warrior looking women. Her eyes flicked to mine as we approached and she nodded her head to the women opposite her, they swiftly stood up and left the table.

"Sit, please" she said with a smile and gesturing to the now empty seats. Alyse slid along the bench seat and I followed, pressing my leg up against hers. I gave her thigh a quick squeeze before putting my hands on the table clasped together and focusing my attention on the Alpha.

"So" she spoke turning her eyes from me to Alyse and back to me again.

"How was your first night in the village?" She kept her eyes firmly on mine now.

"It was very comfortable, thank you Alpha" I maintained eye contact with the Alpha as I spoke, as she initiated it, it would be rude to avert my gaze.

"Excellent, I'm glad to hear that".

An awkward silence filled the gap between us. I could smell the anxiety from Alyse, and I could hear her heartbeat, thumping hard in her chest. The Alpha held her gaze on me, boring into my face. She was testing me, testing my strength and resolve. Although she is indeed powerful, I can feel that much from her, in my thirty-eight years of this life, I have faced others far fiercer than she.

"Well" she finally broke the silence,

"I would like for you to ease some of my curiosity" her facial expression softened slightly, though her eyes continued their assault on mine.

"I can only try, Alpha" I responded.

"Firstly, my name is Hina, and you may call me Hina".

"As you wish, Hina" I responded blankly,

"So, tell me, Moon Light was eradicated, what? Twenty years ago?"

"Seventeen" I corrected her,

"Seventeen, sorry. So where have you been all this time?"

I paused for a moment before answering her question. The inner workings of my mind battling with the decision of how much to tell her and how much to withhold. I still don't know just how trustworthy she is.

"After Alyse nursed me back to health, she joined in my search for any survivors from my pack" I finally answered,

"And? How many did you find?" she responded without missing a beat.

I averted my eyes and lowered my head, the all too familiar feeling of guilt once again waved over me. I had punished myself for years that followed after the attack, though being the sole survivor was a punishment on its own. The Alpha sensed my sadness and blew out a slow breath before she spoke again.

"There were no others" she said stating the obvious. I nodded my head and wiped the tear that had escaped my eye.

"I'm very sorry for your loss" she said softly. I eyed her face, and her expression was soft and earnest, she was sincere in her sentiment. It made me feel a little more comfortable.

"Thank you" I half smiled. She eyed me intently for a while, quickly flicking her eyes to Alyse before resting them again on me. A moment of silence sat between us before she spoke again.

"Is this your first Mate?" Hina asked Alyse with a nod of her head in my direction. One of her dreadlocks fell forward and hung by her cheek.

"She is. I had a boyfriend in high school, but once I had changed, I didn't see him again" Alyse answered. Hina watched her with interest but remained silent.

"I have never felt a connection with another person the way I do with Nae. She is everything to me" Alyse continued once she understood that Hina wanted more.

"And you, Lunaya, is Alyse your first Mate?" Hina asked turning her gaze once again to me. I swallowed hard and answered her question,

"Ah, no, she isn't. I was married to a strong fighter from my pack, you know, before. He was my first Mate and the only other one I've had". Pain radiated through my chest as I spoke about my former love. Micha, my husband. His beautiful black hair and golden-brown eyes, the way his smile reached all the way to his eyes when he laughed. The memory of him was torture to my forever broken heart.

"He was killed in the attack" Alyse interjected, gently placing her hand on my lower back.

"I'm very sorry, I can see this still causes you pain" Hina said softly.

"It's okay, he died protecting his family, and I will always love him for it" I said proudly. I was proud, I still am. Micha was strong and brave, and he always gave his all to his family and his pack, right up until his last moments.

"Thank you both for sharing that with me. I still wonder though, why you didn't join a new pack, you have surely come across a few in seventeen years" Hina asked raising her eyebrow.

"We did try, with a couple of different packs. It just never felt right, we never found the right place to call home" I answered.

"But you have come here. You think that this could be the right place for you?"

"I had hoped so, yes".

"And if I decide you cannot stay, or if you choose to leave, what will you do then?"

"We haven't thought that far ahead. We both had hoped that this would be our last stop"

"I see".

Hina raked her eyes over both of us as we sat silently. She was deep in thought, I assume about what to do with us now. At least she was talking to us and trying to understand our story and our reasoning. We have been turned away from other packs without a single word from the Alpha, so this is a good sign.

"We have a very vigorous initiation process" she finally said, "If you wish to stay, you will both have to go through the trials. If you fail, you leave".

I looked at Alyse and a small glint of hope was in her eye, she wanted this, to stay. I do to. This is basically our last chance. I turned back to the Alpha and nodded my head.

"We understand" I said firmly.

"Well okay then. However, before we move onto that" Hina smirked slightly, flicking her eyes between us.

"Lunaya, Alyse, how did you come to find Luna Eclipse?".

Shit. I knew that she would eventually want these kinds of answers and that I wouldn't be able to hide the truth for long. However, the thought of confessing is still a dangerous and scary notion.

"I uh, I have been told stories of your pack since I was just a child, the great battles you have won and the victories over your many enemies, they are legend" I said with a hint of admiration behind my tone.

"Yes, our history is one of greatness. However, our pack drifted a long time ago into that of myth, believed by most of the world that we are a just fairy tale. So, how is it that you came to know of our location?" Hina asked, her tone now holding more authority.

"I was taught from a young age that your pack and your history is very much real".

Hina slammed her fist on the table and growled, the sound echoing around the hall and drawing complete silence from everyone still present. Alyse gripped my thigh tightly, digging in her protruding claws.

"Stop dancing with me Omega and tell me what I want to know" Hina demanded, glaring over at me. Her mood no longer curious and inviting but now threatening and protective. I expected as much, eventually anyway. She would not have remained in charge for this long by being nice and friendly to anyone and everyone that crossed her borders. Especially as their existence is somewhat secret.

I gulped down the lump in my throat and blew out a slow breath.

"My mother knew of you, and her mother before her, and so on. The women from my line have passed on the knowledge of your pack and whereabouts for generations" I confessed.
"And why is your line so concerned with Luna Eclipse?" she asked gruffly. Well, it's now or never, out with it I suppose.
"My heritage dates back to the beginning of your pack. It was my ancestor, Rhea, that conceived Luna Eclipse. She was the first female Alpha".
Hina and the other women at the table stared at me wide eyed. The entire hall was deadly quiet, I could hear the beating hearts of everyone inside.
"You would do well not to lie to me right now" Hina hissed.
"On my honour, Alpha Hina, I would not lie to you" I assured her, placing my hand over my heart and bowing my head slightly.
Hina looked over my face for any signs of dishonesty. After a few long agonizing minutes, she waved her hand and the woman that called us to the table earlier stepped forward. Hina whispered something into her ear, and she then nodded and walked quickly out of the hall. My mind was racing a million miles an hour. If Hina sees the confession of my heritage as a challenge for her Alpha status, she may execute us here and now. Or she could seek to use me as a tool, if she knows any more about my family history. We sat in complete silence as her eyes bore into my face.
After too long sitting in tense silence, finally, an elderly woman was led into the hall by the same woman that left minutes ago. She brought her to the table and sat her down next to Hina. The woman has long white hair that sat flat down her shoulders. Her skin was ravaged by time and her face was coated in wrinkles. Both her eyes are white and she was looking off into nothing, I believe she's blind. Hina leaned in close to her side and whispered into her ear. She was careful not to whisper too loudly, given I'm a Were and could probably hear her if I tried. After a minute Hina sat back up straight and returned her gaze to me, the elderly lady sat forward and put her hands on the table.
"Give me your hands child" she said with a soft yet crackly voice. I hesitated, looking at the woman and then to Hina. What is this? I pursed my lips and shook my head.

"This is our elder Pappi, she has been with our pack for over ninety years. She is also a Seer and will confirm your story" Hina said with subtle frustration. A Seer, shit. Will she see everything? If I refuse, I'm sure they will either kill us or cast us out. I don't really have a choice here. Alyse squeezed my thigh again and I took a deep breath. I slowly placed my hands in Pappi's, and she gripped them tight. Her head tilted to the side and her breathing quickened.

"So much pain. You carry such guilt and sadness" she huffed, "Ah, I see your lover, so handsome he is" a small smile played on her lips before she took a sharp breath and paused. Oh Goddess, please, please help me here. Her face turned down and her brows furrowed together.

"Pappi, is she telling the truth, can you see her lineage?" Hina asked her.

"Oh yes, I see her line" Pappi answered. My heart began to race, and I took slow breaths to try and steady myself. Alyse rubbed her hand on my thigh to comfort me, but it had little impact. If they discover the truth, they will surely kill me.

"Well, is she from Rhea?" Hina asked with more urgency.

Pappi released my hands and I snapped them away from her, pulling them into my chest. She took slow deep breaths and started to gently nod her head.

"She is" Pappi confirmed. Hina jumped to her feet and stared down at me.

"Have you come to reclaim the seat of your ancestor?" she hissed.

"No Alpha, I assure you, I have no intention of staking any claim to your position. We have come only for a new home, nothing more. You are the Alpha, and I will not challenge that".

Seeming satisfied with my declaration, Hina nodded her head.

"I will arrange for your trials to commence tomorrow" Hina announced, as she begun to walk for the door.

"That will not be necessary, child. This Were needs no initiation, she is destined to be here" Pappi called to Hina.

"It is tradition, Pappi. All she-wolves must go through the trials" Hina stepped back to the table and glared down at the elder.

"You are the Alpha, Hina, and if you wish to put her through the trials, then that is your prerogative. However, I request that you delay the commencement for one week".

Hina growled lowly at Pappi's request, but I could see on her face she was going to accept. Pack elders are highly respected, and to have a Seer is enormously rare. She knew better than to go against her.

"Very well. One week" she huffed and then marched out of the hut, with her warriors following behind her. I looked at Alyse and she was smiling at me excitedly. Was this it? Had we finally found a home? I allowed a glimmer of hope into my chest and a smile pricked at my lips. But Pappi's words were still playing in my mind. Why am I destined to be here and why would she want to delay the trials?

"Uh Pappi" I stammered,

"You have questions, child" she answered me.

"Yes, I do".

"I know you do, but now is not the time for questions. Soon, soon you will have the answers you seek" she said standing from the table.

"But what does that mean, why am I destined to be here?" I rushed out.

"Elaine, please take me back now" Pappi said softly, ignoring my question. She reached her arm out and the woman that brought her here stepped forward, gripping her elbow. Elaine begun to lead Pappi away. She was just going to leave, now? She had told me nothing, only giving me more questions.

"Pappi please, you need to tell me something, anything, I need more than that" I called to her urgently standing from my seat. She paused and turned her head over her shoulder.

"Destiny is coming for you, all you need to do is wait".

With that Elaine and Pappi left the hall. I looked around confused. The hall was now empty, all that was left were four women cleaning the breakfast buffet. What does she mean destiny is coming? The uncertainty is going to drive me crazy. One week she asked of Hina, does that mean I will know more in one week. Ugh, why do Seers have to be so damn vague and secretive.

"Well, they believe you" Alyse said soothingly, pulling me from my whirlwind of thoughts.

"Uh, yeah, I guess so. But I don't think that's enough anymore".

"Nae, I know patience haven't always been your strong suit, but please don't ruin this. I can't keep wondering the Earth forever. We need a home".

I looked down at Alyse, her eyes were pleading with me. She has done so much for me. She saved my life and let me feel love again. I would have given up long ago if not for her. I can do this one thing, for her. I sat back down beside her, straddling the bench seat and looking directly into her eyes. I cupped her cheeks in my hand and looked over her beautiful face.

"I'm sorry my love, you're right, as usual" I said softly as I traced my thumb across her bottom lip,

"I'll reel it in and stay calm. This is our chance" I smiled, and she smiled back at me, the worry from her eyes disappearing. I leaned forward and placed a gentle kiss on her lips. She slid her hands to the back of my neck and held me against her. Tracing her tongue along my bottom lip, I parted my lips, and she pushed her tongue into my mouth. Our kiss became more urgent and needy as we tasted each other and swirled our tongues together. I moved my hands to her hips and lifted her onto my lap. I slowly moved my hands under her coat and up the back of her shirt, gently raking my nails across her skin. She moaned softly into my mouth as she pressed herself against my body harder. I could feel the throbbing in my groin intensify and heat flushed through my veins.

The rough sound of someone clearing their throat pulled our attention back to the present. We both pulled our lips away, panting softly. I looked over to the source of the sound and found Maya watching us with a deep pink flush on her cheeks.

"Sorry to interrupt" she said shyly, moving her eyes to the ground. Alyse giggled and shifted herself off my lap, the loss of her heat made a small growl rumble in the back of my throat. She brushed her fingers across my cheek before standing up to face Maya. I reluctantly pushed down the heat that was growing inside me and stood up as well.

"You have both been assigned kitchen duty" Maya said looking back up at us.

"Do you know how to fillet fish?" she asked us with a discrete smirk playing on her lips.

"We do, yes" Alyse responded.

"Excellent, follow me" she ordered, heading for the door of the hut. I slipped my hand into Alyse's and we followed behind her. Back outside, the snow on the ground was thick but it had finally stopped falling. More women were moving about the village now, seeming unbothered by the snow. We followed Maya around the hall to another slightly smaller building. The smell of fish and roasting meat was surrounding the hut. This must be the kitchen. Maya pushed open the door and stood to the side to allow us entry.

I eyed the large kitchen, well set up and fully stocked. Like the kitchen of a large restaurant. Multiple women were busily moving about the kitchen carrying pots and trays. Maya handed both Alyse and I an apron and pointed to an open counter to the side. Next to the counter sat four large barrels of fish. Did they catch all of these nearby? There wouldn't be a lake this high up the mountain and they wouldn't have been able to drive them in, surely not. I wonder how they got them here.

"Where did the fish come from?" I asked turning back to Maya.

"Our hunting parties bring back a lot of fish, also deer, rabbit and goat. The village has a pen of chickens, though they're only for eggs" she answered as she lifted a large snapper onto the counter. Alyse and I grabbed a fish each and took a filleting knife from the magnetic holder on the wall.

"Let's show them how it's done" Alyse smile, holding the knife up in front of her. She gave me a quick wink and got to work on the fish. Maya was already underway working on her fish. I smiled inwardly, well okay then, let's cut up some fish.

Chapter

Three

Zelena

My eyes flew open and the first thing I see is a sea of burry white. I blinked a few times to focus my eyes, where am I? I blinked rapidly, thinking for some reason that would help my memory. I can remember seeing two glowing silver orbs shining down on me, then nothing. I took a deep breath, and the most deliciously intoxicating scent filled my nostrils. Warm sunshine on a summer's day. I know that smell. I turned my head slightly and my gaze fell upon the most welcome of all sights. Gunner. I involuntarily groaned as I drank in the sight of him. I felt my heart begin to race, and my stomach tighten. Goddess how I love what he does to my body. He stood up slowly and raked his eyes over my body. He looks thin and pale. His hair is longer, and he was sporting some kind of short scruffy beard. What happened to my young and beastly Mate? Where are the rippling muscles and the sharp strong jawline, what has caused him such pain?

His eyes landed on mine, those same blue enchanting eyes that I had come to love. But they felt different now, they held so much sadness. Surrounded by dark purple circles and pale pasty skin, they looked almost dull. He stared at me blankly before rubbing his eyes with the back of his hands.

"Hey handsome" I chirped, my voice sounding so terribly coarse and husky. Gunner fell to the ground on his knees, pressing his hands to his face and slumping forward. His body jolted with ragged breaths as his chest shuddered up and down. Small weeping sounds escaped through his hands and my heart shattered inside me at the sound.

"Gunner?" I choked, trying to lift myself. My head felt light and dizzy, and my body felt weak, but I had to get over to him. I had to hold him. I pulled myself forward as I tried to lift off the bed but was pulled back by a sharp pinch on my arm. I looked at it and saw a cord attached to my skin. I followed the cord over to an IV bag hanging from a silver pole. I was in the hospital. Why was I in the hospital? I tore the needle from my arm and tried to swing my legs off the bed, only to be pulled back again by more cords and wires poking out from all over my hospital gown.

"What the fuck?" I growled. I pulled and yanked at the cords, ripping them off my body. Rapid beeping and alarms started to sound around the room. My attention was caught by two arms grasping my shoulders. I looked up to see Gunner staring down at me. His face was wet from tears and his nose was red. But his eyes now shining a bright blue with a twinkle deep inside them, those eyes were now staring deep into mine.

"You're real" he said like he was convincing himself.

"You're here, you're awake?" his eyes roamed over my body, and he rubbed his hands up and down my arms, squeezing them as he did.

"Of course I'm real" I said in a 'duh' kind of tone. Why would I not be real? What the flipping heck was going on here. He pulled me into his chest and wrapped his arms around my back, holding me tightly as if at any minute I might float away.

"Gunner, what's going on?" I mumbled into his chest. He didn't answer. I could feel his chest vibrating under my cheek. His heartbeat was erratic, and his breaths sounded unsteady. I just let him hold me as I nuzzled my face harder into his chest, feeling perfectly content with this. For now. A loud gasp brought us both back to the room and we turned our heads simultaneously to the source of the sound. There in the doorway, stood a blonde woman in light purple scrubs with her hand over her mouth. Rushing in behind her came a tall man in a white doctor's coat, followed by Roe and Lupus.

"Oh, sweet heavenly Goddess" Roe gasped as she clung to Lupus for support.

"Miss Baxter, welcome back. I'm Doctor Tenner" the doctor said stepping forward. Gunner gently unwrapped his arms and moved to the side, keeping one hand firmly entwined with mine.

"Back?" I questioned looking at the man,

"I didn't know I left".

The doctor chuckled softly as he came to stand in front of me and pulled out a little flashlight that he held up to my face. Holding up one finger in front of my face he moved the flashlight slowly across my eyes. I know the drill, I've done it once or twice before.

"Pupil response good" he said, I think to the nurse who was scribbling on a clipboard.

"Squeeze my hands for me please" he held out his hands and I took them in mine, squeezing hard. He hissed and pulled his hands away with a slight grimace on his face.

"Muscle response good. I need to listen to your chest please, Miss Baxter" he said holding the stethoscope out. I nodded my head and lifted my chin. He placed the end of it down my shirt to my chest. I flinched at the coldness of the metal. I half expected Gunner to growl or hit the doctor, he has never let someone touch me like this before. I looked up to his face, taking a deep breath in and out. He was watching the doctor closely but showed no aggression, he smiled with his lips pressed together and squeezed my hand tighter.

"Lungs and heart sound good" Doctor Tenner said snapping my gaze back to him. He poked around for a little while, looking at charts, writing stuff down, then disappeared. The nurse reluctantly closed the curtains around us, after Gunner refused to leave my side. She removed my catheter, which was horrible, and then pulled a long tube from my nose, which was worse. Once she was done, poking a prodding me, she threw the curtain open to reveal Roe and Lupus chatting with the Doctor.

"How do you feel Miss Baxter?" Dr. Tenner asked placing his hands on his hips.

"I feel fine, I could eat, and my throat is a little sore, but otherwise I feel normal" I answered his question looking around at each of the faces watching me intently. They were staring at me like I was an animal in a zoo. The doctor hummed rubbing his chin with his thumb and forefinger.

"You are a medical mystery young lady" he huffed with a smile.

"What?" I asked confused.

"Zee, you've been unconscious for three months" Gunner blurted out.

"No. No I haven't. That's not funny" I stammered, starting to feel my panic rise. My eyes were bulging out of my head and my breaths were quickening.

"Thank you, doctor, we'll call if we need you" Gunner said not taking his eyes off my mine.

"I think I should..." the doctor started,

"I said we will call if we need you" Gunner snapped. The doctor lowered his head and rushed out of the room, pushing the nurse along with him. Gunner gently placed his hands on either side of my face and turned my head to look at him.

"It's okay Little Wolf, calm down" he said soothingly.

"Three months" I snapped, feeling a sharp heat run up my arms. The windows began to rattle and the equipment and chairs around the bed started to shake and bend. Gunner pulled me into his chest, again holding me tightly against his body.

"Shh, please, it's alright Zee take a deep breath for me okay" he said softly, rubbing his hand up and down my back. The contact made me feel safe, my skin prickled at his touch and his scent slowly calmed my breathing.

"I'm sorry" I squeaked.

"You don't need to be sorry, my love" he soothed me.

"W-what happened?" I stuttered trying to control my breathing.

"We thought it was all over, that they were all dead. Everyone said it was clear. They were wrong, I was wrong, one of the fuckers shot you".

"I was shot?"

"Yes. In the back. It ruptured your spleen and broke some ribs and just missed your kidney. They took the bullet out and fixed everything up, but you had to have a splenectomy".

"What's that?"

"It means they took out your spleen".

"Is that bad? Can I still, like, live, okay?"

"You'll be fine, you're a badass werewolf Goddess remember" Gunner chuckled.

Holy shit, this is a lot to take in. I lifted my hospital gown and looked down at my stomach. A small faint scar was sitting just below my ribcage. I gently traced my finger over the pale pink mark, it was completely healed. But why did it scar, all my old scars disappeared. Why hasn't this one? Gunner grabbed the hem of my gown and gently pulled it back down. I eyed him curiously and he smiled softly at me.

"We'll let you two chat" Roe's voice startled me. I looked over at her. I had completely forgot that she and Lupus were here too.

"Roe" I called, reaching my hand out to her. Gunner let me go and she stepped over in front of me, cupping my cheek with her soft hand.

"Hi Baby Girl" she croaked, as a tear ran down her face. I smiled at her and she pulled me into a warm hug.

"I'm so glad you're okay" she sobbed quietly. I wrapped my arms around her shoulders and hugged her back. Roe is my surrogate mother, the mother I always wished that I had. She pressed her lips to my cheek and left them there for a second. I felt her tears drip onto my skin. She let me go with a sniffle and stepped back. Without hesitation Lupus lunged forward, wrapping me in his giant warm arms and rocking me side to side.

"Hi Lupus" I choked out under the pressure of his embrace.

"Dad, you're crushing her" Gunner said pulling his father's arms back a bit.

"Oop, sorry" he chuckled. He let me go and stood back before grabbing my face in his hands.

"Thank the Goddess you're back" he said with a smile. I noticed for the first time, the new scar across the side of his face. A deep dark pink jagged line ran from the corner of his lip, up over his cheek, and ended above his ear into his hairline. The battle. I forgot, he was hurt. My heart sank and I felt nauseous and overwhelming sadness. He noticed my staring and pulled my face forward, pressing his lips to my forehead before letting me go.

"Lupus, I'm so sorry" I said softly dropping my head.

"Hey now, what do you have to be sorry for?" he cooed, lifting my chin with his giant hand.

"Your face, it's all my fault" I muttered,

"I think it makes me look even sexier, if that was at all possible" he smirked running his hand through his hair. I giggled, wiping my nose, and Roe smiled pressing herself into his side.

"Ugh Dad, really?" Gunner snorted, full of embarrassment.

"We'll be at the cafeteria, and I'll bring you back a little something" Roe winked at me. Not even having to ask anymore. Since changing, my appetite has skyrocketed. I used to eat nothing but table scraps and the occasional school lunch, but once I moved to Gunner's pack, there were never ending meals. I've become accustomed to Roe's cooking, well I had, three months ago I suppose.

Once they left, I turned back to Gunner, he cupped my face and pressed his forehead against mine.

"Hi, my Goddess" he whispered.

"Hi" I returned. I pulled him up to sit next to me on the bed and I tucked myself into his arms.

"Three months, really?" I asked softly.

"Yes. Three. Fucking. Months".

How could that be possible? It felt like only yesterday that we were in the middle of a battle, but now I'm being told that it was months ago. What have I missed in that time? So many questions I need answers to, but where to even start. Let's start with the most obvious.

"Are you doing okay?" I questioned Gunner.

"I am now".

"But before now?"

He paused for a minute, thinking silently. Enough time for me to smell the pain and sadness seeping out of him. I clung to him a little tighter, waiting for his answer.

"No, Zelena. I haven't been okay" he croaked.

My heart tightened and I felt a lump form in my throat. A heaviness pulled at my body and tears welled in my eyes. So much pain and sorrow surrounded him. I could feel it all. I held a breath and clasped my hand over my chest, it felt like my heart was about to shrivel and die. The pain was nearly unbearable. It was his pain, Gunner's. My sweet Mate.

"Gunner" I groaned. Trying and failing to breathe again. He stiffened and took a deep breath calming himself down and stroking my cheek.

"Sorry Babe" he sniffed. The heaviness levelled and I took a deep breath, my body releasing and relaxing slightly.

"Oh, Gunner" I huffed as the tears rolled freely down my cheek.

"I'm so sorry I put you through that" I turned my face into his chest and sobbed.

"Hush now, it wasn't your fault. I just missed you is all. I'll keep it together, I'm sorry" he said calmingly, stroking my hair in long slow motions.

"How many" I asked,

"Babe?"

"How many did we lose?"

"We can talk about that when you're back home, for now, I just want to hold you. Is that okay?"

He was hurting, I could still feel it. He has obviously been through so much and I don't want to push him. I took a deep breath and pressed my cheek into his now wet shirt.

"That's fine" I whispered.

I gently pulled him backwards to lay down on the bed. He understood what I was doing and shifted himself to lie next to me. We lay together on the bed facing each other. His face looks so different. He looks older and worn out. I gently slid my finger over the darkened skin under his eyes and then down to his slightly cracked lips. I moved my head forward and planted a soft kiss. He closed his eyes tight, but a small tear managed to escape through his lashes. I kissed the tear away and kissed his lips again. I pulled back and traced my fingers through the scruff on this chin and smiled.

"I kind of like this" I giggled,

"Oh yeah?" he smiled, scratching the hair with his fingers.

"Yeah, you should keep it".

"You think so, ay?" he leaned forward and rubbed his chin across my cheek and over my face. I laughed and wriggled trying to move my face away from his scratchy hair.

"Okay, okay, maybe it's not that great" I laughed pushing his face away. He sighed heavily and stroked his finger across my cheek.

"Goddess how I've missed that laugh, Little Wolf" he breathed out.

"I'm not going anywhere. I'm yours and you're mine, remember" I whispered,

"How could I ever forget" he smiled.

I leaned forward and captured his lips with mine. I lifted myself up slightly and pressed my lips against him harder. He moved one hand into my hair and the other under my waist and across my lower back, letting his fingers stop over the bump of my new scar. I deepened the kiss, and he didn't hold back, pulling me against him tighter. He groaned into my mouth and I shifted myself up to straddle him. He slid his hands under my hospital gown and up over my thighs. He gripped his hands on each ass cheek and squeezed hard. I could feel his hardening length under me, and I pressed myself onto him harder. My tongue explored every inch of his mouth as my hands found his shaggy hair. I twisted my fingers into his hair and tugged slightly, Gunner growled into my mouth and lifted his hips higher. I slowly ground my hips forward along his length, the feeling sent shivers down my spine and a breath caught in my throat.

"Holy shit" I whispered breathlessly.

I felt Gunner smirk against my lips as he again pushed his hips up into me harder. My body felt like it was about to burst into flames. The heat coursing through my veins felt insatiable. I could feel the wetness pool in my underwear and the smell of my desire slowly filled the room. I tugged hard on Gunner's hair, forcing his head to the side to expose his neck. I trailed my tongue across his jawline over his neck and to the top of his shoulder. His scent filled my nostrils, warm sunshine, I could taste the desire on his skin. Without realizing my actions were no longer my own, I growled deeply and sunk my teeth deep into the crook of his neck. I moved my hips faster and harder against his jeans as the metallic taste of his blood filled my mouth.

"Zelena" Gunner hissed, moving his hands to my hips and forcing me to stop my movements. I growled again and gripped his head to stop him from pulling away.

"Babe, please, you need to let go" he pleaded. Frustrated, I released my grip on his neck and slid my tongue over my bite mark, licking up a trail of his blood. Gunner took the chance to push me back a little and sit up straight. Looking over his swollen pink lips, I had the urge to bite him again. I growled and leaned forward but was stopped when Gunner pushed back on my shoulders.

"Zee, stop for a minute" he groaned, I bared my teeth and snarled before trying to lean forward again.

"Fuck. Zelena, stop" Gunner growled taking hold of my shoulders hard and keeping me in place.

"What are you doing?" I hissed, trying to struggle free of his grip.

"Zee, you've been in a coma for three months, okay?"

"So what?"

"So, you have slept through three months' worth of heat. Your hormones are in overdrive and you're letting them control you".

"Stop talking" I growled.

"Zelena!" Gunner snapped, shaking my body. The lust filled haze cleared slightly and I blinked my eyes rapidly.

"S-Sorry" I mumbled my eyes staring at the red and bloodied mark I had left on his neck.

"It's okay, Little Wolf. Trust me, I want nothing more than to sink my dick deep inside your sweet little pussy". His words sent a new wave of heat washing over me and I bit down hard on my lip to curve the urge to bite him. A low growl rumbled from deep down in my chest, sending vibrations through my body. I breathed in deeply and the smell of his arousal fuelled my own. I clenched my fists together and groaned inwardly, trying to press myself down again on his lap. The brush of his hard dick sent fireworks off in my stomach.

"Mm, Zelena" Gunner moaned, closing his eyes and dropping his head.

"You're being very naughty" he smirked looking back up to my face. His lips were pouted into the hottest devilish smirk. His dazzling blue eyes squinted and dropped slowly to my neck and chest before rising again to rest on my lips. He pressed his fingers into my arms and rubbed them in slow circles. The throbbing fire in my core was causing my legs to shake and my heart to thump erratically.

"P-please, I-I need you" I mumbled, desperately trying to control the urge to rip my claws along his flesh.

"You need more time, to rest" he groaned,

"I've been resting for three months" I bit back. A growl vibrated in Gunner's chest before he huffed and slammed his lips to mine. He quickly flipped us over on the hospital bed so that his body was hovering over mine. His hand slipped down my side to the hem of my gown. He dipped his hand under the cloth and slowly traced his fingers up my thigh until he reached the seam of my soaked panties. He hooked a finger in the elastic and with one swift pull, he tore them from my body.

"Oh god" I moaned, tossing my head back. Gunner took the opportunity to plant kisses across my exposed neck, up to my ear, and across my jaw. My breaths quickened and my body involuntarily squirmed beneath him. I lifted one of my legs and wrapped it around his waist, drawing his hips down on mine. Gunner moved his mouth to his mark on my shoulder and traced his tongue over the raised scar. The sensation sent electric shocks of pleasure pulsing through me, I quivered and took a sharp breath.

"Gun… argh" I groaned breathlessly.

Gunner moved his mouth back to mine and pressed his soft lips against me, biting softly on my bottom lip, he demanded entrance into my mouth. I obliged and parted my lips. His tongue poured into my mouth at the same time he pushed his fingers into my waiting pussy. I moaned deeply and arched my back, Gunner drank in my sounds of pleasure as he continued to move his fingers inside me. Every touch of his skin on mine, every movement of his magical fingers, it all set off an explosion of fire under the surface. I moved my hands to the top of his jeans and fumbled with the button. He lifted his hips a little to allow me more access. I ripped the button off, not worrying about undoing it, and pulled down the fly. I tugged his jeans over his perfectly toned ass and down the back of his thighs. I felt his huge member fling free and hit my stomach.

"P-please… more" I stuttered into his mouth. Gunner bit down on my bottom lip and moved his body lower between my legs. He teased my wet lips with the tip of his cock and hooking his arm behind my knee, he lifted my leg up to my chest. I was spread open and waiting eagerly to feel him enter me. He turned his head and scrapped his teeth along my knee and the inside of my thigh. Moving his gaze back to my face, he looked into my eyes. His eyes were dark and full of lust, it made me ache for him even more. Not taking his eyes from mine, he pushed his hips forward and his entire length slid excruciatingly slowly into my core.

Gunner grunted loudly and I cried out with a pleasurable scream. He pulled his hips back and thrust into me again with a slow measured accuracy. The feeling of fullness was dizzying. I could feel the walls of my vagina clamping around his shaft as my ecstasy built. This wasn't going to take long, I was sure of it. Gunner pushed himself in as deep as he could go with each slow thrust forward, accompanying his movements with a strained grunt. I wrapped my hands around his neck and pulled his lips down to mine. Our sloppy kisses were hungry and urgent as we both neared the edge. Gunner attacked my neck with bites and kisses and amazing sucking sensations. My claws started to protrude out of my fingertips, and I buried them into the flesh of Gunner's shoulders. I lost all feeling in my legs as my stomach began to constrict.

"Gunner" I screamed out as the start of my orgasm hit me. With each wave of pleasure, I felt like I was looking down at my body, writhing underneath my lover. Everything else in the world was gone, it was just me and him, together, in this never-ending entanglement of unconditional love and absolute bliss. With a few last thrusts, Gunner pressed his forehead to mine and tumbled over into his own blissful release. My throbbing clit and aching nipples slowly dissipated into spent numbness as the last of my convulsing orgasm washed away, leaving behind my body feeling weightless and warm.

"I love you" Gunner whispered with a heavy breath. He had one hand gripping the back of my neck and the other wrapped around my waist, he was holding and squeezing me tightly, like he was afraid I would slip away.

"I love you, so fucking much" he pressed his lips to my forehead and nose and cheek and covered my face in sweet kisses.

"I love you too" I giggled.

"Excellent, now can you put us down" he chuckled. Huh? Put us down… oh shit. I looked over my shoulder and we were now floating about three feet above the bed. I looked at Gunner's smug face and couldn't contain my smile. When the sex is so good it makes you levitate, you know you found yourself a sex god. I pulled my claws from Gunner's back and turned my palms to the floor, slowly lowering us back onto the bed. He looked over my red face with a proud smile and I could feel my already flushed cheeks grow a darker shade of red.

"I'm sorry" I giggled,

"I didn't even realize".

"I take it as a compliment" he laughed as he pulled himself off the bed. He held out his hand to help me up.

"Come on, we both need a shower".

I took his hand and moved my feet to the floor. My weak knees gave out the second I stood up, but Gunner caught me and lifted me into his arms, bridal style.

"I was that good ay?" he laughed again. I awkwardly punched his chest and laughed.

"Yeah, keep telling yourself that, nothing to do with the fact that I haven't walked in three months".

"Nah, it's not that. My lovemaking is just too good" he smiled with a wink and kissed my forehead. I rolled my eyes dramatically and buried my face into his neck. He carried me into the little white bathroom attached to my hospital room and closed the door behind him.

Chapter Four

Zelena

Gunner spent that night with me at the hospital, I was more than happy to share the small bed with him. Sleeping in his warm and loving embrace filled me with blissful happiness, and I slept like a baby. Gunner, however, not so much. I awoke at one point in the night to him squeezing the life out of me. He was grunting and mumbling and begging someone not to leave him. I gently stroked his face and whispered that everything was okay. He eventually calmed down and I drifted back off to sleep.

I woke up before Gunner and just gazed at him while he slept. His face was scrunched up and he looked anything but peaceful. There was light coming through the small window and I could hear movement out in the hallways, it must be late morning already. I traced my fingers over Gunner's cheek and lips and tickled the hair on his chin. Slowly his eyes opened and landed immediately on mine. A smile spread across his face and he pulled me tightly into his arms.

"I didn't dream it" he whispered into my hair. He let me go quickly to gaze at my face, then pulled back into him again, and rested his head back onto the pillow. We lay facing each other, my hands gripping onto one of his and his other hand on my hip.

"How'd you sleep?" I asked, already knowing the answer.

"It was fine" he shrugged. Liar. I pursed my lips and furrowed my eyebrows, wondering if I should push him on it or just let it go. There is obviously a lot to unpack here, I can only imagine how hard it would have been after the battle. And I wasn't there to help him with any of it. I only adding to his worries. He lifted his hand from my hip and ran his finger over my scrunched-up forehead.

"What's this about?" he asked softly, tracing the lines on my forehead. I decided to let it go, for now at least, and quickly thought of something else to say. Looking into his enchanting blue eyes, I softened my face.

"What's the date?" I asked him.

"August twenty-seventh, why's that?"

"Huh, I'm nineteen now. Guess I slept through my birthday".

"When was your birthday?" Gunner asked a little shocked.

"It was on August fourth".

"Well, you missed mine too, it was July sixteenth"

"Oh well, just another year right".

"I think we should have a birthday party, for both of us. It can be a welcome-back slash I-was-in-a-coma-for-my-birthday kind of party. What do you think?" he asked with a hint of excitement in his tone.

"I think that sounds totally ridiculous, but also kind of great". He leaned forward and kissed my forehead with a huge smile.

"Perfect, I'll get Mum to arrange it, she loves that sort of stuff".

"Well okay" I chuckled. I've never had a birthday party before, I've never even gotten a birthday present before. The more I thought about the whole thing the more my excitement grew. My very first birthday party.

"What are you smiling about gorgeous?" Gunner asked, running his thumb over my smiling lips.

"I was just thinking" I answered him.

"Yeh, about what?"

"Well, I've never had a birthday party before, I'm kind of excited".

He looked at me wide eyed, before his face dropped a bit and scowl took over. He looked so angry and sad at the same time.

"Hey, what's this for?" I said, using his same line.

"That mother fucker" He growled lowly.

"Gunner, he got what was coming to him"
"He should have suffered more"
"He suffered in the end, that's what matters".
He crinkled his nose and pursed his lips together. He closed his eyes tight and stayed like that for a minute. He eventually blew out a slow breath and relaxed his face. He opened his eyes again and smiled at me.
"Well then, we're just going to have to make sure that this is the best birthday party ever".
I smiled brightly and nodded my head. This is going to be great. A soft knock on the door pulled us out of our little bubble and Gunner sat up straight on the bed.
"Come in" he called.
Doctor Tenner walked in and came over to the foot of the bed.
"How's the patient feeling today?" he asked with a soft smile.
"I'm good, I feel really good" I responded, sitting up on the bed,
"When can I go home?" I asked.
"Ah, well you were in a coma for a long time. We can't just let you up and leave without running a few tests".
Gunner growled lowly from beside me. The doctor noticed and his face paled.
"B-but given the circumstances here, we could possibly release you tomorrow morning" he said quickly while eyeing Gunner.
"Oh, not today? I really do feel just fine. I swear" I said, shifting my gaze between Gunner and the doctor.
"I ah, I-I I'll see what I can do" Doctor Tenner stuttered before quickly turning and exiting the room. I looked at Gunner and he quickly turned his head away from me.
"What's going on?" I asked confused.
"Nothing, Little Wolf" he answered laying back down but still avoiding eye contact.
"Gunner" I growled.
"The Doc knows who we are, more so, what we are" he admitted.
"He what! Isn't that dangerous?"
"We paid him a lot of money to keep his mouth shut, and to do a few other things"
"Things like what exactly?"

"To not do certain tests on you, and to keep your file secret, he also worked on Dad while he was in here as well".

"Oh, so what then? Is he like a secret pack doctor now?"

"He may be. He is terrified of me, so I know he'll do what I want. Plus, he really liked the money we gave him, so I bet he would be up for more should we need him again".

"Hm, okay"

"Okay?" Gunner propped his body up on his elbow and looked at me.

"Yeah okay. You're the Alpha. If you think it's okay, then I support your decision".

Gunner smirked and lowered his head a little so that he was looking at me through his lashes. He quickly shot forward, wrapping his arms around my body, and pulled me back down on top of him. I screamed and laughed as we fell back onto the bed.

"You're my Luna, my Goddess, my equal. You get a say in all this too" he said nuzzling his face into my neck and cheek. I felt a flicker of heat light up in my groin. I love how his skin feels against mine.

"Thank you, my Alpha. Have I told you lately that I love you" I whispered lowly, leaning further into his touch.

"Not recently enough" he mumbled against my neck.

"I've got some making up to do then, don't I?" I half moaned. A seductive growl vibrated through his chest and bubbled out of his mouth. The sound instantly made the heat grow and a small throb began in my panties. He really is deliciously addictive. He licked from the base of my neck up to my earlobe and gently bit down. A moan escaped my lips and I arched my back, grinding my hips into his.

"You smell good enough to eat" he rumbled.

"Go ahead" I egged him on. I felt his smile against my face before he flipped us over on the bed so that he was now above me. He traced his tongue back down my neck, kissing and biting as he went. In a blink he was quickly down with his head between my legs, pressing his face against my pubic bone. He growled again as he pressed his nose and lips into my crotch and inhaled deeply. Oh, sweet Goddess, please take me now. My knees were shaking slightly, and I gripped my hands onto the side of the bed. Butterflies filled my stomach as I waited to feel his strong tongue against my wet folds. He pressed his nose harder against my clit, the sensation sending a wave of pleasure through my already weak legs.

A swift knock on the door and Gunner growled, pulling his head out from under my hospital gown. Agh, for fuck's sake. Really? Right now, things were just getting good.

"Come in" Gunner grunted. Doctor Tenner came in and smiled at the two of us.

"Good news Miss Baxter, I have your release papers and you're free to leave" he announced proudly. I shot up in the bed, my smile taking over my entire face.

"Really, I can go home?" I asked excitedly.

"Yes, you can, as long as you promise that if you show any unusual symptoms, headaches, dizziness, loss of appetite, anything, you come right back".

"I do, I promise" I jumped up onto my knees and wrapped my arms around Gunner's neck.

"Thanks, Doc" Gunner said firmly.

"Any time" Doctor Tenner replied. He put the papers on the table by the door and left again. I was bouncing on my knees squeezing Gunner tightly. Home, thank the Goddess.

"We can go home" I squeaked.

"Finally. Then I can continue with what I was just doing" he said with a smirk.

"Well, in that case, let's not dilly-dally. Get up and take me home".

"Dilly-dally? Really?" Gunner laughed.

"Oh shut up, I'm excited, I can't help what comes out of my mouth" I shrugged. Gunner pulled my face close to his and pressed his lips to mine.

"I'm more excited about what I'm going to put in that mouth" he teased. Holy heck, that's so hot. I couldn't say anything, my mouth just hung open. We definitely need to get home, like right now. Gunner laughed at my expression and kissed me again before standing up off the bed. Getting all the tubes and cords taken off my body was done quickly, and sorting out the paperwork was even quicker. It was like Gunner and I were running a race, the first one home and naked in the bed, won.

When we arrived back at the pack house, I was surprised by how much it had changed. We're in the midst of summer and everything looks greener and brighter. There were flowers and plants everywhere. No trace whatsoever of there ever being any kind of bloody battle here. We hopped out of the car and walked around to the front of the house. Lupus was sitting on the porch swing reading a book. He looked up as we stepped up onto the porch.

"Zelena" he half coughed.

"What on Earth are you doing here?" he called standing up and taking four giant steps forward to wrap me in a hug.

"Doc said I could bring her home" Gunner answered for me.

"Was that the doctor's decision, or yours?" Lupus grumbled giving Gunner the side eye.

"Both of ours" Gunner shrugged.

"Mmhmm" Lupus hummed, not convinced at all.

I got an inkling at the hospital that Gunner was a bit harsh with Doctor Tenner while I was there, Lupus just confirmed all my suspicions. I managed to wiggle myself out of his strong arms and take a breath. Wow, Lupus has really opened up to me, hasn't he? I mean, he was always seriously nice and sweet with me. But now, it's more enthusiastic, and kind of fatherly, like he sees me as his own daughter now. I like it.

"I'm going to take her up to rest for a bit, before we tell the pack that she's back. Can you try to keep her homecoming on the D. L.?" Gunner asked his father.

"Of course, take your time" he responded with a smile down at me. His eyes showing all too well that he knows we won't be resting up there. I blushed and turned my face away. Gunner took my hand and led me through the foyer and up the stairs. I didn't realize how much I missed what this house smells like. How could I miss something that I didn't know I was missing out on? The smell of Roe's cooking mixed with wildflowers mixed with wolf scent, it was exquisite. I breathed in deeply, enjoying each smell as it hit my nose. Mm, home.

We walked through the bedroom door and Gunner quickly slammed it behind him. Lunging forward, he scooped me up in his arms. I squealed with joy as he threw us both down on the bed. He attacked my face with kisses and his hands roamed over my body.

"Gunner, wait" I breathed,

"I want to have a shower first, I still smell like the hospital" I groaned pushing his big head away from my neck. He growled loudly and rolled off my body, throwing his arms to his sides like a toddler having a tantrum.

"Oh, stop it" I giggled kissing his forehead,

"I'll be quick".

"Ugh, fine" he moaned, emphasizing the word 'fine'. I rolled off the bed and ducked into the bathroom. As soon as I walked through the door, I caught a glimpse of myself in the mirror and gasped. I've gotten so thin. I can see my collarbones protruding out and my cheeks look so shallow. All that weight I managed to gain in my first few weeks here, it was gone again. Is this what happens when you're fed through a tube for three months? How I don't feel as weak as I look, is beyond me. I brushed off my unnerving appearance and jumped in the shower.

The water was deliciously soothing. I let it run down my entire body, warming my skin and cleaning away the last of that sterile hospital stench. I tilted my head back and let the water beat down on my face. It is so good to be home, back with Gunner, the pack, and the family. My family. The hot water washed over me, relaxing every inch of my being, I blew out a deep breath and I felt my body lift off the ground. I was no longer under the water of the shower but standing in a dark room. It smelt terrible, like damp and mouldy. I couldn't see anything through the darkness, but I could hear soft sobs coming from the corner of the room. I stepped forward, toward the sound of the sobs but was instantly pulled from my vision. I stepped into the wall of the shower, thumping my face into the wall.

"Oomph" I grunted as I rubbed my hand over my nose and forehead.

"You okay in there?" I heard Gunner call,

"Yeh, all good" I shouted back. What was that? Another Drakos vision, but of what, a dark room? Who was crying and why would I take myself there? I turned off the tap and stepped out of the shower. I'll talk to Gunner about it. I wrapped a towel around myself and walked out of the bathroom. Gunner was lying on the bed holding his phone over his face. He lifted his head and looked at me and sat up on the bed. Just as I was about to open my mouth, the bedroom door flew open with such force I thought it was going to fly right off its hinges. In the doorway stood Nat, with her eyes bulging and her breathing rapid.

"Nat" I gasped, pulling the towel tighter to my naked body. She took four running steps towards me and wrapped her hands around my body.

"You're here. You're actually here, I can't believe it" she squeaked into the crook of my neck. I was pinned tightly in her grasp. My arms stuck to my chest holding the towel and her body pressed hard up against mine.

"I can't breathe" I choked out. Nat didn't loosen her hold but instead started sobbing frantically.

"I was so scared" she cried,

"I thought you were never going to wake up, I just got you and then I was going to lose you. It's been so terrible without you here, Gunner is always grumpy, Mum hasn't stopped cooking, Smith follows me everywhere, repeatedly asking if I'm okay, and fucking Tobias, don't get me started on Tobias" Nat mumbled quickly through her sobs. She always talks a lot and really fast, especially when she is upset or nervous. I think it's adorable.

"Nat, let her breathe will ya" Gunner growled walking over to us. He peeled her arms away and I managed to catch a giant breath. I smiled lovingly at Nat. Her face was now red and wet from crying, her mascara was smudged over her eyes and her nose was bright pink. She smiled back at me and wiped her nose and eyes on the back of her hand. Then Smith appeared in the doorway panting. Smith had quickly become my best friend and always made me feel happy and safe. I stepped toward him ready to pull him in for a hug, but Gunner quickly stepped between us, blocking me and facing Smith, and growled a warning.

"Gunner" I snapped angrily. This overprotective asshole I thought.

"You're naked" he growled at me over his shoulder. I had forgotten that I was still wearing just my wet bath towel. Oops.

"Oh yeh, hold on" I grabbed whatever clothes were on the top of the basket by the bathroom door and ducked into the bathroom to change. I took a pair of my denim shorts and one of Gunner's t-shirts, no underwear, stupid me. I walked back out into the room and wrapped my arms around Nat's shoulder from behind and pulled her down to my level.

"By the way, I missed you too sis" I whispered as I kissed her cheek. She grabbed my arms and pressed her cheek to mine. I walked to Smith who was still standing by the door behind Gunner. I did a little turn and waved my hands over my body to show him that I was now dressed. He rolled his eyes and stepped to the side. Smith had a huge smile on his face and quickly stepped forward to wrap his arms around my body. He picked me up off the ground and spun me around.

"Hey Luna, we fucking missed you around here" He cooed as I spun through the air. He placed me back on my feet and rested his hands on the top of my shoulders.

"Hiya Smith" I smiled brightly at him.

"I know that you're a badass Goddess and all that, but do you think you could not scare us all like that again?" he huffed with a smirk.

"I'll do my best" I said with a soft punch to his chest. I looked at Gunner and he was watching us closely, keeping his eyes fixed on Smith's hands. I remember what happened the first time I hugged Smith, Gunner nearly tore his head off. He has gotten a little better with the whole 'no touching' thing, but not exactly comfortable with it yet. I took a step back out of Smiths hands and stopped when I reached Gunner's chest. He wrapped his arms around my waist and pressed his nose into my hair. A soft growl vibrated through his chest as he pressed his lips to my neck.

"I told Dad not to tell anyone that we were back yet, how did you know we were here?" Gunner asked Nat lifting his head from my neck.

"Oh please" she huffed with a laugh,

"I sniffed her out the second I stepped through the front door. Did you really think that I wouldn't smell her?" Nat laughed again, slapping her brother on the back.

"Of course you did, you're more like a bloodhound than a werewolf" Gunner snickered. Smith roared with laughter, throwing his head back.

"You should see her face when I fart" he snorted. We all started laughing and a blushing Nat punched Smith's shoulder.

"Stop, I just have a better nose than you lot" she whined, crossing her arms and stomping her foot. Her bottom lip dropped into a pout and her eyebrows pulled together, making her look much younger than she is. This just made Gunner and Smith laugh more.

"Ugh, whatever you heathens. Come on girlfriend, let's get some food" she said pulling me from Gunners arms and dragging me down to the kitchen. The sound of Gunner and Smith joking and laughing followed behind us.

I was sitting at the counter with Gunner next to me while Nat and Smith were pulling containers of food out of the fridge, rattling off what they contained as they went. I sat watching them with my head resting on Gunner's shoulder and my arms wrapped around his bicep. They really go well together. Nat and Smith. They are complete opposites and yet perfectly balanced. Smith is sarcastic and cocky, always ready with a joke or a witty comment. Nat is fierce and somewhat neurotic at times, always open with her emotions and generous with her kindness. Smith's hand always found a way to touch Nat as they moved about the kitchen, either on her arm or her waist or backside. And Nat, she was head over heels, you could see it every time she looked at him. It made my heart swell, to see these two important people in my life, finding such love and happiness together.

I was pulled from my wonderment by the kitchen door flying open. Filling the doorway was the monumentally enormous body of my guardian, Tobias. His soft chocolate skin glistened with sweat, and his dark eyes were fixed on me. He stepped through the door and in a blink, he was spinning me around off the stool to stand facing him and had dropped to his knees in front of me. His movements were too fast for Gunner to recognize as he stumbled off his stool and looked down at Tobias with a growl. Tobias had both my hands in his and his forehead pressed against the back of my fingers. The heat from his body was swirling all around the room, but his scent was a mess, relief, sadness, guilt, fear, joy. All of these emotions hit my nose in one quick sweep.

"My Goddess, I beg your forgiveness" Tobias's silky voice was deep and urgent.

"I failed you, I failed the Moon Goddess. I could not protect you and you nearly died because of my incompetence".

What in the world was he talking about? How did he fail me and what was with the begging? It really doesn't suit a man of his stature and power.

"I beg you, my Goddess, I am so sorry. Please forgive me" Tobias pleaded. I quickly glanced at Gunner who was almost smirking at Tobias. I dropped to my knees and grabbed his face, lifting his chin to look at me.

"Tobias, you have nothing to apologize for" I told him firmly. His eyes were wide and full of worry as they stared into my own. He sucked in a sharp breath and pulled his head from my hands with a hiss.

"I am meant to be your guardian, I was meant to keep you safe, but I failed. You were shot and it's my fault" he refuted, exaggerating the words 'I'. He turned his eyes away and lowered his head to a bow.

"I will take whatever punishment you see fit" he said sternly. He really thought I was going to punish him, for getting shot, by someone else. What the fuck.

"Tobias, I more than anyone know when being punished is undeserved. In this instance, it was not your fault. It could have happened to anyone. I don't blame you and you already have my forgiveness, even though there is nothing to forgive" I said as I grabbed his hands again. I pulled him up as I stood. He slowly got to his feet and once again towered over me. My short stature lined me up to his mid to lower chest, I truly looked like a small child standing next to him.

"Please don't punish yourself, you fought hard and I'm okay" I said encouragingly.

"But I…" he started,

"No buts." I interrupted,

"Really, I'm okay, I feel better than okay. It was no one's fault but the hunters, and we took care of them" I smiled triumphantly. He was quiet for a minute, his gaze sweeping over my face and body, searching for signs of insincerity. When I suppose he was finally satisfied with my reasoning he smiled brightly.

"Yeh, you did Little One, you kicked major butt" he chuckled. The anguish I felt from him melted away and the tension in the room lifted. I laughed along with him and squeezed his giant hands.

"Can I have my Mate back now?" Gunner interjected, pulling my hand gently from Tobias's.

"You sure can" Tobias smiled at him and took a small step back. Gunner wrapped his arms around my waist protectively and again pressed his nose into my hair. Okay, so clearly, he hasn't let go of the possessiveness completely. Especially not with Tobias. But they did seem a little different with each other, softer, almost friendly. I wonder what went on with them while I was in my coma. I'll ask him about it later.

"Great, now that all that is sorted, can we eat?" Nat called, breaking my train of thought.

"Definitely, I'm starved" Tobias chimed as he squatted on one of the stools at the counter.

Gunner pressed his lips to my ear and a few more times down my cheek before he let me go to sit down. We didn't bother with plates just picked at the open containers. We sat and ate and talked like it was the most natural thing in the world. Tobias had a mouth full of something and a chicken drumstick in one hand and sausage roll in the other. Smith and Nat were eating and smiling at each other. My friends all together, my family. Just missing one. I furrowed my eyebrows and looked at Gunner.

"Where's Cole?" I asked. There was no answer, just quiet. I looked at Smith who lowered his head, fiddling with the food in his hand to avoid me. Nat also looked down and away from me. The air suddenly felt toxic, thick, and heavy with sadness. Oh no.

"Where's Cole?" I asked again with a little more urgency. Still no replay. I looked at Gunner, pleading with him with my eyes to tell me that it wasn't what I was thinking. I don't remember seeing him at the end of the battle and no one has said anything about him since I woke up. Surely Gunner would have told me if something happened to Cole. It's Cole for fucks sake.

"Gunner, what happened to Cole?" I snapped. He turned his face to look at me and huffed.

"He doesn't want to see you" he finally answered. I breathed a sigh of relief, he's okay. Thank the Goddess. But why wouldn't he want to see me, what have I done?

"Wha-why?" I questioned.

"Zee, it doesn't matter, he'll come around" Gunner stammered.

"Why Gunner?" I demanded. He paused for a minute, clearly struggling with his thoughts.

"He um, after the battle we thought everything was okay" he started explaining,

"Cole's dad"

"Spartan" I interrupted,

"Yeah, Spartan, was with my father after he was injured, he took care of him until he got him to the hospital. It was Spartan that found Doctor Tenner".

"Uhuh" I hummed in understanding,

"We didn't know that he was hurt, he didn't say anything, to anyone".

"What are you saying, Gunner?"

"Spartan was shot in the stomach, he didn't tell anyone because he wanted them to take care of my dad first".

"Is he okay now?" I asked, shooting my gaze from Gunner to Smith to Nat and back to Gunner.

"Was it bad, is that why Cole is angry with me?" I pushed.

"Cole is being unreasonable" Tobias growled lowly,

"Cole is struggling" Smith fired back.

"TELL ME" I shouted,

"Where is Cole, where is Spartan?" I screamed in panic.

"Zelena, Spartan isn't okay. The bullet was laced, and it caused a lot of damage to his organs".

I felt my throat dry, and my chest tighten, and my stomach heaved, like I was ready to throw up. Oh Goddess, no. I gripped the edge of the counter readying myself for what I was about to hear.

"Spartan didn't make it".

Chapter Five

Lunaya

Four days had passed since I told Alpha Hina about my heritage. I tried to steer clear of her where I could and have pretty much succeeded so far. Alyse and I have settled quickly into the village and the pack, taking on our chores and responsibilities each day and getting to know some of the pack members. A lot of the women have become more receptive and welcoming, I think Maya and Trinny, mainly Trinny, had something to do with that. Everything here is so easy and relaxing, I can definitely see us staying for good. Alyse and I have never been more blissfully in love. Each day after lunch half the pack would go for warrior training, Maya included. And since Maya and Trinny have become our shepherds, we get left alone in our hut for three hours. There isn't much to do in a small hut for three hours, so we've been keeping each other warm, so to speak.

I was lying on the bed with my arm around Alyse, looking up at the roof of the hut. Alyse was slowly tracing her finger from my neck down my chest, between my breasts, and back up again. I love the sensation, I just love her touching me. The words of the Seer have been playing over and over in my mind. 'She is destined to be here'. I've been pretty good at staying patient, just like Alyse asked, but as the week's end draws closer, my patience gets thinner.

"You're thinking about the Seer again, aren't you?" Alyse said softly.

"You know me too well" I smiled not looking at her.

"I do. You're being really good, I appreciate your effort"

"Thanks, darling, I'm trying to stay calm and collected"

"I know, and you have been" she cooed proudly. She pulled herself up to press her lips to mine and I moved my hand to stroke her cheek. Her kiss became more passionate and her skin against mine grew hotter. Alyse quickly sprung up to straddle my lap, twisting her fingers into my hair and tugging gently. I ran my hands down her arms and up over her naked back. Her skin is delectable, so soft and smooth. I sat up straight keeping Alyse on my lap and our tongues moving together. I glided my hands down to her backside and squeezed, drawing a soft moan from her lips. I then moved one hand up her stomach to her breast and rolled her nipple between my fingers. She arched her back and pulled harder on my hair. I slipped my hand between her legs and gently stroked her wet folds. Her breathing quickened and her thighs squeezed against my legs. I pushed my fingers inside, slow and deep, and curled them forward pressing against her sweet spot. As I continued the motions with my fingers, I leaned down and took one of her erect nipples into my mouth, sucking gently and flicking my tongue.

A loud bang on the door startled both of us, causing Alyse to jump on my lap. I removed my mouth from her perfect nipples and shouted at the door,

"Go away!" Alyse giggled and rolled her hips onto my hand harder. There was another bang on the door louder and harder.

"Ladies, your presence is requested" the voice called through the door.

"Please come back later" I chuckled taking Alyse's nipple between my teeth. The door nearly broke in half with the next bang.

"Alpha requests your presence NOW" the voice shouted angrily. Ah fuck. I guess I knew I couldn't avoid her forever. Alyse huffed and leaned back on my lap looking at me dejectedly. I took my fingers from inside her and sucked the juice from my fingertips giving her a wink. I lifted her off my lap and stood up to start pulling my clothes on.

"Alright, we're coming" I groaned at the door. 'Perfect fucking timing lady' I cursed to myself. It only took us a minute to throw our clothes on. Still hot and reeling from being interrupted, I opened the door to find a very annoyed and angry looking Elaine.

"The Alpha is not to be kept waiting" she spat as she turned on her heels and stomped away. I rolled my eyes and smirked at Alyse, she elbowed my ribs as a warning to behave. I chuckled and took her hand then we shuffled after Elaine.

We reached a rather large hut, made with large stones on the bottom half and wood panelling on the top. The roof was lightly covered in snow but as we approached, I could feel the heat resonating through the walls. Elaine didn't knock she just opened the door and stepped to the side waiting for us to enter. The hut was undoubtedly the Alpha's quarters, it reeked of power and authority. The walls were lined with furs and there was a fire pit in the centre of the room. There was a leather couch to the left and a desk with two chairs on the right. On the other side of the fire, lying on her side on a shaggy rug on the ground, was Hina.

"Ah there you are. Alyse, Lunaya, thank you for coming. You can go Elaine" I turned to look at Elaine as she nodded her head and threw me a quick glare before turning around and leaving.

"Come, join me" Hina called to us.

We walked around the fire to where Hina was lying, and my mouth nearly hit the floor. It's a wolf pelt, she isn't laying on a rug. It's a fucking werewolf pelt. The shaggy grey fur was long and looked soft. It was sprawled out on the ground with the claws and head still attached. I couldn't hide the disgust on my face as I eyed the pelt. Hina was wearing a flimsy slip dress that exposed her toned thighs and arms. She was brushing her finger through the fur, petting it.

"You don't like it?" she smirked at my horrified reaction.

"No, I don't like it. It's barbaric" I growled, earning me another elbow to the ribs from Alyse. Hina laughed as she stretched her bare legs through the fur.

"What's barbaric is what this beast did to my pack members. Trust me, this was well deserved" she chuckled.

"What could possibly merit this atrocity?" I snapped. Hina stopped her seductive slithering on the pelt and glared up at me.

"This Were kidnapped, raped, tortured, and then proceeded to burn alive eight of my she-wolves. One of which was only nine years old. When I say something is done with merit, I mean it, do not question me" she growled. My stomach dropped and I felt a wave of guilt for my outburst. He did deserve it, and more. I mentally slapped myself, I need to stop being so quick to judge people.

"I'm sorry Alpha, I misspoke" I said softly, hanging my head with embarrassment.

"Sit down and feel the fur. The only decent thing about this monstrosity was his pelt".

Alyse and I kicked off our boots and I helped her out of her coat. Hina watched us with interest until we sat opposite her on the huge wolf's fur.

"Oh wow" Alyse gasped, running her fingers through the hair,

"I've never felt wolf fur this soft before" she exclaimed. Hina smiled at her and then turned her gaze to me. I brushed my fingers through the long grey fur and was taken aback. It felt soft and smooth like a golden retriever puppy's hair. I hadn't realised a smile crept onto my face as I watched my fingers glide through the fur.

"See, delectable, isn't it?" she voiced. I don't know if it's still the heat from my almost sex with Alyse or something else, but something about Hina on this fur and in that dress was sending shivers down my spine.

Do you smell that?

Alyse flashed, I breathed in through my nose and got a full wave of hot desire. I looked at Alyse and lifted my eyebrow. She's turned on right now? She read my expression and smiled with a slight shake of her head.

That's from her

I looked back at Hina who was now on her back with her arms outstretched and her knees bent up. The dress had slid down her thighs, exposing her full leg and resting just below her crotch.

She's aroused
She's beautiful

I snapped my eyes to Alyse who was eyeing Hina. Her mouth was open and her lips were wet. I could hear her heart pounding in her chest and her own arousal filled my nostrils. I know I should be jealous. My Mate was being turned on by someone else. But I wasn't jealous, not at all. Seeing Alyse's reaction to Hina just made my own heat burn hotter.

You want her?

I do

So do I

Alyse looked at me and a delicious smirk played across her mouth. I looked back to Hina who had arched her back as she slithered seductively on the pelt. I see it now, this was a seduction, not an interrogation. Well, two can play that game. Or three. I leaned over and captured Alyse's lips with mine in a desperate and steamy kiss.

"I can smell you, both of you" Hina's voice came seductively. I pulled back from Alyse and gazed at Hina. She showed no signs of anger or disgust, in fact, her eyes were dark and filled with lust. I smirked at her and turned back to Alyse. I gripped the hem of her shirt, lifted it over her head, and discarded it on the floor. I unbuttoned her jeans and began to slowly pull them down her legs. I glanced at Hina and she was watching closely. Once Alyse was left in just her underwear she got on her hands and knees and crawled to me. She began kissing my collarbone, making her way up my neck. I looked over at Hina, she was still watching but now had her hand under her dress, teasing her nipple. As Alyse continued to place soft kisses along my neck she pulled my shirt up and over my head. She moved her lips down my chest, over my breast, and to my stomach. She was now knelt far forward, her head down, leaving her perfectly plump ass waving in the air. Hina edged closer to us and reached out, slowly gliding her hand up Alyse's leg to her ass. Alyse began to work on my belt buckle as Hina's head disappeared behind Alyse's backside. Alyse was pulling down my pants when she took in a sharp breath and gasped loudly. I looked over her face to see if she was hurt, but she wasn't. Her mouth was open, and her eyes were rolled back slightly, she was in a state of euphoria. I moved my eyes down her back to Hina's head, her mouth was working away at the spot between Alyse's legs. The visual set a fire in my loins and throbbing in my clit.

I finished removing my pants, pulling them down my legs and dragging my underwear along with them. Alyse had her fingertips digging into the small of my back. I reached behind me and gently took her hand, gliding it across my hip and down my stomach to my inner thigh. She gripped my thigh tightly as a moan erupted out of her open mouth. I heard a loud slap and averted my eyes back to Hina, she was rubbing her hand in a circle on Alyse's bare butt cheek. She lifted her hand and slapped it back down on the same spot, keeping her mouth working. Alyse squeaked loudly and rolled her hips into Hina.

I can't believe how hot this is, I never thought I would enjoy watching another person pleasure Alyse like this. Maybe it's because it's another woman with us and not a man. Or maybe it's because we were both already attracted to Hina, her power is intimidating and alluring at the same time. There is something about her that makes me feel provocative, I know Alyse can feel it too. My protective nature has always dominated when I thought someone was lusting after Alyse, but this time, with Hina, it feels dangerous and exciting. I don't know why this is different or why this is turning me on so much, but I'm loving it and we both deserve a bit of a respite and some fun.

I slowly moved my hand over Alyse's neck, down her chest, and to her breast. I took her perked nipple between my thumb and forefinger and rolled it, squeezing gently. Alyse gained a little more composure and started kissing around my stomach again. She glided her hand up the inside of my thigh to my moist slit. As she stroked my lips with her fingers, she pressed her thumb against my clit, moving it in slow circles. I entwined my fingers into her hair and tilted my head back. She pushed her fingers inside me and began moving them in and out. My legs started to ache, and my skin burned. The shots of pleasure firing through my body were amazing, but I needed more.

Alyse withdrew her fingers and pushed on my stomach softly, forcing me to lean back on my feet.

"Lay down" she commanded, and I obeyed.

I laid back on the fur pelt and propped myself up on my elbows. Hina made her way next to Alyse and wrapped her hand behind her neck, pulling her in for a passionate kiss. The sight of their tongues dancing together sent a shiver to my core. Hina would still have the taste of Alyse on her tongue and I wanted to taste her too. They moaned and grunted as their bodies pressed together, hands roaming and lips colliding. I reached down and pressed against my throbbing clit, I growled quietly as I gave myself some release. Hina pulled away slightly and smirked at Alyse before slowly flicking her tongue over Alyse's lips. I growled again and Hina turned herself to me. Grabbing my ankle, she pushed it outwards, spreading my legs. Alyse followed suit and took hold of my other ankle. I was spread wide open, ready and eagerly waiting for their touch. They both glanced at each other before trailing kisses slowly up my legs. Each kiss left behind a burning patch of skin that was sizzling into my blood. I was panting heavily with anticipation and desire. Alyse pressed her lips to my pubic bone and continued her trail up over my stomach to my breasts, taking my erect nipple into her mouth.

Hina's tongue dragged up my inner thigh before stopping right before reaching my throbbing nether region. She growled seductively but didn't move any further. The anticipation was torture, I could feel my legs starting to shake. Without warning Hina slammed her face into my groin, pressing her lips to my clit and sucking hard. I tossed my head back and cried out. The burst of pleasure was everything I needed. She worked her tongue like magic, licking and sucking in all the right places. Alyse bit down on my nipple and drew another cry from my lips. My eyes rolled back, and my body was on fire with wave after wave of pleasure. I see now why it was hard for Alyse to compose herself. Alyse moved back down to my stomach and next to Hina. I felt fingers enter me and it just about pushed me over the edge. Hina backed her amazing mouth away and I just about growled in frustration. I lifted my head to look back over at them now kissing hungrily. Alyse curved her fingers hitting my G spot and I moaned at the shock it sent through my body. Hina moved her hand down Alyse's arm and pushed her own fingers inside me as well. The feeling of fullness mixed with the pressure on my clit was staggering. My whole body began to shake as my climax neared. Their fingers moved in perfect harmony and I was revelling in it. Just as I thought my body couldn't take it anymore, a finger slid its way into my asshole. My elbows gave out and I flung back onto the fur, I twisted my fingers into the long hair and gripped hold like I was going to fly away. My toes curled and I felt like every muscle in my body began to contract. I screamed out as the last wave of my orgasm crashed over me. I lay panting on the floor in a state of complete ecstasy. Soft hands were gliding up and down my legs and over my stomach, the sensation was calming and somewhat relaxing. I could just about fall asleep. A soft giggle drew my attention, I lifted my head to see Hina now holding Alyse's ass and nuzzling into her neck. I sat up and watched Hina's hands glide over Alyse's perfect little body. The flimsy straps of Hina's dress had come down and it was now sitting loosely around her waist. Her beautiful brown nipples were fully exposed and perfectly erect. I got onto my hands and knees and crawled over to them. Hina smirked as she looked at me out of the corner of her eye. I stood up on my knees and pressed my body up against Hina's back. I moved her hair from her shoulder and pressed my lips against her neck. Snaking my hand around her waist I took her nipple and rolled it between my fingers. I moved my other hand to her lower stomach and brushed the skin with my fingertips. Dipping my hand further down, I found Alyse's hand, her fingers already buried deep inside Hina's hot pussy. I placed my hand over the top of hers and slowly inserted two of my fingers, moving them in sync with Alyse. Hina growled lowly and moaned, lifting her head back to rest on my shoulder. I bit down onto her exposed neck and I felt a shudder run through her body.

Alyse and I moved our fingers inside Hina, I was biting and sucking along her neck and shoulder as Alyse moved her mouth from Hina's breasts to her lips and back again. The moans, growls, and squelching of our bodily fluids blending together filled the room. The three of us enveloped together in a heated and passionate celebration of our desires. I was fully engulfed in the sounds, the smells, and the fiery sensations coming from each of these delicious women. I could stay locked in this moment for eternity.

"Alpha" someone called from the door, followed by a rough bang. I growled loudly as I gripped Hina tightly around her waist. Alyse squeaked as her head snapped to the door.

"Leave!" Hina boomed. It was quiet for a moment before another bang at the door.

"Apologies Alpha, I have important news" the voice called more urgently. Hina growled viciously and peeled my hand from her waist and her crotch. She stood and stepped away from us, leaving Alyse and I kneeling naked, looking at each other awkwardly. Do we get up as well? I went to stand when Hina pushed down on my shoulder.

"You two, stay" she said gruffly. She was now covered in a large woven blanket. She walked to the door and opened it, not enough to let the woman in but enough to speak. Their hushed voices carried on for a few moments. I looked to Alyse who was watching the door with interest. I brushed my hand against her cheek, and she closed her eyes, leaning into my touch. With my other hand, I took hers, lifted it in front of us, and folded our fingers together. I gently traced my finger over her cheek and bottom lip, down her neck and collarbone to her breast. I circled my finger around her nipple and gave it a little flick. She giggled softly and opened her eyes and looked at me with a crooked smile and her gaze full of lust.

"Ladies" Hina's voice pulled us from our moment, she was standing beside us looking down with a frown on her face.

"I'm afraid we will have to pick this up another time, I have an urgent matter that needs my attention" her demeanour had completely changed. No more of the sensual, flirty Hina, now she was back to firm and hard Alpha Hina. We both stood and grabbed our clothes, dressing as quickly as we could.

"Don't go far" Hina said firmly as we headed for the door. I looked back at her and she had her eyes fixed on me. Her expression was difficult to read, she seemed almost angry. What had the other woman told her I wonder. We walked out the door and found six women huddled together. They were Weres, I could smell that, and they looked to be part of the pack, but I hadn't seen them around before. The woman in front I recognised from the dining hall, she was one of Hina's senior pack members, but the five women behind her were all dressed in warm travelling clothes with strange expressions on their faces. I took Alyse's hand and led her away from Hina's hut and back towards our own.

"What's all that about do you think?" she asked, glancing back at them.

"No idea, did you recognise any of them?" I asked her.

"No, only the one. Do you think they are newcomers like us?"

"No, they are from the pack, but I haven't seen them around the village"

"Hm, weird" Alyse said turning her head back to me.

I looked back at Hina's hut, the women had all gone inside now. I shrugged and continued walking slowly. As we came around the dining hall, I saw Pappi standing in the doorway of a small hut. She was looking off into the distance with a small smirk on her face. I turned to see what she was looking at and almost face palmed myself, she's blind, idiot. I looked back to Pappi who was still staring at nothing. I tilted my head to the side with a curious expression on my face as I studied her. She ever so slightly nodded her head. I stopped walking and stared at her with more intensity. Alyse tugged my hand and turned to see why I had stopped walking. I dropped her hand and went to walk towards Pappi, but she lifted her hand in a stop gesture, how did she know I was there. She then pointed back towards Hina's hut and I followed her hand. After a moment I saw Elaine and three other women marching towards us from around the dining hall building. Elaine looked enraged and the other women weren't exactly smiling either. Oh fuck, we're in trouble.

Chapter

Six

Lunaya

I landed hard on my hands and knees on the fur pelt, the pelt that we were just fucking on not ten minutes ago. Alyse's body was thrown beside me and I grabbed her to pull her into my embrace.

"What the fuck?" I snarled at the woman who dropped her, pushing down the urge to attack was more than difficult.

"Do one of you want to tell me what the hell is going on?" I demanded. I checked over Alyse's face and neck for injuries, she appeared fine, with no visible marks. My question was ignored and when I looked up, I was instead met with glares from the multiple women standing around us. I went to stand but was pushed back down onto my knees. I turned my face and growled at the woman holding me. She pulled her hand back and frowned down at me, her lips curling back over her teeth in a snarl. 'Touch me again' I thought a silent warning glowering back up at her.

"You've been lying to me" Hina's voice came from behind a wall in front of us. I snapped my head back around as he stepped out from behind it. She was now dressed in some kind of woven tribal dress with fur and leather patches, covered by a large fur coat. She stood before us with her arms crossed over her chest, scowling down at us.

"I haven't lied about anything" I spat. She stepped forward and slapped the back of her hand across my cheek, my head snapped to the side and the skin on my cheek throbbed instantly. Alyse growled loudly and went to stand, I grabbed her shoulder and pulled her back down.

Don't attack, I'm okay

She fucking hit you

I'm okay, it's okay

The metallic taste of blood filled my mouth, I moved my tongue and felt a small cut on the inside of my cheek. I turned back to Hina with a frown and spat my blood at her feet.

"I haven't lied about anything" I repeated lowly, my voice dripping with disdain and a soft growl coming through on the last word. She growled and crouched down in front of me, grabbing my chin and lifting my face to look at her.

"I will give you one chance and one chance only, do you hear me?" she growled. I nodded my head as much as I could with her death grip on my chin.

"What do you know of the Triple Goddess?" she hissed. My eyes flew open wide, and my heart just about jumped right out of my chest. Beside me, I heard Alyse take a sharp intake of air. So, she does know about my history, maybe not everything but she definitely knows something. I stared into her face, I didn't know what I was looking for, answers maybe. But to what, I don't even know the questions.

"The Triple Goddess" I said quietly. She squeezed my chin and growled moving her face closer to mine, I could feel her hot breath brush over my cheeks. Her eyes looked wild and full of fury, her lips pulled back over her teeth and her canines extended before my eyes.

"Ahh… okay" I groaned, the pressure on my chin starting to ache.

"The last Triple Goddess died two hundred and sixty-four years ago. She had very limited powers but was able to move small amounts of water. She died in her sleep at the age of ninety-six. There hasn't been another since then" I spoke softly and slowly. Hina let go of my chin and roughly threw my face out of her hand. She stood up and huffed in annoyance.

"I'm not looking for a history lesson, Lunaya. I'm not asking you about the past" she snapped. What could she be talking about if not the past? What else is there to know? I raked my brain trying to figure out what she could know, what is she asking me.

"SPEAK OMEGA!" she boomed, her Alpha power rolling off her.

Alyse instinctually lowered herself to the ground, I however wasn't affected by her Alpha demand. It could be because of Rhea, could be because of my lineage, who knows but I have never felt the effect of an Alpha's anger or command. I looked up at her and she seemed surprised. I guess she expected me to cower from her.

"I'm sorry Alpha, I don't understand. What are you asking me?" I asked her firmly while keeping eye contact. She just about lunged at me, her claws only inches from my face, when a soft voice interrupted.

"Alpha, there is no need for violence".

I turned to see Pappi hobbling through the door and towards us slowly. One of the women ran to her and took her arm to help her walk. They made their way next to us and Pappi sat down on a chair that was placed there for her.

"Pappi" Hina growled.

"My dear" she returned with a small smile.

"What do you know about this?" Hina glared at her, folding her arms across her chest.

"I know that you won't get any answers from this one. She doesn't know what you want to know".

Wait what, what don't I know? Is this what she was talking about the other day? Is this what I was destined to be here for? My mind began to swirl with questions. Excitement and fear swarmed through me and I thought that I may start shaking. I took a deep breath to control myself, the last thing I need right now is more reasons for Hina to kill us.

"What don't I know?" I demanded, moving my gaze from Hina to Pappi and back again. Hina looked down at me and snarled but I didn't back down.

"My scouts have brought back reports of a young woman claiming to be the Triple Goddess" said Hina looking away from me.

"That's not possible" I said softly. My stomach clenched and I could feel the sorrow and anger seeping into my heart. How dare some little no one claim such a divine right. That hope for the world died long ago. Taking with it my own hope.

"And how would you know that?" snapped Hina.

"I just do" I whispered dropping my head.

"I SAID HOW!?" she boomed, her voice bouncing around the room. I could feel her standing over me, her anger was coming off her like hot waves of lava.

"Because I am the last daughter of Selena" I yelled looking up at her.

"Since the destruction of Moon Light, I am all that's left" my voice broke slightly on the last few words. The tears I was holding back spilled over and rolled down my cheeks. Hina looked down at me, her face contorting between anger and pity. The room was deathly silent with only the sounds of my harsh breathing filling the void.

"So, you are from the line of Selene's chosen daughters?" Hina asked, her voice still firm but a little softer now.

"I was" I croaked,

"Either you are, or you are not, which is it Lunaya?"

"I failed the Goddess. She gave me a task and I failed her. I have no right to claim her as my ancestor any longer" I cried out loudly, frowning up at Hina's shocked face.

"No sweet child" Pappi said softly. I snapped my head to look at her and she was looking in my direction with a soft smile wrinkling her cheeks.

"There is another" she said.

"There can't be" I disagreed with a shake of my head.

"Explain Pappi" Hina demanded. Pappi tilted her head to the side and breathed heavily, after a beat she straightened and smiled again.

"Your child lives".

I stared at Pappi's face scrutinizing every inch of skin, every wrinkle, and every line. I was looking, searching for answers, for the truth. She can't be serious, it's not possible. I looked at Hina who was staring at me with a blank expression. I turned to look at Alyse whose mouth was hung open and her eyes bulging, her skin had turned pale and her lip was shaking. Does my child live? My child. It can't be. No. How? No, no, no, no, no. I turned to look back at Pappi but the whole room continued to turn around me. I couldn't see straight, everything was blurry. I tried to take a deep breath, but my lungs wouldn't expand. They stopped working completely. I sucked in a mouth full of air, trying again fruitlessly to breathe. Nothing. My child? Oh Goddess, forgive me.

~

My head felt awfully heavy, and my skin crawled with an uncomfortable heat. I squeezed my eyes together tighter, trying desperately to get my bearings.

"Lunaya" a soft voice sang to me. It sounded like soft bells in my ears. I forced open my eyes and stared up at the ceiling. The face of a beautiful angel came into view above me. My Alyse. I lifted my hand to gently stroke her cheek. She gripped her hand over mine and squeezed it.

"Are you okay love?" she asked, her face furrowing in concern. I didn't answer just stared into her beautiful green eyes.

"Come on, try to sit up" Alyse said pulling at my hand and lifting me up off the ground. She held my hand in hers, gently stroking it with her thumb. Her other hand was placed on my back to support my sitting frame. I looked around and saw the faces of Hina, Pappi, Elaine, and a few other women, all looking down at me. I rubbed my fingers over the back of my neck and cleared my throat.

"What uh, what happened?" I asked stuttering.

"You fainted hon" Alyse answered,

"Don't be stupid, I don't faint" I snapped,

"Well, you did" Hina snapped back.

I looked up at her and she tilted her head to the side. I could swear not moments ago she was full of anger and hostility, now her eyes looked almost soft. Waving her hand over her shoulder, all the other women began to march out of the hut, leaving Elaine and Pappi behind.

"What do you remember?" Hina grumbled. I paused and stiffened as the last conversation came flooding back to my memory. I glared over at Pappi.

"This idiot thinks my daughter is still alive and you think that she is the Tipple Goddess" I grumbled waving my hands between Pappi and Hina.

"Watch your tongue" Hina growled stepping closer to me. I huffed and looked down at my lap. I'm surrounded by nitwits.

They were hunters. Trained, strategic, vicious hunters. How could a thirteen-month-old child survive? Survive them.

"Tell me, my child, why is it you believe your child to be dead?" Pappi questioned softy. I looked up at her and although her white eyes were blank, her expression was warm and comforting. A small feeling of calmness and relief waved over me.

"The hunters killed everyone" I answered in a matter-of-fact kind of tone.

"Did you see your offspring perish?" she answered without skipping a beat.

"Well not exactly" I mumbled,

"Tell me what you remember".

I closed my eyes and breathed deeply. I have avoided reliving this memory for the past seventeen years, with only my dreams betraying me. The pain from just thinking about it still feels as fresh as if it were just yesterday. Everything about the way that my naive twenty-one-year-old self thought my life would turn out, all came crashing down in a fiery explosion that day.

"It was not long after sunrise that we got the call from the Alpha, the hunters had crossed the borders into Moon Light" I began my story.

"We had measures in place for if something like this would ever happen. I would escape one way and my husband, Micha, would go the other. We had practiced and talked about it often, where our supplies were hidden, where we would meet up afterward, and where we would go from there. It was planned down to the last meticulous detail. It was all pointless. The hunters overwhelmed the pack fighters almost too easily. They knew everything about us, from our fighting style to the layout of the village. They knew it all. It became clear that it was no ordinary accidental hunter raid, it was planned, and they were ready. After I said goodbye to Micha, I made it to the edge of the border before I was surrounded. After I realised that I was cornered and had no choice but to change into my wolf if we had any chance of survival, I hid my baby inside a hollowed tree and tried to lead them away from her".

Alyse moved herself close to me and wrapped her arm over my shoulder. I have told her little about the events of that day. She worked a lot of it out herself, but after a while, she stopped asking me about what she didn't know. Hina had sat on the floor next to Pappi, resting one hand on her knee, and was watching and listening with great interest.

"I don't much remember what happened after that, I killed as many as I could, keeping them away from the tree. The weapons they used were unlike anything we had seen before. They had liquid Aconite capsules set in the bullets and smoke canisters with gassed Aconite. In the end, my injuries were too much. I couldn't hold up against the poison, I was weak and just couldn't fight any longer. I remember laying in the snow unable to move, my wolf energy had expired, and I had no choice but to change back. I could see a man holding my baby and walking through the trees. I can still hear her screams." I sobbed as I cradled my head in my hands. My heart ached with every single beat. The earth could open up and swallow me whole right now and I would welcome death. I'm a failure, a weak and useless failure.

"I found Moon Light as the sun was setting" Alyse began, still holding onto me.

"The sight was horrifying, blood and dead wolves everywhere. I couldn't take a step without stepping in blood. The smell of gunpowder and death was nauseating. I was about to turn and run when I heard Lunaya breathing. I didn't think it was possible for anyone to have survived an attack like that, but she did. Every one of my instincts were telling me to leave and run as far from there as I could, but there was something in the back of my mind stopping me. I don't know what it was. Like a voice or some kind of force inside me, pushing me towards her. I can't explain it, I just knew that I had to save her. I dragged her body into a half burnt out house and went about pulling out the bullets and flushing the wounds. To this day, I don't understand how she survived. The wounds should have been enough to end her life, mixed with the amount of poison in her blood, it's a miracle that she is still here" Alyse spoke proudly as she rested her head on my shoulder. I lifted my head and turned to kiss her forehead. She is my saviour, in every possible way. I looked back to Pappi and continued my story.

"As soon as I was strong enough to move, I went to the place I was meant to meet Micha and waited. For weeks I waited, but he never showed. So, I started searching. Alyse took me back to where she found me, and I started there. It didn't matter how nasty I was or how many times I told her to leave me, she didn't, she stayed by my side and helped me the entire time. By then, it had been weeks since the attack, and the wolves were already decomposing. I could barely tell them apart anymore, so I had no idea if one of them was Micha. I never found his body, or that of my baby".

The room was again silent with only the sounds of our beating hearts. Hina edged close to me and reached forward, gripping my arm and squeezing slightly. I looked at her face. She had tears rolling down her cheeks and sadness in her eyes. She didn't need words, everything she wanted to say was said through her melancholy gaze.

"Dear one, the baby from the tree was not killed, just taken" Pappi interjected.

"What? What do you mean taken?" I snapped my head to her.

"She lives and is waiting for you" she smiled.

"That doesn't make sense, why would hunters keep her alive? They knew she was a Were, when has a hunter ever spared a werewolf, baby or not" I rushed out. None of what she is saying makes sense. No hunter has ever shown mercy, so why would this time be different? It's not possible.

"No. I'm sorry but it's not possible" I said stubbornly. Pappi huffed and frowned slightly.

"Alpha, would you please tell us what news your scouts have brought you?" she said turning her head to Hina.

"The story is that there is a young woman, and she is claiming to be the Triple Goddess. In the midst of a hunter attack on her pack, she used some kind of telekinesis power to kill a large number of hunters. Apparently, there are witnesses from other packs. The stories of the newly chosen daughter are spreading around the world like wildfire" Hina answered. She seems to believe what she is saying, she said it with such conviction. Could it really be my baby? My heart raced as a flicker of hope shot through me.

"You're sure?" I asked urgently,

"Of course I'm sure, my scouts have my full trust and have never done me wrong" she snapped.

"Pappi, please, don't do this to me. Tell me straight up. Is it really true, is it my baby? How did she survive?" I pleaded with Pappi, reaching for her to ease my mind.

"These questions are not for me to answer. You must seek the answers from the child".

So, this is it, this is what she meant when she said destiny was coming for me. She knew days ago about this and didn't say anything. Why would she do that, keep such information from me, it doesn't make sense.

"This is what you meant in the dining hall, isn't it? When you talked about destiny and about me being here. Is this what you meant for me to find out?" I asked Pappi, my anger slowly starting to rise. She didn't answer me, she just sat back in her chair and placed her hands in her lap. I edged closer to her and grimaced.

"When you said that you saw my lineage, you didn't mean my past ancestors did you? Did you see her, did you see my daughter?" I growled slowly straightening my posture. Alyse's grip on me tightened and Hina moved herself between Pappi and me. Silence. She offered me no explanation. My anger exploded through my views in a quick heated wave.

"Answer me Seer" I growled, jumping to my feet. Hina stood and grabbed my shoulder, her lips curled back and she growled down at me. A warning, to calm down.

"Come, my love, sit back down and take a breath" Alyse said calmly. It didn't work. The thought that I could have already been on my way to finding my child but wasn't, set off an anger in me like no other.

"I could have left days ago if you had of fucking told me" I screamed at a still and stoic Pappi. She was completely unfazed by my outburst and didn't look the slightest bit concerned.

"Why Pappi, why would you not tell me this right away?" I demanded.

"It was not for me to tell" she answered nonchalantly.

"That's bullshit and you know it. You had the information, you knew the truth, you simply chose not to share it".

My emotions are all over the place. I don't know if I'm still angry that Pappi didn't tell me, or sad that I have wasted all this time here when I could have been with my daughter. I feel overwhelming happiness that my child lives, but deep dread thinking that she may not accept me after all this time. What if she doesn't believe or understand the past. What if she feels that I abandoned her? Well, she would be right, because that's what I did, I abandoned her. I should have continued searching day and night until I found their bodies. Why did I just give up? If I hadn't quit, maybe I would have found her. Maybe I would have found Micha.

I hadn't realised that I was hyperventilating until Alyse pulled me back to reality. I was standing between her and Hina with my hands on either side of my face. Breathing was nearly impossible, I felt like my lungs had completely closed over. The pain in my chest was astounding. It felt like my heart was being torn from my chest and my lungs were dipped in Aconite.

"Shh now, calm down Nae. You need to breathe" Alyse was calling to me, her hands rubbing in circles on my chest.

"Breathe my love, breathe" she called again. I looked down at her piercing green eyes and inhaled a large sharp breath, holding it for a few seconds before blowing it out again. I repeated this a few times over until the pain in my chest eased and my heart rate normalised.

"There you go, you got it" Alyse cooed, still rubbing her hand on my chest. I took her hand and brought her knuckles to my lips, kissing each one.

"I'm okay" I said softly.

"You haven't had one of those in a while" she smiled at me softly.

"I just got overwhelmed, I'm sorry"

"Don't be sorry, you just got a hell of a lot of surprising information. I'd be worried if you weren't overwhelmed" she chuckled.

I turned to face Hina, who was still standing defensively in front of Pappi.

"Are we all good here?" she asked cautiously.

"Yes, I apologise" I said with a nod of my head.

"Okay then" she replied taking a small step to the side of Pappi. I looked down at the old woman and breathed out deeply. I know that she couldn't tell me what she saw, it's not the place of a Seer to divulge information like that. They have to let nature take its course and let the Goddess decide what people know, and when the people know.

"My apologies Pappi, I didn't mean to question your role as a Seer" I said as calmly as possible.

"I know sweet child" she returned with a smile.

"Will you tell me where she is? I need to go to her immediately" I asked as I knelt down in front of her, taking her hands in mine. She smiled and placed her hand on my cheek.

"You will find her in the far East of Canada".

Chapter

Seven

Zelena

The words cut me like a knife. Spartan didn't make it. No wonder Cole doesn't want anything to do with me. It's my fault that his father is dead. The hunters came for me, if I was never here then Spartan still would be. All the dead wolves would be. All I have brought to this pack is death and destruction. I still don't know exactly how many Weres died the night of the battle, but right now I can only focus on the one. I remember, clear as day, when Gunner explained why the packs were so willing to die for me. Because I am a gift from the Goddess, a beacon of hope for all Were-kind. Well, how much hope am I offering Cole now? It's not my place to mourn for Spartan, after all, I only met him a few times. But why do I still feel like I have lost someone dear to me? Is it just the guilt? No, I don't think so. It's Cole. Our relationship had a rough start, but we came around. He came around. And before that damn battle, we were good, we were friends. But now he is hurting, and it's because of me that he is in pain. Maybe that's why I'm feeling this way. I'm mourning for Cole, for his pain.

"Zelena" Gunner had his arm on my shoulder and was shaking me gently.

"Are you alright?" he asked concerned, his eyes searching over my face.

"I'm fine" I mumbled, blinking my eyes rapidly.

"You sure Little One, you kind of phased out there for a few minutes" Tobias said from beside me. I looked at him and forced a smile to my face. He didn't buy it for a second. He reached out his hand and wiped a traitorous tear from my cheek. I took a deep breath and looked at the faces around me. Nat and Smith were across from me with sad sympathetic expressions. I don't know why but it angered me. I looked at Gunner and he was the same. Why are they feeling sorry for me? It's not like my dad just died, it's Cole they should be concerned for. I huffed in frustration and stood up from my stool.

"Where are you going?" Gunner asked,

"To find Cole" I answered firmly before turning to the door, not giving any of them a chance to argue. As I headed out the front door and into the field in front of the house, I could hear their footsteps following closely behind me. As I made my way towards Cole's cabin, I noticed a lot of pack members all starting to crowd around me. At first, I thought they were about to attack, but as they got closer, I saw that their faces held only love.

"Luna" they called to me and bowed their heads. They like me. No, they adore me, how is that possible? I am the reason their former Beta is dead and who knows how many others. How did they not grasp that?

They have been waiting for you

I turned to look at Gunner, he was watching his pack members and smiling and nodding as they greeted him.

Why?

You're their Luna, they were worried about you

I looked around at all the smiling faces. The feeling of their acceptance and their love and devotion seeped into my skin. I could feel how happy they were to see me, and I couldn't contain the smile on my face.

"We're so glad that you're back Luna".

"Thank the Goddess you're okay".

"We've missed you, Luna".

So many happy and adoring faces, and it's for me. I've never felt so much love and happiness before. They really do want me.

They don't blame me?

Of course they don't

But I blame me

Gunner came up behind me, wrapped his arms around my waist, and kissed my neck. The smiling faces looked at us in awe.

They adore you Little Wolf. Just like I do

I turned my head and kissed Gunner's cheek and continued to smile and shake hands with the surrounding pack members. As I looked around the gathered people, my eyes caught a glimpse of someone standing far off at the tree line. I snapped my eyes back and stared at the person.

"Cole" I whispered. I pushed my way through the people and started to run towards Cole.

"Zee, wait" Gunner called as I ran off. Once Cole realized I was coming towards him he turned and dashed into the trees out of sight, but I didn't stop. I ran into the trees and saw the tattered remains of Cole's clothes. He's changed form. I kicked off my sandals as Gunner reached me.

"Just let him be" he pleaded.

"No, I need to talk with him" I rushed out as I pulled off my shirt. I dropped it on the forest floor and Gunner growled. I snapped my head to him, looking at him surprised. Why the heck is he growling at me? I looked down at myself, oh, I forgot that I wasn't wearing underwear. Ugh, whatever. I pulled down my shorts and crouched on the ground completely naked. I closed my eyes and let my change start. Heat flooded my body and then my arms snapped out and back in, and my legs followed right after. My back arched and twisted as my face elongated and then my neck snapped to the side. The pain was nothing like I remember it. This change was almost pleasant, easy. Painful but bearable.

I dug my paws into the dirt and took off in the direction of Cole's scent. Gunner didn't waste any time in running up beside me, nudging into me with his huge body.

Please, I need to talk with him

He's not ready

He doesn't need to talk, I just need to tell him I'm sorry

Gunner growled and huffed, obviously conceding that he wasn't talking me out of this. I continued running and focused my hearing. Drowning out all the other forest noise was hard, mainly because Gunner's heartbeat next to me was ridiculously loud. I pushed him out of my mind and searched ahead. There. I can hear paws hitting the ground and a racing heartbeat. I breathed in deeply, inhaling the scent, and then my eyes flew forward through the trees. I can see him, Cole, his big brown wolf running and prancing through the forest. I dug in my claws and took off faster. It wasn't long until I could see him ahead of us, weaving through the trees. As we got closer, he skidded to a stop and sat down. He was panting softly and looking at a small stream in front of his paws. I slowed down and came up beside him, Gunner stopped just behind us.

Go away Zelena

Cole, I'm so sorry

Please leave

I can't leave knowing that you're hurting

Drop it Zelena

Please Cole, I'm so sorry, if I could take his place, I would

That comment earned a huff and low growl from Gunner. I looked back at him and snarled with a shake of my head. He huffed again and looked away from me.

Just don't, okay, leave me alone

Cole, please listen to me. I can't tell you how sorry I am. I never meant for this to happen, any of this

Yeah, but it did

I know, and it's all my fault, what can I do to help you?

Cole huffed and tossed his head to the side, away from me.

What do you care, it's not like we're friends

I was taken aback slightly by his words, I know he's hurt but I wasn't ready for his bluntness. I lowered my head and whined softly, feeling a little dejected. We sat quietly for a few minutes. I could smell the grief and sadness coming from Cole. I could feel the pain he was in.

Just leave me alone

No. I will never leave him alone, I won't leave anyone who is hurting alone. I was forced to suffer alone for my whole life, I won't let the same happen to Cole. Or anyone that I love.

And I do love him, he is my Mate's best friend and my Beta. I sat up straight and edged closer to him, nudging my head into his neck and resting it on his shoulder.

I won't leave you, Cole, none of us will ever leave you, we love you

Cole growled lowly and huffed before shoving me off of him, he stood up and took a few steps away from me. He stopped and turned around slowly to face me. His sharp canines were borne and his ears lowered, the rage that radiated from him was nauseating.

I will say this once and only once. I don't want your love, your pity, or your friendship. I want nothing from you Zelena

I dropped my head and whined softly, his harsh words slicing me deeply. I felt Gunner's body come closer behind me and his warning growl vibrate through the air.

Tri-Moon Pack is my home, and you are my Luna, because of this and only this will I tolerate your presence.

Watch yourself Cole

Gunner was starting to rage behind me, I could feel his anger flowing through me. I tried my hardest to push it out of my mind and concentrate on Cole and his pain.

Stop Gunner, let him talk

The position of Beta is mine and I won't let you take that from me as well

I would never…

Cole barked and growled in an effort to silence me. Gunner stepped forward and positioned himself ready to attack.

Cole please…

I don't want to be your friend and I don't want to hear your apologies. Just know that when I bow to you, it is out of duty to my Luna and not out of respect for you.

Cole lunged forward snapping at Gunner as he pushed passed him, taking off through the trees. He hates me, he really does hate me. Oh Goddess, what have I done? My body flopped to the forest floor with my head falling on my paws. The sadness inside me was overwhelming and I could no longer hold back the whimpers. Gunner's large wolf lay beside me, resting his head on my back.

Why does this hurt so much?

It's your Luna bond, you can feel his grief

It's so painful

You just haven't learned to cut off the link yet, it will get better. I'll teach you
I don't deserve to feel better
Zelena, it wasn't your fault, you have to know that. Cole is just hurting and is looking for someone to blame. He'll come around eventually
I don't think so
Off in the distance the most sorrowful and pain filled howl that I had ever heard echoed through the trees. It's Cole's wolf. Gunner whined softly before throwing his head back and joining in on the howl. I rubbed my head into his neck before lifting it to the sky and howling as well. Soon the afternoon air was filled with howls from all around us, the pack hearing the mournful cry of their Beta and grieving with him.
Gunner lowered his head, nuzzling into my neck.
I'm sorry he said those things to you
It's okay, I should have listened to you and given him space
No, he should never have spoken to you like that, and he will be reprimanded
I jumped to my feet and barked down at Gunner.
Don't you dare. He needed to say what he said, he didn't threaten me or do anything dangerous, he was just expressing how he felt.
He disrespected you
It's okay, please let it go
I can't do that
Gunner please, just leave it alone
He stood up slowly and shook out his fur, with a huff and a low growl he nodded.
Just this once
Thank you
Come one now, we should head back to the house.

~

Dinner came quickly after we got back to the house and Roe put on quite the spread. Along with the usual family members, she had invited Smith and his mum Deena. I hadn't seen her since the day of the battle, she left on the bus with many of the other she-wolves. She was very excited to sit and gossip with me. Also in attendance was Tobias and a warrior wolf, whose name I believe is Felix. No Cole. After the events of this afternoon, I was exhausted and feeling too dejected to fully get into the spirit of family dinner. I hated that I was being so rude and withdrawn from everyone, but I was just not feeling it. After the main course, Gunner came to kneel by my chair, drawing me from my blank daydream.

"Come on love, let's get you to bed" he whispered, placing a soft kiss on my cheek.

"Your mum…"

"It's fine, don't worry about it" he cut me off.

I looked over at Roe and she nodded her head and waved her hands in a shoeing motion. I smiled weakly and allowed Gunner to lead me out of the dining hall.

"I didn't say goodnight to anyone" I said as we walked slowly up the stairs.

"You didn't need to, anyone at that table could see that you're a walking zombie" he chuckled,

"Was I really rude?" I sighed,

"No Little Wolf, don't fret about it. But before we go to bed, I have a surprise for you".

He led me past our bedroom and to a door a few doors further down the hallway. He let go of my hand pushed open the door and stood to the side to let me in. I stepped into the magnificent bathroom alight with only candles. The smell of lavender and honey filled my nostrils as my eyes fell on a huge bathtub filled to the brim with bubbles. The whole scene looked heavenly.

"You did all this for me?" I smiled back at him.

"Of course I did" he smiled, stepping forward wrapping his arms around my waist, and resting his chin on my shoulder.

"But when?"

"During dinner" he chuckled, and I huffed. I didn't even notice that he left the table.

"I'm not surprised that you didn't notice I disappeared, you look exhausted" he said softly before pressing gentle kisses to my neck.

"Thank you" I whispered, still admiring all the candles and the scents around the room. Who knew my Mate was such a romantic.

Gunner gripped the hem of my shirt and began to lift it over my stomach. I lifted my hands to allow him to pull it up and over my head and then toss it on the floor. He ran his fingers softly up my spine and then unclasped my bra, letting it fall to the floor. His fingers slowly moved over the bare skin of my back before coming up and down my arms. He traced along my collarbone and gently between my breasts. Moving his fingers slowly down my stomach and stopping at my shorts, he unbuttoned them and tugged them down my legs. I stepped out of them and leaned back into Gunner's embrace. He continued to move his fingers, ever so softly, all over my exposed skin. A calming heat and pins and needles were left in the wake of his finger's path over my body. My head was resting back on his chest and my eyes were closed, to better allow myself to feel his touch.

"That feels really nice" I croaked out.

He pressed his lips to the top of my shoulder and moved his kisses up my neck, continuing until he reached my temple.

"Hop in before it gets too cold" he said pushing me forward. I turned and grabbed his hand, looking deep into his eyes.

"Please, will you stay?" I pleaded with him. He smiled and nodded, pulling his shirt off and tossing it to the floor with my own.

I stepped carefully into the tub and lowered myself into the still steaming water. I hissed a little as the heat shocked me, but my body welcomed the hot water. Gunner slid in behind me, pulling me to sit between his legs and lean against his chest. Without saying a word, he picked up a loofah ball, squirted some body wash on it, and began to gently rub my chest. He lifted my arm and dragged the sponge up and down my arm, covering it in bubbles. He moved on to the next arm and repeated the process.

"Sit forward" he commanded, and I obliged. Sitting up I hugged my knees and Gunner began to move the sponge in circles on my back. He was so soft and gentle with his movements, like I was the most delicate thing in the world. He lightly swept his fingers over the mark on the back of my neck, outlining the shape of each moon. I adore this side of Gunner, the caring and romantic side. He is always caring but he usually has a bit more of a protective and passiveness to his love. Right here, right now, I can feel nothing but pure love and adoration coming from him.

He pulled me back into his arms and I rested my head on his shoulder as he gently caressed my arms and stomach. The bathroom was silent, the water was deliciously warm, and the scent of the lavender was seriously soothing. Before I knew it, I was out.

~

I opened my eyes and looked around, I was in a forest of some kind, but somehow different. All the trees and the grass and the sky, everything was white as snow. I walked forward through the trees, as if my body knew exactly where I was going. I came to a clearing, a field of white flowers and white grass. In the middle of the clearing is a figure sitting amongst the flowers. I felt a wave of peace and tenderness wash over me and I continued walking towards the figure. As I got closer, I realized it was a woman. Why did this feel so familiar to me? The woman turned and smiled softly up at me. She was strikingly beautiful. Her pale skin had a glow to it and her eyes were as white as the flowers around us. She reached her hand out to me and I took it, a gentle calmness, like shoots of soothing electricity ran through my arm. I sat down beside her and marvelled at her beauty. Her long and smooth white hair sat calmly down her back. She was wearing a shimmering dress that floated around her like it was caught in a gentle breeze.

"Hello again, daughter of mine" she cooed softly as she ran her long and soft fingers over my cheek. That voice, there was something so familiar about that voice. I was about to ask her who she was when she spoke again,

"It's not time yet, you need to go back" she smiled. Back? Back where? I looked around at the white forest and then back to the beautiful woman, where did she want me to go? Before I got the chance to ask her, she lifted her hand and flicked her wrist.

~

I shot forward and gasped loudly. I quickly spun my head around and realized I was back in the bathroom.

"Whoa, Babe are you alight?"

I snapped my head around and Gunner was looking back at me with worry written all over his face. I launched forward into his body, wrapping my arms tightly around his neck and straddling his lap.

"Hey, hey now" he cooed soothingly, rubbing his hand up and down my back. I was panting hard, and my heart was thumping in my chest. I wasn't scared though, I don't know what I was feeling, exhilarated maybe.

"It's okay, it was just a dream" he said softly.

It was a dream. It felt so real though, was it truly a dream? I've never had a dream that made me feel like this. And plus, everything about where I was and who I was with, it all felt so natural and normal. It felt like I was at home with family. Who was she? Her voice was so familiar, even her face, a face I don't think I have ever seen before, it still felt like I knew her. Gunner continued to make soothing sounds and spoke to me softly as he held me in his arms. Who was that woman?

"Are you okay?" Gunner asked, not releasing his hold on me.

"I'm okay. It was just a dream, or a vision. I don't know" I answered taking a deep breath.

"A vision?" he questioned,

"What kind of vision?"

"I'm not sure, I was in a field of white flowers with a beautiful woman"

"Hmm, I like the sound of this dream" he chuckled.

"Gunner" I growled. I pushed myself back up and slapped his chest. He laughed and grabbed my hands, holding them to his chest.

"I'm just kidding" he laughed.

"You better be".

"Will you show me?"

"Show you, my dream?"

"Yeh, flash me what you saw" he asked. Of course, I could flash him a picture of the field and the woman. I sometimes forget about all my wolfy abilities.

"Sure" I smile at him and place my hands on either side of his face. I see the picture in my mind, the soft smile of the beautiful woman and the white flowers and I push it forward onto Gunner. He inhales deeply and grabs my hands. His eyes flew open and he looked at me like he was searching for something in my eyes.

"Who is she?" he asked, moving my hands back to his chest.

"I'm not sure, I didn't get to ask" I say with a shrug of my shoulders.

"Okay".

"Okay?"

"Yep" he smirked and pulled my hands up to his shoulders so that my body would fall forward onto him. I locked my fingers around his neck as Gunner's hands made their way to my backside. He leans forward and crashes his lips to mine as he squeezes my ass.

"Alpha, if I didn't know any better, I would think you are trying to take advantage of me" I giggle and kiss him back.

"Lucky then that you don't know any better, Luna" he smirked and flicked my bottom lip with his tongue. I kissed him hard, our tongues moving together as I lifted my hips forward and positioned myself on top of his already hard member. I buried my fingers into his hair and pulled just a little hard. Gunner growled and bit on my bottom lip. His fingers found my entrance in the water and he began to slide his fingers along the lips. I grind my hips against his hand, and he slips two fingers inside me, curling them back to hit against my G spot. I moan into his mouth and he moves his fingers faster. After a few minutes, he removed his fingers put his hands on my hips, and lifted me slightly. I felt the tip of his cock brush against my pussy, and I gasped aloud in excitement. I reach down and direct his cock into me as he slowly lowers me down on top of him. I grind my hips a few times, causing Gunner to groan and moan in pleasure. I sit back upright and place my hands on the edge of the bath. I lift myself up and slam back down onto him hard.

"Fuck" Gunner hissed, rolling his head back. I lifted myself and again slammed back down on his dick. The fullness was amazing but the sensation of him bottoming out as I crashed back down was beyond anything else. I continued to bounce up and down on his magnificent cock, the water was spilling everywhere, and I didn't care. Our moans and groans echoed around the bathroom. I could feel the tightness building in my stomach and my walls were starting to tighten around Gunner's dick.

"I'm ready" I moaned as I slammed down onto him again.

"A little more" he grunted as his fingers gripped my hips. He lifted my body and pulled me back down a few more times. I was holding back as much as I could, but I wasn't going to last.

"Gunner" I called out as I felt the start of my release. My clit was throbbing, and my vagina walls were contracting around him. He groaned and bucked his hips upwards and spurted his load inside me. I fell forward onto his chest as my orgasm died down. I was breathing heavily and could feel Gunner's heart thumping against my chest. He wrapped his arms around my waist and held me in place until both our breathing regulated again. A yawn forced its way out my mouth and Gunner chuckled.

"Come one Zee, let's get you to bed" he said as he lifted my hips and slid out of me. He got out of the tub and wrapped a towel around his waist, he grabbed another towel and motioned for me to stand up. He wrapped the towel around my shoulders and then scooped me up out of the bath. I squealed a little and hid my face in his neck. As he walked to the bathroom door, I looked down at all the water on the floor.

"Wait, we need to clean up" I said tapping his shoulder.

"I'll do it later" he grunted and carried me back to our room. He tossed me to the bed, and I landed with a bounce and a giggle. I crawled my way up to my pillow, leaving the wet towel behind. As soon as I laid my head down, I knew that I wasn't getting up again and drifted off straight to sleep.

Chapter Eight

Zelena

"Are you sure about this?" I asked Gunner, still not convinced and feeling a little reluctant.

"Yes" he groaned adamantly, for the tenth time.

"The pack deserves to celebrate and so do you" he said more gently as he rubbed his hands up and down my arms.

The thought of throwing a birthday party, crossed with a new Alpha and Luna ceremony, crossed with the 'arrival of the Goddess' celebration, or so Roe called it, all seemed a bit tacky. Granted the attack was over three months ago and I've been back at home in the pack house for just under two weeks now, try as I may, there was no talking Roe out of this. But I understand, kind of. The pack went through a lot with the hunter attack, and they haven't had the chance to celebrate their new Alpha, with everyone being in mourning. As I have been told many times now, the blessing of the chosen daughter, or me in other words, is a huge deal to all Weres and they need to celebrate. Plus, Gunner did promise me a birthday party, so who am I to rain on their parade. I don't know, I just don't feel good about it though. I feel like we will be dancing on the graves of the lost wolves, on Spartan's grave.

Cole still hasn't said anything to me. And now because of me, Gunner's relationship with him has become strained as well. Gunner hates that his best friend, and Beta, is being so dismissive and disrespectful to his Mate, his Luna. I just keep telling him to give it time, I'm still holding out hope that Cole will come around eventually.

"Ugh, fine" I grunted in defeat.

"Excellent" Roe called happily as she burst through the bedroom door.

"You have finally convinced her to get on board then?" she smiled broadly, her eyes switching between the two of us.

"Mum, we talked about this. Boundaries" Gunner whined.

"Oh shush, I'm your mother, I've seen all your bits and pieces" she said waving her hand dismissively at Gunner.

I couldn't help but laugh at the shade of red his face turned, and the look of his eyes nearly bulging out of his head at his mother's words. Roe took my hands and turned me to face her, smiling at me with a glint of mischief in her eyes.

"Well, now that you've stopped fighting it, you and me need to go shopping" she said with slight bounce of her shoulders.

"We do?" I questioned cautiously.

"Absolutely. We need to find the perfect birthday and Luna dress, something fit for a Goddess" she chuckled and winked at the same time.

"Well, who am I to say no to a shopping trip?" I smiled sweetly at her. Roe's excitement was infectious, and I did really love my last shopping experience. If I'm going to get on board with this big ass party, then I'm going to do it in style.

"Yay" she sung, clapping her hands in front of her while bouncing on her feet. It's hard to remember sometimes that she is basically my mother-in-law and more than twenty years older than us. Her spirit is so carefree, she makes it feel like she is just one of the girls. It's all part of why I love her.

"Nat can come too, right?"

"Absolutely. She's coming, Deena too".

Gunner groaned and rubbed his hand down his face. A look of exasperation crossed his tired face.

"I'll get the car then" he grumbled.

"Uh, no you won't. You're not coming" Roe snapped at her son.

"Yes I am. I'm not letting you take my Mate out of the village without protection" Gunner snapped back.

I took a small step back and pulled my hands out of Roe's. The two of them began to argue about my safety and ability to protect myself. I know better than to interrupt this one. As stealthily as I could, I walked slowly towards the open door. Neither of them taking notice to my retreating figure, as they were too engrossed in their bickering. I made it out the door and dashed downstairs to the foyer. I could still hear them going at it from down here and a smile spread across my face. The door to the hall opened and I was surprised to see Cole exiting with Smith behind him. I stood up straight and looked at Cole, silently praying for him to talk to me. I offered a smile as his eyes connected with mine. He immediately looked away and continued walking towards the front door.

"Luna" he mumbled with a small tilt of his head before leaving. That was it, one word and he left again. Dammit Cole, how am I ever going to fix this?

"Hey Little Luna" Smith smiled draping his arm over my shoulder.

"Hi smith" I said softly, leaning my head into his chest and still looking at the door Cole just left through.

"He'll come around, just be patient" Smith said giving my shoulder a gentle shake.

I shook it off, smiled and gave a weak and unconvincing nod of my head. I left Smith in the foyer and walked to the movie room where I knew Nat was still lounging on the couch.

"What's on?" I asked from the doorway.

"Nothing worth watching" she groaned flipping off the TV.

"Well good, because I would hate to pull you away from something important".

She sat up straight her eyes bright and a smile spread across her face.

"Why, where are you pulling me to?" she asked excitedly.

She, along with everyone else has been trying to convince me that this party is a good thing. She has thrown every possible reason and excuse imaginable at me. I know she is going to hit the roof when she hears that I have finally caved in.

"Looks like another shopping trip is required" I smiled coyly at her.

"You're on board?" she squealed jumping to her feet.

"Yes, you've roped me in" I chuckled.

She jumped and clapped her hands in front of her, just like her mother did. With a high-pitched squeal she grabbed my arms and did another little jump around.

"This is perfect, we are going to find you the most amazing dress ever. Trust me. I am going to make you look like a drop-dead diva. My poor brother won't be able to keep his hands off you. None of those poor unsuspecting little boys will be able to hide their boners. AHH this is so exciting!" her voice steadily rose in volume as her rambling sped up. Her fast babbling is one of my favourite things about her. It's always very entertaining to hear where her mouth takes her before her before her brain can catch up.

"Nat, oh my god will you stop?" I yelled at her with a laugh. I grabbed her shoulders and shook.

"Sorry, I'm rambling again aren't I. I can't help it though, you know what I'm like. I'm way too excited to control myself. O.M.G. I have to go get dressed, we'll need to leave like right now if we are going today. Wait, are we going today? What am I saying, of course we are, the party is tomorrow night".

I pinched the bridge of my nose and shook my head as Nat continued to ramble on. She ended up walking out of the room and up the stairs, still talking, completely oblivious to the fact that I wasn't following her. I laughed to myself at her neurotic rambling. I have never met anyone like Nat, she is positively one of a kind.

The sound of Gunner and Roe coming down the stairs, still arguing filled the foyer. I stood back leaning on the door frame of the movie room. Neither Roe nor Gunner noticed my presence.

"It's done Mum, drop it" Gunner yelled.

"This is completely unnecessary. You're being a helicopter Mate" Roe snapped back.

"I'm being an Alpha, and sending guards is not unnecessary and you know damn well why!" Gunner screamed as he stopped walking and turned to face his mum.

"We can handle ourselves" Roe huffed with a stomp of her foot.

"Well, I'm not risking it. You of all people should understand, her safety is more at risk now than it ever was before".

Why was my safety at risk? I thought we ended the hunters, what other risks are there?

"Gunner, I understand your concerns, I do. But it will just draw more attention to us" Roe spoke a little softer. I don't think I have ever heard Roe use his name with adding a 'baby' or 'darling' or some other pet name to it. She must be either really mad or super serious right now.

"I'm not backing down on this" Gunner said gruffly.

"Compromise with me here, will ya" Roe groaned,

"Just one, a young one that will blend in with us and not look like a bodyguard".

Gunner huffed and groaned loudly as he dragged his hand down his face.

"Fine, one guard. But you are to stay with him the entire time, what he says goes".

"Excellent" Roe said cheerfully.

"I'm serious Mum. You make sure she stays by his side the entire time. Straight there and back, no extra stops and no aimless wondering around. Understood?" Gunner's voice was stern and full of authority. It made tingles run through my legs.

"Yes, my love, I understand. We will be good little girls, I promise" Roe giggled and skipped away down the hall. Gunner rubbed the back of his neck and expelled a long sigh.

"I'm going to regret this" he groaned to himself. He may be the Alpha, but he is still putty in his mother's hand. It's a little amusing that a man of his power and stature could still be brought down a peg by his tiny little mother.

"She has you wrapped around her finger" I chuckled stepping forward.

"Holy fucking Goddess" He screamed, jumping back and clutching his chest,

"You scared the fucking shit out of me. How long have you been standing there?" he huffed heavily walking towards me.

"Long enough to know that you seem to think my life is in danger" I answered bluntly, a subtle question hidden in my response.

"Well, I'd be lying if I said it wasn't" he answered meekly. Wrapping his arms around my waist, he pulled me into his body.

"I thought we took care of the hunters?"

"We did, that clan at least. But there are other dangers in the world Zee. More are slowly coming out of the woodworks"

"What is that meant to mean?"

He unwrapped his arms and pulled me away from him. Gripping my shoulders, he held me in place so that he could study my face.

"Don't worry about it, Little Wolf. Just enjoy your shopping trip and we can talk more about it when you get home".

He bent down and kissed the top of my head before smacking my ass and walking away to his office. Uh what? Excuse me sir, I wasn't done with that conversation. I stood there dumbfounded that he just walked off without letting me speak. Since when was Gunner so dismissive. I felt a small fire light in my chest. He was not going to just brush me off like that, we're meant to be equals in this. I was ready to storm into his office in a crazy rage and demand answers. Luckily, I was pulled from my short rage spiral by Nat running happily down the stairs, donning a short red skater dress with big black ankle boots. She should definitely try out for a modelling agency.

"You ready little sis?" she smiled at me. All my anger towards Gunner and his brutish brush off was completely forgotten.

"Totally" I smiled back.

"Let's go" she grabbed my hand and pulled me to the front door.

"Mum, we're ready" she screamed through the house, maybe a little too loudly.

"Alright, alright. No need to scream the house down girly. Let's hit the road" Roe said walking passed us and out the front door. Deena was waiting for us at the bottom of the porch steps with a bright smile gracing her pretty face.

"Do you want me to drive?" she asked Roe as she glided down the steps.

"Ugh, no" Roe grunted, as she led the way to the front of the house.

"That tyrannical son of mine has arranged a driver, and a personal bodyguard to shadow us".

"Wait seriously?" Nat whined.

"Yes" Roe replied bluntly, clearly unimpressed with the situation. As we walked up to the edge of the driveway, waiting for us by the black SUV was Felix. He was dressed in casual blue jeans and plain black t-shirt, sporting a pair of aviator sunglasses. His chocolate brown hair looks scruffy in the most natural I'm-not-even-trying kind of way. I'd never noticed before how handsome Felix is. He can't hold a candle to Gunner, no one could, but he can definitely steal some hearts. He's well-built and tall like Gunner, and his creamy skin shone brightly in the direct sunlight. Let's hope there aren't too many ladies at the shopping centre today, or else we may get mobbed.

We all climbed into the car, Roe in the passenger seat and Felix driving, the rest of us in the back. Nat, as per usual, hooked up some music for the trip. And we were off. The drive was slow, especially as we got closer to the city. It looks like everyone is out and about, trying to make the most of their last week of summer break before the new school year starts. I am so damn glad that I don't have to do the high school thing anymore. That place was hell. I'm also so thankful to Lupus, he pretended to be my father and told the school that I finished my senior year doing online schooling. I was able to graduate and got my high school diploma. After everything that I had to endure during my schooling, the last thing that I wanted was to be a high school dropout.

"Once we get to the centre, I want you all to stick together. No stragglers, and no one is to walk off alone. Understood?" Felix's commanding voice filled the car. We all mumbled our 'yes, okay, understood' as we pulled into the underground lot.

"You've got two hours before we are to be on the road again"

"Lighten up Felix dear, you're spoiling the mood" Roe badgered.

"Let's go ladies" Felix replied, ignoring Roe's comment.

Roe and Denna led the way, Nat and I walking with our arms linked behind them and Felix bringing up the rear. The first dress shop was horrible. It was filled with tiny slutty dresses that would fit like a second skin. My aversion to tight clothes has most definitely not gone away. The next shop was not too bad. There was a lot to choose from but nothing that screamed 'perfection'.

I was walking the isle of another shop, scanning the dresses on the racks, when a shiver ran down my spine. I felt like I was being watched. I looked around the store but didn't see anything weird. Roe and Nat were arguing over a baby blue chiffon dress, Nat saying it was atrocious, while Roe thinks it's cute. I'd have to side with Nat on this one. Deena was sitting on a pink velvet day bed listening to the exchange and Felix was standing by the entrance to the little boutique. His eyes constantly searching. There were two other young women in the store, but I couldn't see anyone else.

Looking back to the rack, an emerald green silk material caught my eye. I pulled the dress out and held it up in front of me. It looks really pretty. I took the dress to the change room and undressed out of my denim skirt and baggy white crop top. The dress material slid over my skin like water. The cowl neck front accentuated what little cleavage I have, while the silk hung tight on my hips, giving me the illusion of having curves. I turned to see the back in the mirror and fell more in love with the dress. Thin spaghetti straps connected to the front of the dress and came over my shoulders and down my back in a criss-cross pattern, ending at the small of my back. The thigh high spilt made the dress feel a little more flowy and less constricting. This is definitely the most revealing thing I have ever worn, but I love it. I could not stop staring at myself. The dark green made my pale skin glow and in contrast with my raven hair, I looked like some kind of modern-day Snow White.

I stepped out of the change room and stood in front of the wall to ceiling mirror in the common dressing area. The change of lighting made me love the dress more again. Twirling in slow circles in front of the mirror and swaying the train of the dress around my legs, I felt like a princess.

"You look lovely" a deep accented voice came from the entrance to the dressing area. I turned to see a dark-haired man leaning against the wall with his arms crossed over his chest. He was tall and a bit burley, kind of like a lumberjack with better fashion sense. Wearing a leather jacket over a crisp white t-shirt, matched with black jeans, he looked very bad-boy dangerous. His eyes were sweeping over my body from top to bottom and back again, a sly smirk playing on his lips. His hungry gaze immediately made me feel uneasy.

"Uh, thank you" I replied softly.

"You should get it" he said still staring at me.

"Excuse me?"

"The dress, you should get it" His English was brilliant but there are hints of an accent hidden among his words.

"Oh, okay". I couldn't look away from the man. I wanted to, I wanted to turn back to my dressing room and slide the lock in place. But something deep inside me kept me still, my feet planted and my eyes on the mystery man.

His tongue peeked out and grazed slowly over his bottom lip as his eyes bore their way through my skin. He wasn't just looking at me. He was looking into me, deep inside me. Staring at something buried way underneath. He smacked his lips and tensed his jaw, pressing his plump lips into a tight line.

"You look ravishing" a low growl rumbled through the word ravishing as it fell from his full dark pink lips.

The man stood up from the wall and stepped towards me and I promptly took a step back. He smiled, a look of lust twinkling in his dark eyes. He took another step forward, I again stepped away. We continued this dance until my back hit the mirror. With two more steps, he was now standing right before me. A Were. I can smell the wolf inside him, the scent of fur still hung to his skin. Not just a Were, power, a powerful Were. I froze, fear swimming through my stomach. Where is Nat, where is Felix? The man placed one hand on the mirror next to my head and leaned closer to me. He smelled of wet earth and stale cologne, but the scent of his desire was more potent than anything else. He reached down and grabbed my hand. I fought him, trying to pull my hand from his grip but it was pointless, his grip was locked. He lifted my hand to his face and firmly pressed his nose against the inside of my wrist and inhaled deeply.

Do something dammit! Use your force field, push him away, something. I was screaming at myself internally. But it didn't work. I was stuck, unmoving, my fear taking full control of my body. The tall man pressed his lips to the back of my hand and held them there for a little too long.

"My Goddess" he whispered, lifting his eyes to mine. His pools of dark brown bore into my soul, my nerves sending shivers through my arms and legs. He knows who, or what I am. My skin broke out in heated goosebumps and body shook uncontrollably. The mirror on the wall behind me began to shake and the display table and pink armchair in the dressing room creaked and cracked as they rose into the air. The man didn't take his eyes from mine, his smirk now spread across his face. One more chaste kiss to my hand before he dropped it again. In a blink, he was gone. My body fell to the floor, a wave of exhaustion and numbness blew through me. The armchair and display table dropped down with a loud thump. Roe, Nat and Deena came bursting into the dressing room. Nat quickly rushed to my side while Roe and Deena distracted the shop assistant. I could hear what they were telling her. Their voices faded away into nothing while my mind flashed images of the mystery man.

"Hey, what happened, are you okay?" Nat asked me, her voice laced with concern.

"I, I don't know" I mumbled. I buried my face in my hands and tried to take deep breaths. My body trembled with each strained inhale. Who was he? How did he know who I was? I wanted to cry, to scream, to punch something. How could I be so weak, why didn't I fight back. Something about that man rubbed me the wrong way. I thought I was done being the scared little girl that didn't know how to defend herself. I'm a fucking werewolf with superpowers, why didn't I use them?

Felix appeared in front of me and gripped my hand. I shuddered and tried to jerk out of his hold on me. His touch taking me back to the stranger and how powerless he made me feel. A stray tear rolled down my cheek and Nat growled at Felix.

"Let. Her. Go" she demanded.

"We have to go, now" he replied, ignoring her request and instead scooped me up into his arms, bridal style, and began walking for the door.

"Hey, you have to pay for that" the shop assistant yelled.

"Here darling allow me" Roe said to the girl, dragging her over to the registers.

Felix marched through the shopping centre like a man on a mission, the crowd of shoppers parted like the red sea to let him through.

"Did you see who it was?" his firm voice asked me.

"Wha-what?" I stuttered.

"Did you see who attacked you?" he asked not missing a beat.

"I wasn't attacked".

Felix stopped walking and looked down at me in his arms. His brows were furrowed together, and the stink of anger was seeping out of his pores.

"You weren't attacked?" he echoed me.

"No, I mean yes. I don't know. He didn't attack me, he said he liked my dress and kissed my hand and called me Goddess" I said looking away from Felix's heated gaze.

Felix growled, I felt the vibrations rumble through his chest. The intimate position that we were in made the whole interrogation that much more uncomfortable. Roe, Deena and Nat caught up to us, still standing in the middle of the walkway. Shopper gazed at us as they passed. Curious eyes and full of question. The added attention made me shiver.

"What's going on Felix?" Roe demanded, her voice hard and agitated.

"We will talk in the car". With that Felix continued his marching to the parking lot, me still in his arms. We got to the car and Felix finally placed me down in the back seat. Roe and Nat slid in on either side of me while Deena and Felix climbed in the front. They all turned to me, eyes expectant and waiting for answers.

"What happened, Sweetheart?" Roe asked lifting my hand to her lap and stroking it gently.

"I was trying on the dress when this man said I looked nice" I started,

"Did you know him?" Felix asked,

"No, I'd never seen him before. He said that I should get the dress because it looked good. Then he backed me up against the mirror. I don't know what happened, I just froze, I didn't push him away, I didn't use my powers, I did nothing. I just stood there like an idiot. He grabbed my wrist and smelled me before he kissed my hand and called me his Goddess."

"He smelled you?" Felix asked with a cocked eyebrow,

"Yes, he pressed his nose to my wrist and inhaled"

"And he called you Goddess?" Roe asked,

"Yes, he said 'my Goddess'. After that I lost my control and that's when I broke the chair and table"

"And the man?" urged Felix,

"He was there one second, kissing my hand, and the next he was gone. That's when Nat came in".

"None of you saw anyone exit the dressing room?" Felix asked looking at the others.

"No, no one" Row replied while Deena shook her head,

"She was the only one in there when I went in" Nat answered.

"Okay, we need to get back and report to the Alpha" Felix turned on the car and started to pull out of the parking garage.

"Do we have to tell Gunner? Nothing happened, I'm fine" I whined. Once he finds out about this, he will lock me in the room and not let me leave again. That, or he will handcuff himself to me. Ugh, this is a disaster.

"Yes" was all Felix said in return.

"Sorry sweet girl, but I'm with Felix on this one" Roe said soothingly, still holding my hand.

"Me too. He will legit kill me if he found out I kept this from him, sister or not" Nat scoffed.

Great, this is going to be a total shit show.

Chapter Nine

Lunaya

Staying true to her Seer ways, all Pappi told me was Canada. Well East Canada, but nothing concrete. No town name, not the name of my daughter, nothing. I wonder if the hunters kept her birth name, engraved on a dainty bracelet worn on the wrist. I wonder how she escaped them. So many questions. A frenzy of emotions swarmed through my body. Joy, because she lives. Fear, that she will reject me as her mother. Anxiety, being forced to wait even longer before seeing her. Pride, that the Goddess has once again risen, and from my child. But above all, hope. It has been a long time that I felt true unadulterated hope. There have been flickers and small glimmers of it over the years, but they dissipated as quickly as they arrived. This time, the hope stays. It warms my body, prickling over my skin and coming to rest deep inside my heart.

Although I fought to leave Luna Eclipse right away, I reluctantly agreed to wait a few more days. Hina has ordered that her Beta, Elaine, join us on the trip to Canada. Along with three other warriors from the pack. Arrangements have been made for flights out of Queenstown, but we can't depart until Tuesday. It'll take a full day to get down the mountain and then a few hours to get to Queenstown, we'll stay overnight before departing the next afternoon. After that we will be plane hopping for the next two days. Auckland, Kuala Lumpur, Dubai, Toronto, then Montreal. After that, we search. Pack by pack, rumour by rumour, until we find her. Forty-eight hours, six flights, four countries and countless hours driving and searching. One step closer to my daughter. Hina's attitude toward me was like a wild roller-coaster ride. She started off with intimidation and fear, then she moved to seducing my Mate and me. We've seen her fury and rage, her sympathy and compassion. After the revelation of my daughter, she became unexpectedly supportive. All of our travel arrangements have been taken care of by her, or the pack. Our flights to Montreal, the accommodation at the bottom of the mountain, hire cars and enough cash to support the six of us for two weeks upon our arrival. I expect her kindness has a lot to do with the possibility of building an alliance with the Triple Goddess, formed through me and my motherly connection. But Luna Eclipse have always been, and will continue to be, a supporter of she-wolf empowerment. Regardless of my connection to the Goddess, they would have still sought her out.

"Are you going to eat that or just stare at it?". Alyse's voice broke me from my tense daydream. I lifted my head and looked at her with a weak smile. She placed her hand on my leg to stop it from bouncing. I have been acting like a nervous wreck, there's no doubt about it.

"Sorry, I was just thinking" I mumbled. I stabbed a piece of fish with my fork and plopped it in my mouth. Turning my nose up with a grunt, it had gone cold already.

"You've barely eaten or slept in nearly two days. I know that your anxious but you're not doing yourself any favours" Alyse scolded while pushing my barely touched plate of food closer to me.

"I know, I know. I'm sorry love" I said, picking up her hand and pressing my lips to her knuckles.

"There's nothing more you can do until we leave tomorrow morning. So please will you at least try and eat" she gently cupped my cheek and glided her thumb over my bottom lip.

"I will" I smiled at her. It was a weak attempt at a smile, and I bet it didn't even nearly convince her, but she nodded and turned back to her own plate anyway. I ate as much as I could stomach, which wasn't much and before long we slowly made our way back to our little hut.

"Miss Lunaya, Miss Alyse".

We were just about to walk through our door when someone called for our attention. We turned around and came to see the breathless face of Trinny, trudging her way through the snow and over to us. Her sister wasn't far behind her. Trinny's pale white skin was flushed wish red cheeks and a red nose from the cold wind. Her hands were folded over her small body and her dark chocolate brown hair poked out from beneath her beanie.

"Is it true?" she asked wiping fresh snow from her cheek.

"I'm sorry?" I questioned her,

"Is it true you're going to meet the Triple Goddess?"

"Oh, well yes that is true".

"Wow wee, how'd you manage that, you've only been here for like two weeks. I don't think anyone has ever gotten on the good side of the Alpha so quickly" Trinny rushed out as her sister came up to her side, eyeing us both curiously.

"Yes, I was thinking the same thing" Maya said. She failed miserably to hide the somewhat jealous nature of her tone. Alyse scoffed and slapped her hand over her mouth and disguised the sound with a cough. I smirked down at her before turning my gaze back to the two young girls.

"The Alpha believes we could be of use on this particular journey" I lied. Well kind of lied, it's not exactly untrue but it is far from the total truth.

"And what is it that you can offer that all of the actual pack members of Luna Eclipse cannot?" Maya said emphasizing the word 'actual'.

"Maya" Trinny hissed, elbowing her sister's ribcage.

"What? They haven't even had their initiation yet and they are already selected to go on a charge as important as this one. It's not right" Maya huffed. She looked at her sister as she spoke but made no attempt to hide her words or hush her voice. She wanted us to hear her, and she wanted us to know that she wasn't exactly happy. I can imagine that many of the other she-wolves feel the same way.

"It's quite alright Trinny, your sister is entitled to her opinions" I said with a tight smile. Maya was a beautiful young girl, pale skin like her younger sister and the same grey almond shaped eyes. She had plump pink lips and a small, upturned nose. Even with the scowl that never left her face, she still held a youthful beauty.

"We are going because we were roaming omegas for nearly twenty years, we have been to every corner of the globe. We have met many Weres in that time and made many friendships and alliances. The Alpha believes that our connections could become of use".

Both the young girls looked us over for a minute. Trinny smiled and bobbed her head with excitement. Maya's eyes still held a little contempt, but her frigid expression had eased.

"Well, I suppose that makes sense" she said sternly.

"This is so exciting" Trinny squealed, her pale grey eyes sparkled with joy.

"I can't believe that she has actually risen and that you get to meet her".

I offered her a kind smile. Her excitement is exactly what I needed. I have been so busy focusing on the possible negatives and my nervousness at the whole thing, that I have not truly let myself bask in the amazement that the Triple Goddess has risen once again. It is exciting. And it is an amazing time for all of Were kind.

"Yes, it is very exciting isn't it?" I held my hand out for her and she took it, squeezing tightly and bouncing on her feet.

"I'm going to make you some cookies, do you think you could give them to the Goddess when you see her?" Trinny asked, her voice holding so much hope.

"Well dear, we don't exactly know where she is. It may take a while for us to find her" Alyse spoke with a gentle motherly tone.

"Oh of course" Trinny giggled, slapping her forehead with the palm of her hand.

"I'll make the cookies for you then, to enjoy on your trip. You can pick them up from the kitchen before you leave".

"That is very sweet of you darling, thank you" said Alyse with a very slight tilt of her head.

"Come on Trinny, it's late" Maya said pulling on her sister's elbow.

"Travel safe and best of luck. I hope to see you again soon" Trinny smiled as she was pulled away.

"Us to Trinny" I called to her. I looked down at Alyse and she watched fondly as the two sisters walked away. I could feel her longing and sadness, even if she would never admit it to me.

"Come on" I said pulling her into the warmth of our hut. Alyse sat down at the bed and begun undoing her boots. I sat on a chair by the small table and watched her work her boots off. Her face was free of emotions, but I could see the sullenness in her eyes. I love her. I dearly love her, but the regret that she had become stuck with me all these years, it runs deep. I never forced her to stay, I actually tried many times to push her away, but she never left. She gave up so much for me and I still don't believe that I was worth it.

"I'm sorry" I whispered through the air of the hut while looking down at my feet.

"What's that?" Alyse questioned,

"I said I'm sorry".

"Whatever for?"

"I'm sorry that you became bridled with me. I'm sorry that you never had children of your own. I'm sorry that you didn't get the life that you deserved".

Alyse became quiet, though I could feel her eyes boring into me. After a moment, she came to kneel in front of me and took my hands in hers, placing them on her chest.

"Lunaya, I am not stuck with you, I chose this life. I chose you. I knew when I chose to remain with you that I would not carry my own child, and I accepted that. You are worth it. Being loved by you is enough".

"You can't say that I am enough, I saw how you were looking at Trinny just now. I see how you look at all the children you come across. It makes you sad. You long for one of your own but being with me has taken that choice away from you".

"No my love, no. I love children, I always have. Do I still sometimes wish that I had my own? Yes. Do I sometimes imagine what my stomach would look like swollen with life? Of course. But you have taken nothing from me. You have given me everything. Before you, I was alone, lost and scared of life itself. But with you, I have seen the world and gotten to experience things that most can only dream about. Lunaya, you are my world. Without you I would be wondering through the darkness. Believe me when I say that you, this life with you, is most definitely enough".

Tears flowed freely down my face. This isn't the first time that we've had this talk, we spoke of it often in the early stages of our mating. It has been a while since our last talk on the subject but each time I see that longing look in her eyes, guilt floods my veins. She would be a fantastic mother. She has so much kindness in her heart and is fiercely protective. There was a time that we thought of adopting, but the roaming life that we lived was in no way suitable for raising a child.

"You would be an incredible mother" I said softly as I ran my finger down her cheek.

"Are you kidding? Of course I would be. I'm amazing" Alyse giggled with a cocky shrug of her shoulders. I chuckled and grabbed her under the arms and lifted her onto my lap. She sat with her legs on either side of mine and arched her back so that her breasts pushed against my own.

"And I'd bet my left leg that your babies would have been the most beautiful creatures in the world" I said wrapping my arms around her back.

"Only your left leg huh, not your right one? You mustn't be too sure then".

"You joke but I'm dead serious".

"Oh, you're always so serious" Alyse frowned and pouted her lips with a playful gleam in her eyes. I lowered my eyes and smirked. So, she wants to tease me. I leaned forward and look her bottom lip between my teeth and growled. She hummed and snaked her hands up my neck to my hair, slowly pulling out the band to release my golden-brown tresses. I let go of her lip and she stuck out her tongue, flicking it over my lips. Moving my hand to the back of her head, I crashed my lips to hers and hungrily kissed her. She slipped her tongue into my mouth and deepened the kiss.

I stood from the chair, keeping Alyse in my arms and carried her to the bed. I gripped her backside to keep her body against mine and gently laid her down, perching above her. I unbuttoned her jeans and pulled the zip down. Leaning my weight on one arm, I kissed her eagerly while moving my other hand under her jeans and to her sweet spot. I traced my fingers across her moist slit, and she moaned into my mouth.

The fire of my desire exploded with just that one beautiful and erotic sound from her, a desperate and hungry need set in and I couldn't wait to taste her.

I pulled my hand from her pants and knelt up on the bed. I quickly shook off my jacket and kicked off my shoes as Alyse pulled her jumper and shirt over her head, discarding them on the floor. Then unclipped her bra and dropped it by the bed.

"Take your pants off" I growled lowly while standing up to pull down my own. Once I stood in my singlet top and underpants, I looked down at Alyse laying on the bed. She was now completely naked and all mine for the taking. She watched me rake my eyes over her delicious body and slightly opened her legs, giving me a perfect view of her glistening pussy. A lust filled growl bubbled from the back of my throat as I stalked back down between her legs. I gripped her thighs and pulled her down the bed so that her knees were over my shoulders. The smell of her arousal was exquisite, enticing me in ways I couldn't understand. I leaned down and breathed in deeply through my nose, getting a lung full of her luscious nectar.

I flicked out my tongue and drew small circles around her clit, tearing a moan from Alyse. I licked from her clit down her slit to her asshole and back up again. I sucked her bundle of nerves into mouth and slid my hand up her torso to her perked nipple. Teasing her nipple between my thumb and forefinger, I sucked hard on her clit. Alyse wriggled underneath me, moaning and groaning loudly. I held down her hips and continued to work my tongue over her clit. Letting go of her nipple, I moved my hand back between her legs and slowly slid two fingers into her entrance. I pumped my fingers in and out as I worked my lips around her clit.

"Keep going" she moaned breathlessly.

I added another finger and pushed them in further. I could feel her muscles tensing around my digits and I knew she was close to her first orgasm. Still moving my fingers, I gently bit down on her clit and tugged slightly. Alyse cried out in pleasure and bucked her hips as she came.

"Fuck yeah" she giggled relaxing into the bed.

I took my fingers out and slid them up and down along her slit. Sitting up so that I could she her flushed face, I smirked.

"Ready for number two?" I asked her. She looked up at me with wide eyes and threw her head back on the pillow, with a smile engulfing her entire face. I pushed my fingers back inside her and moved them slowly. With the extra slickness from her orgasm, I easily added a fourth digit. I worked them in and out while holding her hips down with my other hand. I watched her eyebrows furrow together and her lips part as she moaned.

"More" she pleaded. Her hands gripped the bed cover, and she tossed her head from side to side.

"Are you sure?" I asked a little excitedly. I've always loved doing this to her.

"Yes. Please" she huffed breathlessly. I readjusted my hand into a beak shape and pushed slightly at her entrance. I was met with some resistance at first but continued to ease my fingers in out, stretching her open. I worked my hand and added a bit more pressure, my hand slid into her vagina.

"Oh god!" she screamed.

The look of her lips around my narrow wrist was a sight I would never tire of. I twisted my hand inside her, ever so slightly. The pressure of her walls gripped around my hand was erotic and I was dripping wet at the sight of it. I began to pull my hand back, stretching her entrance over the wider part on my palm. Before I pulled all the way out, I pushed back in again. Alyse's screams of pleasure resonated around the small hut. Her face was flushed, and her chest heaved up and down with quick and deep breathes. Her head was bent back but I could still see her parted lips and closed eyes. I twisted my hand around and moved it back and forth in small quick movements.

"So beautiful" I said softly watching my hand move inside her. In what felt like no time at all, her inner walls clenched down on my hand like a vice grip. She flew up and grabbed my forearm halting my movements. Her bottom lip was pulled between her teeth and her eyes bore deeply into mine. Her cheeks were red, and her eyes held a look of euphoria. I felt the spasms around my fingers and Alyse's eyes rolled back in her head before she collapsed back on the bed with a blissful groan.

"Holy fucking shit" she breathed out, lifting her arms above her head. I pressed my hand down on her lower abdomen and slowly and gently pulled my hand out from inside her. She groaned and hissed but immediately melted into the mattress as soon as she was empty again. I grabbed a small hand towel to wipe Alyse's juices from my hand and then came back to lay beside her on the bed.

"I should take care of you now" she said rolling over. She flopped a hand over my chest and rested her head on my breast.

"No love, I'm happy with what I just witnessed. You get some rest" I said affectionately.

"You're sure?"

"Of course I'm sure. That is one of my favourite views in the world. So damn sexy"

"You're too good to me" Alyse huffed and closed her eyes. I could tell she was exhausted, that was one hell of an intense orgasm.

"You deserve all the orgasms you want my love. And I am more than happy to give them to you".

She giggled but didn't respond or open her eyes and in mere seconds she was peacefully asleep. I ran my hand up and down her bare back, enjoying the feel of her soft delicate skin.

The Were community has only started accepting same sex mating over the past few decades. Though there are still some packs and individuals that continue to frown on the pairing. Polyamory has always been common amongst Weres, probably because we are such sexually driven creatures. A male with multiple she-wolves is more common than a female with multiple males. I put that down to the fact that men are so damn possessive. I just hope that the pack we find my daughter in is accepting of Alyse and I. My heart would tear apart if I was forced to choose between them.

Chapter

Ten

Lunaya

Only twenty more minutes. The alarm will go off in twenty minutes and then it's time to get up, get dressed, and leave Luna Eclipse. I have been lying in bed wide awake for just over an hour now, the excitement running through me just won't let me sleep. Just falling asleep, to begin with, was difficult. Alyse, as usual, is passed out and curled up under my arm. She needs the sleep, so I won't move yet and risk waking her.

Seventeen minutes. If only I had the willpower to stop staring at my watch. I closed my eyes and tried to imagine what my child might look like today. Would she resemble me at all? I picture her with soft brown hair like my own but with Micha's pale skin and bright golden-brown eyes. Both Micha and I are tall and muscular, so I would assume that our offspring would fare the same height and strength. Though, being the chosen daughter of the Goddess and being blessed with the power of telekinesis, would be strength enough alone.

"I can basically hear your thoughts flying around like rabid bats" Alyse grumbled. I tightened my grip and looked down at her. She still had her eyes closed and her face held a small smile.

"How'd you sleep beautiful?" I asked her,
"Mm great actually" she moaned rolling onto her stomach.
She lifted her body slightly and rested her head on her
crossed arms over my stomach.
"Did you sleep at all?" she asked with a frown.
"A few hours, not as many as I should have though".
"I can tell".
"You wound me, are you saying I'm not pretty?"
"No, I'm saying you could have used an extra hour or two of
beauty sleep" she chuckled. I fake gasped and pretended to
swoon, placing my hand across my forehead.
"Oh, stop it. You know you're always beautiful in my eyes"
she laughed and pinched my cheek.
"Lucky. You nearly broke my heart" I chuckled sitting up on
the bed.
Right then, the alarm went off and startled us both. I looked
at the beeping watch on my wrist and tapped the face to
silence the alarm. I smiled back at Alyse and held my arm out
to show her the time.
"The watch has spoken" I said with a smirk.
"Okay boss watch" she replied with a smile and sat up on the
bed with her feet off the edge.
We both quietly got dressed in our thick coats and double
socks, lost to our own thoughts. If Alyse could change forms,
we all would have travelled in our wolf form. It would have
been quicker to get down the mountain but also harder to
carry our bags in our jaws. I pulled on my boots and tightly
folded the small blanket and put it in my backpack. I had our
bags packed and ready to go the moment we found out that
my child was alive. Styling my hair into a low ponytail, I
secured it with my hair band and pulled my beanie down over
the top. I tucked my gloves into my coat pocket and looked
over at Alyse. She pulled on her coat and turned to face me
with a closed lipped smile.
"Ready?" I asked her,
"Ready" she nodded.
Picking up our bags, we headed out into the cold and to the
dining hall. Elaine and the three other warriors were already
there eating breakfast, accompanied by Alpha Hina. We
dropped our bags by the door and walked over to the table of
women. With the five of them sitting there in close

proximity, the large picnic table looked like a child's playset. Hina is tall and muscular but, Elaine, she has a very large frame for a she-wolf. Her short black hair melted into the base of her thick neck and wide set shoulders paved the way for her large bosom and square torso. She towered over me, which is impressive given that I am just shy of six feet tall.

"Good morning ladies" Hina smiled as she stood up to greet us.

"Good morning Alpha" I replied with a small nod.

"Your breakfast is here, ready for you" she motioned to two plates in the middle of the table. One of the warriors grabbed the plates and passed them up to us.

"Oh, thank you" I said taking the plates. We sat down at the end of the group of women and ate our bacon, eggs, and pancakes.

"Everything is ready for your trip, I have been discussing the finer details with Beta Elaine" Hina said as she moved down the table to sit next to me.

"Thank you for that" I mumbled with a mouthful of eggs,

"It's not a problem. All you have to do is seek out the Lua Chei pack in the Southwest of Nova Scotia. I have come to understand that the pack runs the Trout Point Lodge, it's their main source of income. I've booked you a few nights at the lodge, so once you make it there it shouldn't be too difficult to make the rest of your travel plans. Given that the Alpha cooperates".

"Thank you Alpha, that is very kind of you" Alyse spoke from beside me.

"You're most welcome" Hina replied, throwing Alyse a wink.

"Excuse me?" Elaine called from the end of the table and all three of us turned to see her.

"Once you have finished eating, we need to set off. It will take at least nine hours to get down the mountain in human form" she said standing at the end of the table.

"Okay. We'll be ready in ten" I responded, trying my best to ignore Elaine's somewhat hostile tone. She is still not exactly happy about travelling with Alyse, a half-breed, but because her Alpha has okayed it, she has no say in the matter. Her digs at Alyse have been subtle and she has placed her hatred, or caution, or whatever it is she feels towards Alyse, to the side for the time being. We will just have to wait and see how this whole adventure with her turns out.

Alyse and I finished our breakfast under the watchful eye of Hina. I gathered our plates and was about to stand when Hina placed her hand on my shoulder.

"If I could have a minute" she said gently, forcing me back down,

"Of course" I nodded, sitting and turning to face her. She kept her hand on my shoulder and leaned forward slightly.

"I just wanted to tell you that if for any reason things don't work out, or if you don't wish to stay with your daughter's pack, you are always welcome here".

Hina averted her eyes to Alyse and smiled softly.

"I mean the both of you. I am still very curious about your half-breed abilities" she said with a lustful smirk. A pang of jealousy ran through me, but it was quickly washed away by the memory of our almost threesome. Holy fuck that was hot! I would definitely be up for another go.

"But besides that fascinating and mysterious aspect, you are both wonderful she-wolves and I can see your permanent residence at Luna Eclipse having an excellent effect on our community. Please think about returning, even if only for a visit".

Alyse placed her hand on my shoulder and leaned forward so that her chin was on her hand. I rubbed my cheek against the top of her head and smiled. I believe that we could make a really good life for ourselves here with Luna Eclipse. The pack already feels more like a home than anywhere else we have been so far. As much as I could enjoy living here, there is something pulling us away. Even if my daughter doesn't accept us and doesn't want me to stay there, I could never live so far away from her. And New Zealand is a world away.

"Thank you, Hina. You have no idea how much that means to us" I said softly as I placed my hand over her own.

"I can assure you that you haven't seen the last us. Not yet anyway".

Hina gazed at us for a moment, rubbing her thumb over my hand. Without a word, she stood up from the table and halted at my side. She leaned over and placed a kiss on the top of my head and gently rubbed her fingers through my hair, then repeated the act for Alyse as well. With that, she left the dining hall.

I turned to Alyse to see that tears had stained her cheeks. I pulled her onto my lap and wrapped my arms around her waist. She sobbed quietly into my shoulder for a minute while I soothingly rubbed my hand up and down her back. There was nothing to say. I know we are giving up a good thing here to chase a long-lost dream, but how could we not. It could turn out shit. My child could reject us, imprison us, or just kill us. But Alyse knows that I will never, could never, truly rest until I see for myself.

"It's time to go ladies" Elaine called from the door.

"Thank you, Elaine, we're ready" I replied with a nod.

"Come on love, let's get a move on" I said softly, prying Alyse from my chest. I wiped the tears from her pink cheeks and smoothed down her stray hair. I cupped her cheeks and placed a soft kiss on her full lips.

"We will come back" I said firmly.

"I know, it's just this place is the best we have come across. I'm worried is all".

"I know, me too".

After a brief pause, Alyse got up off my lap and walked to our bags by the door, with me following behind. We picked up our bags and headed out into the small clearing in front of the dining hall. The snow had stopped falling through the night, but the ground was covered in knee deep fresh powder and the wind was harsh against my bare cheeks. It was still dark and too early for the other pack members to be awake. Pappi stood holding onto Hina's arm, as they said their goodbyes to Elaine and the warriors. Alyse and I stood to the side to give them some privacy. It didn't take long for Elaine to embrace Hina, kiss Pappi on the temple, and turn to walk over to us. The other warriors joined her, and we all started to make our way out of the village. I stopped at the edge of the tree line and turned back to look at Hina. She was still standing and watching us closely. I offered her a wave and in reply, she nodded her head slowly. I turned my back to her and caught up to the others. It took Alyse and me three days to climb this mountain and find Luna Eclipse. Now, we were going to try and get back down it in just one.

~

"This next part of the mountain is dangerous and requires your full and undivided attention" Elaine said sternly as we gathered in behind her. We were about four hours into our hike and had come to a stop at a cliff that appeared completely impassable. The thick snow had been left behind us a while ago, though the air was still cold and held a hint of moisture. I looked up at the rocky cliff. We couldn't go back up, that would defeat the purpose. I walked to the edge of the small flat that we were currently on and looked down. Unless Elaine brought rock climbing equipment, there is no way that we can go this way.

"I don't remember coming this way on our way up" Alyse said quietly, intended for my ears only, as she stepped up beside me.

"You wouldn't have" Elaine responded over her shoulder, "This section of the path is obscured from view on the ascent and not easily found by accident when hiking down. Only a select few know how to access it". Elaine turned to face us with a 'shut-up-and-listen' kind of look on her face.

"I will go first, followed by Alyse and then Lunaya, the rest of you will bring up the rear. The path allows for only one at a time, so do exactly as I say, stay in line, stay close and no messing about".

With that, Elaine turned around and walked to the furthest side of the cliff face and disappeared behind a large boulder. I rushed over to see where she went and found her standing on a narrow path. If you can call it that, path was generous, ledge was more appropriate. The uneven ledge looked completely unstable and scattered with loose rocks. It ran along the edge of the cliff, carved out of the side of the mountain like nature's perilous staircase. This can't possibly be a good idea.

"You've got to be fucking kidding me!" Alyse gasped behind me.

"Apparently not" I said with an equal amount of shock.

"Let's go, ladies, I said to stay close" Elaine called. I looked along the path and over to Elaine. She had her back pressed up against the cliff face, taking slow side steps.

"Don't look down and follow Elaine's lead. Back against the wall with slow and steady steps. I'll be right beside you" I said pulling Alyse in front of me. She responded with an obviously strained swallow and a shaky nod of her head. Heights have never really been her forte. She stepped out onto the ledge and I followed closely beside her. One of the warriors was right beside me, watching my every step closely. We shuffled along, catching up to Elaine quickly. The tiny path, no, the tiny ledge, was eight inches wide at its widest section. The rocks were still wet from melted snow, making them slippery as well as unsteady. Small groves in the side of the rockface allowed for slim hand holds but our backpacks weren't exactly helping.

"How long does this go for?" Alyse shouted to Elaine,

"You don't have to scream at me, I'm right beside you" Elaine responded with annoyance.

"Sorry" Alyse shouted again, she cleared her throat and spoke a little softer,

"Sorry, how long does this go on for?"

"About six hundred meters".

Alyse froze and turned to stare at me with panic and fear in her eyes. Her eyes grew three times in size and her face turned a shade of pale green. Her mouth hung slightly open, and an uncomfortable squeaking sound fell from her lips.

"Hey, hey. It's okay, you got this. It's not that far and you're killing it. Just keep going one foot at a time. We're all good".

I tried to speak as encouragingly as possible, but I don't think it was too convincing. Alyse closed her mouth and slowly nodded her head but her colour didn't change, and a sweat had now broken out on her forehead.

We kept going, nice and slow. All six of us, one after the other. It feels like we have been up on this damn ledge for an hour already, but probably more like twenty minutes. My legs were starting to get shaky, and my fingertips were feeling raw from gripping the rock face so tightly. I avoided looking down as much as I could but seeing as I had to look where I was putting my feet, looking down was nearly impossible. The cloud cover around us had started to clear a little more, giving us a beautiful view of the New Zealand landscape. To say it was breathtaking, would be the understatement of the century. Huge snow-covered mountain tops reached up to the clear blue sky, while rivers of crystal water weaved around the valleys below. Fields of lush green spotted the landscape in the most beautiful way. It was awe-inspiring.

"Look at that" I whispered to Alyse without taking my eyes off the view.

"Oh wow" she gasped beside me,

"It's beautiful" she said softly.

"It really is" I agreed.

There was a cracking sound, a scattering of rocks, followed by a high-pitched shriek. I looked over to where Alyse was standing, but she was no longer beside me. It took me less than a moment to realize that the shriek had come from her. I snapped my head down towards the shrieking sound and in what felt like slow motion, I saw Alyse's body falling. Her face twisted in terror and her arms outstretched for me. Just like a movie in freeze frame, the picture of Alyse falling down the mountainside seared itself into my brain forever. I just about launched myself off the ledge to grab at her slowly descending hand. Her fingers grazed along my own and disappeared. I'd missed her. Her harrowing scream came to a sudden halt as a set of hands pulled me back against the wall. I glared at the woman holding me back. Looking back to Alyse she was gone, in her place was Elaine. Hanging from the narrow ledge by one hand. I ran my eyes down her body to her other arm. There holding on with knuckles turning white, was Alyse. The sight of her hanging by the balls of death snapped me back to reality.

"GRAB MY BAG!" I screamed at the woman behind me, and she obeyed immediately. I crouched down and forced my fingers into a small grove on the ledge. If there was any skin left on my fingertips before, it was all gone now. I began to lower myself off the ledge but was met with a scream from Elaine.

"Don't you fucking dare!" she growled. I snapped my eyes to her and snarled. How dare she try to forbid me from saving my Mate. I looked down at Alyse again and she looked to be on the verge of passing out. Her face had lost all colour and her eyes were rolling around in her head. I continued to lower myself down, getting closer to Alyse.

"Cleo!" Elaine yelled. I was instantly hauled back up the cliff by my bag and forced up against the rock face.

"Let me go" I said with a deadly venom to my tone.

"I have her" Elaine snapped back with equal ferocity.

"Alyse" she called, no answer.

"Alyse!" she called again with added volume. Alyse grunted in reply and groaned a fear filled sob.

"Alyse, I want you to climb back up to the ledge, okay?" Elaine demanded.

"I-I can't".

"You can and you will".

"P-Please" she sobbed. I tried to get back down to the ledge and reach out for her but the grip on my shoulders was not letting up.

"Alyse. You are a Were. You are a strong she-wolf. You can do this! Use my body as a ladder and climb the fuck back up to the ledge" Elaine all but yelled. She tried to be encouraging but it came out strong and too hard. After a minute of not moving, Alyse looked up to lock her eyes with mine. I tried again to reach for her, but I risked falling myself if I struggled too much against the vice grip on my shoulders. I nodded and pleaded through my eyes for her to do it. She ripped one hand from Elaine's hand and threw it higher up her arm. She did it again with her other hand and gripped onto Elaine's shoulder. She continued with these movements until she was only inches from the ledge.

"Okay" Elaine grunted and the hands holding me back released. I leaned down and grabbed for Alyse's hand. Once I had both my hands locked around her wrist and forearm, I began to stand myself back up, pulling her with me. The woman behind me had her hands around my waist to ensure I didn't topple forward. With a few grunts and groans, Alyse was back up on the ledge, with Elaine right behind her. I guess I severely underestimated Elaine's strength and power. With our backs pressed against the cliff, I threw my arm around Alyse's shoulder and pulled her head in under my armpit.

"Thank the fucking Goddess" I huffed in relief. Alyse sobbed quietly into my jacket for a moment before lifting her head and staring into my face.

"I can't do this" she sobbed.

"Yes, you can, we're nearly there and we can't turn back now" I said firmly.

"No, please I can't. I want to go back" she pleaded.

"We can't do that love, you know this".

She roamed her eyes over my unwavering face and finally sucked in a tight breath and wiped the tears from her eyes. She nodded and turned back to face Elaine. Elaine was beyond furious.

"I said to pay fucking attention. I don't care how fucking pretty the sky is. Watch where you are going or I will let you just fall next time" she growled, her angry eyes looking over us both.

"S-sorry" Alyse mumbled softly. A growl bubbled up through my lips and rolled across the rocks. But Elaine ignored me and started sliding along the ledge again. Alyse just nearly died, I nearly lost the love of my life. Again. And she dares scold her right now, while we're still standing on this fucking cliff. If we were anywhere but here right now, I would have ripped her face off.

It's okay love, she's right

No, she is not

She is, I wasn't looking where I put my feet

She has no right

Nae, calm down. Let's just get off this damn fucking mountain

This isn't over

Of course it's not

Alyse began moving again, following closely behind Elaine and paying extra careful attention to her foot placement. I wasn't wrong when I said we were nearly there. The small ledge started to spread out a little until it came out on the side of a deeply slopped rocky field. From there, we could see all the way down to the bottom of the mountain. It was still a long way to go but the path from here on out was a hell of a lot less life threatening.

~

We made it to a small stone cabin at the foot of the mountain just as the sun began to set. We spent the night all squished together in the tiny single room hut. It was tight, though I was thankful for the warmth that the combined body heat provided. I learned that the three warriors who joined us were named Venus, Cleo, and Phoebe. Venus was born in India, though she didn't say much about her upbringing or how she came to be at Luna Eclipse. She is younger than the rest of us, tall and slender, with long deep black hair and smooth tanned skin. She is a little quiet, but her eyes never stop watching. Phoebe has been with Luna Eclipse her whole life. She was found abandoned as a baby by an Omega and they came to the pack together. Phoebe is the image of a typical Barbie, but her skills in tactical warfare and hand to hand combat could rival that of an Alpha male. Cleo is an interesting woman, the strong and silent type. She came from a Māori pack somewhere in Raukumara, but that was all I got out of her. It's clear that she is fiercely loyal to Hina and Luna Eclipse, but there is something sinister in her silent nature. It makes me feel a shiver slide up my spine each time I catch her staring at me emotionlessly.

Hina really did have everything organized. There was a minivan waiting for us at the little hut, but by the looks of it, it lived there permanently. Just in case the time comes for it to be needed. The drive to Queenstown airport was about four hours and we made it with an hour and a half to spare. Now, Alyse is browsing magazines and buying out half the little airport shop of its confectionaries. I've never known someone to have a sweet tooth quite like Alyse. But after the day we had yesterday, I would buy her all the sweets in the world if it meant she kept that smile.

Elaine came to sit beside me, she didn't say anything, just sat next to me watching Alyse. My anger at her reaction on the mountain had subsided somewhat but she was still not my favourite person right now. We sat quietly for a few minutes, the awkward tension growing significantly.

"I have to apologize" she finally broke the silence.

"You do?" I questioned. This, I was not expecting. At all.

"You didn't need my scolding on the cliff. I was just worked up and couldn't hold it back".

"You know that's not an apology?" I poked, glancing at her out of the corner of my eye.

"I am sorry" she huffed, leaning forward to rest her elbows on her knees.

"Thank you. But you were right. We were so taken in by the view that we weren't paying full attention to our footsteps".

"I can't blame you for that. New Zealand is the most spectacular place in the world" Elaine said leaning back and smirking at me.

"You've travelled?"

"Not a lot, no. But I don't need to travel to know that this place is beyond beautiful".

"That's a fair assumption. Take it from someone who has seen the world, this place is unlike any other. I almost wish we could stay"

"You could you know. Stay".

"Hina said the same thing, but I couldn't. Not if it really is my daughter. I would never be able to leave her again".

"And if she doesn't want you there?"

"Well, then I would just watch over her from the shadows".

Elaine was silent for a brief minute, nodding her head and still watching Alyse flitter around the small store.

"You're a good mother" she finally spoke,

"I beg to differ".

"It wasn't your fault, you did all that you could do".

"It just wasn't quite enough though, was it?"

We returned to a comfortable silence. I appreciated her apology and her honest opinion, even if I don't fully agree with it. I could have done so much more to protect my offspring. But there is no point in living in the past, it can't be changed. But I can make damn sure that the future is bright.

~

We boarded our first flight of the trip and settled in for a long, and sure to be tiresome journey. We slept when we could on the flights and the stopovers were spent stretching our legs and walking around. Dubai was our longest stopover, so we decided to let our wolves out for a run. Being cooped up in a flying metal tube for hours on end has a way of messing with you, especially with creatures that are born to be in nature. The run was desperately needed and thoroughly enjoyed by all of us, except Alyse of course, though she did enjoy her walk.

Arriving in Montreal sent wave after wave of anxiety through my bloodstream. She is here. My child is here, somewhere. I am so close and yet still so far. I wish I could flash with her. I wish I knew where she was, so that we could go straight there. I wish a lot of things. I just need this whole search part to be done with, I need to hold her in my arms and make sure she knows that everything will be alright. We picked up our two hire cars and split up. Elaine, Alyse, and I were in one car. Cleo, Phoebe, and Venus in the other. Then, we started on our search along the St Lawrence River, slowly making our way to Nova Scotia and the Lua Chei pack.

Chapter Eleven

Zelena

"Where the fuck were you? I told you to stay next to her the entire time. Was that really so fucking difficult?" Gunner's angry voice filled the entire office, bouncing off the walls and reverberating back through my ears.

Roe sat in the matching chair next to me, her hands placed in her lap and her head bowed down in shame. Felix stood between the two chairs with his shoulders held firm and high, but his head bowed, and hands clasped behind his back. Gunner has been raging now for nearly twenty minutes. First at Felix, then his mum, he gave me a few stern words and is now back to screaming at Felix.

"I told you, I fucking told you that more would come for her. But no! You had to leave the village, you just had to go shopping".

Gunner was pacing back and forth behind his desk, waving his arms around as he yelled and cursed at the three of us. Though, I don't see how this is my fault. How was I supposed to know that there were Weres out looking for me? Besides overhearing him speak with his mum this morning, this is the first I'm hearing of it.

"I'm sorry, Sweetheart, what more can I say?" Roe rebutted again.

"You could stop talking for a change and listen to me. For fucks sake Mum, I'm the damn Alpha now. You need to stop treating me like a child and let me do my fucking job" Gunner yelled turning to face her. His face was red with anger and his eyes were wide and darkened in his rage. I was dumbfounded, I have never heard such disrespect from Gunner, especially aimed at his mother. His mother, who has never been anything other than welcoming and supportive. The gall of this guy!

"Stop swearing at your mother! I know that you're upset but that doesn't mean you get to be disrespectful" I yelled back at him, slamming my hand on the armrest of my chair.

He flicked his eyes to me and frowned. Shit. Maybe that was a bad idea. I could be in trouble here. I basically just challenged the Alpha. Do the same rules apply to a Luna as they do to other pack members? Gunner stared me down as the room sat in silence, waiting for his next move. After a few agonizing seconds, which felt more like hours, he took a deep breath in and released it slowly. His shoulders seemed a little less tense and his face relaxed ever so slightly.

"You're right. I'm sorry Mum, you didn't deserve that" he said in a much calmer tone. I nearly choked on my own saliva and slid off my chair. I was not expecting him to concede his anger, let alone apologize for his outburst. Mind blown. Roe muffled back a sob and wiped a tear from her cheek.

"No, you're right. I keep overstepping. I spent the last twenty-five years speaking and acting like a Luna, it's a hard role to let go of so quickly. I will back off and let you do your thing, no more sticking my nose where it doesn't belong" Roe said with a stringent nod of her head.

"That's not what I mean Mum" Gunner huffed, collapsing into his chair.

"Your opinion is still welcome, you just can't dispute every decision that I make" he leaned forward in his chair as he spoke, placing his folded hands on his desk.

"Alpha, I take full responsibility and will accept whatever punishment you deem necessary" Felix drew our attention back to his stoic presence.

"I really don't think that is needed, Gunner. It wasn't his fault. I was in the damn dressing room, you didn't expect him to follow me into the changing rooms, did you?"

Gunner growled at my last comment, the thought of another man seeing me semi naked brought out his possessive side. I knew I'd get him on that. He leaned back and raked his eyes over Felix. After a few more moments of silence, he breathed out another heavy breath.

"No. No punishment is necessary. You handled the situation swiftly and with diligence. It is my own responsibility for allowing you to travel with only the single guard".

I smiled at Gunner when he flicked his eyes to mine and gave him an appreciative nod. He turned back to Felix and waved his hand.

"Thank you, Felix, you're dismissed" Felix bowed with his hand to his chest and then turned to me and repeated the same action, then swiftly left the office.

"Gunner, I think…" Roe started but Gunner cut her off, holding his hand in the air.

"Mum, if you don't mind, I need some time with my Mate" he grumbled not looking at his mother. She hesitated but nodded her head and headed for the door.

"I'll prepare a late lunch for you" she said before closing the door behind her.

We sat awkwardly in silence for a few minutes. Gunner sat at his desk staring at his hands on his desk. I slumped in my chair and crossed my arms over my chest. There is definitely a lot we need to talk about. The main point being, what in the hell happened while I was in my coma? Something big must have occurred for him to get so worked up over my safety. And Felix's first assumption at the mall was that I was attacked. So, does that mean they were expecting an attack? The identity of the strange man and his intentions were tormenting my mind. Why did he reveal that he knew who I was, was the whole point of that interaction just to scare me?

"I like the dress" Gunner's purring voice rolled across the table.

"Huh?" I asked, looking up to meet his adoring gaze.

"I said, I like the dress. You look absolutely beautiful" he said with a small smile.

I haven't had the chance to change out of the dress since we got back from the shopping centre. Felix flashed with Gunner before we got home, so he was ready and waiting for our interrogation the minute we pulled into the driveway. He was beyond furious and ripped into us the second we stepped out of the car. Nat and Deena slinked away, leaving Felix and Roe to cop the most of his rage.

"Oh, yeah thanks. I did love it" I replied indifferently.

"Did?" he questioned,

"Yeah. Now, after the… uh, incident, I just feel dirty in it" I mumbled back, smoothing out the wrinkles that had gathered in my lap.

"Don't let him ruin it Little Wolf, the dress is yours and you look magnificent in it" Gunner stood up and walked around in front of me, perching on the edge of his desk he crossed his arms in front of his chest. He looked more delicious than ever. It has taken no time at all for him to fill back out, his muscled chest now swelling from under his button-down navy-blue shirt. His arms have grown, and his biceps were now straining under the thin material. Becoming Alpha really agrees with him. My hungry eyes travelled the length of his body before returning to his eyes. He was watching me explore his physique with a smirk etched across his full lips.

"Do you like what you see Little Wolf?" he purred seductively. Well, two can play this game. I stood from my chair very slowly, keeping my eyes locked on his. Taking one small step forward I reached my hands towards him and rested them on his chest. Gunner uncrossed his arms and set his hands on the desk at his sides. I dragged my hands down his chest, feeling every curve and twitch of his muscles. I let them stop at the top of his pants and fiddled my fingers with the buckle of his belt.

"I do" I answered softly, looking up at him through my dark lashes. His smirk widened and his eyes flashed with a mischievous lust. Undoing his belt, I began to slide it out of the loops in one slow and steady motion.

"You look good enough to eat actually" I preened at him as I flung the belt to the floor. I pulled the hem of his shirt, untucking it from his pants, and began undoing the buttons. Working my way up to the collar, I let my fingernails graze over the exposed flesh.

"My, my, Zelena. Are you trying to seduce me?" Gunner asked with a cocky smile painting his face.

"Who me?" I gasped in mock surprise,

"I would never" I snickered and pressed my lips to his hard chest. I roamed the intoxicating flesh of his chest, leaving a trail of small hickeys and kisses in my wake. Moving my lips down slightly to the rippling muscles of his six pack, I traced each outline with a swish of my tongue. Gunner's breaths were slow and deep, his chest heaving with each intake of air. Yet he didn't move. After undoing his pants, I pushed them down slightly until they dropped to the floor.

A low growl rumbled through his chest as my hands ducked under his boxer briefs, squeezing the firmness of his glorious ass. I slid his underwear down his hips until his erect dick sprung free, slapping against his stomach. I lowered myself to my knees and let my tongue brush against the base of his dick before I sat back.

"You're being very naughty" he grumbled with his head tilted back. His hands gripped the edge of his desk so tight that his knuckles were turning white. I wrapped my small hand around his shaft and licked at the small bead of precum that had escaped.

"I suppose I should stop then" I teased, blinking up at him through my lashes. He snapped his eyes down to mine and grabbed the wrist of my hand that was holding his throbbing member.

"Don't you dare" he growled. His breathing quickened and I could feel the heat radiating from his skin. I smiled back at him and licked my bottom lip. His eyes widened before growing dark, finally realising that I was just playing with him. He released my wrist and twisted his fingers through my hair, another growl shook through his chest.

Keeping my eyes on Gunner's, I leaned forward and dragged my tongue from the base of his dick to the tip. I opened my lips and slid them down his shaft, hollowing my cheeks and massaging my tongue against him.

"Holy fuck" Gunner moaned tossing his head back again. I fought against my smile and began to bob my head, sliding my lips up and down his shaft. Gunner's grip on my hair tightened and his grunts and moans increased, ringing through the office. The sound sent shivers down my spine and an excited tingle between my legs. I pushed my mouth down his shaft taking in as much of him as I could. I could feel the tip of his penis hit the back of my throat and I resisted the urge to gag. I groaned, sending vibrations down his dick, which only made Gunner moan louder and push at the back of my head. I pulled back, sucking on the tip, before sliding all the way back down again, rubbing my tongue along his shaft as I went.

"Fuck Zee. You're gonna make me cum" Gunner groaned. His legs were shaking slightly, and I could feel his stomach tense. I continued to move my mouth back to the tip of his dick before sliding back down, again and again. His dick swelled inside my mouth, he bucked his hips with a breathy moan and shot his load down my throat. I expected not to like it, I thought it would be kind of gross. But the salty taste was better than I imagined, in fact, I liked it. I could feel myself craving for more. I licked his dick clean and swiped my tongue over my lips, licking up any excess semen.

"Holy fucking shit. That was amazing" Gunner moaned breathlessly. He slumped back on his desk slouching his shoulders forward. I stood back up and rested my hands on his chest, looking over the sated expression on his face. In a flash, he gripped hold of my waist and pulled me flush against him, burying his face into the crook of my neck. His lips and teeth teased the sensitive skin below my ear.

"How did I get so lucky?" he whispered between kisses. I curled my arms around his neck and tilted my head to the side, exposing more of my neck.

"Will you now let me return the favour?" Gunner asked with a lustrous excitement to his tone.

"Not wearing this dress" I giggled,

"Don't want to get it all messy, seeing as I won't be able to get another before tomorrow night".

Gunner paused his attack on my neck and stood up straight, looking into my eyes. His playful and seductive demeanour quickly changed to one of seriousness and frustration. He looked over my face for a moment before huffing out a long breath.

"I'm sorry this happened" he sighed while pulling his pants back up.

"Why did this happen, what aren't you telling me Gunner?" my voice came out a little harder than I intended it to. I didn't mean to be so brazen, it just kind of slipped out.

"Zee, please. I'll take care of it, I don't want you to worry about it" he replied with exasperation coating his tone.

"You said we were in this together, you said we were equals. How can we be if you keep things from me? This clearly has something to do with me being the Triple Goddess, therefore I have a right to know. I can't be a Luna if I'm left in the dark on important issues".

Gunner stared down at me, not saying a word. I could see the gears turning behind his eyes, he was having some kind of internal struggle. Finally, he released his grip on my waist and gently pushed me backward to sit back down on the chair.

"Okay" he sighed heavily.

"Okay?" I repeated,

"Yep" he paused, blew out a breath, and began.

"About a month before you woke up, we had some Weres visit. They came completely unannounced and with more Weres than a usual delegation. They were from a pack in Italy" Gunner explained, and I nodded along as he spoke.

"The pack they came from is called Origin Wolf. History books say that the pack was created by one of the children from Lycaon, therefore they see themselves as royalty"

"Are they? You know, royalty?"

"Lycaon was the first born werewolf but he was not a crowned king. Origin Wolf is the closest thing that the Were community have to royalty, but there is no official government or crown or anything like that"

"So then why do they think that? That they're royals?"

"Well because before you were discovered, the world thought that the Alpha was the last remaining direct bloodline tied to Lycaon, and in turn Selene. The children of Lycaon are a big deal in the Were world. Origin Wolf's power has been growing exponentially over the past two centuries. But the discovery of you and your continued bloodline has tipped the world on its head".

"And what did they want?"

"To be short, you".

"Me?" I choked. Why in the hell would they want me? Well, I mean I can take a guess at why, but what could I possibly offer them?

"You, the Triple Goddess. They wanted to test you"

"Test me? For what?"

"To confirm your bloodline or status of the Triple Goddess, we're not completely sure"

"And did they?" The thought of strangers poking and prodding me, taking my blood and whatever else they wanted, all while I was unconscious and defenceless. It made my skin crawl. I felt sick to my stomach and I knew that the colour had drained from my face. Gunner pulled the other chair in front of me and sat down, taking my hands in his.

"Of course they didn't. I wouldn't let anyone near you. My dad, Artemis, Tobias, and everyone else that they spoke to, all attested to the fact. They weren't exactly happy to leave without physically seeing you, but I didn't give them the choice" he traced his fingers in slow calming circles over the back of my hands.

"This is a lot" I sighed, choking down a sob.

"I know Babe, I'm sorry".

"You should have told me, Gunner. You should have told me everything right away" I scolded him.

"You're right" he conceded.

"But what does this have to do with the man from the mall?"

"Could be nothing, could be everything"

"I don't know what that means"

"It means, he could have just been a visiting Were from another pack or a roaming Omega that heard the stories about you". Gunner paused but continued rubbing those delicate circles on my hands. He was hesitating.

"Or..." I drawled out,

"Or he could have been sent from Origin Wolf to track you down".

Track me down? Had it really got to the point where I was being tracked? Like some kind of rare and exotic wild animal. My skin broke out in goosebumps and I felt an icy shiver snake its way up my spine. How could someone from Italy find me, in Nova Scotia of all places. We're not exactly advertising our location. But Origin Wolf still managed it. So did the mystery man from the mall. But with him, he found me, not the pack or the village. Me.

"But he knew who I was, he came right up to me. How did he know what I look like if you didn't let them see me?"

"That there lays the issue" Gunner snapped standing up and restarting his previous pacing.

"They shouldn't know what you look like. A Seer or a Prophet or maybe a really powerful healer may have been able to sense your powers, but they would have to be close to you or touch you or have some kind of link to you for that to happen. You said you never saw this man before and I haven't seen him before either. So, how did he know to approach you? How did he even know where you were going to be?"

My mind ran rampant with all the information Gunner was throwing at me. A few things I knew for sure. One; this Origin Wolf was bad news, I could feel it in my soul. Two; the news of my arrival (or so Roe called it) had already spread far and wide. Three; not everyone is exactly happy about it. Four; I have no idea what a Seer or a Prophet is. And five; no one should have known where I was today or what I look like. Unless... There is really only one way that information could have gotten out. I looked up to Gunner, he had stopped pacing and was now standing still, staring out of his office window to the memorial. Anxiety, fear, anger, it was rolling off him in giant waves. It would seem that he has come to the same conclusion that I have.

"Gunner" I said softly.

He turned to face me, his eyes heavy with dread but held a hidden rage. His jaw was rigid and tight, and his brows were furrowed together.

"We have a traitor" he said through clenched teeth.

~

A few hours later I sat on the porch swing looking over the village, the sun had disappeared behind the trees and the summer air was thick with anticipation. Set up for the party tomorrow night was well underway. Some big brawly pack members were nearly done building what looked like a raised platform or stage, and long picnic tables were being laid out in rows before it. Big tents were being set up around the outskirts of the village, for the members of the visiting packs to stay in. A lot of Blue Moon members were coming, one of which was Marius, Tobias's younger brother, and Beta. He had become good friends with Gunner while I was in my coma. I don't think Gunner knows about my first interaction with Marius and the comments that were made, hopefully, he never will. After all, it was just innocent flirting. Nothing worth jeopardising a friendship and strong alliance over.

This afternoon I managed to catch parts of a tense conversation between Gunner and Cole. Apparently, quite a few packs have been offered an invitation to the party, and almost all of them had accepted. I'm not stupid, I know that Gunner is hoping to cement a lot of new alliances during this party. As well as ensuring and strengthening the ones we already have. Some of those alliances are with the Waning Wolf pack and the Howlers pack. I heard them say a few others as well, but I don't remember what they were called. Now, I don't know much about either Waning Wolf or Howlers, except for what Nat has told me about the Howlers. Apparently, the pack members are nearly all male and they can get very rowdy.

Roe has been extra stressed with preparations, I think she is trying to make it up to Gunner by ensuring that everything is beyond perfect. Well that's my assumption, but she said it's because allied packs don't usually come to Alpha ascension ceremonies. They are all coming because of me, because they want to meet the Triple Goddess. Being the centre of attention is still not one of my favourite things and my nerves were bashing at the roof of my sanity.

My talk with Gunner was still plaguing my thoughts. A traitor. A traitor here, in Tri-Moon. It doesn't seem possible. We decided to keep that theory just between the two of us, for now at least. We need to work on finding out who it could be and who we can trust to help us find out. Gunner has completely stopped all communication with Cole, unless it was for urgent pack business, like security during the party. He hasn't said it directly, but I can feel what he is thinking. He thinks the traitor could be Cole. I disagree. I just hope that I'm right.

Tobias walked over and plopped down on the swing next to me. The old wooden chair creaked and groaned under Tobias' added mammoth weight.

"Hey Little One, what's got you all strung out?" he asked cheerfully nudging my side with his elbow.

"Oh nothing, I'm just enjoying the show" I said as I gestured to the hustle and bustle taking place in the large clearing.

"Yeah, tell you what, my ascension ceremony didn't look anything like this" he said leaning back and crossing his arms over his chest.

"Are you excited to see your brother and pack members? You haven't been home in a while".

Tobias sighed and rubbed his hand over his bald head and scratched at the back of his neck.

"Yeah. I uh, I want to talk to you about that"

"Oh yeah?"

"I um, I... Ah fuck" he dropped his head and shuffled uncomfortably in his seat. He was anxious and struggling with something. Being my guardian, we share a bond and that makes us a lot more in tune with each other's thoughts and feelings. And right now I could feel that something was making him feel guilty.

"Tobias, breathe. Tell me what's going on" I said placing my hand on his forearm.

"I'm handing over the Alpha position to my brother" he blurted out.

"You're what! Why?" I couldn't contain my shock. Being an Alpha is a huge honour, why would he give that up?

"I can't run a pack when I'm not around. I've been spending all of my time here. Do you know how many times I've been home since the battle?" He paused but I didn't answer.

"Three times, three times in nearly four months. My pack deserves better than that. They deserve an Alpha that will make them their top priority, and I can't offer them that anymore".

"Tobias, you don't have to stay here, I don't want you to feel obligated because you're my guardian. I can look after myself, and besides I have a whole pack of werewolves here to look out for me" I told him, trying my best to sound sincere. But the thought that someone in this pack is doing the opposite, hit me where it hurts the most.

"No Little One. I don't feel obligated, being your guardian is the highest honour imaginable. I haven't been able to go home because when I am away from you the world doesn't feel right. When the Goddess first sent me to you, I thought she intended for us to Mate, but that wasn't the case, clearly. She sent me to you to be your guardian, your best friend, your confidante, your big brother. She sent me to you to be your protector and I can't do that from another pack. I love you Zelena and I belong here, with you".

A breath caught in my throat at his last words. He loves me. Is he in love with me or just loves me? Because there's a huge difference. There is no denying the bond that we share. When I am around him, I can breathe easier, think clearer, and I feel calm and safe, right down in the depths of my being. I do love him. He's like the brother that I never had, but the love I have for Gunner is unmatched in every way. Tobias has become extremely important to me and the selfish part of me warms at his words. But I don't know if I can handle being the reason that he abandons his family and home pack. Could I live with that on my conscious?

"Tobias, I…" I blanked, how do I respond to that. My face heated up and a cold sweat broke out on my brow. Tobias chuckled a little and elbowed my side again.

"Don't get it twisted Little Luna. I love you like my little sister, I don't want to Mate you" he laughed again, a big throaty laugh that made the porch swing rattle. I sighed a massive sigh of relief and grinned at him.

"Oh, thank the Goddess" I giggled.

"Hey now" he grabbed his chest and feigned hurt,

"Would being my Mate really have been that bad" he pouted and followed it with a chuckle.

"No of course not. But it sure would have made shit complicated"

"Fair point, fair point"

We both sat quietly for a minute, looking out over the darkening sky.

"Just for the record, I do love you. But Tobias, I don't want you to leave your family. Not for me" I said breaking the silence.

"Zelena, I'm not leaving my family. They will always be my family. I have spoken with Marius about this a lot. He, my father, and my other brothers all understand my decision, and they support me. They know what I've been chosen for and they understand the importance of it. I'm giving up my role as Alpha, not my role as big brother or eldest son".

Tears were flowing freely down my face as he spoke. A pang of envy hit my heart. To have a family that love and support you so unconditionally must be truly amazing. He's lucky to have them and I am beyond lucky to have him.

"Don't cry Little One, this is supposed to be good news" he said wrapping his arm around my shoulder and pulling me to lean on his chest.

"Are you sure?" I blubbered, wiping my cheek with the back of my hand.

"Absolutely"

"Thank you" I squeaked. I wrapped my arms around his waist and buried my face into his chest. I cried into his warm shirt as I hugged him. Why am I crying? I have no idea. I just feel so overwhelmed by love and acceptance that it just started pouring out of me. Tobias laughed and squeezed me a little tighter.

"Why are you crying?" he asked, smoothing down my hair.

"I don't know, I'm just happy, they're happy tears" I sniffled. He laughed again and rested his cheek on the top of my head. "Well, I'm glad".

After a few minutes I had calmed down again and the tears finally stopped flowing. Tobias now has a huge wet stain on his shirt, but he either hasn't noticed or isn't bothered by it. I sat up straight and wiped away the wetness from my cheeks and tried to calm my hair with my fingers.

"One more thing" He said standing up and holding out his hand for me. I growled lowly, taking his hand and he pulled me to my feet. What else could there be?

"What?" I groaned.

"Well, now we have to convince your possessive and overprotective Mate to let me join your pack, permanently" he smiled down at me and laughed.

Zelena

I stabbed my fork into the piece of steak and swirled it around my plate, stirring it through the thick gravy. The dinner table was full of chatter about the upcoming celebration, excitement was buzzing through the air. This is going to be the biggest ascension ceremony that Tri-Moon has ever seen. The fact had been mentioned many times. I am excited. To officially take my place as Luna and legitimately announce my arrival, or the arrival of the Triple Goddess. But I'm terrified also. Gunner has been running things since the day we announced ourselves to the pack, his father has been helping with the transition. But come tomorrow night, we will both be formally taking our place as leaders of the pack. Though at this point, it is just a formality.

"You're very quiet tonight" Gunner said softly leaning over his chair, closer to me.

"Got a lot on my mind" I half smiled at him.

"Like that favour I need to repay you?" he smirked. I frowned at him and quickly glanced around the table. If anyone else was listening to our conversation, they weren't showing it.

"Stop it" I grimaced through clenched teeth. He laughed to himself and sat back up straight.

"Actually, I do need to talk with you after dinner. It's important" I told him firmly.

"Sure, we can talk after dinner, before bed" he replied before eating another mouthful of food. He had completely missed the firm and concerned tone in my voice.

"In your office please, Tobias will be joining us".

Gunner paused his chewing and looked at me. His brows furrowed together and his eyes held unspoken questions. He flicked his eyes to where Tobias was sitting and then back to me and answered with a curt nod.

I know that their relationship has improved tenfold, but it is plainly clear to anyone that wished to take notice, Gunner stills holds jealousy over the bond that Tobias and I share. That being said, I don't think that he would turn Tobias away. He is too important, he was handpicked by the Goddess herself and Gunner would never throw that away. At least I don't think he would. The anticipation of the conversation to come was messing with my nerves and scared away what remained of my appetite.

While Gunner was working with his dad in his office, I slipped away for a shower before I met with him and Tobias. A hot shower can melt away all the stress in the world, at least it can for me. The smell of my strawberry conditioner wafted around the large steamy cubicle. I tipped my head back under the water to let the conditioner wash out. With my fingers rubbing over my scalp, relaxation soon took over. My body became weightless as I felt a Drakos-Mati vision take hold. I opened my eyes and was standing in that same dark room. Why here? Why are my powers bringing me here, what is so important about this place? The smell hasn't changed, still damp and mouldy but with hints of blood now. I stood in place and looked around the dark room, willing my eyes to adjust.

"Who's there?" a small yet fierce female voice whispered. I turned my head in the direction that the voice came from, still not able to see anything. Who could she be talking to? No one has ever been able to see me when I'm in a vision. At least I don't think they could.

"I know you're there" the voice whispered again. She had a hard sharpness to her tone, it made a shiver run down my spine. I breathed deeply through my nose trying to get a sense of the girl's scent. The smell was horrific. Something dirty and rotten dominated my nostrils but a hint of something familiar lurked in the background. What is that? I breathed in again, focussing all my energy on that peculiar scent. Where do I know that from? I strained my eyes in the darkness. A swish of something to the right caught my attention. It was like a dark shadow flew across my line of vision, bringing with it a swift breeze. The full scent of the mystery girl hit me like falling piano. I know this person. I'm sure of it.

Zelena

I gasped loudly, inhaling the shower water unintentionally. I spat the shower water out with a choked cough. I was back in the shower, like I'd never left. I glanced around the shower cubicle and sighed with relief. I'm alone. But what the actual fuck was that? I've never felt a vision so real before. Usually my visions are only visual, this time I could smell everything. Not just the overbearing foul stench but everything it that dark room. But that voice, it was like it was directed at me, like the girl could see me or sense me. This was a completely different kind of experience.

Zelena, are you okay?

Gunners voiced filled my head, instantly calming my erratic thoughts.

I'm okay, just in the shower

I've been calling your name for like five minutes

Sorry, I was off in my own little world

Okay, well Tobias is here, we're waiting for you

I'll be there in five.

Until I can figure this vision out a bit more, I'm not going to tell Gunner about it. He will not like it, I'm in no sense of denial about that. But I think it's for the best. He is already stressing about so much, a potential traitor in our pack, the possible threat from this Italian wannabe royal pack, the party, and of course his strained relationship with Cole. I'm sure there is so much more going on, but he won't tell me about all of it, not without my pushing him too anyway.

I threw on a pair on sweatpants, a singlet top and one of Gunners hoodies. I let my wet hair fall down my back, it'll dry on its own eventually. I ran down the stairs and stopped in front of Gunner's closed office door. I knocked lightly and it was immediately followed by Gunner's voice,

"Come in".

I pushed open the door and stepped in, closing it again behind me. Gunner was stretching back in his office chair, a big smile on his face and a glass of amber liquid in his hand. Tobias was sitting in a chair opposite the desk, also holding a glass of liquor.

"Ah, there she is" Gunner chuckled raising his glass in my direction. Wow, he seems unusually cheerful.

"Here I am" I chuckled nervously. I sat down in the chair next to Tobias and threw him a weary glance. His face was also sporting a huge smile. What is going on here?

"What have I missed?" I asked looking between the two of them.

"Nothing Little One, we were just having a chat" Tobias shrugged with a smile.

"Huh, I didn't realize that you two were so chummy" I smirked, throwing a wink to Gunner.

"There is a lot that you don't know, my love" Gunner winked back.

"Okay… anyway, should we get on with it then?" I said slowly. The happy and cheerful energy was making me uncomfortable. It shouldn't though, I should be happy that these two men are getting along. They are both ridiculously important to me and I love each of them in different ways, so their friendship should bring me joy. But right now, it doesn't, it makes me nervous that I am missing something huge.

"Yes, what's on your mind Zee?" Gunner said as he placed his glass on the desk and sat upright.

"Well uh…" I began but was cut off by Tobias.

"I'll take this one if you don't mind?" he said placing his hand over mine. The notion didn't go unnoticed by Gunner, his eyes zeroed in on our connected hands.

"Alpha Gunner, I would like to join the Tri-Moon pack" Tobias blurted out. No delaying, no dancing around the subject and no easing into it. I nearly swallowed my tongue and my eyes just about burst out of my head as I whipped around to face Tobias.

"You want to join our packs?" Gunner questions leaning back in his chair, his eyes still focused on Tobias's hand on my own. Tobias chuckled and took his hand away from mine.
"No, I have passed the Alpha title onto my Beta, my younger brother, Marius"
"Yes, I know who he is".
Gunner paused, moving his eyes between the two of us. I could feel the confusion swirling around his thoughts.
"Why would you give up something as important and honourable as your Alpha title?"
"I am under no assumption that being an Alpha isn't of the highest honours granted to a Were. However, I have been granted a position much more important".
Silence enveloped the room as Tobias waited to see if Gunner was understanding him. Gunner was definitely understanding. His anger was starting to rise and his gazed narrowed at Tobias.
"Being guardian to the Triple Goddess" Tobias nodded coaxing a response from Gunner, however he didn't bite, he just stared blankly at Tobias.
"I can't successfully run a pack and continue my guardian duties to the best of my ability. Not with the distance between our territories"
"I am perfectly capable of protecting my Mate" Gunner growled. His dominance and power rolled off him and just about suffocated me.
"I am not questioning you, young Alpha. I know how fiercely you will fight for your Mate and it is not just my duty to protect her, but you as well. Without you she will fade".
I had never really thought of it that way. I had always thought Tobias was to just look out for me, but to do that, he would have to look out for the ones I love as well. Including Gunner. He was right, without Gunner I would die, no question about it. With the dangers of the Origin Wolf and the mystery traitor, the more strong and capable warriors we have, the better. Especially one who's loyalty is no question, someone who is bound to me. The realisation just made me that much more determined to convince Gunner to accept Tobias.
"Gunner, we need him. I need him" I said softly.

Gunner's growl filled the room. Shit, I could have worded that better. His eyes moved to me and he slowly stood from his desk, glaring at me.

"Tobias, give us a moment please" he said with a growl incorporated in the last word.

Will you be okay?

Tobias flashed before standing up. I looked to him and gave a slow and certain nod. He stood from his chair and eyed Gunner for a moment. Gunner paid him no mind and kept his gaze firmly on myself.

It's okay, we'll only be a minute

I flashed him. He slowly walked for the door and looked at us both before leaving. As soon as the door closed behind Tobias, Gunner leaped over his desk and had me pressed up against the wall. My hands were held tightly above my head by one of his hands and his other hand was gripping my jaw. His body was pressed hard up against mine, I was trapped and unable to move.

"Gunner" I huffed, partly from surprise, partly from annoyance at his roughness.

"What is going on?" he growled down at me,

"What do you mean?" I squeaked,

"You expect me to believe that an Alpha as strong and powerful as Tobias would just give it all up?"

"He explained that to you. What don't you understand?"

"Are you fucking him?" Gunner hissed viciously. His chest vibrated against me and it immediately sent a rage burning through my body. How dare he.

That fucking prick! Drawing in the energy of the night, I used my powers to push Gunner back and away from me. He tumbled over one of the chairs but quickly jumped back to his feet.

"How dare you!" I yelled. He stepped towards me and I lifted my hand, closing my fist tightly. I pictured my fingers wrapped around him, holding him in place as if he were a doll in my hand. The gravitational pull poured out of me and wrapped all around him. He was completely frozen, unable to move his arms or legs. The heat of his furious gaze burned into my face.

"Let me go" he growled through gritted teeth.

"Calm the fuck down" I yelled. His anger was starting to seep into me, if I don't get him to relax, I'm afraid that it will overtake me.

"LET ME GO!" he roared again.

His anger was palpable, it prickled seductively across my skin. I could feel my claws push through the tips of my fingers. My gums ached with the need for my canines to extend. I rolled my head back and the heat of his fury crawled up the back of my neck. My eyes narrowed and heaviness filled my heart. I flexed the fingers of my outstretched hand, squeezing Gunner tighter. He roared again and tried to thrash fruitlessly under the grip of my power. The feeling of rage felt good under my skin. A darkness clouded my vision and I welcomed it. It was seductive, pulling me deeper under its spell. I could feel a tightness in my chest and my heartbeat accelerated. The feeling was intoxicating.

The office door suddenly flew open with a loud crash, and two gargantuan arms wrapped around my waist.

"Breathe Little One, you need to calm down" Tobias's calm voice echoed through my ears and his warm breath fanned across my cheek. He wrapped his fingers around my outstretched wrist but didn't try to move it. The touch of his skin offered some relief to the anger, but I fought against it. I want to stay with the darkness, the anger, the numb feeling of nothingness.

"Get your filthy hands off my Mate!" Gunner screamed, still in the grasps of my power.

"Alpha, you need to calm down. Can you not see what you are doing to each other?" Tobias pleaded.

I struggled against his hold on me, but it was pointless. Being wrapped in his arms was like being tied down by ten-inch steel bars.

"Get off me" I screeched, trying my best to wriggle from his arms. The glass of the windows blew out with an almighty explosion. The air of the room grew heavy. The weight of it pulled Tobias towards the ground. His grip on me held firm, therefore, he was pulling me downwards with him. Gunner's desk creaked and cracked and snapped in half, sending pieces of wood splintering through the air.

"Release her now" Gunner growled, his voice low and deadly.

"I can't do that" Tobias remained calm and collected in the face of a raging Alpha and a powerful Goddess on the edge of exploding.

"Look at your Mate, little Goddess. Look into his eyes and find the love you have for each other. It's in there, just remember Zelena".

I squirmed and moved as much as I could, growling and grunting with each failed movement. Parts of the shattered desk were flying through the air at dangerous speeds. Tobias grabbed my face and turned my head towards Gunner. His calming presence was almost soothing, but the seduction of the anger and darkness was too much. I looked over Gunner, the position of his body looks somewhat awkward, legs pinned together and arms crossed over his chest. His face was red with anger and his blue eyes were wide and held a deadly warning. Even in his rage he is unbearably handsome. I stared deeply into his furious eyes, looking for a glimmer of the love I know we have.

"Gunner" I half growled, half huffed. His enraged gaze wavered for a moment, it was only a brief second, but I saw it. That was all it took. The rage within me dissipated almost instantly, and a deep regret filled its place. Broken pieces of wood rained down on the floor of the office. I breathed out a slow and ragged breath and relaxed into Tobias's arms. The heaviness was gone from the room and the downward force with it.

"Alpha, I beg you please, you need to expel your anger before it consumes you"

"You need to take your hands off my Mate".

"I promise you, I am offering her no more than the support of a friend or a big brother. I have been chosen by the Goddess herself to protect her and that is what I will do. We have spoken of this, there is no kind of romantic feelings between either of us. You know this. You need to trust in your Mate and believe in the will of the Goddess".

Gunner huffed and growled and struggled against my hold on him. After a minute of that he realised it was pointless. He looked up to me and stared into my eyes. I don't know how long we gazed at each other, could have been seconds, minutes, or even hours. An array of emotions ran through me,

I know he was feeling the same as me. We finally came to rest on remorse, guilt and love.

"Please Zelena, will you release me?" Gunner asked, he sounded defeated and full of shame.

"Are you okay now, Alpha?" the concerned Tobias asked, gently removing his arms from around me.

"He's okay" I answered for him and pulled back my hold on Gunner. He slumped forward and fell to the floor on his knees. I rushed over to him, dropped to my knees and placed my hands on either side of his face. I gently lifted his face to look at me, and as soon as he did my heart broke a little. Tears streamed down his face and his lip quivered.

"I'm so sorry" he choked,

"I don't know what happened, I just lost all control".

I pulled him into my chest and rubbed my hand through his hair.

"It's okay, we're okay" I soothed. He pulled me onto his lap and buried his face in the crook of my neck. His breaths were ragged, and I could feel his chest shake with each expel of air. Tobias stood behind us near the door, not yet fully trusting that the situation had eased. I continued to run my hand in slow calming circles on his back for what felt like hours. With me still in his arms, Gunner began to stand up. I wrapped my legs around his waist and held on to his shoulders. He walked us over to his large leather office chair and sat back down, shifting me so that I now sat across his legs.

"Tobias, I apologise for my outburst" Gunner said gruffly, returning back to his Alpha wolf mode.

"Not a problem Alpha, I understand" he replied stepping closer to us.

"I did not intend to offend you. Of course you can become a member of Tri-Moon and can remain in your current room in the main house".

"Thank you, Alpha". Tobias placed his hand over his chest and bowed low. I released a breath and relaxed further into Gunner's chest. I looked up to him and smiled to show my appreciation. It took a minute but we got there, eventually. I just hope that Roe doesn't learn of this little incident. I don't think I could handle her disapproving gaze and strong scolding about the dangers of giving into the anger. Gunner gently traced his finger down my cheek and over my lips, his beautiful blue eyes held a sparkle of adoration.

"But please refer to me as Gunner. You're important to my Mate, so you are important to me" he said averting his gaze back to Tobias.

"As you wish Alpha Gunner" Tobias answered with a small bow of his head. Gunner chuckled and any remaining tension melted away.

"I would like to offer you a role in the pack Tobias. How do you feel about commander?"

"It is really not necessary. I am happy to just be accepted"

"I insist. You deserve a title of some sort"

"With all due respect Alpha Gunner, if I were to accept a commanding role, I fear it will serve as a distraction to my guardian duties".

Gunner paused and ran a hand through his hair. He was clearly thinking of another role he could offer. Gunner already has a Beta in Cole and a Delta in Smith. I'm still not completely educated about all things Were, but I don't think there is any other kind of title.

"Well, I suppose guardian to the Goddess is a pretty good title" I piped up. Gunner smiled down at me and Tobias chuckled quietly.

"It is a pretty good title, isn't it?" Gunner agreed. I sat up straight and readjusted the placing of my butt on his legs. Gunner gripped my hips tight and eased me back on his lap. I could feel the outline of his semi hard dick underneath my ass cheeks. A slight blush blew across my face as I turned away from Tobias.

"How do you feel about Lead Advisor?" Gunner asked reverting his attention back to Tobias.

"Advisor?" he repeated.

"Yes, you're a strong and highly capable Were. You were an excellent Alpha and I feel like you could offer a lot to this pack. I can't offer you my Beta position as you know, but I do want to incorporate you into the organisation and running of this pack. Being my leading advisor is a good way to make that happen".

Tobias looked between the two of us for a moment before his eyes settle on me. I nodded my head and smiled with encouragement.

"Thank you, Gunner. I will do my best not to disappoint you" Tobias stood and bowed again with his hand over his heart.

"As long as you continue to be a loyal guardian and trusted advisor, I have no doubts about your capabilities".

Gunner lifted me from his lap and stepped around large pieces of his broken desk to stand in front of Tobias. They took each other's forearms and pressed their foreheads together. They held the position for a few seconds before breaking apart and smiling at each other. The two most important men in my life have finally come together. And they did it for me. I couldn't keep back the smile that spread across my face as I watched them. Gunner turned to me and smiled.

"If you don't mind Tobias, Zee and I have a few things to discuss" Gunner said to him as he walked back over to my side and placed his hand gently on my shoulder.

"Of course. Have a good night" Tobias said, offering a small smirk before walking out of the door. Gunner picked me up and I wrapped my legs around his waist. He pressed my back up against the wall and pushed his hips into my own. He pressed his lips to the base of my neck and I angled my head back to give him more room.

"I'm so sorry my love, you know I would never intentionally hurt you?" Gunner mumbled into the soft skin of my neck.

"I know" I answered in a strained voice.

"I think I should show you just how sorry I am" he teased, tracing his tongue up my neck to my earlobe and biting on it softly. I gasped and arched my back, pressing my chest into his.

"I think you should too" I moaned softly. Gunner released my ear and pulled back before pressing his lips to mine. Our lips moved with an insatiable hunger as our tongues danced together. I squeezed my thighs tightly around his waist and dragged my fingers through his hair. He pulled me off the wall, bracing me by my ass and headed for the door.

"Where are we going?" I mumbled into his mouth.

"To bed. Once I start my apology, I don't plan on stopping until you are fully satisfied"

"Mm well this may take a while"

"Oh baby, I'm planning on it".

Chapter Thirteen

Lunaya

The first pack we came across was in La Mauricie National Park. They didn't open their pack grounds and offered us nothing but a swift death if we didn't immediately "fuck right off". No sign of friendly Canadian hospitality there. It was a hit to my confidence. I knew being turned away was a very high possibility, some part of me even expected it. But that first refusal was crushing. I had it in my mind how this was going to go. The first pack we find would welcome us in with smiles and open ended answers to all our questions. They would know where the Goddess was and how to get to her, and they'd tell us without hesitation. Clearly, that was some kind of fantasy fever dream. So we very swiftly retreated out of their pack lands and continued on.

Phoebe knew of a smaller pack that lived somewhere in the Hautes-Gorges-de-la-Rivière-Malbaie National Park. Though she claimed them to be recluses, a little on the wild side. She was very much against us tracking them down.

"They won't help us. I doubt they even know of the Goddess' arrival, they don't commune with the outside world beyond what's absolutely necessary. They live completely off the grid, one hundred percent reclused" Phoebe argued.

"It's worth a try at least" I retorted. She scoffed and turned to glare at Elaine, I assume expecting that she would back up her argument. Elaine looked between us, hesitating, calculating. After a few minutes, she breathed out deeply.

"We'll give it a go" she conceded. Phoebe threw her hands up with a shake of her head.

"This is a bad idea" she snarled.

"Also, no cars can enter the park, what are we going to do, just run around blind and hope we stumble on them?" Phoebe asked sarcastically.

"Watch your tone" Elaine growled.

"Sorry Beta" she quickly huffed and dropped her head.

Elaine leaned on the bonnet of one of the cars and took her time to go over a couple of maps. The only input she would allow came from Cleo. Phoebe answered what questions she could about the reclusive pack, which wasn't a whole lot. But after an hour Elaine and Cleo packed away the maps and came to where the rest of us were sitting and waiting.

"Okay, here's what's going to happen" Elaine announced.

~

The plan was solid. Elaine had decided on a secure location to stash the cars and an entry point to the park. She and Cleo did their research, marking walking trails, bike trails, camping spots, and any other known and accessible areas within the vast expanse of the park. Cleo, as it turns out, has a mind for off the grid type. It's something I want to learn more about her. Between the two of them, taking into account things like easy access to fresh water, heavy tree coverage, inaccessibility to the general public, and local game hunting, they managed to mark out only two possible locations for the pack.

Once we got to the entry point, we stashed the cars and readied ourselves to head for the first location on the map. All the women changed into their wolves, opting to leave bags and such with the cars. I let myself fall towards the ground, and with a few cracks and breaks, I landed on the soft dirt on my paws. I shook out my long black and white fur and let the fresh air wash over my wolf body.

Alyse ran her hand through my coat, up and along my back. The sensation sent a shiver shooting down my spine. I turned my giant head and licked her smiling face. I do still wish she

139

had a wolf form. I've never really gotten used to the fact that we can't run together, we can't mate in wolf form, and can't connect on that extra level. Alyse though, it's never bothered her. She never had a wolf, so she never truly knew what she was missing. For her, she was happy with her heightened senses and strength and speed. Plus, she makes good use of her claws. But I don't think the longing for her non-existent wolf side will ever leave me.

"Feel better" Alyse chuckled as she scratched behind my ear. I tilted my head to the side a little to allow her better access. A quiet growl crossed with a purr fell from my mouth as her fingers worked their magic. I lifted my head and shook out my fur to get rid of the tingles that her fingers left on my pelt.

Come on, you

I flashed and knelt down low enough so that she could climb onto my back. Alyse nimbly climbed up my front leg and onto my back. Leaning forward, with her chest pressed between my shoulder blades, she wrapped her arms around my neck. Well as far as her arms could reach, my wolf is a lot larger than most she-wolves. Once I felt that she was secure, I nodded to the other wolves. Together we bounded off through the trees. I was more careful with my movements, to not knock Alyse around too much. I ran and jumped and ducked under branches, over fallen trees and large boulders. Keeping up easily with the others. The freedom of the run was exhilarating. The air flowing through my fur is unlike any other feeling in the world. It's enough to make me forget, if only for a second, the importance of our mission.

The run was easy enough, at least for the first few miles. The deeper we went into the forest, the more difficult the paths became. There was no discernible pathway, not any visible to the naked eye. Though I suppose if I had grown up in these woods, lived, ran, and explored them on a daily, it would be like a second nature. The land is beautiful. Thick and dense with so much greenery. I can understand how a whole pack could get lost in here.

As we approached the first location on the map, it became clear quickly that this wasn't the right place. At no point were we intercepted by patrols or warriors. There were no obvious sections of the forest developed to make trespassers turn around. No downed trees, large boulders or cliffs, no thorned vines precariously planted to block the way, nothing. We continued on, just to be sure. And just as I suspected, there wasn't any kind of village, or anything that can be misconstrued as such.

"They're not here" Alyse called to the gathered Weres. Elaine's wolf huffed and shook her head in response. Her head bent back and she reformed into her large intimidating human form. Alyse slipped off my back so I could change as well. Elaine stood with her hand outstretched to Alyse as I stood back up on my human legs. Alyse handed the folded map to Elain. She looked over it quietly while the other females sniffed around the trees, choosing to remain in their wolf forms.

"To the next location then?" I asked as I walked to Elaine's side, peering at the map she held in front of her.

"Yes" she answered gruffly. I could see the two small circles on the map, the possible locations of the pack. We were at the closest one. The other marked spot was at least an hour away at best, two hours if the forest was harder to navigate still. Elaine slid her finger along the map, starting at where we were currently standing, weaving and curling a path to the next marked place on the map. Once she selected a route she looked up at me wordlessly and I nodded in my agreement. I have a feeling it's going to be hard to get there regardless of the route we track. Elaine refolded the map and handed it back to Alyse who was hovering close by.

"Let's go" was all Elaine said before she changed back to her wolf. Alyse slipped the map back into the small fanny pack she had strapped across her chest and climbed up onto my back again. The other wolves came back over and watched us, waiting for Alyse to position herself before we again took off through the trees.

Unsurprisingly, the run was brutal, nearly impassable. A natural path in the land would end in either a rock face, a thicket of trees, a pile of boulders, or some kind of body of water. Finding a way through was beyond difficult. Many times the she-wolves would have to change back into their human forms to navigate the terrain. A one point we all had to scale a sheer rock face. It would have been a sight to see.

Six women, all but one of them stark naked, climbing up a cliff.

Over an hour had passed since we left the last area, we hadn't come across a single wolf. But the signs of them were around. The traps and tricks designed to guide travellers into moving away were becoming more frequent. Though every few hundred meters we got closer, an ominous feeling in the woods began to rise. We hadn't come across any patrols. Plus, it was too quiet. Even the sounds of nature seemed to be silenced. This is not the kind of atmosphere one would expect this close to a supposed pack. The silence can't even be blamed on the natural food-chain. Though Weres are at the top of the list in the forest, animals still tend to keep close to where we gather. Perhaps as a way of protection, or some other manipulation of natural animal instincts. This silence was unnatural, haunting. It sent a cold shiver along my spine. "I don't like this" Alyse whispered softly to the back of my ear. I huffed softly so as to not make too much noise. I agreed with her one hundred percent. We slowed to a careful and watchful walk. Each step was hesitant and cautious not to make a sound. Without needing to discuss it, the females all drew in tightly, keeping together in a small circular formation. Alyse and I were strategically placed in the centre of the ring. The further we walked the more off it felt.

"We should have been stopped by now" Alyse whispered again. Elaine bobbed her head in agreement. The fact that we hadn't yet made my stomach tight. A gentle breeze picked up the underbrush and blew through our group. The scent was undeniable. Blood. A lot of blood.

We paused in unison, noses lifted into the air sniffing at the scents the wind was carrying our way. Beside the blood, there was decay and ash, and the unmistakable scent of gunpowder. The females grunted back and forth, clearing flashing about what they wanted to do next. Good Goddess I wish I could hear them right now. It's not safe to change into my human form to communicate. Although I'm confident in my ability to fight and defend myself in human form, the wolf is unparalleled in every way. And this was obviously a time to be ready for anything. Cleo's wolf nudged me from behind, pushing me to follow Elaine as we continued our approach.

The way into the outskirts of the village area was excruciatingly slow. Every ear was focused on the sounds of the forest, straining to hear anything of consequence. Every eye was trained on the trees, the ground, the surroundings, searching for signs of danger. Each and every one of us was ridged with tension. Our animal bodies readying themselves for the possible threats that we could feel in the air.

The first body came along the forest way just twenty minutes after that first scent of blood found us. The mangled wolf corpse was riddled with holes, its fur stained red with thick crimson blood. The bodies were a steady stream after that, like a path leading to the heart of the village. Sprinkled throughout the many, many corpses were human forms dressed in black battle armour. A Hunters armour. The bodies were in a great variety of disarray. Some were nearly split in half by the amount of bullet holes, a couple looked completely untouched. In normal Hunter fashion, many of the remains had been desecrated. A wolf's head hung from a tree branch by a giant hook through its eye. Another wolf form was tied between two trees in an X shape. Its limbs had been snapped in a way to allow the unnatural movement. A woman's body had been stripped bare and tied to the trunk of a tree. Her flesh was sliced and peeled back in large sections. There wasn't an inch of her skin that wasn't coated in crusted dried blood. Bile rose in my throat as I took in the scene around me.

Seeing what remained of the slaughter, the trees painted red, the brown earth blackened with blood and ash, the discarded bodies, and the scent of death. It brought it all rushing back to me. The memory of my own pack. The aftermath of that massacre. It was so much like what had been done to these poor souls. This wasn't a simple battle. This village wasn't just massacred. This was an extinction. This chaos was caused by the hands of pure evil. The vow I made all those years ago, the promise I made to the Goddess, that I would kill every hunter involved in the extermination of my pack. It felt renewed in my soul. The heat of that hatred, the burning desire to bring retribution down upon these monsters, it engulfed me once again.

The sound of Alyse whimpering drew my attention away from the dead hunter, and to a pile of small bodies. Children's bodies. The mountains of ash that remained showed a map of how the village once stood. Rows of scorched wood and rubble were piled in two lines down the middle of the village space. It was just a small village, at least as best as I could tell. And so far, not a single sign of life.

Two of the female wolves beside me began growling ferociously, their heads whipping around at the destruction surrounding us. It was Phoebe's pale blonde wolf that broke rank first. She darted forward to the closet body, shoving and snuffling with her snout. Then moved to the next, and the next, and the next. She came up with the same lifeless result from each body, and with each confirmed death, her body began to shake and tremble with the unshed emotions. Cleo's foreboding wolf form stalked around the small space, gazing at the endless stream of bodies. As Alyse slipped from my back and made to walk to the bloodied mess of children, I quickly changed and caught her arm, stopping her.

"I have to" she sobbed. I pulled her back to me, bringing her wet face to my chest. Her body heaved with silent heavy sobs. I stroked my hand down her back in a soothing motion. I knew there was nothing to soothe this pain in her heart. There were no words to say that could comfort her. Alyse's feelings ran deep, it's one of the many things I love about her. But her compassion and love for children was unmatched in every way. I knew seeing this was going to hit her extremely hard.

"Let me" I strained out as I gently lifted her head from my chest. I gripped the sides of her face and tilted her head to look at me. Her eyes were pressed closed tight, but the tears still found their way down her cheeks. I rubbed one away as it rolled to the corner of her mouth. She heaved a sigh and without opening her eyes, Alyse shuddered and nodded weakly. I hesitantly let her go and stepped around her body, leaving her, standing there alone.

Elaine was already there, gently lifting and sifting through the mound of children. I came to her side and took a small body from her hands. The boy couldn't have been more than four years old. His tattered and bloodied clothes barely contained the gaping hole in his chest. I laid him on the ground and placed his hands across his body, his head straight. Elaine moved to place a young girl next to where I laid the boy. She was older, perhaps ten. Her throat was cut so deep it was a wonder that her head was still attached. Each child was more of the same. Each one died a horrible gruesome death. Each body covered head to toe in blood.

I looked over my shoulder to find Venus and Phoebe laying out the bodies of the adults. I turned in search of Alyse, but she was no longer behind me. I paused and searched the area with a hurried whip of my head. She was among the trees, shovel in hand, standing slightly back as Cleo's wolf dug savagely at a hole in the dirt. The earth flew around her body at such speed, it was like a wave of dirt. Slowly, Cleo's body drifted lower and lower into the hole as she dug deeper and deeper. Alyse moved around Cleo and continued to dig at her side. She must have felt my gaze upon her. As she looked up, her red and tear stained cheeks glimmered in the gentle sun that managed to break through the tree cover. Although the grief and devastation was clear on her face, she was still beautiful, even among the desolation. She nodded her head, telling me she was alright. Well, as alright as you could be in a moment like this. Then swiftly went back to digging.

The hours ticked by and the bodies kept coming. Venus and Phoebe took down the naked woman from the tree, at which point Venus spewed behind a tree. I get it. It was truly sickening. Not just what they did to that woman, the whole thing was horrendous. We had the members of the pack laid out as respectfully as we could. The Hunter's bodies were discarded in a pile out of site. When there was no one left, the rest of us joined Cleo and Alyse with the hole. Five sets of giant paws clawing at the earth got it done much faster. When we were content with the depth and size, we moved on to the next task.

We started with the men and the larger wolves, Elaine and Cleo waited in the hole as the rest of us passed them the bodies. Each body was carefully laid down, side by side, at the bottom of the grave. Then we moved on to the women and the smaller wolves. And then finally, the children. We took the time to place and arrange each and every one of the pack members to look as peaceful as possible. We closed their eyes and laid their hands and paws together, so they could all remain connected, even in death. We covered up those we found naked and cleaned the blood off all their faces. When there was no one left, we all just stood there.

What could be said to bring comfort to the dead? What could be done to remember people we never met? What more could we do beyond that which we had already done. Cleo picked up a handful of dirt and held it out over the open grave. She let the dirt fall slowly between her fingers as her deep mournful voice sang out. The other females joined in as they picked up handfuls of dirt and scattered it over the bodies. Alyse took my hand, with tears falling freely down her face, and rested her head on my shoulder. Cleo's voice wailed beautifully into the darkening sky, carrying through the trees and filling the forest around us. With the deep melody of the other females accompanying her operatic voice, the melody was beautiful. I didn't understand the lyrics, she was singing in her native Māori tongue, but somehow, I understood. It was a farewell. It was the least we could offer this pack as they returned to the Goddess.

The women sang and sang and sang. As we filled the grave, they sang. As we replanted wildflowers around the burial site, they sang. As we collected trinkets, soft toys, and other small items from around the village and placed them atop the grave, they sang. Only once the sun was gone, the moon was high and the forest was silent once again, the singing stopped. We stood together again, sullen and grieving. The light from the moon seemed to shine in a beam over the top of the grave, like the Goddess herself was welcoming her children home. A shiver ran through me as a gentle breeze swept around us. It tickled across my skin, and it warmed the air ever so slightly. Fallen flower petals were picked up in the breeze and carried in an upward spiral motion to the tips of the trees. A small smile graced my lips as I tilted my head back to the sky. Selene was here, she was taking these souls back with her. We watched on silently for a while longer. When the breeze was gone, and the moonlight disappeared behind the clouds, we finally turned from the grave.

"What about them?" Phoebe sneered in the direction of the pile of hunter bodies.

"We should burn them, they don't deserve peace" Venus growled lowly.

"We can't risk a fire" Elaine said sternly.

"Then leave them" Cleo clipped. I turned to her, surprised to hear her speak.

"Let the animals have them" she added after a second. I looked to Elaine who seemed to agree wordlessly. The other females nodded their agreement.

"They hate the natural line of life so much, they hate the beasts they claim we are. Well, now they can feed those beasts, they can contribute to that natural line that they have tried so hard to break" Alyse hissed through her teeth. I squeezed her hand and nodded.

"We should take their armour and boots off first" I said. Cleo didn't respond, she just marched to the pile of human bodies and began shedding their armoured vest and thick combat boots. In no time at all we had a pile of shredded items. They got no care from us, not extra time to untie laces and unzip coats. We clawed at their bodies until the balk of their coverings was gone, leaving the rest open to the forest. Once satisfied with the work, we left them there. Alone, cold and vulnerable.

"It's time to go" Elaine called. There was no argument and no hesitation. The females changed back into their wolves and readied themselves to depart. Alyse climbed onto my back and we set off, back the way we came.

"Lua Chei is where we're headed next, yeah?" Alyse called to my ear as I ran through the trees behind Phoebe.

Yes, that was the original plan. I flashed back in response.

"Do you think they know about this?" she asked.

There's no way to know, though I assume they wouldn't have left them like that if they did

"True" she mumbled and pressed her cheek to the back of my head, shielding herself from the elements of the forest.

~

The sun was rising when we made it back to the vehicles. Each of us was exhausted, both from the running and the emotional turmoil of the past night. Elaine and Cleo may have hidden their fatigue better than the rest of us, but the eyes never lie. And all of ours were bloodshot and droopy.

"We should rest" I called to Elaine.

"Yes. Take your packs and find a tree, you've all got three hours to sleep before we're on the road again" she called back, loud enough for all of us to hear. Venus and Phoebe wasted no time and curled up together against a large tree truck. Cleo grunted something to Elaine, too softly for me to hear, before she changed into her wolf form and sauntered off through the trees. Elaine turned back to look at me and I gestured to Cleo with my chin, a quiet question about where she was going.

"Cleo will take first watch" Elaine answered knowing my unspoken curiosity. I nodded and took Alyse's hand, pulling her to another tree near the other females. We laid down and I pulled her head to my chest. I leaned my head back against the trunk of the tree and closed my eyes. The day's events and the emotions they brought rammed through me like a freight train. As I gently stroked my fingers through the ends of Alyse's hair, her quiet sobs shook her body. We both fell into a fitful sleep with tear stained cheeks and aching hearts.

Chapter

Fourteen

Lunaya

We entered Nova Scotia over four hours ago, and finally turned off the highway and onto a dirt road at the Trout Point Lodge sign. This was the beginning of the Lua Chei pack borders. We drove much slower along the bumpy gravel road, with the sun hidden behind the tall trees and the roughness of the road, it was way too dangerous to maintain our previous speed. After only five minutes on the track, a flash of something dark darting past the window caught my attention. I searched the darkening surroundings for whatever it was when I spotted another.

"Wolves are surrounding us" I said not taking my eyes off the pale brown wolf running through the trees alongside our car.

"Yes, I noticed" Elaine responded, seeming somewhat unfazed.

"And what if they don't accept us on their land? Hina only booked the accommodation, she didn't contact the Alpha to alert him of our arrival" I said turning to glance at Elaine's stoic face.

"We will deal with that if it comes to it" she said lowering her eyes and tightening her grip on the steering wheel.

"You saw the same thing I did, you know there's going to be some kind of trouble. There's no way they don't know of the attacks" I argued.

"I said we'll deal with it" Elaine growled back.

As we pulled up to the front of the lodge, I searched around the trees before exiting the car. I could no longer see the light brown wolf or any other wolf hiding in amongst the trees. All the front and interior lights were on, but they were of course expecting a group to be checking in, they just didn't know that it was a group of Weres. Elaine stepped out of the car first and I followed after her. I opened Alyse's door and blocked her between the car and my body the best I could. The other car pulled up and the three warriors didn't hesitate to get out of their car and stand by us. Walking together in a tight circle towards the door, to anyone else, we would have looked like idiots, but I do not doubt that the pack fighters could recognise our defensive circle. Elaine opened the front door and we all filed in. Standing in front of a reception desk, I took the chance to look around, it was completely empty but I knew they were all there. I could smell them. Just as I'm sure they could smell us.

Elaine hit the bell on the top of the desk, and I spun around to glare at her. The sound of the bell echoed through the eerie quiet lodge, waking all the ghosts and telling anyone who didn't already know we were here, exactly where we were. A big grey wolf stepped out into a large open doorway that led to what looked like an extravagant living area, another appeared at the top of a set of stairs. A dark brown and grey wolf stepped forward from around another corner and more now stood outside around our cars. We weren't going anywhere. They had made sure of that.

Growls and barks filled the lodge, and even more swept in from the other wolves outside. We are severely outnumbered. The warriors and Elaine concealed Alyse and me between their bodies and took a defensive stance, keeping us tucked away in the middle. The movement irked me a little, like we couldn't take care of ourselves. Please. We have lived as Omegas for a long time. We know how to hold our own. But right now is definitely not the time for a show of strength.

"Please be calm, we didn't come for trouble" I called out pushing my way through the hard and strong protective women.

"We mean you no harm" I said to try and convince them to stand down. I held my arms up in surrender and shot my eyes between the wolves on either side of us.

"State your business here" a voice bellowed from the living area. A tall blonde woman came to stand next to the grey wolf. She was a little older, perhaps in her late fifties, or early sixties, but still held an aura of power.

"We have a booking" I said turning my back on the wolves behind me and giving my full attention to the woman. This was a risky move, leaving myself open to attack from behind, but I needed to show her that we really did mean them no harm.

"And why should I let you onto my lands, you have come here unannounced and uninvited" the woman said firmly.

"Luna" I said with a small bow of my head. She lifted her nose in the air, scenting us. Her lip curled as she growled.

"I can smell the death on you" she hissed.

"Regrettably, your pack is not our first stop" I announced, letting the pain and sorrow fill my voice.

"Given your security and hostility, I can only guess that you know what we found".

"That you found or that you imparted?" the Luna growled. The other wolves surrounding us growled in unison.

"I think you already know. That decimation was not caused by Weres. In this, we are on same side" I said as I stood up straight and lowered my hands.

"We have come from Luna Eclipse. We are on a diplomatic mission to offer our greetings and support to the newly risen Triple Goddess" Elaine barked sternly.

The woman hissed but was quiet for a moment, her eyes raking over each and every one of us from head to toe. She was sizing us up and searching for signs of danger or deceit.

"How do I know you are being honest? Luna Eclipse is said to be just a legend".

"All legends start somewhere. In this case, from the source itself" Elaine rebutted.

"Hm" she mumbled. She crossed her arms over her chest and stared at me with an emotionless face.

"I swear on the Goddess herself, we mean you no ill intent. And we really do want to keep our booking" I chuckled with a large smile. Anything to lessen to thick tension swirling around the room. After a moment the woman laughed and stepped towards us.

"Thank goodness. I didn't want to deal with dead bodies today" she joked and patted my shoulder. Elaine growled lowly but stood up straight from her attack stance. She stepped up next to me and offered her hand to the woman.

"I am Beta Elaine to the Luna Eclipse pack".

"Wow, you are a big lady" she chuckled and took Elaine's hand then stepped closer to initiate Sevasmo. Elaine bent down and pressed her forehead against the woman's. After a brief second, they split apart, though she still held Elaine's forearm.

"I am Luna Astéri. Welcome".

I motioned for Alyse to step forward and she came to my arm, pressing herself into my side. Astéri watched us closely before a bright smile took over her face.

"You must be the couple?" she said nodding her head in our direction.

"This is Alyse, and I am Lunaya" I said with a short nod.

"Ahh, perfect. We have your special room all ready for you" she said turning around,

"I'm sorry. A special room?" I questioned before she could walk away.

"Yes, as requested on your booking information, two double rooms and one suite" she confirmed and walked around the desk.

I looked down to Alyse who was now smiling at me with excitement. It has been a very long time since we have stayed in anything that could be considered a suite. My excitement began to bubble through, and I could feel the corners of my mouth turning up into a smile. Astéri stepped back in front of us and handed me a big old-fashioned key. She then handed two more keys to Elaine.

"Come now, I'll let you get settled in before you have dinner. Please follow me".

Astéri walked off towards the stairs but bypassed them and instead opened a set of double doors to the left. We followed her into a room that could only be described as magnificent.

There was a large queen canopy bed made of hand-crafted wooden logs. The other side of the room boasted a large stone fireplace, surrounded by plush sofas. The high ceiling was held up by exposed log beams and alight by a gorgeous small chandelier that hung above the bed. Another set of double doors opened out onto a stone patio that overlooked the most beautiful running river. The sounds of nature enveloped the room in a luxurious cosiness.

"This is for us?" Alyse gasped as she stood in place and turned in a circle, examining the marvellous room.

"Sure is" Astéri nodded as she glanced around the room, clearly proud of the luxurious space.

"Your separate bathroom is through that door. However, if you want something a little extra relaxing, there is a woodfire sauna or hot tub located by the river. You lot are our only guests at the moment, so you will not be disturbed. Your bags will be brought to you and I will let you get settled. Dinner will be served in two hours".

With that, she left the room taking Elaine and the others with her. Alyse went to explore the vast room while I went and sat on the couch in front of the dimly lit fireplace. The weather was warm enough without needing the fire, but it made the room feel so much more comfortable. Just as I lifted my feet to relax, a knock sounded at the door. I stood up and walked over, opening the door to find a teenage boy with our backpacks.

"Hello, I'm Akela. I've brought your bags" he said handing me the first bag,

"Thank you" I said as I took them and placed them by the door. I looked over the young boy. His blonde hair accentuated his sharp young features. He couldn't be more than maybe sixteen. His face held characteristics of the Luna, Astéri.

"Are you related to the Luna?" I asked him.

"Uh yes, I'm the youngest of six Alpha-sons and three Alpha-daughters"

"Well shit, your parents have been busy" I chuckled. He laughed awkwardly and rubbed the back of his neck.

"Yeah, it's gross" he sneered avoiding eye contact. I could tell he didn't want to talk about his parent's mating habits, but the blush on his cheeks and his awkward demeanour made it hard to resist teasing him a little more.

"No, it's a beautiful thing" I provoked him with a smirk.

"Not when you have to catch them banging it out all over the forest and the pack house" he huffed with a groan. I let out a laugh from the pit of my stomach, my whole body shaking with fits of uncontrollable laughter. The poor boy.

"What's going on here?" Alyse asked as she came over to my side. I wrapped my arm around her shoulder and buried my face in her hair to stifle my laughter.

"I was just talking with this young Alpha-son about the mating habits of his parents" I mumbled, trying to soothe my over-excited heartbeat.

"You were not" Alyse gasped. I couldn't respond as another bout of laughter came on after seeing how red poor Akela's face had gotten.

"I'm so sorry, I think her exhaustion has made her delirious" Alyse yelled over my obnoxious cackling. Akela nodded his head and just about ran away from us. I closed the door and turned to see a glowering Alyse.

"You're so mean, you know that?"

"I couldn't help it. Did you see how red the kid got?"

Alyse's hard face shattered as a giggle ripped from her but she quickly masked back over it and slapped my arm.

"That poor boy" she chuckled.

"Nah, he'll be fine. After nine kids, I reckon he is pretty used to it".

"Nine kids?" Alyse gasped with her mouth hanging open.

"That's what he said, six boys and three girls".

"Oh wow, can you imagine the noise at dinner time" she giggled with her hand on her cheek.

"Good Goddess no!" I huffed as I slumped back down on the couch by the fireplace. Alyse came to sit next to me and lifted her legs to my lap. I pulled off her boots and let them drop to the floor with a thump.

"So, my love, are you going to give that bath a workout or would you like to join me at the wood fire hot tub?" I asked as I rubbed my hands over her calf muscles.

"Mm, hot tube sounds so relaxing" she moaned with her head bent back and her eyes closed.

"Well then, we have an hour and a half until dinner, so let's get to it". I tapped her leg and pushed them off my lap, before standing up and holding my hands out for her. Alyse huffed and groaned but took my hands and I pulled her up on her feet. I gave her ass a smack, I then walked out the double doors to the stone patio and eventually found the hot tub.

After over an hour in the hot tub, making the most of our privacy and optimal location, we reluctantly made our way back inside to change and prepare for dinner. In no time at all Astéri's voice called from the other side of the door along with a sharp nock.

"Ladies, dinner is ready when you are" she said through the solid wood door.

"Thank you, Astéri, we'll be right there" I called back to her.

~

The dining room was designed just like the rest of the lodge. Exposed wooden beams along the ceiling with a few hanging chandeliers that bathed the room in a warm light. The walls were made of both large stone bricks and thick wooden beams, scattered with windows overlooking the forest and parts of the river. The large table was made of one large piece of treated wood, running the entire length of the room, with matching wooden chairs placed around it. The atmosphere of the dining room was like a warm blanket of luxury, just like you would expect of a five-star restaurant in Paris.

"Holy crap" Alyse exclaimed as we walked in. Elaine and the others were already seated around the table, each with a large glass of wine. Astéri, Akela, and a few others I hadn't met yet joined them. Astéri and Elaine both turned to see us as we stepped into the room.

"Ah, there you are ladies, how did you like the hot tub?" Astéri called as she stood up and walked over to us.

"It was incredible, thank you" I replied taking her outstretched hand. She led us to two empty seats towards the head of the table. As we walked past each of the people that I didn't recognised she named them.

"These are some of my children; Akela, you know. Aleah, my youngest daughter, Analah, Ahmad, Aston, and my eldest son, Ares".

Ares stood and offered his hand to me, I took it and he pulled me forward for Sevasmo. After a brief pause, we separated, and he did the same for Alyse.

"It's a pleasure to have you all here" he said in a deep and rumbling voice. I roamed my eyes over the eldest son, Ares, he is a tall man with slim muscles. Possibly in his early thirties. He must look like his father as he held nearly no resemblance to his mother. My curiosity spiked as I took him in, if he is of age, why has he not ascended to the Alpha position yet?

"It's a pleasure to be here. This is quite the establishment you have, you must be proud" I said to Ares as we took out seats at his side.

"This lodge has been run by Lua Chei for generations. It is our pride and joy" he confirmed with a nod. As I looked around the table, I noticed that all the place settings had been filled, meaning the Alpha was not joining us.

"I have to ask, is your father not joining us tonight?"

"No, he won't be with us unfortunately, he has been called away on pack business" Ares said in a very final tone. Clearly not a subject he wants to discuss.

"I hope you don't mind, but we have arranged a set menu for tonight" Astéri called out as she stood up in her seat beside Elaine. We smiled, nodded, and agreed without hesitation and then a line of waiters walked through the doors, each holding three dishes. They placed them on the table in front of each of us and the smell attacked my nose, leaving me salivating. I have no idea what it is, but I can't wait to eat it, holy shit does it smell good. After each person had a plate, the waiters left and Astéri waved her arms.

"Please, dig in".

I didn't hesitate and picked up a small round ball and plopped it in my mouth. I moaned as soon as it hit my tongue. I still had no idea what it was, but I didn't care. I just want more. Alyse elbowed my ribs and I turned to glare at her.

"Can you at least pretend not to be a heathen" she scolded while gesturing to her knife and fork. I smiled meekly and nodded, picking up my fork.

"Sorry love" I whispered. Ares was watching our exchange closely, his brows were furrowed together and his lips were pursed in a straight line.

"So, you two are Mated" he commented, not exactly posed as a question.

"Is that a problem?" I ask sternly, reading into his curious gaze and matter-of-fact tone.

"No, not at all. Lua Chei is not opposed to polyamory, however, I don't believe we have had a lone same sex Mating before. Do you not wish to procreate?" he asked with a lift of his brow. Alyse half choked on her current mouthful of food, and I tried desperately to hold in the growl working its way up my chest. The audacity of this man.

"I don't believe that is any of your concern or your business" I snapped, placing my fork back on the table before I used it to gouge out his eyeballs.

"My apologies, I meant no disrespect. I am just simply curious" Ares rushed out with a small wave of his hand.

"Uh huh" I huffed. I raked my eyes over this obnoxious Alpha-son. My anger bubbled away in my stomach. Like a slow burning furnace. It's not like he is one to talk, where is his Mate and offspring?

"Well, if you don't mind my asking, where is your Mate young Alpha-son?" I sneered. He laughed and leaned back in his chair, resting his hands on the edge of the table.

"My wife has just given birth to our second child not a week ago, I instructed that she stay home to rest" he smiled. I expected him to be smug or condescending, to take pleasure in his showing up my attitude. But he didn't. His smile was genuine, and his tone was pleasant. I swallowed my pride and bit back my desire to push on the topic of his ascension.

"Oh, congratulations" I choked, I could feel my shame turning my cheeks a shade of pink.

"Thank you. She is a beautiful and healthy baby girl, just like her big sister" Ares cooed. His eyes held a brightness to them, and his tone flooded with pride and love. In that moment he reminded me so much of Micha. A pang of pain and jealousy stabbed through my heart, but I pushed it down as per usual. After our plates were cleared, another course was brought in and it smelled and tasted just as delicious as the first. This course was trays of oysters, lobsters, and small pieces of fish. The seafood spread was incredible. The conversation throughout dinner flowed nicely and we all got to know each other a lot more. Astéri and her daughters were very interested in learning more about Luna Eclipse. Unsurprisingly. An all-female pack would get any she-wolf's interest turning. Although Elaine told them enough to sate their curiosity, it didn't escape my notice that she withheld a lot of information.

Ares and I got to speak a lot more. I judged him too quickly, he is actually a remarkable Were, a great father, and an even better son. He explained that he has been ready to take the role of Alpha for some time now, but his father insisted that he spend the first few years focused on his new family, without the distraction of running a pack and a popular travel lodge. It impressed me that he chose his family over the power of Alpha rank. Very few Weres would take that road. My respect for Ares skyrocketed when he explained his decision to me.

Dinner and dessert wound down, and the three youngest children; Akela, Aleah, and Aston, headed off for bed. Leaving Ares, Astéri, Analah, and Ahmad with the six of us.

"So, you are fond of the A names, Astéri" I joked. She chuckled and nodded.

"After number seven we were running out of ideas, but we had to uphold the tradition. Ambrose, my husband, and both his brothers had A names, as did his father and grandfather. So, we just stuck with it".

"I like it, I think it's sweet. Traditional" Alyse chimed in.

"Thank you, darling. Tell me, do you have any children?"

Alyse tensed up and shook her head before picking up her wine glass. I gently squeezed her thigh and shuffled a little closer. Astéri caught on to the slight increase of tension in the air and quickly changed the subject.

"Well then, I remember you mentioned that you've come to find the Triple Goddess" she said, loudly, her voice carrying an aura of power across the table. Finally, the topic I have been waiting for. Please, please, please, tell me you know where she is.

"We have" Elaine confirmed, her voice holding just as much strength and power.

"How do we know that you don't mean the Luna any harm?" Astéri asked, her gaze set squarely on my own. Luna, she called her a Luna. Unsurprising I suppose. I have no doubt that once her pack found out she was the Goddess they would have raised her up to leadership immediately. Thankfully it didn't go the other direction, with them attempting to hide her and lock her away.

"As I said, we only wish to offer our greetings and hopefully form an alliance. You know that Luna Eclipse will support any woman of power. You can't get more powerful than the Triple Goddess" I replied without breaking eye contact.

"I heard you, but we still don't know a lot about you. If we tell you where she is and you harm her, the Goddess herself will take her wrath out on Lua Chei". She stared only at me, clearly a smart woman, and could clearly tell that I was the most invested in this topic.

"So you do know where to find her?" I retorted with a raised brow.

"Ahh, I didn't say that now did I?" Astéri chided with a finger pointed in my direction.

"What will it take for you to believe that we have come peacefully?"

Astéri was quiet for a moment, she eyed me up and down and rolled her eyes over Alyse as well. Alyse had gripped my tense hand, trying to calm down my erratic heart. Elaine and the others too sat stiff and anxious, awaiting Astéri. She brought her gaze back to me and tipped her head to the side, her stare boring into my soul.

"This means a lot to you" she remarked.

"Of course it does, it means a lot to the entire Were existence" I replied bluntly.

"Yes, but you especially. Why? What has got you more invested in this than any of your companions?"

Don't Lunaya, she could be baiting you

I know, but I need to give her something. She can already sense it

Fine but don't tell her the whole truth

I won't

I looked at Elaine and she was watching me with an intense glare, she also didn't want me to tell the whole truth. Fuck. How am I meant to spin this? I desperately raked my brain for something. Anything. I have an idea.

"I came across a Seer, she told me that I needed to seek out the Goddess" I spat out. It was a partial truth. Even if it's only zero point five percent of it.

"I see" Astéri mumbled while rubbing her fingers over her chin and eyeing me sceptically,

"And what else did this Seer tell you?" Ares butted in. I turned my gaze to him, and he appeared more curious than sceptical. He had a softness to his face. He must definitely take after his father.

"She didn't answer the questions I asked, she told me that only the new Goddess could give me answers I sought" again a partial truth. I'm getting good at this whole deception thing. I'm not sure if that is something I should be proud of though.

"Well, I'm convinced" Astéri laughed and slapped her hands together. Her daughters laughed and Ares smiled wide, and I felt Alyse relax beside me.

"So, you'll tell us then? You'll tell us where she is?" I asked urgently.

"I will, on one condition" she nodded. Oh great, of course there would be a catch.

"You will take my daughter Analah with you. And then, when you leave, she will accompany you to Luna Eclipse. There she will reside for a minimum of one year. In order to form an alliance between our two packs".

I snapped my eyes to Elaine, as the highest ranking Were in attendance, this proposition was all her call. A scurry of thoughts berated my brain. She will never agree to this, Luna Eclipse are too secretive. She has to agree, it's our only way to find her. This would never work, Hina would hate this idea.

"Agreed" Elaine said standing up and taking Astéri's forearm. My mouth hit the floor. I thought it would take a hell of a lot longer for her to agree than that, or that she would need to consult Hina or something. Relief washed through me and I smiled to Alyse. But wait, Astéri just threw this offer out there so quickly, did she discuss it with her daughter at all or is she just being thrown to the wolves. Literally. How could she be ok with leaving her family and her home to travel halfway across the planet. Also, would she stay there indefinitely or come back again after the year is up and the alliance is secured? I looked up to Analah who was sitting next to her mother. She had a wide smile across her face and was happily talking to her brothers. She looks pretty excited about the deal. Maybe she is more in the know than I thought.

Then again, it is absolutely none of my concern or my business anyway.

"Well now that that is settled, I suppose we should talk details" called Elaine, rubbing her hands together and sitting back down.

"I think we have all had enough excitement for one day. Perhaps we could call it a night and set up talks and further arrangements tomorrow when we are well rested and not piled with wine" Astéri suggested. I immediately went to refuse but Alyse gripped my arm and held me in my seat.

She's right, we've both had a bit to drink

I don't want to wait any longer

What's one more day going to hurt?

I groaned and sat back in my chair. Elaine eyed me carefully before turning her attention back to Astéri and agreeing. Analah talked very animatedly with her brothers, her excitement was palpable and a little contagious. I couldn't help but smile at her excitement. She looks very much like her mother. A young fresh face with bright grey eyes and soft blonde hair. She was tall and lean and had some defined muscles in her arms. I would bet she is a skilled fighter or climber. She'll fit in well at Luna Eclipse, for however long she stays there.

"Well ladies, if you'll excuse me, I think I'll call it a night. I have three very lovely women at home waiting on me" Ares called as he wrapped an arm around his mother's waist and planted a kiss on her cheek.

"I'm proud of you sis, you'll do great" he said pulling Analah in for a tight hug.

"Ladies" he bowed to Alyse and I, then turned and left the dining room.

"I like him, he's a good man" Alyse said quietly into my ear.

"I agree" I smiled and rubbed my hand over her back.

Ahmad, Venus, and Phoebe all headed off as well. Elaine, Analah, and Astéri were deep in conversation, but I was too tired to follow it properly. Plus, the sooner I get to sleep the sooner it will be tomorrow, and I will find out where my daughter is.

"You ready love?" I asked Alyse as I pressed my lips to her neck.

"Sure am" she whispered. We both stood up and bid goodnight to the others. Cleo sat quietly and kept her gaze firmly on the both of us as we departed the dining room.

"Cleo kind of creeps me out" Alyse whispered as we got to our bedroom door.

"Me too, she is always watching and barely speaks" I agreed.

"Come on, let's have a nice hot shower before bed. It'll help you relax" Alyse said as she pulled me into the bathroom.

Finally, Alyse and I climbed into the oversized bed. She sighed heavily and snuggled her head into the pillow, pulling the covers over her. She let out a content groan and smiled without opening her eyes.

"This is really nice" she moaned,

"You're really nice" I teased and slid in under the covers next to her. I pulled her into my chest, and she reciprocated by snuggling into me.

"I love you" she said sleepily.

"I love you too beautiful".

Alyse's soft snores quickly filled the room. With the warmth of her body and the calmness of the crackling fire, I soon drifted off to sleep.

Chapter Fifteen

Zelena

"Oh my god" I moaned loudly as I flopped back onto the mattress. My every muscle ached, and every inch of my skin was glistening with hot sweat. I feel completely spent and exhausted. I turned my head to gaze at Gunner puffing beside me. Just the sight of his sweat slick skin, the flush of his face, and the way his chest muscles rippled with his heaving breaths had me ready and raring to go again. I rolled onto my side and traced my finger over his chest and circled his nipples.

"Do you forgive me yet?" he huffed with his eyes closed.

"Hmm… almost" I teased and tugged lightly on one of his nipples.

"I don't know how much more I can offer you" he said with a wince and grabbed my hand off his chest. Oh, I could think of many, many more things he could do to me. But we've been at it for hours and we both need to sleep. Eventually. I planted my hand on his pec and pushed myself up to straddle the lower half of his chest. Gunner's hands came to rest on my hips, his fingertips digging into the tender flesh, and he growled softly.

"You are insatiable" he groaned. I giggled and leaned down to scatter kisses along his neck and collarbones.

"At this rate, we're going to end up with you pregnant or with me dead" he grumbled with a slap to my bare backside. I flew upright and glared at him.

"You said she-wolves could only get pregnant during the early stages of their heat" I bit at him.

"That's true. But when you're having sex multiple times a day, every day, who knows what could happen" he huffed with a weak chuckle.

"And let's get really real, you and I haven't exactly been a usual paring".

"That's not funny Gunner. We're too young to be parents" I growled and slapped his chest.

"Luckily I know a little something we can do that doesn't result in pups" he smirked. He gripped my hips tighter and pulled me forward until I was over his head with one leg on either side of his face.

"Now be a good little girl and sit that fine pussy on my face" he growled and pulled my hips down until I was literally sitting on his face. He wasted no time in burying his tongue deep inside my drenched slit. He pressed his nose into my clit and rubbed against it while his tongue darted in and out of my entrance.

"Oh shit" I gasped and threw my head back. The urge to grind myself hard against his face was strong, but he was already sending waves of pleasure through my stomach. He reached his hands around and gripped my ass cheeks tight. He squeezed and moulded my cheeks and spread them wide to give himself more access to his favourite playground. As he worked his magic on my throbbing pussy, his finger slid to my back hole, and he pressed the tip of his finger inside. It was only to his first knuckle, but the sensation drove me wild, and I screamed out for more.

He mumbled and growled into my crotch creating little vibrations, all the while he slid his finger further into my back entrance. The tightness in my stomach grew and I was on the tipping point of my orgasm. I grind my pussy into his mouth and dug my nails into the headboard. My legs began to quake, and I could feel my body giving over control to the pleasure. With his finger moving back and forth inside my asshole, I rode Gunner's face into my release and screamed out as I came over his tongue. He lapped up everything I gave him, drinking my juices like he was dying of thirst. My shaking body fell back onto the mattress, and I heaved with heavy breaths.

"Okay" I said with a shaky and puffed out voice,

"I forgive you now".

My legs rested over his chest and my shoulders and arms hung off the bed above my head. We were a tangle of limbs and bed sheets. Gunner gently massaged my calf muscles, slowly bringing back their full feelings and sensations.

"Mm, that feels really good" I mumbled, feeling sleep creeping up on me.

"Better than what I was rubbing just a minute ago?" he asked,

"Oh no, nowhere near as good as that. But if you want to rub that part again, I won't stop you" I chuckled.

"Who would have guessed that the shy and quiet little girl I bumped into in the school hallway, was actually a seductive temptress, hellbent on draining the life out of me, through my dick"

"Gunner, don't be so crude".

"Babe, you just rode my face to infinity and beyond, I think we have passed the point of crude".

"I rode it where?" I gigged at his turn of phrase.

"Ah fuck. Of course you haven't seen Toy Story. You know we really need to dedicate a week to getting your cinematic knowledge up to scratch. The amount of movie innuendoes you miss is just appalling" he chuckled while slapping my thigh.

"Well in case you forgot, I was a little preoccupied during my childhood".

"I'm well aware" he grunted, this topic always gets his anger soaring.

"Gosh, that feels like a whole other life ago now" I sighed heavily,

"It was, basically".

"We'll be okay, right?"

"What do you mean?"

"I mean you and me, Alpha and Luna, True Mates and Triple Goddess. It's a lot, you know. I don't want to lose these moments with you. The happy, peaceful, blissful moments".

"I will never let that happen" Gunner said sitting up on the bed.

"You. This. Us." he annunciates each word clearly while gesturing between us.

"It's too important" he mused while gazing lovingly at my sated body.

I sat up and smiled at him. I never knew love like this was possible. That it even existed. Or that I could ever have a love like this for myself. A year ago, I would have never dreamed of this future for myself. Now, it dominates my every thought, my every fibre. Loving Gunner is the best part of my life. He is my life.

"I love you" I gushed.

"I love you" he replied, grabbing my arms and pulling me onto his chest. We fell back on the bed, and I wrapped myself around his body. Gunner ran his fingers up and down my bare back, the sensation left little electric goosebumps across my skin. The sound of his heartbeat, the smell of our arousals mixing together in the air of the room, and the taste of him still on my tongue, it was getting my body hot again. Holy Goddess, this man truly has a way of driving me wild. I am like he said, insatiable. I forced myself to ignore the need in my stomach and tried to concentrate on sleep.

It must have worked, because when I opened my eyes again, the morning light was shining through the window. Gunner's soft snores sounded beside me. I looked over my shoulder and his handsome face was smooshed into his pillow. It was a completely unguarded and youthful look that I don't get to see on him anymore. As I sat up on the edge of the bed a tightness panged through my stomach. Ouch. Okay, so maybe we did go a little too hard last night. I ducked into the bathroom and did my business. As I sat there, the pull of the shower and its hot water was too much to ignore. After flushing, I climbed into the shower and let the scalding water run over my tired and aching body. I took my time washing myself, enjoying the relaxing effect the hot water had on my overworked body.

I finally dragged myself from the shower, only to realise that I left my towel out near the bed. I stomped my feet on the bathmat to shake off as much of the water as I could and then waltzed out to the bedroom. Gunner was sitting up on the edge of the bed, scrolling through his phone. He turned his head with a smile, about to say 'good morning' but froze once he noticed my wet and naked body in the doorway. His smile dropped and his eyes darkened. Using his speed, he was off the bed and had me pressed up against the wall in less than a millisecond.

His lips pressed roughly against my own and his hands roamed my wet skin. I tossed my hands around his neck and threw myself into his hungry affection. I pulled my legs up and around his waist, making way for his throbbing morning wood to dig into my stomach. Gunner moved his hands to my ass cheeks and lifted me a little higher. In one strong thrust, he buried himself deep inside my pussy. He grunted and growled with each strong thrust, as he kissed, sucked, and bit the skin of my neck, chest, and shoulders. His movements were savage and desperate, but I revelled in his dominance. Moaning and crying out with my own pleasure.

He carried me away from the wall and threw me down on the bed. His eyes were dark and full of untamed lust. His canines were extended and set into a seductive smirk. I could cum alone from just the look of him. He grabbed my hips and flipped me over onto my stomach, gripping hold of my hair he pulled my head back, lifting me onto my hands and knees. Without hesitation, he slammed back into me and continued to thrust wickedly. The sound of our skin slapping together echoed alongside the sounds of my pleasurable screams and Gunner's dominating growls. Gunner released my hair and leaned forward over my back, wrapping his large hand around my throat.

"Holy fuck!" I scream as I jolt forward with each thrust of his merciless impaling. I could feel his teeth scratching over my shoulder blades. The sensation elicited an animalistic urge from deep inside me.

"Bite me" I choked from under the slight pressure he placed on my throat. He continued to scrape his teeth gently along my skin, ignoring my plea.

"Gunner, bite me!" I demanded with a moan following close behind. After a few more deep and hard thrusts, I felt his teeth sink into my skin. Right between my shoulder blade and armpit. The pain was delicious, mixed with the pleasure from his rough assault on my pussy. Without further warning, I came. I came harder than I felt I ever had before. My whole body shook as my muscles contracted around his dick. With his teeth still buried in my skin I couldn't move. Even if I could, I would be writhing uncontrollably underneath him. Gunner roared out as he pulled his teeth away, his hips bucked against my backside as he met his own release. His body slumped over mine, letting me feel his rapid heartbeat and course breathing. Still reeling from my orgasm, my spent body was still shaking, riding out the last of my spasms. Gunner pulled out and flopped down on the bed.

"Ah, Zelena. The furniture" he huffed breathlessly. I looked up and saw that the bedside table lamps were spinning rapidly in mid-air. I looked over my shoulder and the desk chair and desk were also floating off the floor.

"Sorry" I chuckled and relaxed my hold on the bed. The items slowly made their way back to the floor and tabletops. I'm getting so much better at that now. Letting my hold on the power go gently, instead of letting it drop away in a blink, making the furniture drop to the floor to smash apart. I flopped myself onto the bed beside Gunner and heaved for air.

"What got into you?" I half laughed half gasped.

"What do you expect when you go walking around naked and wet?"

"I just had a shower".

"That's not my problem. You don't want me to ravish you, then don't tempt me with that tight little body of yours".

There was a brief pause, then we both cackled with laughter. Gunner pulled me into his arms and kissed my cheek as he laughed.

"If you're going to fuck me like that, I will never wear clothes again" I laughed, grabbing his jaw and kissing his plump lips.

"Now look who's being crude" he chuckled, wrapping his arms tighter around my waist. A loud bang on the door had us both flying upright in surprise.

"What the heck is going on in there?" Nat's voice screamed from the other side of the door.

"Nat?" I called back.

"Do you want to tell me why all the doors and cupboards in the house were flying open and closed like someone released a hoard of demonic pissed off poltergeists loose in the house?" she screamed again. I looked at Gunner with a terrified and embarrassed look on my face. He stared back at me with wide eyes and an open mouth. At the same time, we both burst out laughing again. I laughed so hard that tears streamed out of my eyes. I heard Nat mumble something along the lines of 'you guys are gross' as she stomped away.

"Okay, okay, okay. I'm convinced, that was a really good wakeup call" Gunner laughed and fell back onto the bed. I stared at the door and laughed as well. My laughing stopped abruptly as it dawned on me. Everyone in the house knows what we have been doing this morning. And seeing as it's the day of the party, there are a lot of extra people in the house. Holy shit-balls. I felt the embarrassment flood my cheeks with a hot flush. Gunner lifted his head to peek at me and it only set off another round of laughter from him.

"You've turned so red" he choked out between breaths.

"Gunner, it's not funny. Everyone will know what we were doing" I said hitting his chest.

"Relax, we're Mated, they already know that we have sex. A lot of sex. And with how often we do it, it would be weird if you didn't smell like sex anymore".

"Okay yes, that's true, and also not helping the situation. And I smell like sex? Seriously? Not the point. The point is, losing control of my powers, is no longer confined to just our bedroom"

"Or hospital room" he interjected,

"Or hospital room. This is so embarrassing. I don't want your parents to know that sort of stuff".

"Zee, who do you think taught me about the birds and the bees? They were just as bad at our age. Don't worry about it. And besides, it was just a few slamming doors, maybe they will think it was from a fight or a nightmare or something".

"Ugh, whatever" I groaned. Gunner sat up and crawled over to me. He planted a few soft kisses on my pouting lips. Then proceeded to nuzzle his nose into my neck and hair, inhaling deeply.

"Fuck you smell good" he groaned then pulled back to look over me again.

"I love you" he cooed and kissed me once more.

"I love you too" I sang in a mocking tone.

"Seriously though, you smell fantastic, don't have another shower" he smiled, jumped off the bed, and walked over to his dresser.

"Seriously?" I whined.

"Yes seriously. There are a lot of visiting males around the village and if the mark on your neck and now the mark on your back doesn't clue them into the fact that you're taken, the smell of me all over you should do the trick" he pulled on a pair of blue jeans and a tight black t-shirt while he spoke. I watched his every movement carefully. The way his muscles twitched and bulged with each lift or pull of his arms and legs, it made my stomach flutter and my lady bits tingle all over again. I know the possessiveness should make me angry or something, but it doesn't. If anything, it makes me feel loved, safe and protected. I was only ever seen as a burden or a possession growing up. So, being seen as something to be protected is a nice change.

"I don't know if I should be turned on or completely disgusted by your possessiveness" I teased Gunner, my arms crossed over my chest and a playful pout on my face. He smiled and leaned over the bed so that his face was only inches away from mine.

"Why can't you be both" he snickered and pecked my lips and stood up again.

"Come on, get dressed. We've got a big day before the party starts. I'll meet you downstairs".

Gunner dashed out the door before I could argue further. As much as I would love to go back to bed and sleep off the tiredness from last night's round of sexual escapades, it wouldn't be very 'Luna like' of me to sleep through the preparations for my own party. With a disheartened groan, I pulled myself up and out of bed and went to the closet. I want to show off my new mark a bit, so I chose a pale blue strappy sundress that shows my back and chest and sits just above my knees.

I pulled the dress on and tied my hair up in a high ponytail to expose the mark on the top of my shoulder too. I did a little twirl in front of the mirror. Showing this much flesh would have made me wince and cower not six months ago. And now I'm flaunting myself for the entire village to see. Okay, so not flaunting myself, just being confident. Gunner may not like how much skin I exposed but he won't beat me half to death like my father, well pretend father, used to. And now that I don't have horrible scars and bruises to cover up anymore, I'm starting to like wearing stuff like this. I guess not being afraid of getting murdered at the end of every day encourages a little self-confidence and personal growth.

The pack house was alive with activity, she-wolves running back and forth and big burly men coming and going. Roe's voice could be heard echoing through each room and hallway, calling out instructions and demands. I followed the sound towards the kitchen, the busy noise got louder and louder the closer I got. The kitchen was a maze of moving bodies and carts of food. I could hear Roe's voice above all the others, but I couldn't see her through the crowd of people.

"Roe" I called out, standing on my tippy toes. I don't know why I bothered. With my short legs, I'd need a step ladder to see over all these giants.

"Roe!" I called again with added volume,

"Zelena. What are you doing in here? You can't be in here. Out!" she screamed over the rest of the noise.

"I just wanted to help" I yelled back,

"Not in here you won't, now out".

"But…"

"OUT!" she screamed. A chorus of laughter filtered through the kitchen as I exited through the door. 'Well now what?' I thought as I jumped out of the way of a man carrying a large box. Maybe Gunner could use my help, so I headed for his office, but it was empty. Next, I tried the hall, but that was empty too. Maybe I can help outside with the tents or decorations or something. I wasn't exactly expecting it to be less busy than the kitchen, perhaps the same. But boy was I wrong.

Standing on the porch, I scanned the chaos going on before me. The fire pit was like a bug zapper, drawing in all the bugs to congregate around it. The entire clearing down the middle of the village was full. Full of Weres, long picnic tables, tall standing tables, benches, and much, much more. It was all lined up and facing the stage, like some kind of wedding altar. I swallowed hard at the sudden nervousness that got stuck in my throat. This isn't a wedding. Is it? If I'm too young to be a mother, I'm definitely to young to be a wife.

Off in the side field beyond the last row of cabins is where the majority of the tents were set up, other tents were scattered around the outskirts of the village. Again, way more than I was expecting. Just how many Weres have been invited to this thing? I spotted Nat weaving around the tables, placing decorations as she went. I ran down to catch her before she ran off again.

"Nat" I called. I hopped up onto one of the bench seats and waved at her over the top of all the other people. But of course, I didn't just get Nat's attention, no, I got everyone else's attention as well. Most of them were from our pack, and thankfully, they had gotten a lot better at not swarming me when I wandered around the village. I guess that the novelty of living with the Triple Goddess had worn down significantly. The visiting Weres though, that's a different story. Those that didn't know for sure who I was, whispered and sniffed the air as I walked past. The rest, those who already knew me, or at least what I looked like, bent to a knee with their heads down and hands out.

"Nat, wait" I yelled as I got a little closer. I smiled and waved timidly at the kneeling and staring Weres as I made my way toward her.

"Lena, what are you doing out here?" Nat growled and grabbed my hand, pulling me close to her body.

"I came to help" I replied, a bit confused at her harsh tone.

"Firstly, holy shit! You reek of my brother, like his essence is all over you. Secondly, eww you're fucking my brother" Nat sneered with her nose scrunched up. But she quickly lowered her head and raised her brows in a sly teasing kind of way.

"But lastly, get it girl. You're getting that good kind of loving, aren't you. I mean if the display this morning was anything to go by, you're getting it in real good" Nat crooned at me playfully with a smirk on her lips. My eyes blew wide and my face flushed with embarrassment.

"Nat!" I whisper-hissed and darted my eyes around at all the people in the clearing.

"Oh please, as if they don't already know you guys are fucking like rabbits high on Viagra" she laughed.

"Stop" I hissed again. My embracement had taken on a lift of its own and I could feel my entire body heating up with my shame, making a bead of sweat sprout on my forehead.

"Pft, whatever" she scoffed with a wave of her hand.

"Anyways, you're not supposed to be out here. And I wouldn't let you set up for your own party even if you were" she grumbled with a shake of her head and started pulling me back towards the house.

"That's not fair, I should be helping with something. Your mum won't let me in the kitchen, I can't find Gunner and now you're forcing me back inside. What gives?"

"Has no one told you yet?" she snapped and stopped walking, turning back to face me.

"Told me what? What the fuck is going on?" I demanded. My panic started to rise with my first thought being that something bad had happened.

"Babe, the new Luna isn't meant to be seen until the ceremony when you're officially introduced to the pack".

"So, what, I'm just meant to hide out inside until the party starts?"

"Well yeah, except you won't be hiding out" she chuckled and continued pulling me back to the pack house.

"Okay, explain" I huffed.

"Mum and I have arranged something a little special for you, Gunner was meant to tell you. Obviously, he forgot. He's been doing that a lot lately. Though this time I don't think it was entirely his fault" she smirked at me over her shoulder.

I shrugged in response. I can't blame him, a lot has been going on. Both with him and with the pack. Of course things are going to slip through the cracks. I am a little excited about this surprise though, even if my excitement is a little overshadowed by my guilt. I should definitely be helping with preparations.

"Anyway, no biggy, not too many people saw you thankfully. Head to my room and I'll send your surprise up" Nat continued. As we reached the porch steps she stopped and turned to face me.

"I'll be up in an hour or two".

"Nat, this isn't right, I should be helping" I whined.

"I know your whole pay-my-own-dues thing and nothing-is-for-free mentality is hard for you to shake, but this is tradition, a kind of important one. Do you think you can just go along with it? Just this one time?" She was harsh and the bluntest that I have ever seen her. It kind of kicked me back a little.

"Wow, when did you become so straight forward?" I asked, reeling back a little.

"Don't take it personally sis, I have a fuck tone of shit to do, and if my mum finds out that you were out here, she will literally tear me a new asshole".

I snorted and laughed a little harder than I expected. I have never heard Nat speak like that. She is always so sweet and innocent, a little sarcastic and sometimes cheeky, but not so 'Wham' in your face.

"Okay, I better be quick and sneaky then" I giggled.

"I'd appreciate that. Now go, you're already behind schedule" she said pushing me up the first stair.

"I have a schedule?"

"Zelena, go" she chuckled and walked away.

I stuck my head in the front door and listened. Roe's voice was still booming from the kitchen and the foyer was empty. I bounded through the door and up the stairs and made it to Nat's room without anyone seeing me, well at least I think no one saw me. I took a deep breath and pushed open the bedroom door. Smack bang in the middle of the room was a giant leather recliner chair with a big tub, spa like thing attached to the bottom. Oh, I know what this is, it's like a spa for your feet. I've seen them in the shops. Shit yeah, this will be awesome.

"Finally, I thought I was going to have to come and find you" a feminine voice came from the bathroom, followed by a small woman carrying a hose thing. She plugged the hose into the chair's bath and turned the tap on.

"Hey hon, I'm Clary. I'm going to give you a pedicure and full foot treatment" she smiled and stood with her hands on her hips. She was just a tad taller than me with dark brown skin and deep brown eyes. Her hair sat in gorgeous nappy curls in an afro style, giving me a bout of major hair envy. She is beyond gorgeous.

"Well, sit down girl, let's get this show on the road" she smiled and waved her hand for me to sit in the chair. I did as I was told, kicked off my shoes, and plopped my feet in the water. My smile was splitting my face in two. I'm so excited for this.

"Come on ya'll" Clary called, and two more people walked out from the bathroom. One wheeling a cart with nail polish and other bits and bobs on it. The other carried a big bucket with products and tubes and bottles, and a whole bunch of stuff I didn't recognise.

"You ready for some pampering?" Clary asked and smirked up at me.

"Hell yes I am!"

Chapter Sixteen

Zelena

Okay, pampering has become my all time favourite thing ever. Okay, maybe the second favourite thing. Clary did my feet and toenails, while Scott gave me a full facial and Trisha did my fingernails. Being fawned over by three people at the same time was the most awesome feeling. I felt like a princess or a queen, or even just a super-rich important person. Nat came up towards the end of my little indulgence and started setting up her makeup desk. Once the pampering was done, she started on my makeup while Scott did my hair. Turns out he is a man of many talents. By the time they were all done, and I was standing in my dress in front of the mirror gawking at myself, it had been seven hours, and the party was in full swing.

"Oh my Goddess. Lena, you look so beautiful" Nat cooed as she stood behind me, looking over my shoulder at my reflection in the mirror.

"I really do" I gushed. My feet were encased in golden strappy heels, with my new red toenails glimmering in the light. My new dress had been steamed and sat, wrinkle free, delicately over my body. My fingers donned the same red polish as my toes, and the bracelet that Gunner gave me dangled on my wrist. Around my neck was a dainty gold chain with a small red stoned pendant. My deep ebony hair was curled and twisted up into a loose and delicate updo. Small tendrils of hair hung free, framing my face and caressing my shoulders. The makeup was light and natural, brightening all of my features in the most deliberate way. My eyes glittered with a gold shadow and held full and luscious lashes. A light pink blush made my pale skin glow, and a vibrant red lip completed the look in the most impeccable way.

I stared at myself for a long moment, taking in every dazzling aspect of myself. A deep flush flew through me, heating my body slightly. I've never looked so pretty before. The mark on my shoulder sat openly for all to see. I turned around and saw the fresh mark on my back. It was circled by a red ring of irritated flesh, but it also sat in an uninterrupted view of anyone who wanted to see it.

"Ugh, I can't believe he bit you again. And on the day of your birthday, Luna, Goddess party, thing. What are we calling this party again?" Nat asked eyeing the new mark on my back. She was wearing a strapless royal blue high-low dress that accentuated her chest and clung to her slim waist. Her hair was braided over her shoulder and her jewellery and makeup were simple and classy.

"No, I love it" I replied gazing at myself some more.

"Really? You don't think it's like really possessive and demeaning?" she asked with a bit of an accusatory tone.

"Goddess no. I'm his and he's mine. Why wouldn't we mark each other?"

"I suppose it's probably different 'cause you're True Mates".

"Nah, we just know our love is forever. You wouldn't let Smith mark you?"

"Heck no" she laughed bitterly,

"I love him, I really do, but I don't think he is my forever".

I turned to gape at her. When did this happen, I thought that they were happy. Are they not happy anymore? Have I really not noticed that they were having issues?

"Wait what? Nat, what's going on?" I asked urgently.

"Oh Babe, it's not like that. We are very happy, and we love each other, a lot. But both of us are under no illusion that we are just comfortably settled together right now. We're young and have plenty of time to find our end-game Mates. Until then we can just be together, and what happens, happens" she said so blasély.

"That sounds so sad though. What if you change your mind?"

"It's not sad, and if we change our minds then we stay together. You're overthinking it".

"I think we need to unpack this"

"Nope we don't. We need to head downstairs, the ceremony is about to start".

"Maybe tomorrow? Can we please talk about this some more?"

"Sure Babe, now let's go".

Nat grabbed my hand and we headed down to the foyer where Roe was waiting for us. She looked up as we got to the bottom of the stairs and slapped her hands over her mouth. Tears started to pool in her eyes, and I could hear her whimpering behind her hands.

"Oh, my girls. Look how beautiful you are" she sobbed and fanned her face.

"Thanks Roe" I smiled at her,

"Thanks Ma" Nat cooed.

"Come here you two" she held her arms out for us and we stepped into them simultaneously, wrapping her up in our arms. Roe wound one of her arms around my shoulder tightly and squeezed.

"My daughters" she gushed with another sob.

"Mum, cut it out or you'll ruin your makeup" Nat jeered as she pulled away.

I stepped back and grabbed her hands, looking over her beautiful and kind face. She may be twice my age, but you wouldn't tell it just by looking at her. Roe is wonderfully preserved for her age and could easily pass as a young thirties. Maybe that is why I have been able to bond with her so well. I don't see her as the scary mother-in-law and instead just see a friend, a confidante.

"I love you, you know that. You're the Mum that I always wanted" I told her. The sincerity in my voice was undeniable. Because it's true. I adore her and couldn't have asked for a better motherly figure.

"Oh Zelena, I love you too, Sweetheart" she blubbered and fanned her face again.

"Don't cry. I didn't mean to upset you" I chuckled awkwardly,

"I'm not upset darling, I'm just happy. Happy that you can think of me as a mother. I want to be that for you. You deserve it, and so much more".

I wrapped my arms around her neck and pulled her into my body for a long tight hug. We stood together for a few moments, just enjoying the embrace. Beside me, I could hear Nat sniffling.

"Nat, are you crying?" I asked, teasing her a little.

"I'm not crying, you're crying" she snapped back. Roe and I laughed and pulled apart to look at Nat, who was very carefully wiping a tear from her eye without smudging her makeup.

The front door opened and with it came a whirl of noise and inaudible chatter. Lupus's head poked through and he held a wide smile over his face, the scar at his lip tilted his smile to look a little crooked, but he was still ruggedly handsome. Just like his son.

"They're ready for you" he spoke looking over each of us, then pulling his head away again.

"Let's not keep them waiting any longer" Roe said as she smoothed down her dress and patted away the tears on her cheeks. Nat grabbed my hand and gave it a quick squeeze while smiling at me, then disappeared out the door.

"You ready love?" Roe asked looking over my face, which I'm sure held a look of mixed terror and excitement.

"I think so" I answered trying to exude confidence, but no doubt failing miserably.

"Don't panic okay, you're already the Luna, this is just a formality. The rest, the Goddess part of the stuff, just try and go along with it. Even I don't know the full scope of what will happen".

"What?" I half shouted,

"Zelena, you'll be fine. We're all here with you".

"O-Okay" I forced a smile and Roe softly cupped my cheek before she left through the door as well. I took a deep breath to steady my nerves and gave myself a once over in the mirror in the foyer.

"I got this" I said out loud to myself. I pulled open the front and found Lupus standing there waiting for me. Smartly dressed in a dark grey suit and his hair combed back.

"You look absolutely stunning, Zelena" he gushed, holding out his arm for me.

"Oh, stop it" I smiled and wrapped my arm through his.

"Thank you" I said with a smile, as we turned to face the stairs.

"What for?" Lupus asked in return,

"For being my surrogate father" I told him as I looked up at him with adoration. He stared back down a me for a moment, not saying anything. I could see the softness in his eyes as he looked me over. That is a description few would use for Lupus. Soft. But right here, at this moment, I could see all the mushy parts of him. He blinked a few times and cleared his throat, then turned his head and straightened himself up. I leaned my head on his arm and squeezed his elbow.

"Let's go and show you off a little" he said as he patted my hand fondly. I giggled with a little embarrassment and nodded.

Lupus led me down the porch and out into the clearing. Strings of white lanterns hung from one side of the clearing to the other, filling the space with beautiful glowing lights. A red carpet had been laid out from the bottom of the porch, all the way to the stage, making me feel like some kind of movie star. The crowd of Weres was huge. Must be double the size of Tri-Moon. They gathered on either side of the carpet, bunching in together to get as close as they could to the stage. As we walked through the middle of them, they knelt to their knee with their heads bowed and one hand over their heart. It was deathly silent, with only the sound of my thumping heart filling my ears.

"Breathe" Lupus whispered. I sucked in a sharp intake of air, unaware that I had been holding my breath. As we came to the stage, Gunner stepped forward. He wore a dark grey suit and emerald green tie that matched my dress. His hair was combed neatly and he shaved, giving his face a fresh look. The soft glow of the lanterns made his bright blue eyes shine. He held his hand out for me and I just about jumped forward to reach him. He chuckled at my eager reaction and clasped his fingers around my own. He leaned in and kissed my cheek, holding his face against mine.

"You look positively delicious" he whispered and then leaned back with a devilish smirk. We left Lupus at the edge of the stage and Gunner walked with me into the middle, where we stood in front of Artemis. He was wearing his usual brown fur coat that hung past his knees. He was holding a giant silver cup that had two large handles on either side. He held the cup forward and Gunner took it from his hands.

Grab the handle closest to me and hold the cup in between us. Gunner flashed.

I did as he said and looked out over the crowd. All eyes were on us. I saw a few familiar faces from our pack and a few that I recognised from Crescent Wolf. Right in the front next to Roe and Nat, stood Tobias, with who I could only assume were his brothers and parents. His smile took up half of his face and his huge stature took up half of the crowd. I smiled back at him and gave him a small nod.

"Tonight, we welcome the new Alpha and his Luna" Artemis's heavily accented voice called out loudly.

Just follow my lead. Gunner flashed me and winked.

"Alpha, do you swear to protect your pack, care for them, love them, and lead them with justice and kindness. Forsaking all others" Artemis asked.

"I swear" Gunner answered, smiling down at me.

"Luna, do you swear to protect your pack, care for them, love them, and lead them with justice and kindness. Do you swear to keep your Alpha, ensuring his rule will always be just?"

"I swear" I answered.

"Your hand Alpha," Artemis said stepping up to Gunner. Without taking his eyes off me, he held out his hand and Artemis grabbed his index finger. Using a long needle, Artemis pricked the end of his finger and squeezed it over the cup. A single drop of blood fell into the liquid.

"Luna" Artemis said asking for my hand.

It's fine, it doesn't hurt

I know it won't

I held my hand for Artemis and he repeated the same thing with my blood.

"Now drink" he demanded taking a step back.

I drink first, then you, then the pack will cheer

Okay

Keeping my hand on the handle of the cup I tilted it to Gunner's lips. He drank a large mouthful and then smiled down at me, shifting the cup to my mouth. I drank a sip and smiled, it's just wine, really good wine. Artemis took the cup from us and Gunner held my hand, turning us to the pack and throwing our joined hands into the air. The moment that they hit the sky, the entire crowd before us called out in screams of joy and celebration. After a few seconds, their happy cries turned into scattered howls. Soon enough the entire village was a chorus of howls, echoing through the early night sky. Gunner tugged me into his chest, wrapping his arm around my waist, and threw his head back and howled. Roe, Nat, Lupus, Tobias, everyone, they were all howling to the sky. A soft wind flew around my body, sending a shiver crawling up my spine. My skin prickled with goosebumps and an urge to cry to the moon filled me to my essence, taking hold of every part of me. I lifted my chin and howled to the night, to the moon, to the stars, to the Goddess herself.

As the chaos died down and the howling stopped, all the people in the crowd were buzzing with excitement and adrenalin. Their wild eyes stared up at us and their chests heaved with heavy breaths. The atmosphere was electric, and I wanted nothing more than to throw myself to the wolves, pun intended, and revel in their elated passion. I stepped forward, just a little, keeping my hand in Gunner's. I could feel the tingling sensations running through my arms and legs. My powers were surfacing. Only, it wasn't me calling them forth. It was something from deep inside me, something I didn't know was there. The force of the energy burning through me was unlike anything that I had felt up until this point. This force, this energy, it was primal.

I lifted my other hand in front of me to study my fingers. They felt alight with fire. I twisted and curled my fingers and pale blue light, similar to electric sparks, began to burst from my hand. I released my hold on Gunner and brought my other hand to my face. The same thing happened. The sharp electricity shot through my skin and up along my arms and the back of my neck. I felt a tingling in my scalp and a weightlessness, the feeling shifted back down my neck to my chest, and stomach. I looked up to the moon, its pale glow bathed me in a warm light. With one final blow, the energy surged through my entire body, encasing me in light, wrapping around my every cell, and flowing out of me. My head flew back, and my arms flew out beside me. A feeling of absolute power exploded out of me, a power unlike anything I had experienced before.

The power rolling through me was not mine, it was hers. She's here. The Moon Goddess. She is here with me now. I can feel her arms wrapping around me, holding me. Her love and her blessing, it's suffocating in the most intoxicating way. Her presence was a shining light in the dark, a gentle hand, love. She is love.

I opened my eyes and looked back over the crowd. Though I was no longer on the stage. I was now flying about eight feet above it. The pale blue light now shone over my entire body. Without giving it a second thought, I willed my power to move me, to let me glide over the crowd below. And I did. In a slow and deliberate motion. I held my hands out with my palms facing down and let the lights and energy fall from my fingers, bathing the people below me in tiny sparks that danced across their skin. I circled over the crowd and came back to the stage. With a pull of my hand, Gunner floated up to my side. His eyes were wide and full of wonder.

"What is this?" he spoke.

"It's the Goddess" I smiled at him. I grabbed hold of his hand and the energy, the power, the sparks, they filtered through my fingers, I could feel them seeping into him. He hissed and bent his head back, lifting his eyes to the sky. The blue light that surrounded me slowly enveloped him too. After a moment he looked back at me. Only this time, his eyes were glowing a bright silver. They have done this before, during the war with the hunters. He's accessing the power of the Goddess. Through me. He told me once that when I tap into my powers, my eyes glow yellow. When he taps into my powers his eyes glow silver.

You're accessing my power

How do you know?

Trust me

I shouldn't be… we can't

The Goddess wouldn't allow it to happen if she truly didn't want you to. Can't you feel her?

I don't know what I feel, it's just warm and soothing

That's her. That's her love, her blessing

Are you certain?

I am

Gunner gazed at me as we floated above the stage together. His eyes glowed dazzlingly, I could come to love this colour on him. He smiled and nodded his head in agreement. I closed my eyes and said a hushed prayer to the Moon Goddess, to the All-Mother. 'Thank you, Mother' I whispered. A warm feeling flooded my chest, and a feeling of love and adoration took hold inside of me. She is a part of me. Now and always. We came back down to the stage, our feet landing at the same time. I turned to Gunner, completely elated at the thought that the Goddess approved of him using her power. I launched into his arms, crashing my lips to his and kissing him deeply. He lifted my legs to wrap around his waist and held me by my thighs. I ravaged his mouth, my tongue exploring the deepest parts of him. Hungry and desperate to feel any part of him pressed against me.

"For the Alpha and the Goddess. The True Mates" Tobias's voice called out of the crowd of shocked and stunned Weres. At his proclamation, they once again broke out into a sea of howls and cheers. As hard as it was to break away from his lips, we did. He kept me in his arms and rested his forehead against mine. I took heavy breaths to calm the unsatisfied need for more of him. My heart ached to feel him inside of me, to feel his lips and tongue and hands roam my body. I don't know if it was the shared use of the power, or the new surge of energy, but the heated desire I felt for him was near unbearable.

Gunner let my feet back on the ground and pulled me into his side, gripping my body tightly to his. He turned us to face the pack, placed his hand over his heart, and bowed his head. I mimicked his action without hesitation. I know that it is to show respect. And I adore our pack, and I respect our allies. The crowd didn't follow suit though. Instead, they all got down to their knees, held their hands out, and lowered their heads, a pose that I have become a little more accustomed to now.

"For the Alpha and the Goddess" they sang out in perfect unison. After a moment they stood and watched us for what to do next. I looked up at Gunner and winked. He smiled back and turned to the pack.

"Let's have ourselves a party!" he yelled throwing his arms above his head and laughing loudly. The crowd cheered and started to break apart. Standing on the stage, I could see the village better. The long picnic tables were overflowing with mountains of food. Bathtubs were placed around the space filled with ice and cold drinks. The lanterns provided just enough light, but the candles in vases set out on all the tables added to the ambiance. This is going to be one hell of a party. Gunner's arms snaked around my waist and his head came to rest on my shoulder. He pressed his nose into my neck and inhaled harshly. A growl rolled out of his mouth as he trailed his tongue up the side of my neck to my jaw.

"You smell so fucking good" he rumbled. I pressed myself back against him, my ass rubbing against his crotch.

"Think we can slip away for a few minutes?" he whispered grazing his nose across my neck and cheek. I growled with excitement. The thought of having him pounding inside me, with hundreds of people close by, with the possibility of getting caught, set a fire in my panties.

"Alpha, Luna" Lupus called over to us. I growled again with annoyance. Gunner bit my cheek gently before following it with a kiss.

"Duty calls, love. We gotta go shake some hands and kiss some ass, and then, I'm going to bury myself inside that sweet little ass of yours" he growled the last bit, and I nearly came just from his words.

"Gunner" I whimpered. I don't know if I'll be able to hold out that long. He chuckled and took my hand, leading me to a long table set up at the side of the stage. Roe and Nat were already seated, along with Tobias and Smith. No Cole though. In fact, I haven't seen him at all yet. We sat down, Tobias, Nat, and Smith at my right and Gunner at my left with Lupus and Roe next to him.

"Gunner?"

"Yes, my love" he replied as he passed me a glass of wine.

"Where's Cole?" I asked, watching his face carefully. His jaw tensed and his eye twitched a little.

"He is leading the fighters and border patrols. Someone needed to make sure that all our guests remained safe tonight and that we didn't have any unwelcome visitors. He was more than happy to volunteer" he answered with a monotone and uncaring attitude. Though I could tell he was bothered by it.

"You didn't want him at the ceremony?"

"He wanted to ensure our safety, how could I argue with that. Here eat, the diplomats will start coming up to us any minute now and I want you to eat" he brushed passed the topic of Cole, I could tell he didn't want to talk about it. Even if he pretended that he was okay with it, I could tell he wasn't. He pushed a large plate of food in front of me and nodded for me to eat. He wasn't wrong about the diplomats. The first visiting ambassador came right over to our table, shadowed by four other Weres.

"Hello Alpha, my Goddess" the man smiled and bowed his head with his hand over his heart, then stood up again and spoke with his arms out by his side.

"I am Gregor, Beta wolf of the New Moon pack. On behalf of my Alpha, may I say, we are truly honoured to hold an alliance with the pack of the Triple Goddess. I give my word that if you call, we will answer".

"Thank you, Beta Gregor. I appreciate you coming in your Alpha's absence and hope that you can pass on our thanks" Gunner smiled and nodded.

"If I may?" Gregor asked as he stepped closer to the table. Growls erupted from behind us and also from Tobias. I looked over my shoulder to see Felix and a row of big buff and scary looking Weres, acting as our guards. I looked over the row of men and they each held an aura of fierceness and intimidation. Oh. They're not acting. They're warriors. They are actually here to guard us, or me, or both of us maybe. I can't imagine Gunner would need a guard. But who am I to question it.

"Apologies, I only wish to offer the Goddess my personal greeting" he rushed out, pausing his forward movement and bowing again.

"It's fine" I waved off the guys behind us and stood up, Tobias followed suit, standing beside me like a giant protective grizzly bear. Gregor stepped forward, leaned over the table, and took my hand, placing it on his forehead.

"For the Goddess, I live" he said softly before quickly releasing my hand and stepping back.

"Enjoy your night of celebration Alpha, Luna".

With that, he turned around and quickly shuffled off with his entourage. I sat back down and continued to eat.

"I'm not exactly thrilled with a bunch of men putting their grubby hands all over you" Gunner growled lowly.

"He touched my hand, that was it" I huffed and held back a laugh. Another man walked forward with a young woman and a few other people behind them. He must be in his early thirties maybe late twenties, with dark brown hair and a manicured beard. But the woman was clearly much younger, around our age I would think.

"Howdy Alpha Gunner, Luna Zelena. Thank you so much for having us here to join in this glorious celebration" the man spoke with a pep in his voice and a smile on his face. He wasn't nearly as scared or intimidated by us as Gregor was.

"Alpha Travis, Luna Maryann, thank you so much for coming" Gunner beamed, standing up from his seat and walking around to the front of the table. He embraced the Alpha and they both leaned in for Sevasmo, holding the position for longer than usual. When they broke apart, they hugged briefly before Gunner bowed his head to the Luna.

"Zelena, come here Babe" Gunner waved me to him. I stood up and walked over to where they were standing, with Tobias following closely behind me.

You don't have to get up, you can keep eating

Wherever you go, I go Little One

I chuckled over my shoulder at Tobias and came up next to Gunner. He pulled me into his arms and smiled brightly at the Alpha and Luna.

"Travis, this is Zelena, my Mate. Zee this is Alpha Travis and his Luna, Maryann, of the Waning Wolf pack" he said pointing to Travis and Maryann.

"Hello" I smiled and nodded.

"Phew, she's a looker. Tell me darlin' how did a scrub like him manage to wrangle a woman like you?" he chuckled to himself. Gunner laughed and punched him lightly on the chest. I giggled and smiled at the two of them, totally loving this interaction. They appear to be very close, but I don't recall Gunner ever mentioning a Travis.

"Well, you can't fight fate" I chuckled and rested my head on Gunner's chest, smiling at the Alpha.

"Unfortunately for you Sweetheart" Travis laughed a big throaty laugh. Gunner let me go and leaped onto Travis, tackling him in a headlock. The two of them laughed and growled and wrestled around.

"Hi, it's so nice to meet you" Maryann said stepping closer.

"You as well, thank you for coming" I replied as we watched our Mates play fight.

"Are you kidding, it's not every day that you get invited to the Triple Goddess's birthday party. Oh, happy birthday by the way" she smiled and gently placed her hand on my forearm. I felt Tobias move in closer behind me at her movement. She noticed and quickly pulled her hand back again.

"Oh, thank you" I chuckled awkwardly.

"So, these two are close then?" I asked,

"As close as two competing Alpha's can get. Gunner used to spend summers at Waning Wolf and Trav would spend some summers here. They grew up together I suppose, even though Travis is seven years older than him".

"What an amazing way to build an alliance" I remarked, watching the two guys come to a rest and start walking back over to us, still bumping and shoving into each other.

"One of the purest alliances we have" Maryann agreed.

"You two done measuring dicks?" she teased as Travis pulled her into his side.

"Yep, I won of course" Travis chuckled.

"You wish" Gunner snorted.

"Alpha" a strong and deep voice rumbled over to us. The sound sent a flutter of butterflies to my neither region. Weird, not my normal reaction to a stranger's voice. A tall bulking man stepped forward followed by a rather large group of men. They must be the Howlers. The man in front was bigger than Gunner, but by no means as big as Tobias. Curly light brown hair sat on top of his head and tattoos covered his arms. His aura of power was a little off putting and made my stomach pang and turn in on itself. He stood waiting for Travis to leave before he came closer.

"I'll be around, we'll catch up more later" Travis winked at Gunner.

"My Goddess" he said turning to me with his hand out. I placed my hand in his and the feel of his skin immediately sent tingles up my arm. He felt it too because his grip on my fingers tightened to a painful level. Oh no. I know what this is. I think. Please, please, please don't be what I think this is.

Chapter Seventeen

Lunaya

The morning light filtered through the large windows and the sounds of nature beyond filled the space around my head with happiness and contentment. I groaned and rolled over, feeling for Alyse's sleeping form beside me. The bed was empty. I shot up and looked at the empty space beside me and then moved my eyes around the room. She sat on the armchair between the window and the fireplace. The light from outside shone through and hit her face in the most picturesque way. Her skin glowed and her eyes sparkled under the light. She was holding a cup with steam rising from it while reading a book.

"Good Goddess you're beautiful" I gushed. I pulled my knees to my chest and let my hands hang over them.

"Good morning, how'd you sleep?" she smiled and placed her book on the coffee table in front of her.

"I slept better than I have in a really long time" I said smiling wide and stretching my sleepy muscles.

"I could tell, it's after ten".

"Is it really?"

"Yep, I wanted to let you sleep. You needed it"

"You were right, as usual".

I crawled to the end of the bed and kicked my legs out over the edge. The room looks just as magnificent in the daylight. The sunlight and the feel of the wilderness outside was calling to me. As I sat looking out over the trees through the open double doors that led to the patio, my stomach growled with ferocious hunger. Alyse giggled and set her cup down.

"Breakfast was brought in about half an hour ago, they figured we were still sleeping" Alyse said as she picked up a tray and carried it over to me.

"I didn't even hear it" I replied, slightly surprised and annoyed with myself. I should never have slept through something like that, what if it wasn't a friendly visitor. There has never been a time that I'd not woken up at the sounds of other people entering or coming near to where we sleep. It's just the way I was trained and raised. Always sleep with one eye open.

"Thanks love" I said as I took the tray from her. There were two pieces of, what I suspected to be, cold toast, a bowl of cereal, and a small glass jug of milk.

"You're not eating?" I asked Alyse.

"No, I already ate, while it was still hot and fresh" she chuckled.

"As you should have" I answered with a quick wink. I smiled at her before shoving the toast in my mouth. It was cold and had lost most of its crunch, but the cinnamon and butter was still delicious.

"After you've eaten, we've been asked to go meet with Elaine and Astéri. They're chatting in the main sitting room" Alyse said cheerfully as she turned and walked off to the bathroom.

"They're waiting for us now?" I asked urgently with my mouth still half full of partially chewed toast.

"No, they're just chatting, told me to bring you out when we're ready" Alyse called back from inside the bathroom.

I swallowed what was in my mouth and jumped from the bed to dress in a mad rush. I was pulling on a pair of denim shorts when Alyse reemerged from the bathroom. She had her brown hair pulled up into a high ponytail, showing off her freckled face. She had on a pair of cargo shorts and a dark blue tank top. She walked over to me and pressed her lips to my cheek. I could still smell the fresh toothpaste on her breath.

"Calm down" she cooed,

"They're waiting" I mumbled while doing up the button on my shorts.

"No, they aren't. They are discussing Analah and her transfer to Luna Eclipse. I assume they're also having a bit of a history lesson. I think Astéri is a little worried about where Analah will be living and who she'll be living with" Alyse explained as I pulled my boots on.

"How do you know all this?" I questioned breathlessly.

"I listened in for a little as I ventured out to the dining area earlier this morning" she answered with a shrug. I mumbled in response and launched myself towards the door, half tripping over my untied shoelace.

"Let's go" I called as I held the door open for Alyse. She didn't answer, just smirked and walked through.

We found Elaine and Astéri in an overtly large living space, and that is an understatement. The room is massive. It boasted a high ceiling with exposed wooden beams and chandeliers. Two large stone fireplaces give the space warmth and coziness. Beautiful rugs littered the floor with a multitude of armchairs and sofas spread around the room. Elaine and Astéri were seated on a large leather couch that curved around a beautiful antique looking coffee table.

"She lives" Astéri exclaimed with a sly smirk playing on her face. I chuckled awkwardly and sat on the other side of the large couch, pulling Alyse to sit close beside me.

"Astéri and I were speaking about our travel plans" Elaine spoke, capturing my attention away from Astéri.

"Oh, and what have you come up with?" I asked, taking the bait.

"We didn't get too far into it, we were waiting for you to rise" Astéri cut in.

"We're here now, so let's get to it" I said leaning back into the soft leather.

"The Triple Goddess is on Cape Breton Island. She and her Mate took the positions of Alpha and Luna before the hunters attacked" Astéri began.

"She has a Mate?" I flew forward on the couch, my voice becoming a little too loud and a little too high pitched. She can't have a Mate yet, she is still just a baby. The thought that a Mate was in the picture didn't cross my mind. Not once. I had assumed that she became Luna after her Goddess status had been realised. It was naive of me to believe a pack would make a lone she-wolf their leader. But mated? No.

"She does, he is, or was the Alpha-son, so the accession makes sense".

"And you said an attack, we knew they were attacked but we don't know the details. Is she okay? How bad was it?" I demanded.

"I am happy to share these details with you all, but I ask that you stop interrupting me" Astéri said with a low growl. Alyse gripped my forearm and pulled me back on the couch. I gave Astéri a curt nod and she continued.

"The hunters were searching, that part is obvious. They slaughtered packs from Vermont to Prince Edward Island, and everywhere in between. They knew who or what they were looking for, they just didn't know the where part. Thank the Goddess they didn't move to the South, to us, and instead started in the North. That's where they found her. But she wasn't alone. Not by a long shot. She had amassed an army of her own and they overpowered the hunter's clan. I don't know all the details myself, only the small parts that have followed the chain of whispers. But apparently, she took on up to fifty hunters all by herself. Some of the hunter's bodies were so mangled and broken that they didn't even look like humans anymore". Astéri paused gazing out the windows to the forest.

"And then what?" I pressed.

"Well, there is no more. No one has seen or heard any more from the Goddess since the attack. Some speculate that she died, others say she has retreated to the sky after fulfilling her purpose to defeat the hunters".

"That's ridiculous, there is more than just one clan of hunters. There must be hundreds of them across the world" Alyse spat.

"I agree, that theory is crap. But people believe what they want to believe".

"And what do you believe, Luna Astéri? If you really think that she is dead, why are we here?" I asked, my anger and frustration pushing to the surface.

"I never said she is dead. I said that some speculate that she may be" Astéri grinned at me and crossed her legs.

"But you know differently?" I spoke. I could see it on her face. She knows more, she is just trying to lead us on an emotional journey. She's enjoying the storytelling.
"I do" she answered smugly.
"Care to share it?" Elaine asked, finally speaking up.
"What did my son say, when you asked where his father was?" she asked me, leaning forward and resting her elbows on her crossed legs.
"He said he had to go away on pack business, that was all" I answered, holding back on my annoyance.
"Mhm" She hummed,
"Ambrose is acting as pack diplomat for the next few days. We were invited to a birthday party".
"Oh my Goddess" Alyse whispered harshly.
"Enough games Astéri" I growled,
"Either tell us or don't but stop with the suspenseful storytelling already".
"Watch yourself Omega. This is still my pack, and you are still a guest here" she roared as she stood up and glared down at me. Omega. She called me Omega. So, somehow she knows that we, or at least that I, am not a part of Luna Eclipse. She is smart and intuitive, she has proven that much, but this is a dangerous revelation she has stumbled upon.
"I apologise" I said eyeing her stubbornly. Alyse's grip on my arm tightened and Elaine shifted in her seat. I won't confirm nor deny her assumptions that I am an Omega, I will just let it go as if I never heard it. If I pay it too much attention, she could become more curious or worse, defensive. Astéri sat back down and crossed her legs again.
"Lua Chei was invited to a birthday party, but not just any birthday party. It's an ascension ceremony".
"Since when do other packs get invited to those?" I snapped. Astéri lifted her brown and eyed me intently. As if to say 'last warning'.
"They do when it's for the Triple Goddess and her Mate" she said firmly, a smirk twitching at her lip. So, she is alive. And she's throwing a party. What better time for us to go, we can act as diplomats and meet her that way. If they let us in. If they have invited packs from all over, how would they even know if a few extra guests showed up. Who am I kidding, she's the Triple Goddess and they will have high ranking

members from multiple packs. Security will be tighter than a nun's asshole.

"When's the party?" Elaine asked.

"Tomorrow night" she answered without hesitation.

"Then we'll go to the party" I announced standing up from the couch.

"You won't be able to cross the pack border. Not if they aren't already expecting you".

"We can just say we are diplomats from Luna Eclipse, because that's what we are" I huffed in annoyance.

"Listen love, I'm a very open-minded woman. I'd like to think anything is possible, but that doesn't mean that everyone else does too. Just because I believe that's where some of you are from, doesn't mean that they will too. They will kill you before you get the chance to prove it" she made a show of eyeing me as she said 'some of you'. A hint of nerves and frustration filtered through my blood.

"How do you know that for sure" Alyse asked.

"I don't know it for sure, but I do know that everything changed after the hunters. All the packs in this region, even the ones further out, have all upped their security measures. Just as we have. I'm sorry but you can't just show up there".

"Then what do you suppose we do?" Elaine asked, coming to stand at my side. Her show of comradery really boosted my mood and feelings towards her.

"I suggest you take Analah and use her to contact her father. He will vouch for you and then they will be a little more accommodating" Astéri announced, looking up at us. I looked at Elaine, I could see her mind working. She has already agreed to take Analah back to Luna Eclipse, so it makes sense that she comes with us now. Even if Elaine and the others stay there longer than anticipated, Analah could always just come back home again, and then they could pick her up on their way back through. I like the idea, but I don't have the final say.

"Okay" Elaine said firmly.

"Excellent" Astéri clapped her hands and stood up,

"Ingonish is an eight-hour drive, so you will need to leave first thing".

"Ingonish?" Alyse asked as she stepped up to my other side.

"Yes, that is where the Tri-Moon pack and its new Luna are located".

~

Sleep was near impossible, I think I may have drifted off for a total of two hours through the entirety of the night. The anticipation of the day to come was too much for my brain to handle. The things that Astéri was saying, the things that she said she did and was able to do. Only one other daughter has ever had that much power before, and that was Selena, the first daughter. My mind was alive with the possibilities, the potential that she could have. There is still so much that I don't know, but there is definitely a lot that I could teach her. If she accepts me. If she allows me to teach her, a whole new world of power could be opened up for her.

We didn't leave Lua Chei until after ten in the morning. A fact that annoyed me more than I care to mention. As much as I wanted to yell and scream and stomp my feet, I held my tongue. Astéri and her daughter are already doing us a great favour by helping us get into Tri-Moon, I couldn't risk angering them, not when I'm this close.

We've been on the road for roughly eight hours and we're nearing the pack border. With each kilometre that we get closer, I get more anxious. Alyse sat with my hand in her lap, stroking her fingers across my skin. She could feel my nervousness. I think at this point it was noticeable to everyone in this car. Which was comprised of Alyse and I in the back seat, and Elaine and Analah in the front. The other three were in the car behind us.

I wound down the window, hoping that some fresh air would make me feel a little better. The sun had long set at this point, so I couldn't see much, especially while we were driving. The air flowing through the window had a hint of sea salt mixed with pine and wet earth. It was a relaxing scent. Full of nature and wildness. The car began to slow down, by a lot. We hadn't passed a town yet, a few farms yes, but we hadn't reached a town. Which must mean the pack lives on the outskirts or further out.

I pulled my head away from the window and looked between the front seats and through the windscreen. About eight men stood across the road, blocking the path of the car. Elaine stopped about twenty meters away from them. I sniffed at the air from the window and caught their scent. They're Weres. The border patrol. Increased security measures. As we sat in the car watching the men on the road, a few wolves ran up alongside them. With more visible off towards the tree line. One of the wolves changed form, right there out in the open. But if I can smell them, I imagine they smell us too. The man that changed pulled on a pair of loose shorts and stepped closer to the cars. He waved at us to get out.

"Exit the vehicles" his firm voice demanded. We did as we were asked. Elaine and Analah stood in front with Alyse and I behind them. I felt Cleo come up behind me, with Venus and Phoebe on either side of her.

"State your business" the Were called. I looked the man over, as he stepped towards us, a few of his men flanking him. He has a tall build with long arms and legs, taunt muscles flexed on his chest and stomach as he walked. His light brown hair hung shaggily over his forehead and his eyes were dark. Not in colour but like he was holding something dark behind them. He is a young one, still a teenager, early twenties at the most. But the aura of power he emanated was obvious. Beta Were.

"I am Analah, Alpha-daughter to Alpha Ambrose of Lua Chei. We were invited to the festivities tonight" Analah announced taking a small step forward, Elaine matched her step, not letting her go alone or appear to be the leader.

"Alpha Ambrose and his Luna were invited, and Alpha Ambrose has already arrived. He said nothing of his daughter coming, or any others" he called eyeing each of us carefully, his eyes landed on me for longer than I liked.

"So, give me a reason why I shouldn't kill you where you stand?" he growled, turning his eyes back to Analah.

"My father has been notified of my arrival and is on his way to the border to confirm our identities" Analah replied, maintaining a perfectly authoritative tone.

"That may be so, but I doubt that you are all daughters of Alpha Ambrose. Now I ask you again, state your business here".

This time Elaine stepped forward, and Phoebe quickly went to stand at her side. The rest of us shuffled closer as well, trying to remain inconspicuous.

"I am Beta Elaine of Luna Eclipse. We have come to offer our greetings to the newly risen Goddess" she called out loudly, loud enough for all of the Weres gathered to hear. I guess Luna Eclipse isn't so worried about staying hidden away from the world anymore. The young Were stilled, I could see the surprise flicker across his face, momentarily breaking his stern facade. But a look of recognition quickly settled in his eyes. He knows about them, Luna Eclipse, maybe he was told stories as a kid, but he definitely knows something.

"If it weren't for your tattoo, I would be inclined to call you a liar. Do you have proof of this impossible claim?"

"Only this" Elaine said as she pulled an envelope from her back pocket. She held it out in front of her, for the Were to take. He walked forward until he stood right in front of Elaine. He is a tall kid, but Elaine is still bigger. He took the letter and opened it, pulling out a piece of paper.

We stood quietly as he read over the letter. I looked over the young man, his youth was more present in this close proximity. His fresh face and untouched skin make him appear innocent, just a greenhorn. But his eyes told a different story. His eyes held pain and anguish. There is so much darkness hidden behind his firm glare. The young Were held the letter to his nose and sniffed deeply, his harsh glare sticking to Elaine the whole time.

A shiver ran up my spine and my skin broke out in goosebumps. Something strange hung in the air. A spark. A heaviness. An energy. I could feel the electricity run over my body. No one else seemed to notice, except Alyse, she noticed the change in me.

What is it?

I'm not sure, I think something is happening

What kind of something?

I don't know, but I feel something strange

Like a bad feeling?

No, nothing like that, it's an energy in the air

I don't feel anything

I think it's her. My child

Do you really think so?

I do. Something is going down

Like what?

There is magic in the air. The Goddess is around us.
Alyse gasped audibly, catching the attention of Cleo. I looked around in the air. There is definitely something going on, some kind of force or power. A small breeze ruffled the trees and swirled across the road. It curled its way around my legs and up over my chest and neck. A soft whispered voice kissed at my ear, so quiet I almost didn't hear it. 'Our daughter'. My heart jumped and my stomach fell to the ground. That voice, that angelic celestial voice. It can only belong to one being. The Moon Goddess. She is here, and she is calling me forward.

"She's here" I whispered out loud. Elaine snapped her head back to me, her eyebrow raised.

"Nae?" Alyse called softly, stroking my face.

"She's here, I feel her".

The man lifted his head from the letter and gazed at me curiously. He let his eyes travel to Alyse who was watching me intently, still stroking my face and trying to comfort me.

"Who's here?" he asked, no, he demanded.

"My child" I answered him without hesitation.

"And who might that be?" he questioned turning his body to me and crossing his arms across his chest.

"The Triple Goddess" I said firmly, not backing down from his gaze. This boy doesn't scare me, not in the face of my daughter. He huffed and barked out a contemptuous laugh.

"Fuck off" he spat pushing the letter back into Elaine's chest.

"You won't keep me from her. I can feel her, through the trees. She's calling to me" I growled stepping forward, now only inches from the boy.

"I said, fuck off. Her parents are dead, so go spin your bullshit somewhere else".

"Who told you that?" I demanded, my voice raising in power and volume.

"The one who raised her" he answered glaring into my eyes.

"They were wrong. I am right here".

"Tell me her name, her hair colour, her eye colour. Tell me anything about your supposed child".

My lips curled back over my teeth and my claws pushed at the tips of my fingers. A growl ripped from my throat as my anger burst forward.

"Lunaya, be calm" Elaine barked at me, but I ignored her.

"My child was stolen by hunters as a babe, I would assume her looks have changed since then, unless you're telling me the Triple Goddess is an infant. Even her birth name may have been thrown away for all I know. I will see my daughter and you won't stop me. If I have to fight my way to her, then it is a fight you will get".

I let my canines extend and my claws push through. The change was upon me. One more push and my wolf will be tearing them to shreds. The boy snarled and dropped his arms, his stance was ready to attack. Alyse growled from beside me and Cleo from behind me. This wasn't going to end well for these Weres. Or for us. We're all in trouble now. Before I got the chance to attack, the boy shot up straight and turned to face the forest. The pending fight with me and my crew was lost, and his attention was now elsewhere.

The breeze crawled up the back of my neck, my skin once again broke out in goosebumps and I felt the prickle of electricity on my skin. That same voice called to me again. 'Go to her'. The boy whipped around, his eyes meeting mine. A look of terror filled his face. Oh. This was bad. He took off for the trees, changing into his chocolate brown wolf in an instant. Half of the other Weres followed closely behind him. "Something is wrong" I said before taking off after them, changing into my wolf mid stride. Elaine, Cleo, and Phoebe flanked me on both sides as we trailed the other wolves.

Stay with Venus and Analah, I'll find you after

Don't worry about me, just go

I flashed Alyse as I ran on the heels of the brown wolf. He looked back at me and huffed with a growl but didn't stop. We ran for a minute or two until I began to see lights through the trees up ahead. The sound of howling and growls filled the air. There is a fight happening, a big one, that much I could tell. As we approached a large clearing, where the party had been well underway, I could make out an extremely large pitch-black wolf tossing men left and right. I stopped a few meters away from the tree line and observed the chaos unfolding. Quite a few Weres were scattered about, growling, fidgeting, and flinging themselves around like they were trying to get bugs out of their ears. They looked deranged and downright crazy. Some of them were still in their human form, being restrained by she-wolves, and others were lying unconscious on the ground. As I scanned the area, one thing became glaringly clear, it was only the males that were losing their minds. The scene before us was just bizarre. Like something from a movie. What in the hell is going on here? The brown wolf and his men didn't stop to take it in like I did, they barged their way through the madness towards the far end. I growled to Elaine and we quickly followed after them. We skirted around the large group, watching what was unfolding. One very muscular Were, covered in tattoos, was being held down by four she-wolves and one very large older man. His canines were fully extended, and he was in the early stages of the change. He looked completely out of it. In fact, he looked near feral. I cracked my head to the side and back again, enacting the change. I stood upright and snarled at the unruly men.

"What the fuck is going on?" I growled. I walked into the crowd, Elaine and Phoebe now in their human form, stayed beside me. Cleo remained as her wolf and walked behind us.

"I said, what the hell is happening here?" I screamed, catching the attention of a few women. A male growled and snarled at me, launching forward. I snapped my elbow out, colliding it with the male's nose. He fell to the ground with a thud. A woman came forward, handing me a large grey t-shirt and more clothes to the others.

"We don't know how it happened. Everything was fine and then in an instant they all went mad" she said, her voice shaky.

"What caused this?" I demanded.

"And who are you?" another woman asked coming over to us. She was a tiny lady, with her brown hair once styled nicely, now in a state of disarray haggling over her shoulder. She held a certain amount of strength and power though, it came out with her voice. A Luna, or former Luna perhaps?

"I'm just a diplomat, here for the party, we arrived late" I told her, bowing my head slightly.

"Ah, well you missed quite the show then. Her heat came on so bloody quick. We had no time to get her out" the woman said as she stood firm with her hands on her hips. I didn't respond, the fear gripped hold of my vocal cords. I didn't need to ask who she was talking about. I knew already.

"I've never seen a female in heat have this effect before. I didn't know it was possible" she huffed, looking around at the frenzied Weres. I knew this was a risk. It was one of my many lessons as a descendant of Selene. When a Goddess goes into heat, she emits a pheromone that will signal the primal instincts of a male, calling forward the most powerful of Weres in a near crazed state of dominant need. The effect only grows in intensity as the power of the Goddess grows. There are records of only a rare few males that can deny the effect, mostly those males were mated in deeply intimate bonds. This should never have happened, she should have been removed from the vicinity of all males while in her heat period. I should have been here. I was meant to teach her this. I failed again.

"The chosen daughter is very different from any normal she-wolf" I murmured softly. The woman's head whipped back around to me, her gaze roamed my face as she scrutinized me carefully.

"What makes you think I was talking about her? If you were late like you say you were, then how would you know that?" she challenged.

"Call it female intuition. Where is she now? The Goddess, where did she go?"

"Her Mate carried her away".

I nodded in response and gazed around the party. The male population was looking a little calmer now, though still not fully okay.

"Why so interested?" the woman asked stepping closer to me. Elaine growled and Phoebe edged closer. The woman's eyes darted to Elaine and her brows lifted curiously, as if just noticing her for the first time.

"What pack did you say you were from?" she asked, keeping her eye on Elaine,

"I didn't" I answered.

"Well consider this me asking, where have you come from?"

"And why should I tell you?" I snapped looking down at the woman, she may hold a little power, but I know I could still defeat her if necessary.

"Because I'm the Luna-mother and I'm asking. Now where are you from and how did you get in here?" she growled back, her protective energy filtered across to me. The Luna-mother. My child's mother-in-law. And now I have pissed her off. We're getting off to a great start here at Tri-Moon. Elaine put her hand on my shoulder and stepped forward.

"We have come from Luna Eclipse" Elaine said sternly. The woman's eyes bulged, and she swallowed heavily.

"Luna Eclipse?" she questioned,

"Yes. I am Beta Elaine, we have come to offer our greetings and support to the Triple Goddess".

"Oh my, you're being serious?" she gaped.

Elaine didn't reply, only nodded once. The woman opened and closed her mouth a handful of times before she regained her composure with a slight shake of her head.

"Forgive me, I am Romeá, former Luna and mother to the new Alpha" she said finally.

"Pleasure. This is Lunaya, Phoebe, and Cleo over there" Elaine spoke, pointing to each of us.

"Hello, welcome" Romeá beamed at each of us.

"We came with three others, but we had issues getting through your border patrol".

"Yes, well, we had to up our security over the past few months. Plus, as I'm sure you are aware, the majority of the Were world believes that you're, you know, not real".

"That is the way we liked it, but given recent events, the Alpha has decided it was time we reemerged from the shadows".

"I understand, and you have no idea how pleased I am that you're here. I've heard stories about Luna Eclipse since I was a child, and being a big history buff and the pack history teacher, this is a huge deal. You have come so far" she began to ramble, and I lost interest quickly. There was only one person I wanted to talk about.

"Excuse me" I interrupted,

"Yes, Lunaya right?" she said looking up at me.

"Yes. You said the Triple Goddess had left with her Mate?"

"She has yes, they have gone to a safe house".

"And are they guarded?"

"Not currently, I don't think. We haven't had the time to organize something"

"Allow us" Elaine inserted,

"Excuse me?" Romeá mused.

"Your males can't be near her, and she needs protection, especially in her current state. Your females are best to remain here and keep the peace" Elaine continued,

"We are perfectly capable of protecting our own Luna" she snapped back.

"We are not questioning your capabilities, simply offering our assistance. You said you know of Luna Eclipse, so you know that our she-wolves are the fiercest warriors. We want the best for the girl, that is all" I added.

Romeá eyed us over for a little bit, her eyes trailing over Elaine's large and intimidating frame. After a minute she conceded, her shoulders slumped, and exhaled a forced breath.

"Okay. You're right, I'll take you to them".

Chapter Eighteen

Lunaya

The woman, Romeá, led us on what felt like a wild goose chase through the thick of the forest. We walked for at least half an hour, the village and the party were long behind us. The roars of the male wolves and the constant howling rang through the trees until we were too far away to hear them. Whatever this girl did, it clearly had a lasting effect. I have heard of a few other daughters through our history that had similar effects on the male population, but nowhere near to this extent. This kind of reaction is off the charts. Such a large range of Weres, all of them spread out over an expansive space, and all suffering the same incredibly intense reactions. It was like she released her own chemical weapon. To cause such chaos, she must be the most powerful daughter since Selene herself.

Soft screams could soon be heard through the forest up ahead. I picked up my pace, walking a few steps in front of Romeá now. A small hut slowly appeared through the trees, the screams were coming from underneath it.

"What is this place?" I asked, turning back to glare at Romeá. The little cabin was dirty, and small and looked like it could fall down with a stiff breeze. Definitely not suitable as a safe house against horny and uncontrollable Weres.

"This wouldn't have been my first choice either" Romeá answered, screwing up her nose.

"This is your safe house?" Elaine blanked from beside me.

"No, this is a holding cell. We use it for dangerous Ferals and the occasional prisoners" she answered, a hint of anger seeped through the word 'prisoner'. What has happened here for her to have such an adverse reaction?

"It's deceptively sturdy at the core of the structure" she grunted.

"Why here, son?" Romeá whispered softly, probably not intending for us to hear her. I couldn't help but wonder what has got her so worried about this cabin, something must have happened here. Another scream carried through the walls, it was filled with torment and pain. I ran for the door and pulled it open roughly.

"Stop!" Romeá called, running after me. The room was dusty and clearly unused. A small wooden table sat up against the far wall, along with two chairs. A bench top ran along the other side with a dirty sink and rusted out oven. How could she call this shack sturdy. The screaming was pouring into the small room nonstop. A bulky wooden door caught my attention, nestled away in the corner. The cries were louder coming from there. Before I got to pull open the door, Romeá jumped in front, blocking it with her body. I growled and bared my teeth.

"She is in heat, locked in a room, alone, with her Mate. What do you think you will be walking in on?" she growled back. I paused and straightened my back. Shit. She's right, I'm not thinking clearly. I stepped back from the door, putting some space between us. Elaine stood in the main doorway, her hard eyes watching me carefully.

"You are here to guard the building, nothing more. This child is my responsibility, and I won't have you putting her in any kind of uncomfortable or compromising positions. Are you understanding me?" she asked firmly, with the full authority granted to a strong Luna. I felt both hatred and admiration for the small she-wolf. She is clearly very fiercely protective and has taken to the role of mother effortlessly. My role. It should have been me protecting her, watching over her, making sure no one else caused her harm or shame. It should have been me.

"I will watch over the Goddess and her Mate, Phoebe can stay with me. You need to go back and collect your Mate and our other companions. Take a minute to calm yourself" Elaine spoke as she took a few steps into the small room.

"No, I will stay, she needs me here" I refuted.

"No, you will go. Don't forget your place Lunaya" Elaine spoke with authority and a heavy firmness. Romeá watched our interaction closely. Her curiosity towards me hadn't escaped my notice. I could see the gears of her mind working, trying desperately to figure out my secret. A secret I wasn't yet ready to tell.

"Very well" I conceded. Not because I agreed with Elaine, but because I needed to separate myself from the situation. I need to put some space between Romeá's curiosity and my all-too-revealing emotions.

"I will come back in two hours" I said with conviction.

"Three" Elaine rebutted,

"Two" I repeated, crossing my arms and squaring off against Elaine.

"You will come back in three hours with either Venus or Alyse, two of us will remain on guard at all times. If Tri-Moon wishes to send some of their own guards, you will accept them and work together".

"No…" I began to argue but Elaine growled, a large rumbling growl that shook the creaky old floorboards.

"Enough, Lunaya!" she bellowed, leaning her massive frame towards me. I stood straight and glared at the Beta. Her stubbornness is definitely one of legend. We could fight it out, but I will still not win this one. I yielded and let my surrender flow from me.

"Well then, sounds like we have come to an agreement" Romeá spoke, breaking the rising tension. The wooden door behind Romeá swung open, and a tall and muscular Were stood in the open doorway. His eyebrows were pulled together in a frown and his lips were pressed into a tight line, revealing his frustration. The screams of pain rolled through the room from the open door. He stepped through the doorframe, glaring at myself and Elaine. His blue eyes were hard and red rimmed, and a hint of wildness flashed deep in the back of his burning gaze.

"Who the fuck are you?" he growled stepping closer. Elaine came to my side and hissed at the man's threatening stance. Romeá jumped forward, placing herself between us. She placed her small hand on the Weres large chest and held him still.

"Gunner, this is Elaine and Lunaya, they have come to offer their protection to the Triple Goddess" Romeá spoke looking up to the face of the Were.

"Ladies, this is the Alpha of Tri-Moon and my son, Gunner". The Alpha. She is Mated to the Alpha. That means this is her Mate. He stood tall and strong. His white button-down shirt sat untucked and crumpled over his large muscular chest. His dark blonde hair was scruffy and a little long, coming down close to his shoulders. As I gazed over his handsome young face, I saw the remnants of a scar leading towards his ear. The skin was healed but had left behind what looked like a burn mark. His ear itself was missing the top section. A dark pink and jagged semi circle remained where the piece of flesh had been ripped from. A battle wound perhaps.

"Where have you come from? I don't recall seeing you at the ceremony" his hard voice trailed across the space between us. His fists were clenched tightly at his sides and his body trembled all over. His nose and the corner of his mouth twitched incessantly. The heat was affecting him, more than he cared to show. The cries of pain from my child had not stopped. Burying their way into the depths of my soul.

"Why are you not with your Mate?" I snapped.

"I asked you a question" he growled, pushing against the hold of his mother.

"She is screaming, in pain. Why are you not comforting her?" I demanded, my own growl filtering through. Gunner gripped his mother's hand and forcefully removed it from his chest. In two large steps, he came to stand in front of me. His chest was pushed out and only millimetres from pressing against me. I stood tall but he was a few inches taller. He tried to assert his Alpha dominance, I could feel it bouncing off my immune skin. Elaine flinched from beside me, her head lowering ever so slightly. Romeá whimpered from behind her son, feeling the full effect of her Alpha's dominance.

"Who are you?" he demanded, a wary and somewhat confused look flashed across his face. He has clearly not met someone who could resist the command of an Alpha.

"I am Lunaya, I have come to protect the Goddess. Now, why are you not taking care of her in her most desperate hour?"

Gunner released his threatening stance and pulled back his Alpha control. He stepped back slightly and his stiff shoulders slumped forward. Defeat. He was completely lost and overcome with defeat.

"She isn't conscious, and I can't get her to stop screaming" he said dejectedly. His mother came to his side and wrapped her small arm around his waist.

"You haven't laid with her?" I asked, my voice coming out a little too hard.

"She isn't conscious. I'm not going to rape my Mate!" he yelled. His feral eyes opened wide, and his cheeks turned a shade of red. Anger, frustration, anxiety, and a huge amount of sexual need flowed from him. I stared at him, shocked. Dumbfounded. With all these other random Weres damn near losing their minds over this girl's scent, yet here, her own Mate, has been able to sit at her side and not lose control. My respect for the boy, no, the man, it skyrocketed. I knew in that moment he too would have my loyalty and respect, not just my blessing.

"I apologize" I said placing my hand over my heart and bowing my head. As I stood back up, a baffled look sat on both Gunner's and Romeá's faces. I looked to Elaine and she had her brow raised, scrutinizing my action.

"Thank you for coming, where did you say you are visiting from?" he said a little softer, still looking at me with bewilderment.

"We have come from Luna Eclipse" I told him. He snapped his head to his mother and she nodded enthusiastically with a broad smile. I heard him whisper to her 'really?' and she continued to nod, placing her hand on his forearm.

"Well, okay then. Please let us arrange a meeting once my Mate is feeling better" Gunner said quietly.

"Of course, Alpha Gunner" Elaine finally spoke. He eyed her up and down as if just noticing her for the first time. His eyes widened slightly before a calm composure covered his face.

"If you'd excuse me" he said as he turned away, he brushed his mother's shoulder then went back through the large wooden door, closing it behind him. He seems like a good man, a good Were. I have a feeling my daughter is in good hands.

"I will go find the others then" I said as I looked to Elaine. She nodded her head and backed out the door. Cleo was lying on the ground, still in her burgundy and grey wolf form, while Phoebe leaned up against a tree.

"Phoebe, you will stay with me and we will take first watch over the Goddess. Cleo, you will accompany Lunaya back to the village to find the others. We will be refreshing guards every three hours" Elaine directed. Cleo stood and took a few steps closer as Elaine spoke. Phoebe nodded and walked around the other side of the cabin, scouting the perimeter, I assume.

"I will send more she-wolves out shortly. Thank you, Beta Elaine" Romeá spoke kindly. Her soft and genuine words were a stark contrast to the constant firmness that I have grown used to from the Luna Eclipse she-wolves.

Elaine moved to stand in front of the cabin door and crossed her arms over her wide set chest. Romeá walked past Cleo and I and started back towards the way we came. Cleo nodded to Elaine and turned to follow behind her. I hesitated for a moment, eyeing the cabin.

"Go, Lunaya" Elaine rumbled, leaving no room for argument in her tone. I turned and jogged after the others without saying anything further to Elaine. I walked next to Cleo's wolf, a few steps behind Romeá. We were all silent. A few scattered howls echoed through the quiet forest, slowly getting louder as we got closer to the village.

"Are you not going to change back?" I asked Cleo. She looked up at me out of the corner of her eye and shook her large head.

"You prefer the form of your wolf" I said, not asking her, just stating the fact that I had noticed. Cleo has spent a lot of time in her wolf form. Coming down the mountain, at Lua Chei, around the village back at Luna Eclipse. She is almost always in her wolf form. She huffed and snorted and continued walking.

"You aren't worried about not being able to change back? About becoming a Feral?" I asked looking down at her. She didn't look at me or growl or huff or anything. After a moment she stopped walking and snapped her head back, then stood up on her human legs. She began walking again, coming in step with me.

"The wolf is who I am, not the human. The form of the wolf is free and wild, it is the way I prefer. I do not fear becoming what you call, a Feral" Cleo said as she looked ahead. I stared at the side of her face, wide eyed. I have never heard her speak so much before. I almost couldn't respond, almost.

"If you don't call it Feral, what do you call it?" I questioned her,

"I call it Kūwao. Which in your tongue means to be untamed. In my birth pack, the wolves were our natural state, our preferred form. We only changed to the human body to keep a hold on it. To ensure the change could still happen when called upon. More than half of the Weres that were born would go on to live permanently in their wolf skin".

"Kūwao" I mimicked, tasting the name on my tongue. I mean, wow, I had no idea that packs like this existed. In all my years of roaming, I had never come across one. What a terrifyingly beautiful way to exist. It's admirable. I watched Cleo walk with awe in my gaze.

"They didn't become violent or too wild?" I asked,

"No".

"Every Feral I have come across is rabid. Or at least overly aggressive".

"Not in my pack"

"But how?"

"We accepted our wolves. We understood that they were the natural way, the pristine predator. The human was weak and small. The wolf is more, in every way".

"I accept my wolf" I said incredulously.

"No. You live with your wolf, tolerate it. You have not fully accepted that the wolf is the natural form".

"For me, it's not, it is only half of who I am. I am human as well".

"And that is where we differ" Cleo spoke firmly and with the utmost conviction in her words. She truly believes in what she is saying. I am a strong woman, but even I have never felt as sure about something as Cleo is about this. In a way her assuredness is enviable.

"Why did you leave? It sounds like you still want to live that way. So why would you give it up?" I asked her, watching over her facial expressions.

"I had no choice" she grunted,

"What do you mean?"

"Hunters killed my pack. Every wolf, every pup. The young, the old, all of them. All but me and my sister" she replied without hesitation. She held no emotion in her voice, no hint of grief or anger, just completely blank.

"I'm sorry" I said softly.

"I got my revenge, in the end".

"And your sister?"

"She is gone now".

"Cleo, I'm so sorry. I don't know what else to say".

She stopped walking and turned to glare at me. I stopped and faced her, watching her movements carefully. She stood rigid and tense, her hands by her side and her upper torso leaning towards me ever so slightly.

"I do not want your pity. I don't need it. I did what I had to do to avenge my family, and now you will do the same. I will help you to do the same".

Avenge my family. A thought I have always had kept in the far back of my mind. For a long time, I longed to rage against the hunters, to take them on, all alone. To destroy them as they did to me. But I never did. Or, at least, I never could. I hold too much love in my heart. I know that going to war with the hunters all on my own is never what Micha would have wanted. He would have wanted me to live, to move on. With or without my family. It took me a very long time to resign myself to that fact and to let go of my anger. Even if it still lives inside me.

"Thank you, Cleo. But revenge is not what I want anymore. I did, a long time ago, but I have let that part of me go. I just want my baby back, and I have that now" I said as I placed my hand on the side of her shoulder, to offer some kind of gratitude for her show of support.

"And if she wants to avenge them? If she wants to tear them down and take back what they took from her? Would you stand against her?"

"I don't even know how much she knows of what happened, if anything at all. But I will never stand against the Goddess, or my child. If that is her wish, I will help her achieve it".
"Even if it is not what you want?"
"What I want is her. Her happiness, her prosperity, her life to be everything it was meant to be. I will do anything and everything to make that happen"."
"You didn't answer the question" Cleo barked. Fuck me. When did she become so talkative, I think I prefer creepy silent Cleo.
"No" I sighed heavily.
"I wouldn't stand against her. If it's what she wanted, I would help her get it" I answered honestly. Cleo tipped her head to the side. Her curious gaze searched my eyes.
"And I will help you" she said with a nod. The response surprised me. I didn't even know Cleo liked me. Yet here she was declaring her assistance should I go to war with the hunters. I stood silently staring at her, rethinking every harsh criticism I had previously had. I had no idea how to respond to her decree, so I just opened and closed my mouth a couple of times, before landing on a contemplative frown. Cleo watched me for a moment before shrugging and setting off walking again. I caught up to her and we both found Romeá waiting for us up ahead. The rest of the walk was silent. As we got to the village, it had been cleared of nearly half the crowd. The mess was slowly being cleaned up by multiple Weres, male and female.
"I'll go get something for you to wear" Romeá said over her shoulder before walking off through the tables and chairs. I looked around at the mess and the dishevelled appearance of a lot of the Weres. This party clearly didn't turn out like they expected. I spotted Alyse and Venus among the pack members, helping with the cleanup by picking up chairs and rubbish.
"Alyse" I called out and waved to her. She looked up and smiled and waved for us to come over. I was walking across the clearing when the Were from the road, the Beta I presume, stepped in front of me.
"Where did you go?" he demanded, scowling at me.
"Excuse me?" I snapped back.

"Where did you go and where are the other two?" he asked again, raising his voice a little more.

"None of your business" I growled and went to sidestep around him. He stepped back in front of me and grabbed hold of my shoulder. I looked down at his firm grip and then back up to his hard eyes. Cleo stepped forward and growled. The sound echoed around us and filled the clearing. Everyone stopped working and turned their attention to us.

"Remove. Your. Hand!" Cleo growled at the Were, stepping right up to my side.

"Don't forget where you are, she-wolf. You have not been invited here and you can't just go wandering around my pack as you please" he hissed, glowering at Cleo. I shoved off his hand and stood up tall and straight, pressing my inflated chest to his. We growled back and forth at each other, neither one making the first move to attack. His canines slowly extended as his lips curled back over his teeth.

"Where were you? Spying, sabotaging, planting something? Where!?" he yelled in my face.

"Cole, that is enough!" Romeá's voice called as she came running over. She tried to push him away from me, but he shoved her off him and came back in my face baring his teeth and growling.

"They are trespassing" he hissed.

"They are here to protect the Goddess, now back off!" she snapped at him and tried again to pull him away. The Were, Cole, turned and raised his claws to her, but froze before he brought it down.

"Cole Thomas! Have you lost your damn mind?" Romeá screamed. She looked up at him with wide eyes, filled with sadness and confusion. He dropped his hand and took a step away from me. He blinked rapidly a few times while looking at Romeá.

"Cole" she whispered softly and reached out for his hand. He pulled away and hardened his gaze once again.

"Has this she-wolf told you who she is?" he asked her, his voice hard and angry.

"She is from Luna Eclipse, they all are, and they're here to offer their greetings to the Triple Goddess" Romeá answered.

"But has this one told you who she is?" he snapped pointing his finger at me.

Oh no. He is about to blow my secret wide open. I knew it wouldn't stay secret for long, but I was hoping to have at least met my child before they all found out.

"What are you talking about, Cole?" she asked sounding exasperated.

"Has this she-wolf told you who she claims to be?" he said again, turning to stand back in front of me. Romeá looked up at me in confusion. Her eyes darted back and forth between Cole and me.

"Who are you?" she asked me. But I didn't answer. I glared at Cole and bared my teeth.

"Who the hell are you?!" she demanded.

"What's all the yelling about, and why is this one naked?" a tall brooding Were asked as he came to stand beside Romeá. I shot him a quick glance, it was the same man that was holding down the tattooed Were earlier. He is very tall and muscular, with a dark pink scar that runs along the side of his face. If it weren't for the beard, I would say he looks just like my daughter's Mate only older. He rested his hand on Romeá's shoulder as he watched us. He must be the former Alpha, Gunner's father. I turned my glare back at Cole and growled a warning.

"Cole, explain" he demanded. No, no, no. Please don't.

Cole glared at me for a second, his eyes moving all over my face before staring back into my own. An evil smirk spread across his face. He is going to tell them. I pushed aside my pride and fury and pleaded with him through my eyes. I conveyed as much begging as I could, without speaking a word. His smirk slowly disappeared, and his gaze seemed to soften, the anger and pain on his face didn't leave though. It stuck with him like a scar. From the moment I met this man, I hated him. But now, in this moment, with him examining my pleading face and the hurt written all across his own. I felt for him.

"It's nothing" he grunted and quickly turned on his heel and stormed away. I expelled a harsh breath, my secret is safe for the moment.

Chapter Nineteen

Zelena

Warmth twisted in my stomach. A deep ache and a sheen of sweat quickly covered my body. Travis leaned forward, my fingers still grasped tightly in his. I thought he was going to bow but instead, he pressed his moist lips to the back of my hand. The feel of his lips and a small fleck of saliva as it touched my flesh, burned against my skin. My stomach tightened and I nearly doubled over in pain. I tried to rip my hand from Travis's, but he wouldn't let go. I looked up at his face and his eyes had turned dark and his lips curled back. His tongue dipped from his mouth and moved over the back of my knuckles. A low growl slowly bubbled through his clenched teeth, getting louder, until it rolled all around us.

"Trav, what the fuck are you doing?" Maryann demanded, grabbing hold of him and trying to get his attention. I struggled to pull my hand free, but he fought against me. The pain in my stomach and the burning of his saliva on my skin intensified ten-fold.

My heat!

I screamed through my flash to both Gunner and Tobias. At first, I thought it was just Travis growling. I was wrong. He wasn't alone. It was all of the Howlers pack men, all the ones that had come over to greet us, they were now slowly circling around us. Around me. Surrounding me. Growling and glaring at me and me alone.

My heat!

I flashed again, and this time I got a response. Gunner roared. He roared so loud that I swear the ground shook under my feet. Tobias pressed himself right up behind me with a protective arm around my waist, and together he made us take a few steps back. The contact of his body on mine hit me with a deliriously intoxicating feeling and I found myself pressing my body harder up against him, anything to lessen this pain. And boy, does his body feel good. Gunner was standing in front of us, slightly crouched in an attack stance, with his claws at the ready. Felix had come to stand by his side with the other guards, though I could see they too were affected by my heat. Some of them would glance back at me, they would snarl and growl, and then turn away and shake their head. As if fighting their basic instincts.

"If you wish to leave my land with your limbs intact, I suggest you step the fuck away from my Mate" Gunner roared at the surrounding men. Lupus came barrelling over and tried to pull some of the men away, trying to get them to snap out of it. I wonder why he doesn't seem affected by it at all.

"I can't leave" Travis growled, his voice full of pain and contradiction. Maryann was trying desperately to pull him away but failing at every attempt.

"Not when she smells like that" he added just for good measure. The curly haired man that led the Howlers stepped closer, a wicked smirk playing across his face. He was ignoring Gunner's threatening growl and eyeing me up and down, like a juicy piece of meat he wanted to sink his teeth into. His stare should repulse me, I know this. But my need for someone, anyone, to ease the desire and the pain coursing through me, it was stronger this time around.

"Gunner" I moaned leaning my head back onto Tobias's chest. I pushed my back and ass further into Tobias and his body froze. I could feel his muscles tense and his chest vibrate as a deep growl slipped from his mouth. Gunner's eyes whipped around to where I stood, and he growled a warning up at Tobias.

"Get her out of here!" he ordered.

"I can't do that Alpha. Her scent is too strong, if I leave with her, I can't guarantee that I will be able to control myself" Tobias groaned. He pressed his fingers into my lower stomach and pushed his hips forward into my back. If I thought his stature was large, it followed through to the giant snake in his pants. His erection pressed up against me, like a third arm hidden between his legs.

"Oh fuck" I groaned. The moisture in my panties increased tenfold. The scent of my arousal flooded through the air, invading the nostrils of all the Weres nearby. One of the men managed to get by Lupus and came running forward. Gunner caught him by the neck and in one swift movement, he spun him around and threw him with such force, that he went hurtling through the air, eventually crashing back to the ground almost fifteen metres away.

I couldn't think of anything other than Tobias's hands and the burning sensations they were sending through me. He tightened his arm around me once again, then he leaned down and pressed his nose into the crook of my neck. I could feel his tongue sliding along the sensitive skin leading up to my earlobe. It burned in the most wonderful of ways. I tilted my head to the side, allowing him more access, and moaned out loud. My hand came up to the back of his neck, to hold his mouth against me. Another roar sounded and it made my knees weak. If it weren't for Tobias holding me, I would have crashed to the ground. I was suddenly ripped from Tobias's arms and encased in a new pair. A pair that set off a round of sparks and fire flooding through me. I saw Tobias fall to the ground on his knees, taking slow and heavy breaths. A white haze flooded my vision, blurring out all my worries about the possible dangers, and any care I had about being taken by any of the men present. They all dissipated. Consumed by the fireworks that came from the arms now pressed against my burning skin.

Another Were came running towards me and the person holding me flung out his leg in a flying kick, connecting it against the side of the man's head. He dropped to the ground with a thump. As I rubbed myself up against whoever was holding me, more of the Tri-Moon pack stepped up to fight back the men. Most of which were women. Luckily, we have a lot of strong female fighters in our pack.

A strong hand gripped my jaw roughly, forcing my eyes to theirs. Gunner. Everything inside me screamed at me to take him, to end this torture. I jumped up into his arms, wrapping my legs around his waist, and forced my lips to his. I dove my tongue deeply into his mouth and wound my arms around his neck. We growled and moaned as our lips moved together hungrily. I could feel my canines pressing against my gums, begging to be released, to be buried in my Mate's flesh.

"Gunner, get her out of here!" Travis's country voice roared. I turned my gaze in his direction, he was further back now but still struggling against the hold of his Mate. More of the Howlers had closed in now. With our guards partially distracted and the she-wolves struggling to hold back the hoard of uncontrollable, lust filled men, we were in trouble. I was about to become tonight's main entertainment. Passed around the mob of horny Weres like the donation tray at church. And right now, in this very moment, the idea excited me more than scared me.

Wrapped in Gunner's arms, with my heated body aching for his touch, he was caught between trying not to take me right here right now and trying to pay attention to the slowly enclosing crowd of would-be rapists. Would we call them rapists if at the moment I welcome it? I know that I don't really want this, I know it's the heat affecting me. But right now, I am desperate for any kind of stimulation or release, from whoever wants to give it to me.

The curly haired man launched forward, right at me and Gunner. I closed my eyes and waited for the collision of our bodies. But nothing happened. An enormous rumbling roar filled the sky, like a crack of thunder. I opened my eyes and found Tobias's monstrous black wolf, tearing into the hoard of men. He made deliberate and precise strikes, being careful not to kill anyone, but there is definitely going to be a lot of scarred up Weres come tomorrow morning.

Tobias provided the perfect distraction. Catching the attention of the hoard long enough for Gunner to start running, with me still firmly in his arms. The after-effects of his feet hitting heavily against the ground with each stride sent a shockwave of reverberations echoing through my body. I drank in the feelings greedily, my body reacting like a wanton whore.

Everything after that is somewhat of a blur. We ran and ran for I don't know how long, I don't even know if we were being followed. The heat from Gunner's skin occupied what remaining space was left of my thoughts. I recall being laid back on a soft surface and Gunner's hands and mouth roaming over my aching body. I could hear him talking to me, trying to soothe me. But his words were just blank space, a fuzzy sound buzzing in the back of my mind. The need and desire was all consuming. It was beyond painful. The beatings I once got from Hank, and the pain he inflicted on my body, it is nothing compared to this. This unrelenting burning, the twisting ache that I could see no end to. It felt like a death devouring monster, made of pure lava and glass, was trying to tear her way out of my body.

I could hear wailing and screaming echoing all around me. I didn't even realise that it was coming from me until I could feel the burn in my throat. I was crying out for any kind of release from the pain. Gunner's body was hanging over mine, his face holding an expression of fear and heartache. His hands travelled the length of my body, but his eyes remained fixed on my own. It was too much. Too much pain. Too much desire. Too much heat. I tried to focus on Gunner, but it was a lost cause. My eyes closed and I lost consciousness.

~

My body feels like I have rolled down a tall mountain, hitting every bump, every boulder, every pointed and sharp surface along the way. Everything felt tight and constricted. My stomach had turned in on itself, and just the thought of rolling over brought me more pain. I struggled to open my eyes, even my eyelids hurt. I couldn't move, I didn't have the energy and I didn't have the strength to face more pain.

"Zelena" a soft melodic voice called to me. The sound was blissful and soothing. I groaned in response, begging to hear more of it.

"Hey, Little Wolf, are you awake?"

Ah, that voice. The voice of my love, my life, my mate. I forced open my eyes and blinked rapidly, trying to bring them into focus. Gunner sat on a chair in front of me, leaning forward and staring down at me. My first thought was 'why are you so far away from me right now'. I was laying on the floor, or on a mattress on the floor, I'm not sure. I just know that I was low to the ground, and he wasn't with me. I opened my mouth to speak but my throat felt like it had lost a battle with a bucket of hot razor blades. Next option, I tried to reach out to him. I removed my arm from around my stomach and very shakily stretched it toward him. He didn't take it though. Instead, he moved further away from me. He leaned back in the chair and made it slide further back across the floor. The act filled me with shame and defeat.

"I'm sorry" he mumbled. His body sat stiff and rigid in the chair. His fingers dug into his thigh, so much so that I knew he was going to have bruises. He was looking at me, but he wasn't seeing me. His eyes were far away and, dare I say, scared.

"What's" I coughed roughly, clearing the swollen dryness of my throat.

"What's going on?" I croaked out. My voice sounded like that of a seventy-year-old grandma who has smoked four packs a day since she was thirteen.

"I can't" Gunner growled lowly,

"Can't what?"

"I can't be next to you".

The statement stung like lemon juice over a fresh paper cut. A right kick to the stomach. He's repulsed by me. I pulled my arm back and curled myself tighter into the foetal position. I closed my eyes tight, but it didn't stop my tears. I knew this day would come eventually. How could he ever love me? Want me? I'm horrid.

"I'm sorry, I just can't control myself. Your smell, Zelena" he groaned and growled again,

"You smell so fucking intoxicating. You have no idea how hard it has been not to have my way with you over and over and over again" Gunner growled painfully. I opened my eyes again and wiped away the tears so that I could see him more clearly. He was hunched over in the chair with his hand placed firmly over his mouth and nose.

"What do you mean?" I asked, holding back a sob. Gunner flew up from his chair faster than I'd ever seen him move. He stood over where I was lying and glared down at me. I stared back at him blankly, surprised by his furious expression. It took me a moment to see through the pain, to see him. He wasn't mad at all, he was full of wild lust. I could feel the way it was eating at him. I could practically taste the desire on his tongue.

"I have never smelt something so fucking delicious. I have never wanted something so fucking much. But fuck me, I love you too much to just rape you while you're unconscious".

His hands sat in tightly balled fists by his side, his legs wobbled and his whole body was shaking. The sight of him like this, filled with so much desire that it drove him to the brink of madness. It was enough to set a new wave of heat through my body. My skin broke out in a sweat and my groin throbbed. It was like a tap had been turned on between my thighs. My slick desire just poured out of me.

"I'm awake now" I whispered.

"No" he growled, stepping back slightly.

"Please, Gunner, I need you".

"You're too weak. I'm not some uncontrollable animal"

"Please".

There was silence, the tension between us was thick. I could feel his resolve slipping. His hesitance was barely hanging on. "It hurts, Gunner. Please" I begged. It was enough. Gunner was on me in an instant. His lips crashed to mine hungrily and I wrapped my arms tightly around his neck. I was still wearing my green dress from the party. I'm beginning to think this isn't a very lucky dress. Gunner sat back and using his claws he tore the dress from my body, discarding the ripped fabric on the floor. He was back on me in a second. Trailing his lips down my neck and over each breast. He sucked hard on each nipple and they pebbled at the touch of his firm tongue. His lips continued south to the flimsy fabric of my panties, and he wasted no time in ripping them off. Then he dived headfirst into my pussy, eating me like his last meal. I screamed out with pleasure and gripped his hair. My hips bucked against his face at their own accord. He drove his fingers into my entrance and worked them back and forth, rough and hard, while his mouth sucked, licked, and nibbled on my throbbing clit. My orgasm came fast and hard and yet provided no solace to the aching heat.

"Gunner" I screamed, and that was all that he needed to hear. He picked up both my legs and threw them over his shoulder so that my ass was lifted off the mattress. Without a moment of hesitation, he drove his pulsating dick into me, in one hard long thrust. I screamed with a mix of pleasure and pain. The fullness he provided was perfectly stimulating, but I want more, I need more. His hips moved erratically and yet in utter sync with the lift of my own hips. Gunner's upper thighs slapped against my ass cheeks and his dick found every inch of my vagina. Hitting every bit of sensitive flesh. I grabbed my nipples and toyed with them while Gunner rammed into me mercilessly. I pinched and pulled and twisted my aching nipples. It added to the stimulation but was still not enough. "More" I cried out. Gunner's hips moved faster and hit harder. If he wasn't holding onto me, I would have gone flying across the floor. I could feel my walls contracting and my orgasm looming. I just want that one extra hit to help me explode. And like he read my mind, Gunner reached down and pinched my clit between his fingers. He pulled, pinched, and twisted, and it was everything I needed. My orgasm washed over me, pulling Gunner along with me. I felt his hot seed cover the walls of my pussy and it was like an extinguisher over the flames, providing instant relief to the pain. He bucked his hips a few more times, emptying himself inside me. Then he collapsed onto the mattress beside me.

"Thank you" I huffed, my chest heaving for air,

"Did it help?" he asked, sounding just as breathless,

"More than you know".

He pulled me up so that I laid half across his chest and then lifted my leg up over his waist so that my bare pussy was pressed against his upper thigh. We huffed and puffed until we both caught our breath again and calmed down.

"I'm sorry" he said quietly,

"For what?" I asked a little confused.

"For a lot of things, but mainly for not helping you like that sooner".

I held in a chuckle. It's funny to think fucking like that is helpful. But a gut feeling told me this was not the time to laugh at his unnecessary apology.

"It was like you said, I was unconscious, there was nothing you could have done".

"I could have got you away from that fucking situation a lot quicker. Could have got you to safety sooner, before you got to the point that you were in so much pain you fucking passed out".

"That wasn't your fault, you didn't know I was in heat. If anything, I should have realised long before it hit".

"Yeah, but I should have known too. It affects me just as much as it affects you, and the fucking we did the night before the party, that was no normal fucking, it was animalistic. That should have been enough to clue me in. Fuck. I'm so sorry Zee".

'The night before the party'. Why did he say it like that, wasn't that just yesterday?

"Gunner, what day is it? How long have we been here?" he lifted his head and looked at me confused, like I'd just grown a second head.

"The party was two nights ago" he answered and dropped his head back down,

"You've been in and out of consciousness the whole time but barely stopped screaming for more than half an hour at a time on the first night".

"You're joking?" I demanded. It can't have possibly been that long. I don't remember any of it.

"Afraid not love. A lot has happened".

"Like what?"

"Well first off, the scent you let off was unlike anything that anyone had ever encountered before. The effects of it drove a lot of the visiting Weres a bit crazy. There were a lot of fights and injuries. Some needed to be sedated or locked up, just to keep them from fucking you raw. A lot of them have left already but most are still here".

"Oh". It was all I could manage. 'Oh' that's it. Gunner could have worded that a little better, but I understand he has been through a lot these past couple of days. What is wrong with me? How could I cause so much chaos and damage?

"If it's been two days, why are they still here, shouldn't they have gone back to their own packs by now?" I asked looking over his face. He was looking up to the ceiling as he talked, slowly stroking his hand up and down my back.

"They are waiting for you. They barely got to meet you, and they want to make sure that you are happy with them".

"Happy with them? Why does that matter?"

"Well, you're still the Goddess, and they still want to offer their greetings. Plus, I think they are afraid you will punish them or something".

Ah, so they are afraid of me. I have been worried this would happen. I never wanted anyone to be scared of me. I lived my whole life in fear, I would hate to inflict that on anyone else. But if they are so fearful now, I doubt that they would enter into an alliance. I could have ruined everything.

"And the alliances? Did I ruin the chance of making alliances?" I asked, scared of the answer but needing to know either way.

"The alliances are fine. If anything, the visiting packs are so terrified of us that they are clamouring to get on our good side. Especially the Howlers. The Alpha thought that they may have started a war".

"Did I meet the Howlers Alpha?"

"Not exactly, no. He was there when your scent first hit and he nearly got to you, but Tobias held him off".

"Tobias did?"

"Yeah, he snapped out of the haze reasonably quickly. Lucky for him".

"What do you mean, lucky for him?"

"You don't remember any of this?" Gunner asked as he lifted me off his chest and sat upright.

"No. I'm sorry" I said, dropping my head. Gunner cupped my cheek and gently tilted my head back up so that I could look at his face.

"Don't be sorry love, it wasn't your fault. Not even close".

"Don't say that, of course it was my fault".

"No Zelena, you couldn't have known. There were meetings, once we got you far enough away, and the rest of the male population could calm down enough to think rationally. It was all mutually agreed upon, and backed up by Artemis, we think it's because of your blood. Your personal connection to the Moon Goddess, that's what made us all go nuts. You're more powerful than anyone expected. So of course, once your heat hit, it only made sense that that would be more powerful too. We just weren't ready for it. Obviously".

"That's a lot to take in, Gunner" I said softly, my head spinning with the information. I knew something felt different at the ceremony. I felt different, it was a whole new and unexplored feeling of power. Something unlike anything else. And now I'm being told that I'm a walking talking disaster zone. Once a month, ready to drive the male population of Weres bonkers. Great.

"Zee, everything will be okay. I can see it in your eyes, you're blaming yourself. I know that you're going to be thinking about everyone else and what will happen to them, and I'm telling you, they will be okay. You will be okay" Gunner soothed as he pulled me onto his lap. The feel of his flesh against mine made my skin crawl with desire. I wrapped my legs around his back and my arms around his neck, pressing my chest up against his. My lips found the soft skin of his neck and I sucked and nibbled my way up to his jawline. I pushed my hips forward into his and Gunner's erect dick pushed back.

Gunner gripped my hips and held me firm against himself. Tilting his head up and back, he allowed me room to move my mouth all over the delicious skin of his neck. He pulled my hips forward, making my pussy slide along the base of his dick. I moaned softly and Gunner growled quietly. I lifted myself a little and I felt Gunner position the tip of his dick at my slick entrance. I lowered myself back down, slowly sliding down his shaft until he was fully sheathed inside me. Gunner wrapped one arm around my lower back and the other he placed at the back of my head. And I began to move. Lifting my hips, slow and steady, and then bringing them back down just a slow. Each time I pressed myself back down, I could feel his entire cock deep inside me, hitting all the right places. We stayed like this for a long while. Making slow and passionate love. The closeness of our bodies and soft and gentle moans, it was beautiful. Gunner slipped his hand between our bodies and began to rub slow hard circles on my clit. My orgasm had been a slow build, growing and growing inside me until it was ready to burst. I was ready to burst.

"I love you" I moaned into Gunner's ear. My hips started to move a little faster, hitting back down on his dick a little harder. The muscles in my stomach were constricting. The walls of my vagina were gripping around him.

"Cum with me baby" he whispered with a groan, increasing the speed of his hand on my throbbing clit. I gave myself over to the pleasure and my orgasm crashed over me hard. I threw my head back and cried out as I buried my fingers into his thick scruffy hair. I ground my hips forward, drawing out my orgasm and helping Gunner find his own release. He grunted and bucked his hips into me, emptying himself deep inside me. We were both panting, still wrapped up in each other's arms. I laid my head on the top of Gunner's shoulder as he stroked my hair. We stayed tangled together for a while, just getting lost in the embrace.

"I think it's over" I said softly, not lifting my head.

"Possibly" he replied.

Chapter Twenty

Zelena

I lay with my head resting on Gunner's chest. We decided to stay here for a few more hours, just to be on the safe side, to make love a few more times, and to make sure the heat was really over. As I looked around at the small room, a familiar feeling came to me. I've been here before.

"Gunner, where are we?" I asked as I sat up,

"Huh?" he mumbled.

"What is this place?"

Gunner sat upright and glanced at me. He bit his lip and rubbed his hand over the back of his neck, something I have noticed he does when he is nervous or uncomfortable.

"It's uh, it's the cabin" he said meekly.

"The cabin? What cabin?" I looked around the room again. The cold concrete floor, the steel walls, and the iron bars covering the door. I have definitely been here before. A sick feeling filled my stomach and the urge to vomit hit me hard and fast.

"Gunner, why?" I grunted as I slowly stood up off the raggedy mattress on the floor and onto my wobbly and unstable legs. My heart rate accelerated, and my chest tightened. Why would he bring me here? Here! Of all the places we could have escaped to, he brought me to the place where I murdered my childhood caregiver and torturer. I could picture it clear as day. Hank's sneering face and evil smile. The blood on his shirt. His body, crumpled and broken on the floor. The memory of what I did to him still haunts me.

"I'm sorry Zee, I panicked" he rushed out. He stood and wrapped his arms around my waist, pulling my head into his chest. I can't be here, I need to get out. I could feel my panic rise and I started to hyperventilate.

"I don't... want... to be here..." I gasped for breath.

"Okay, okay. We'll go home. Wait here a second". Gunner let me go and walked out the door. I lowered myself back to the floor and tucked my knees into my chest. I forced myself to take deep intakes of air, but the feeling of my throat constricting was stopping the air from reaching my lungs. Gunner came back through the door holding a pile of clothes. He knelt down in front of me and pulled my hands away from my legs. He placed his hand on my cheek and rubbed his thumb over my bottom lip.

"Slow down, Little Wolf, just breathe" he said softly as he looked deep into my eyes. I leaned my face into his hand and let the warmth of his skin soothe me. We stayed like that for a little while, just staring into each other's eyes, me copying the movements of his chest and the breaths he was taking. After a few minutes, I could breathe normally again.

"There, that's better" he smiled sweetly at me, swiping his thumb over the curve of my cheek.

"Here, put these on, and then we can go" he said putting the clothes on my lap. I pulled a grey t-shirt over my head and then stood up, I pushed my feet through the legs of the sweatpants and turned to Gunner. He held his hand out for me and I took it. He pulled me to his body and lifted me into his arms. I buried my face into the crook of his neck as whisked us out the door and up the stairs, leaving that hellish nightmare room behind. We came up to the top floor but didn't stop, we went straight out through the front door.

As we came outside, Gunner carefully put me down again. But as soon as my face was out of his protective hold, I had to shield my eyes from the bright sunlight. Two days in artificial lighting can mess with your eyes. I squinted and tried to blink away the brightness. Gunner took my hand and led me a few steps away from the front door when a shocked voice caught my attention.

"Oh, my word" the feminine voice whispered. I turned to see who had spoken but I didn't recognise her. A small statured woman stood by the front door of the cabin. Her chocolate hair sat messily atop her head, showing off the freckles that littered her face. She's not one of our pack members, I haven't seen her around the village. Perhaps a visitor, here for the party, or what was meant to be the party. The stranger took a step towards us, but Gunner pulled my hand, bringing me into the side of his body. Another woman jogged over from around the side of the cabin. This one was very large, the biggest woman I have ever seen. Not large as in fat, large like Tobias. Wide set shoulders and bulging muscles. Her size wasn't the intimidating thing about her though, it was the tribal tattoo that covered her chin and bottom lip. I know for sure that I've never seen this woman before, I would have remembered.

The moment the huge woman spotted me, she dropped to her knee and bowed her head. The smaller woman quickly followed suit, placing her hand over her heart.

"My Goddess" the big woman spoke, her voice was loud and hard, and it carried a powerful aura with it.

"Beta Elaine, Miss Alyse. This is my Mate and the Triple Goddess" Gunner said to them. They both stood and walked a little closer to us.

"Oh, she's beautiful" the small woman whispered and covered her smiling mouth with her hand. Her eyes filled with unshed tears and a small sob escaped her. I can't say someone has become this emotional when meeting me before. Excited, shocked, maybe joyful, but not emotional like this. It's strange.

"Goddess, I am Beta Elaine of the Luna Eclipse. It is the highest honour to meet you" the larger woman spoke, meaning the small crying one is Alyse. Makes sense, she's built like a Beta, if not an Alpha.

"Hello" I smiled and nodded to both of them.

"The diplomats from Luna Eclipse have been guarding you since the night of the party. We are very lucky to have them here" Gunner said proudly. He almost sounds like he is gushing over them.

"Thank you for that. It is very kind of you" I smiled again and stepped forward with my hand outstretched for a handshake. Alyse squeaked quietly and stepped back, and Beta Elaine eyed me curiously. After an awkward moment of me standing in front of them with my hand outstretched, Beta Elaine stepped forward and gripped my forearm. She placed her other hand on my shoulder and leaned way down in order to reach her forehead to my own. I have seen Sevasmo between many male wolves, but I have never done it, and I've never seen a she-wolf do it. I should ask Gunner about that. Is it a male wolf only type of thing? We stood together for a moment, with our heads touching lightly. Being this close to another Were, I could feel everything she was feeling, I could smell all of her emotions. The highest of them all was pride and joy. She is happy to be here, to meet me. The feeling made me happy.

We broke apart and I stood back at Gunner's side. He smiled down at me fondly and gently traced his finger over my cheek. Another sob came from Alyse.

"Are you okay?" I asked her. She nodded her head furiously and cleared her throat.

"I'm sorry, I just can't believe you're actually here, you're real. You have no idea how often we thought of you" she said as a few tears streamed down her face. I couldn't understand what she meant by 'how often we thought of you'. The world hasn't known about me for that long, so how could she have thought about me? And who does she mean by 'we'? Is that like a general we, including all Weres, or a more specific we? Anyhow, what a strange statement to make.

"Ah, yes. Well, I'm here and I'm ready to go home" I replied meekly.

"Your heat has ended?" Elaine asked.

"It appears so" Gunner answered her,

"We are headed back to the village, you're welcome to walk with us" he said as he took hold of my hand.

"We will, thank you Alpha" Elaine said with a curt nod.

The walk back to the village was quick and basically silent. Not much more, beyond basic pleasantries, was said between us. I did though catch the she-wolf Alyse staring at me a few times. Something about the way she was watching me worried me. It was as if she knew who I was, like she knew everything there was to know about me. It was weird and unnerving. But she couldn't really know me. It's probably just the whole Goddess thing getting her emotional and excited. The village itself was clean and tidy now, if you hadn't been in attendance, you'd have no idea that there was a party here the other night. All the chairs and tables have been packed away. And the decorations have been taken down. It looks just like it did before.

As Gunner said, there was still a lot of visiting Weres around. A lot of the larger tents are still up around the outskirts of the village, just nowhere near as many as before. As we got to the fire pit in the middle of the clearing, Roe and Lupus came barrelling down the porch steps toward us.

"Sweet girl, how are you feeling?" Roe fussed as she smooshed my face between her small hands.

"You gave us quite the scare" Lupus rumbled as he gently squeezed my shoulder.

"I'm sorry, I'm so sorry, I didn't know" I mumbled, I could feel the lump in my throat working its way up and tears welling up in my eyes.

"Nonsense, it wasn't your fault dear. We're just glad that you're okay" Roe cooed as she pulled me into her arms and hugged me tightly.

"You're not mad?" I choked out from within her constricting embrace. She may be a small woman, but damn she is strong.

"Don't be ridiculous" she huffed, and Lupus laughed from behind her.

"We should have known you had another surprise up your sleeve" Lupus chuckled,

"We never quite know what to expect with you do we?"

Roe released me from her iron grip, and I snorted and smiled up at Lupus.

"I gotta keep you on your toes" I mused.

"Well, you definitely did that. You should have seen the chaos that went on around here. Those poor bastards didn't know what hit them" Lupus roared with laughter, he leaned over and slapped his thigh. The sound of his laughter filled the clearing. He's really getting a kick out of this, isn't he?

"Oh enough" Roe chided and hit him on the back of the head.

"Go and do something useful" she groaned in annoyance and gave him a firm shove. Lupus continued to laugh as he waltzed away.

"I see you met some of our esteemed visitors" Roe smiled as she looked at the women behind me. I hadn't realised that Alyse and Beta Elaine were still standing there,

"Have I told you much about Luna Eclipse yet darling?" Roe asked as she turned her gaze back to me. I shook my head meekly. Before today I hadn't heard the term Luna Eclipse mentioned once. Their pack is a total mystery to me. Seeing Roe this excited has me curious though, there must be something important about them.

"Thank you again, ladies. We are so truly honoured to have you here at Tri-Moon. Will you please join us for dinner tonight?" Roe asked stepping in around me to stand before Elaine.

"That is not necessary. As I said, it is our honour and our duty to protect the Goddess" Elaine replied. Does her voice always hold such hardness? I get it, she's a Beta and she has to keep that tough guy persona. But seriously woman, lighten up. I smiled to myself as I thought about the stone-faced Elaine cracking a joke, what a sight that would be. I noticed once again, that Alyse was staring at me. She is by no means scary, but she is really starting to creep me out.

"Well, that being said, I insist" Roe spoke in her usual chirpy way. Roe almost always gets what she wants. I don't think even the tough Elaine can get out of this one.

"Please come, I would like to get to know you better, and I would like to hear about your pack. It is the least I can do to say thank you after you spent two days watching over me" I said looking up to Elaine. She watched me carefully as I spoke, and I knew then that I had her. She didn't reply, she just nodded her head.

"Are there more of you?" I asked,

"Yes, there are four others" Elaine confirmed in her usual hard tone.

"Excellent, please bring them too" I said, as I turned to look at Roe. She was smiling as she watched the conversation, with her hands on her hips and a proud look on her face.

"If that is okay with you, Roe?" I asked her,

"That sounds absolutely perfect" she mused and clapped her hands together,

"I had better go start cooking. I will see you ladies in the dining hall at six o'clock" she said with a curt nod before turning on her heels and marching off into the pack house.

"We will see you all tonight?" I asked once more, just to make sure.

"Yes, my Goddess. We will be here" Elaine confirmed.

"Perfect, now if you don't mind, my Mate needs some rest" Gunner spoke as he snaked his hand around my waist and pulled me into his side.

"Of course, Alpha" Elaine said with a bow, she turned and ushered Alyse along with her.

"Gunner, I have slept for two days, I don't need to rest" I argued.

"You do need to rest, you expelled a lot of energy at the ceremony and then went straight into one of the most intense heats I have ever heard of. You need to rest if you want to be functioning properly at this dinner you have just arranged".

"I didn't arrange it, I just made sure that the Luna Eclipse diplomats would join us" I said somewhat confused. He was there, he saw his mother ask them for dinner,

"You almost arranged it. You did use your charm to ensure that important guests will be in attendance. Just like a Luna would. You're a natural to the role" he mused and kissed my temple.

"Really" I asked, my excitement rising. I suppose I have kind of taken to this Luna thing pretty well. Especially considering I was in a coma for the first three months of it.

"Yes really" he chuckled and pulled me into his chest.

"You really don't know anything about Luna Eclipse?" he asked, peering down at me.

"How could I? All of my werewolf knowledge has come from you and your parents. If you haven't told me, then I wouldn't know. Why? What's the big deal with this pack? Are they dangerous or something?"

"Yes and no. Until the night of the party, the entire world thought that they were a myth".

"What do you mean? Why would you think that?"

"Well, because they kind of were. No one really knew for sure where they were or if they were still alive. The only information we have is the stories and the tales, and you can't really rely on a fairy tale".

"A fairy tale? What are they, witches or magical she-wolves or something?"

"No love, they are an all-female pack. No men allowed. But not just that, they are rumoured to have the best, fiercest, most deadly fighters in the entire world".

An all-female pack, what a thought. I have come to realise that the Were world can be pretty sexist. I haven't lived in it for that long, but I can already tell that they have that aspect in common with the humans. But an all-female pack. Everyone equal. How amazing. And an Alpha she-wolf, a woman in such a position of power. I kind of want to meet her. If she is anything like her Beta, I can only imagine how fierce she must be. But all-female would mean no babies, right? No family legacies. Who does the Alpha position pass to if not an heir?

"All-female, how would that work? If they don't have males they can't procreate, how do they maintain their numbers and choose positions?" I asked with a tilt of my head,

"They recruit" Gunner answered in a very blasé kind of way.

"Recruit how?" I demanded.

"I don't know Zelena, that's why I am just as excited about this dinner. I have been wanting to talk with them since they got here" chuckled Gunner as he nuzzled into my hair.

"Oh, well then, I suppose that if even *you* don't know, this is kind of a big deal, huh?"

"This is a huge deal. They have come out of hiding for you, for the Triple Goddess".

"They have?" I gulped. That is a lot of pressure. A mythical all-female pack to reveal themselves to the entire Were world, just so that they could meet me. Holy shit. This is a huge deal.

"I assume so, yes. I have to admit though, I am slightly concerned" he said a little softer now, not wanting anyone else to hear us.

"About what?" I whispered back,

"About whether or not they are really just offering their greetings, or are they trying to recruit you".

"Do you really think so?"

"I don't know, Little Wolf, I'm not leaving anything out. I don't know what they are possible of yet. But I can tell you one thing, if it comes to a fight over you, I will die before I let you go" Gunner said gruffly as he squeezed his arms tighter around me.

"I will never leave you or Tri-Moon, not willingly" I said adamantly.

"I know that, but I don't know anything about them. They may not take no for an answer".

"And if that happens?"

"Never mind about that now, let's just see how dinner goes" he smiled, kissed my head, and then dragged me upstairs to bed.

~

"Do you like this one?" I asked Gunner as I twirled in a circle in front of him, showing off my baby blue silk skirt and soft brown cami top. I had my hair up in a high ponytail, mainly because it was getting long and gets in the way too much. But also because I wanted to show off the mark on top of my shoulder. Now that Nat had shown me the basics and I was feeling alright with my abilities, I put on a touch of light makeup. I can't deny it, but I have actually been enjoying my lessons with Nat about the joys of makeup and beauty products. And I love that my lessons usually end with us in fits of giggles, lots of junk food, and full glam makeup. Spending time with Nat has quickly become one of my favourite things to do. I've never felt overly comfortable with people. That changed with Gunner, then Smith, now Nat. I never feel compelled to hide away or keep my mouth shut with her. I don't have to worry about angering her with what I say or do. It's like I can truly be myself. And I'm starting to like myself more and more.

"You look beautiful, as always" Gunner cooed as he eyed me up and down,

"But the outfit, do you like the outfit?" I asked with a pout. Gunner smirked and strode over to me, his black slacks clung to his muscled thighs and sat low on his hips. That tempting V that rolled from his firm abbs to the band of his pants, had my crotch throbbing. He reached me and leaned down to cup my ass cheeks.

"I like the way it sits over this" he said with a firm squeeze. He then leaned down further and licked over his mark on my shoulder.

"I like the way this is out for everyone to see" he mumbled with his lips pressed against my sensitive skin.

"And I like the way these sit, tempting me from under this flimsy fabric" he groaned as he moved one of his hands to cup my breast and roll his thumb over my nipple. It immediately pebbled at his touch. A fire lit up inside me and my skin crawled with desire.

"Gunner" I moaned. He continued to move his mouth over my exposed neck and collarbones.

"What?" he answered and pulled my earlobe between his teeth.

"Haven't you had enough today?" I groaned with a tolt of my neck.

"There's no such thing when you're involved" he mumbled back.

"You're going to make us late" I hissed. He moved his hand to my inner thigh and pulled my skirt up. His fingers now teased at the seam of my panties and I could feel them slowly becoming wetter.

"We have time" he said softly and moved my underwear to the side so that he could slide his finger along my slick slit. I moved my hands to Gunner's bare chest and scratched my nails along his skin. He hissed and pushed one of his fingers inside me.

"Gunner" I moaned and moved my hips against his hand, forcing him to go deeper.

"Zelena" he groaned back. I pushed hard against his chest and stepped out of his hold. He nearly toppled forward at my quick retreat and growled lowly.

"Time's up, let's go" I smirked at him and fixed my skirt. He glared at me but stood up straight. With his eyes firmly locked on mine, he slipped his finger in his mouth and sucked my juices off.

"You're a tease" he growled and threw me a crooked smirk.

"I learned from the best" I smirked back and slipped on my sandals.

"I'll get you back for this you know?"

"Aw my poor big Alpha baby" I feigned pity,

"I'm counting on it" I chuckled with a wink and turned for the door. Gunner came up behind me and slapped my ass, hard. I squeaked and glared up at him. He kissed my nose and smiled.

"That's just a taste baby doll. And there's a lot more coming your way" he chuckled and walked past me and down the hall.

~

Nat, Smith, Roe, and Lupus were already in the dining hall when we got there, all talking and laughing adamantly. I quickly looked around the room, looking for the one face I hoped would join us. No luck. It seems Cole is still avoiding me. Dammit.

"Hi everyone" I smiled as we walked in and sat down, Gunner now taking the seat at the head of the table and me to his left.

"Hello gorgeous" Nat called as she suggestively wiggled her eyebrows at me.

"Look who's been following my fashion advice" she mused proudly as Smith wolf-whistled.

"Do you like it? I just love this skirt" I said, throwing Gunner a sly smirk.

"You look beautiful, sweet girl" Roe cooed. She sat by Lupus, who gently rubbed his hand up and down her back. They are seriously couple goals. The amount of love that they have for each other is indisputable and I can only hope that Gunner and I are still as close after twenty years.

"Aww, you guys" I chuckled and waved my hand at them dismissively. Tobias walked through the door, letting it slam closed behind him. He turned and glanced at the door, like he was questioning why it slammed so abruptly, then looked back to the table.

"Whoops" he smiled with a shrug of his shoulders. Everyone else went back to their conversations as Tobias walked over to my seat. He placed a kiss on the top of my head and slapped Gunner on the shoulder. Gunner watched Tobias's show of affection and curled his lip back in a snarl, but didn't growl out loud.

"Glad you're feeling yourself again, Goddess" Tobias smiled down at me as he moved around my chair.

"Thank you. And thank you for your help with… that whole thing" I said quietly, feeling a little embarrassed.

"Anytime. So, is this it? I thought you said it was a dinner party, Little One" Tobias spoke loudly and took his seat next to me, leaving the side of the table at Gunner's right empty.
"Who invited you?" Gunner asked sourly,
"I did. And they said they're coming" I answered both men. I placed my hand on Gunner's thigh and squeezed. He gripped hold of my hand and squeezed it back tightly.
Calm down, you know there is no need to be jealous
I flashed Gunner and looked up at him through my dark lashes. He grabbed my throat, wrapping his fingers around my neck, and pulled my head to his. He pressed his lips hard against my own and moved them hungrily. I heard Tobias start laughing and say to Roe and Lupus,
"He still hasn't forgiven me for my actions during her heat then" he said boisterously. I smiled and Gunner slipped his tongue into my mouth right as the door opened once again. A rough coughing sound forced Gunner to let me go and we both turned to see who was standing at the door. The Luna Eclipse she-wolf, Elaine, stood in the doorway, with a tall and very beautiful blonde woman just behind her.
"Beta Elaine" I called and stood up quickly. I walked to her and offered my hand, this time she took it without hesitation. Gunner stood and waited by his chair.
"Goddess" Elaine nodded and stepped further into the room to allow the women behind her to follow.
"My Goddess" the blonde woman bowed low,
"I am Phoebe. I offer you my loyalty, from now until my last moon".
"Thank you, Phoebe, and thank you for coming. Please take a seat" I said, motioning to the empty chairs at the table.
"My Goddess. It is an honour to meet you, I too offer my loyalty" the next woman spoke. She was tall, slim, and quite striking to look at. Her deep black hair and dark caramel skin made her look very exotic, though I couldn't place where she might be from.
"Thank you, what's your name?"
"My apologies, I am Venus, my Goddess" she said and bowed with her hand over her heart.
"It's a pleasure to meet you Venus". The next woman through the door was just as intimidating as Elaine. Tall, large and with very serious dark eyes.

"My Goddess, I am Cleo. I offer you my loyalty, my servitude, and my life when you require it" she said firmly, her voice was rough and held a wildness to it.

"Thank you, Cleo. However, let's hope that time never comes" I replied, a little shocked at her proclamation. Are Weres really willing to die for me? I recognised the next woman, Alyse. Her face held a wide smile though her eyes looked nervous.

"My Goddess" she said with a small bow of her head.

"Nice to see you again Alyse, please have a seat" I said as I turned to the table. Once I did, I realised that none of the women had sat down yet, in fact, they all stood with their eyes firmly set on me. The tension they were exuding was strained and somewhat unsure. Like they were all collectively holding their breath. I turned to the next woman with a smile. She stepped through the door and a strange sensation swept through my body. A warmness, a lightness. Something familiar. We both stood, unmoving, gazing at each other. Her clear tanned skin and soft brown hair, the way her brown eyes searched deep into my own, I feel like I've seen it all before. Somewhere.

"Hello" I finally spoke, stepping forward and holding out my hand for her,

"I'm Zelena".

Chapter Twenty-One

Lunaya

I'm not completely out of the woods yet. The Beta didn't confess my secret this time around, but that doesn't mean he won't spill it later. I gritted my teeth and clenched my fists as Cole turned and stormed off.

"What's his damage?" Alyse asked quietly as we watched him go.

"No idea" I replied. Something is very wrong with that boy, and I think it runs much deeper than he is letting on.

"What is he talking about?" Romeá demanded of me.

"As he said, it's nothing" I threw back at her.

"I don't believe you" she grumbled, edging closer,

"I assure you, everything will be revealed in due time. Until then, you will just have to trust me" I said staring at the small she-wolf blankly. Her lips curled back and a small quiet growl came from her, but she didn't argue further. After a minute, the man I assumed to be Gunner's father, whispered in Romeá's ear. She nodded her head and he walked off again.

"Where is Beta Elaine?" a voice called from behind us. I turned around to see Analah with a group of Weres following close behind her. The large man at her side was quite obviously her father. I thought she held a resemblance to her mother, but seeing her next to him, she clearly shares more of a likeness to her father. They were both tall and well built.

She had the eyes of her mother, but everything else was from her father, from the shape of her mouth to the tip of her nose. "She is with the Goddess" I answered and eyed the Alpha at her side.

"Lunaya, Cleo, this is my father Alpha Ambrose, of Lua Chei" she said, gesturing to her father. The man stepped forward and offered his hand. I took it and he pulled me forward for Sevasmo. Not something an Alpha male usually initiates with any random she-wolf.

"My daughter has told me all about you and your travel companions, and I must say, it is an honour to have housed members of the elusive Luna Eclipse on my pack land" he spoke without letting go of my arm.

"Thank you, Alpha, you have a very beautiful home and family" I smiled at him kindly.

"Alpha Ambrose" Romeá said stepping forward.

"Luna-mother. You grow more lovely each day' he laughed and bowed slightly.

"Oh, stop it, don't let my Mate hear you talk like that, he may get jealous" she giggled and waved her hand. Was she flirting with him?

"Thank you for the invitation, what a party it turned out to be huh?" he huffed and looked around at the disastrous area.

"Ah yes, thank you for your assistance. Your strength and self-control are something to marvel at" she said fondly. She is flirting with him. There's some kind of history between these two, they are too familiar, too comfortable for there not to be. They talked and giggled and flirted back and forth for a few minutes, and as much as I wanted to walk away, I still didn't know where we were meant to be staying.

"Excuse me" I butted in,

"Yes, dear?" Romeá cooed overly sweetly, seeming to forget the hostility she held towards me not minutes earlier.

"I wonder if you had any room left for us to bunk down?"

"Oh, of course we do. You can take one of the larger tents, come I'll show you". She turned to Alpha Ambrose and gently touched his shoulder,

"It's good to see you" she smiled and turned to walk away. I eyed the long look on Alpha Ambrose's face as he watched her walk off. I took Alyse's hand and followed after Romeá. Venus and Cleo followed along behind us.

Did you catch all that sexual tension? Alyse Flashed.
I did, there's history there
I wonder what happened between them
Don't intrude, it's not our business
I know, but aren't you curious?
Of course, but she is the mother of my daughter's Mate. I need to keep the peace
Ugh, fine, I'll leave it alone
Thank you

I flashed with Alyse as we walked to the edge of the village, stopping in front of a large tent.

"This one is now empty, the six of you will fit just fine" Romeá said as she stepped to the side and let us through the tent door. It was very large with eight cots in two lines across the floor, the roof was high, allowing us to stand up without interference.

"There is still a lot of food remaining, so if you are hungry or thirsty head over to the first cabin on the right, right in front of the pack house".

"Thank you for your hospitality" I smiled down at her before she turned and left again.

"Well, it's no suite at Trout Point, but it'll do" Alyse laughed and plopped down on a cot.

"I'm pooped" she yawned and curled onto her side.

"Have a rest love" I said softly and pulled a blanket up over her shoulder.

"You said that Elaine and Phoebe are with the Goddess?" Venus asked as she sat down on her own cot.

"Yes, they are guarding the small hut that her Mate has taken them to. Two of us will go and relieve them in just over two hours" I replied,

"I suppose you will be next on watch" she said with a small chuckle.

"Yes" I confirmed, not finding the humour in it.

"Well, in that case, I'm going to relax for a bit. Come find me when it's time to change out, I'll be taking the next watch with you" Venus said smoothly as she ruffled through her bag.

"I'm going for a walk" Cleo grunted and left without a response.

~

I still had an hour to kill before Elaine would let me take over the watch. Alyse was asleep and Venus was lying down in the tent reading a book. After sitting anxiously for an hour, I couldn't take it any longer, I decided to go for a walk and have a look at the place my daughter had made her home. The clearing that held the party was now tidied, back to what I assume was how it normally looked. A few she-wolves were taking down the last of the decorations that hung from trees and posts. I walked through the middle of the village, small houses lined the area, with more lined behind those. All in all, this was a very beautiful pack. But beauty is only skin deep, there could be dark secrets buried here. And I'll be damned if I don't find out everything about this place before I even think about leaving her here. As I reached the tree line, I was about to turn around when a lone figure in the dark caught my attention. It was the Beta Were, Cole, sitting alone on the trunk of a fallen tree. I hesitated for a moment, but something inside me pushed me forward.

I walked over to where he sat and perched myself on the trunk beside him. He didn't greet me or acknowledge my arrival. I sat quietly and watched him from the corner of my eye. The lights from the clearing shone on his face, highlighting the sharp angles of his jaw and nose. But still, the shadows made the dips of his face accentuate the shallow and gloominess. Though he is a handsome man, his eyes hold so much darkness. After a while, once I realised he was not going to speak first, I broke the silence.

"You didn't tell them" I spoke, looking back to the village.

"Tell them what?" he answered, sounding uninterested.

"About who I said I was here for"

"It's not my story to tell" he said leaning back and crossing his arms over his chest.

"You know it's not a story though, I can tell that you believe me" I said, now looking at him.

"Yeah, and?"

"And why didn't you tell them?"

"Because I don't care" he said harshly. I watched the corner of his mouth turn up and his eyebrows furrow together. He's angry. But about what?

"You are the Beta, aren't you?"

"Yes".

"So, isn't it your duty to report all critical information to the Alpha and Luna?"

"Not about this".

"How is this different? I don't understand".

"Then drop it" he snapped.

We sat quietly again for a while. His emotions were all over the place. He was stricken with grief and sadness, and yet it mixed deeply with anger and fury.

"The she-wolf with the freckles, you two are close?" he asked, not looking at me.

"Alyse, yes, she is my Mate" I confirmed. He spun his head and gazed at me for a moment.

"Where is your male?"

"There is no male. It's just us, me and her".

"Alone? Just two females?" he asked again. He didn't sound appalled or angry, he sounded confused or, more so, interested.

"Yes, a lesbian couple. No male".

He turned away again and looked back to the village. After a few minutes of silence, and letting him take in the news of my Mating, I studied his face carefully. He was very interested in my Mating. But I don't think it's just normal horny boy interest. He is invested. Perhaps for a more personal reason.

"Do you have a Mate?" I asked tentatively. He didn't answer, just glared silently at the village before us. His silence only piqued my interest.

"There is someone though, isn't there? Perhaps someone that doesn't feel the same way that you do" I questioned in a soft tone. He whipped his head to me and growled with exposed fangs. I put my hands up and leaned back.

"I'm sorry, that was a private question" I quickly shot out. He relaxed his face and watched me for a second before turning away again.

"If there was someone, someone that maybe other people would disapprove of, or not understand your choice of Mating with, may I offer a piece of advice?". I waited for his response, watching his chest rise and fall in quick succession with his rapid breathing.

"Don't wait. Life is short and uncertain. If you have someone you want to be with, make it happen". I let my hands fall on my lap and linked my fingers. I held back from Alyse's affections for far too many years. Years that we could have been sharing our love. But I was afraid of judgment, of the unknown, of giving myself over to someone new after losing everything I loved. It is one of my greatest regrets.

"He doesn't want me like that" Cole whispered. He spoke so quietly that I almost didn't hear it. But the sorrow in his scent was hard to miss.

"There will be another" I said as I brushed my fingers over his hand in an attempt of comfort. When he didn't recoil, or immediately rip my head off, I considered it a win. We sat side by side, in solemn silence. It must have been at least half an hour, though it could have been longer, that we simply sat together and watched the world pass us by.

"How did you do it?" he asked me quietly.

"Do what?" I answered with a breath.

"How did you live all these years without her, without your family?".

Wow. Where did that come from? How do I even answer that? I knew immediately he wasn't talking about Alyse anymore. I took a sharp breath and thought about my answer. I guess the short answer is Alyse. She didn't let me wallow in my grief as much as I wanted to. She gave me a reason to keep going. But Cole has so much sadness inside him. He is grieving. I don't know how I didn't see it before. He must have lost someone in the attack on his pack. My instincts told me to wrap my arms around the young Were and hold him. I want to soothe him, make him feel better, and tell him everything will be okay. This boy, he's still just a kid, and the mother in me wants to settle him.

"You lost someone?" I said out loud. He didn't answer me, and that in itself was an answer.

"It was recent, wasn't it?" Again, no answer. His breathing became short and harsh and the sadness seeping out of him was painfully obvious.

"Cole, there is no short answer and there is no quick fix. After the hunters attacked and I lost everything, I wanted to die. I prayed for it. But I had Alyse, she gave me something to live for. She lessened the pain, even if I still live with it every day, she made it bearable".

I turned my head to see him, and he was hunched over with his face in the palm of his hands. His chest heaved up and down with ragged breaths and I heard muffled sobs coming from him. I lifted my hand and gently rubbed his back.

"Who did you lose?" I asked him softly. He shook his head and sat upright, wiping his eyes and nose roughly with the back of his hand.

"They killed my mother when I was five, and then they took my father. All because we had to protect her!". He really spat the word 'her' and it made me rear back. Is that who he is angry with? The Goddess, not the hunters?

"You blame her?" I asked, my confusion at the front of my mind. How could it possibly be her fault and how could he honestly believe that it is? Surely, I am misreading this.

"Of course I do. If she never showed up here, everything would still be fine. My father would still be here, and I'd still have my best friend" he hissed angrily.

"It was not her that killed your father, it was not her that brought them here, it certainly was not her that made them kidnap her as a pup. All of that was done by the hunters. Because of their greed, their hate, and their desperate desire to wipe out all of Were-kind. They only saw her as a means to an end, and if she wasn't here, the hunters still would have come eventually. They still would have killed your father and many more. They still would have continued in their mission to kill us all".

He glared at me as I spoke, obviously not liking that I was putting him in his place. His nostrils flared and his lips pressed together hard. After he didn't respond, I continued,

"I understand grief and pain and anger. Trust me, I have known a lot of it. But I also know that your anger is misplaced. You are looking for a reason, for some way to make it all make sense, but you will never find it. The hunters are ruthless, merciless, and unreasonable, they are the true enemy here. Not the Goddess".

Cole sat quietly seething in his anger. I kept my hand on his shoulder, feeling the heat slowly leave his body. After a few minutes, he seemed calm enough, so I decided to continue.

"I can see your side, your reasoning. Yes, they wanted her, and they came to find her. In doing so, chaos reigned down on this pack. But my boy, that was not about her, that was about them. Don't let your anger and your grief take control of your life. If you do, they win. If you do, your mother and your father have died in vain".

"Why are you helping me?" he asked glancing at me quickly.

"Why wouldn't I?" I threw back at him,

"She's your daughter, and I've just told you that I hate her. Why would you continue to talk with me after that?"

"Because I know you don't really hate her. That is just your grief talking. In fact, I think you feel the opposite, I think you care for the Goddess a great deal".

He huffed and growled quietly but didn't respond.

"I think you like her. I also think that you have suffered, you are suffering. A lot is changing, and your usual support system isn't available. But you haven't lost everything, Cole. You still have your best friend, now you have that sweet little girl too".

I can see so much of my young self in this kid. The anger he holds, the grief, and the pain. I felt it all too. And if not for Alyse, I would have given over to it also. Just like Cole is on the precipice of doing.

"Why does it feel so easy to talk to you? I don't even know you?" he asked accusingly.

"Well, that's just because I'm amazing. Can't you tell?" I chuckled and slapped his back. He chuckled a little and I finally saw a light inside his broken soul. After a few moments of sitting together peacefully, a wave of guilt washed over me. I sat straight and turned to look at Cole, it wasn't my guilt I feel, it came from Cole.

"Something is bothering you" I noted.

"I did something" he said softly.

"What kind of something?" I asked, keeping my tone level,

"Something bad" he clipped out.

"Do you want to tell me about it?"

"I can't" he whispered. I sat quietly and thought about what he said. It was no doubt adding to his anger and sadness, whatever it was that he'd done.

"Is it something you can come back from?" I tried to push him as gently as I could, but his words were now making me feel very anxious. What could he have possibly done?

"I... I don't know" he replied, slumping forward once again.

"Look, I don't know what you have done, but I can see you, Cole. You're a good Were. I'm sure that whatever it is, you can find a way to make it better. All you can do is try".

"I don't know about that" he said dejectedly.

"You'll figure it out" I said standing up and patting his shoulder.

"In the meantime, if you want to chat, come find me. We'll be hanging around for a while" I put my hands in my pockets and turned to walk away,

"Wait" he called and stood up also.

"You are going to tell her though, aren't you?" he asked as his eyebrows pressed together, creasing his forehead.

"I will, when the time is right" I assured him.

"Don't wait too long, ay. You've both already missed a lot. And like you said, life is uncertain".

"See, I knew you cared about her" I smiled and walked off back through the clearing. It was time to get Venus and head back to the hut.

Venus was already up and waiting for me, sitting on the edge of her cot. It was just about midnight, Cleo wasn't back, and Alyse was still asleep.

"Ready?" I asked Venus quietly, so as not to wake Alyse. She nodded, stood up, and walked out of the tent. As we walked through the forest an uncomfortable feeling rose in my stomach. The forest itself is quiet and dark. The trees are tall and strong, their thick branches shield the ground from the moonlight. It was eerie quiet. Usually, the sounds of animals fill the air, owls, bugs, and creatures of the forest. But tonight, there was nothing. Nothing but an unpleasant feeling of being watched.

Venus was walking a few paces behind me, lost to her own thoughts. I slowed my pace and allowed her to catch up so that we now walked in step with each other. I scanned the tree line around us, trying not to move my head too much. I lifted my eyes to the tops of the trees and across the earthen floor, searching for any signs of life. There was nothing visible, but something told me that my eyes were being lied to.

"Venus" I whispered, stepping closer to her side,

"Yes" she replied, just as softly,

"Something doesn't feel right" I told her.

"I know, I feel it too. Act normal, don't draw attention and keep walking". We walked for another ten minutes and the feeling only intensified. The unmistakable sound of a twig snapping pricked my ears to attention, but I resisted the urge to turn to the source.

"Did you hear that?" I whispered harshly,

"I did" Venus replied.

"We can't go to the hut, someone is following us".

"We won't. Instead, we are going to go in a large circle. What way is the hut?"

"Straight ahead and to the right, about a half hour further at this pace" I told her as another snap sounded. Whoever is following us is either untrained or just sloppy.

"Okay, we will start to veer left and circle back around to the other side of the territory. No matter what happens stay at my side and stay mutual".

I followed her lead and very slowly we started to move to the left. The feeling of eyes on me remained. After about fifteen minutes the winds changed direction, now coming in from behind us, and the foulest of all smells hit my nose. A Feral. Hot garbage, rotting flesh, and chemicals. The scent changes from Feral to Feral depending on the depth of their wildness, but the key elements always stay the same.

"Can you smell it?" I whisper-hissed,

"Yes" Venus whispered back.

"If it's just a Feral we can take it down".

"We don't know if it is just one Feral. There could be more than one or it could be a trick"

"Ferals don't do tricks" I huffed quietly, my frustration taking centre stage.

"No, but smart Weres that know how to manifest the scent do".

I didn't think of that. I need to give Venus more credit, she may be young but she is smart. We continued on our long walk, the Feral didn't get any closer. In fact, after the winds shifted, the smell slowly disappeared, the further we continued to walk. It's smart, probably still has a hold on its humanity. This means it's either still on the cusp of becoming full Feral or it has only recently lost its human. Or Venus is right, and it is just a ruse to make us let our guard down.

"It's gone" Venus spoke, still staying quiet but no longer whispering.

"It's smart" I replied,

"What are your thoughts?" she asked,

"Meaning?"

"Meaning do you really think a rogue Feral stumbled into the territory at the same time the Goddess made her appearance?"

"You don't think it was a Feral" I said. I didn't need to ask, I could hear it in her tone.

"I don't. I think there is a bigger game at foot here"

"You could be right" I agreed,

"And you? Do you think it's just random?"

"Nothing is random when it comes to the Triple Goddess" I said firmly.

~

Once we arrived at the little hut, over an hour later than originally planned, we greeted Elaine and Phoebe and briefed them about the near encounter in the forest. Elaine decided she would do a full sweep of the forest before heading back to the village. Phoebe agreed easily and Cleo was called to join them through Elaine's flash. My argument about Alyse being left alone in the village was nullified. Finding the scout in the forest was more important, as much as I hate to admit when I am wrong, this time I was. Alyse is surrounded by warriors and diplomats, she'll be fine.

Midway through our debrief, the screaming started up again. The girl's pain filled screams were dulled by the layers of the hut, but I could still hear them, as if she were screaming directly into my ear. It ripped at the pieces of my heart, and I so desperately wanted to comfort her. I can't though, and that caused me more pain than the sound of her torture.

"You will not enter the hut" Elaine demanded, looking directly at me.

"I won't" I assured her weakly.

"I mean it Lunaya. The Luna-mother made it very clear, we are to guard only. Can you be trusted with this?" she admonished me.

"I won't go inside, I swear it" I replied, giving my tone the extra firmness that Elaine was chasing. After seeming satisfied with my response, she continued,

"Okay then, two more she-wolves from Tri-Moon have come to guard. They are currently running a small perimeter. They seem capable enough, but under no circumstances are they to be left at the cabin alone. Understood?"
"Yes Beta" Venus confirmed, and I nodded along.
"We aren't to trust the Tri-Moon pack?" I questioned. My imagination filled me with questions and reasons as to why Elaine would make such a call.
"Until we can be certain of their loyalty and faithfulness to the Goddess, only us, only the Weres I trust will be left alone with her".
I felt warmed by the fact that Elaine just inadvertently said that she trusts me, but cautiously wary of her stance on the Tri-Moon pack members. There is a lot of good here, I can see that much. But we really don't know anything about them, any of them, my child included. Elaine is right to be cautious. And dammit, I just handed it to her again. Shit, maybe my aversion to Beta Elaine is slipping, if not already gone. Fuck, I like her. I had come to respect her since our descent down the mountain, but I wanted to hate her so badly.
"Keep in contact via flash and keep your eyes open" Elaine said looking from Venus then to me, obviously because I can't flash with her.
"We will" both Venus and I said at the same time. She smiled and turned to look at me and mouthed the word 'jinx'. I chuckled softly and shook my head, it's easy to forget how young Venus is. She always comes across as so mature and serious, when in fact she is only a couple of years older than my daughter.
Without saying another word, Elaine and Phoebe jogged away into the forest. Venus took her stance at the door, and I began my walk around the hut, scoping out the structure. There is only one window on the building, the broken glass has been bordered over by a plank of wood. To anyone else, it would just look like a decrepit run-down building. If wanderers were able to get this far into the woods without being chased out by the pack patrol, they would probably just waltz on past the structure. If not, the singular boarded window and thick padlocked front door should deter them.

I stood on the opposite side of the hut to Venus and scanned the surrounding forest. After a good twenty minutes, two she-wolves came jogging through the trees towards where I stood. I leaped forward, my claws sprung free and I growled a warning to the two women.

"Stop where you are" I demanded of them,

"Chill lady, we're of Tri-Moon, here to watch over the Luna" one of the she-wolves spat with her palms up in front of her. I roamed my eyes over both of them, looking for signs of insincerity. They were a little shocked, if not fearful, but they showed no signs of dishonesty. I stood up straight, nodded my head, and withdrew my claws.

"Your names?" I asked them, still holding onto my authoritative tone.

"This is Casey, and I am Faylene" the first one spoke, first pointing to the girl beside her and then at herself.

"What news around the perimeter?" I asked them firmly.

"Two males from Howlers were wandering around the forest. After a brief interrogation, they admitted to wanting to get away from the village and the scent of the Goddess in order to stay loyal to their mates. We sent them back to the village with assurances that the Goddess was no longer there" Faylene told me. She was tall, slim built, and possibly in her early thirties. Clearly the leader of the two.

"You told them her location?" I growled lowly,

"I'm not fucking stupid. Of course I didn't tell them where she was" she snapped back. The younger woman next to her, Casey, almost broke her neck with how fast she turned to glare at Faylene.

"Watch your disrespect she-wolf" I roared letting the full power of my voice roll over them. Faylene shied away, turning her head to the side and dropping her shoulders. Casey trembled and bowed. Like an actual bow. No one has ever bowed to me before. I didn't know that my voice could elicit such a response.

"I'm sorry, it's just been a long night" Faylene mumbled softly.

"Apology accepted. And good job on the Howlers. My packmate and I will watch over the cabin, I want you two to continue to scan the surrounding forest area. Keep a three-kilometre radius and one of you needs to report back every half hour. Understood?"

"Yes Miss" they chorused and turned and walked back through the trees.

I took my place back by the window and let my eyes roam across the foliage, up the trees, and deep into the darkness. The screaming was intermediate. Loud and shrill one minute to moaning and groaning the next, but there was hardly any respite. Casey came back first and reported that there was nothing to report. Faylene came back next with the same. After she left, I heard movement from inside the cabin and ran around to the door. Gunner stood in the doorway with his teeth bared, growling down at Venus who was growling back.

Chapter Twenty-Two

Lunaya

"Alpha Gunner," I called to him as I approached. He turned to me, and the aggression on his face dissipated instantly.

"I'm sorry, I have forgotten your name," he said quietly, running his hand over his face. The look of exhaustion was evident in his dark eyes.

"That's okay, Alpha. You've had a long night. I am Lunaya, this is Venus, she is also from Luna Eclipse. Two of your she-wolves are scouting the perimeter," I told him eagerly.

"Which she-wolves?" he asked, his voice sounding somewhat disinterested whilst still holding a demanding tone.

"They told me their names were Casey and Faylene".

"Okay good, Faylene is second in command to my highest-ranking commander. You can trust her" he said tiredly.

"Yes Alpha" I replied. He went to turn back inside but stopped and turned back to me again,

"I forgot, I have called for my sister, she is bringing us some supplies" he mumbled, swaying a little on his feet.

"Alpha, have you had any rest?" I asked him, stepping forward and gingerly taking hold of his shoulder. He threw his eyes to where my hand met his arm, and a wary look came to his face. After a second, he turned his eyes to mine, and with a suspicious frown, he slowly stepped out of my reach.

"I haven't been able to calm her" he admitted softly.

"She hasn't woken long enough for you to mate together? You know that is the only way to ease the pain?" Venus said accusingly. Gunner glared at her and snarled.

"Yes, I'm perfectly aware and as I have already stated, I will not rape my unconscious Mate" he spat.

"That is admirable Alpha Gunner, many in your position would not be so... accommodating" Venus said smartly, crossing her arms over her chest. She was testing him or pushing him. But for what, I wasn't sure. I threw her a cautious glance and she responded with a small shoulder shrug.

"Thank you" Gunner growled lowly, well aware of Venus's hidden overtone. Gunner went to turn back to the door but paused.

"One more thing" he said turning back to face me,

"Yes, Alpha?" I asked.

"There will be a meeting at daybreak for all the lead diplomats. My Beta, Cole, is organizing it and running point. I would like for yourself and your Beta to attend" he said firmly. It was clear that the invitation was non-negotiable.

"As you wish, Alpha Gunner" I agreed with a small bow of my head. He huffed lowly, glared at Venus over my shoulder, and then went back into the hut.

"What was that?" Venus asked with a sly smirk,

"What was what?" I groaned, turning to face her.

"The whole 'as you wish' thing" she said in a mocking tone.

"He is the Alpha of this pack and Mate to my daughter. We need his approval to stay on pack land and I need his acceptance if I am to get to know my child. Your attitude is not helping" I snapped.

"Okay, you're right. I'm sorry" Venus smirked with her hands up in surrender.

"I just... I don't like males, especially Alphas. But I'll try to ease up on him, I swear" she said with a little more softness. I watched her face fall and her eyes dart away from me at her confession. She looked around the forest, to the ground, to the sky, anywhere but back at me. I don't know anything about her past, only that she came from India. But I wasn't going to shake the comment she made about Alphas. The motherly instincts in me want to push, to get her to open up about what happened to her. But I know it isn't my place and forcing her to talk won't help her. We aren't exactly friends, just travel companions. But damn me and my maternal instincts, the urge to soothe her thoughts and protect her from harm is strong.

We stood together at the front door for a little while longer. As much as I wanted to, I didn't press Venus for details on her comment. Casey came back again with nothing to report. Soon a tall she-wolf with short blonde hair, carrying a sports bag, came through the trees. She wasn't surprised to see us, but she approached slowly and cautiously anyway. I could see the likeness between her and Gunner, and need not ask who she was.

"Hello" she said as she approached,

"I'm Alpha Gunner's sister, he's expecting me". She came to a stop a few steps in front of where Venus and I stood. She straightened her back and rolled her shoulders, allowing her to stand taller and more confident.

"The Alpha is with the Goddess" Venus said from beside me.

"I know that. He asked me to bring these for him" the sister replied and dropped the bag at our feet. I smirked at the huffing sound Venus made and swallowed the chuckle that bubbled in the back of my throat.

"I will make sure he gets it" I said stepping forward and picking up the bag. The screaming started again at that moment, and the sister snapped her head to the door. Concern engulfed her face, her eyes wide and anxious. She took a step forward and Venus blocked her path. The girl growled lowly and hissed.

"Move" she seethed edging closer again.

"You've done your duty, now go" Venus growled back,

"She is my sister, this is my pack. You don't give the orders around here she-wolf" the sister roared. She has quite the bark on her. But does she have the bite to back it up? As entertaining as a showdown between these two youngsters would be, I doubt the Alpha, Alpha-mother, and Beta Elaine would appreciate it. I placed my hand on Venus's shoulder and held firm.

"The Goddess is with her Mate, she is in heat, and they are alone. What do you think you would be walking in on?" I said to her, using the words that Roe said to me not a few hours earlier. It worked, just as it did on me. The she-wolf stopped growling and put her canines away. She shook her head, blinked rapidly, and scrunched up her nose.

"Right, of course" she said with a disgusted scowl. Probably picturing her brother in the throes of passion with her sister-in-law, judging by the repulsed look in her eye.

"We will take care of it. Best head back to the village" I told her as I moved in front of Venus. She looked me over for a few moments, studying my face and body carefully. Her head tilted to the side, just slightly, a look of recognition or familiarity graced her features, and I immediately went on alert.

"Have we met before?" she asked me pointedly,

"Not that I am aware of Alpha-daughter" I replied without hesitation. She eyed me again, and Venus growled quietly.

"You're sure?" she questioned me. A slow panic began to fill my stomach. Perhaps my child looks a little too much like me, and this she-wolf is the first to notice. If they are as close as I assume they are, then it would make sense that she can spot the characteristics that a mother and daughter share. The Mate would have been too consumed in the heat to take notice, but the sister. She would see it.

"I promise that we have not met, young one" I assured her and turned my gaze away.

"Okay" she said slowly, still eyeing me curiously before turning away.

"Make sure my brother gets that" she called over her shoulder and began to jog off through the trees.

"That was weird, what's that about you think?" Venus wondered out loud.

"Not sure" I quipped quickly. I turned and went for the hut door. I placed the bag on the only piece of furniture in the space, a little wooden table. I paused in the middle of the room, letting the screams of pain echo around me. The poor child. She is nineteen now, she would have had dozens of heats by this point in her life. Could each bout of heat have been as intense as this one? Surely not, the pack was unprepared and unaware of it. Why is this one so different? I should have been around to teach her, to show her ways to alleviate the pain. I shook my head and went back out the door. The sun was not far from rising. The eastern sky was slowly starting to lighten. The next two guards should be arriving at any time now. Cleo and possibly Alyse I imagine. I took my place next to Venus at the door crossed my arms over my chest, and let my child's screams and wailing fill my ears.

~

I was right, Cleo and Alyse appeared not long after the sister left. The sun was now visible through the trees, meaning the meeting that Alpha Gunner spoke of would be starting any time now.

"You need to go, the diplomats are gathering for the meeting. Beta Cole is expecting you, and Beta Elaine is already waiting" Cleo said as they came to stop in front of us. I looked to Venus, and she nodded her head, indicating she was okay to return to the village alone.

"I'll debrief, you go" she said with finality. I quickly kissed Alyse on the cheek and ran off through the trees. The run would take a while in this form, and it's time I don't have. I cracked my head to the side and then to the back. My nose elongated into a snout and my body fell forward, landing on four paws. I picked up my speed and dashed through the forest in a blur. I came to the village edge in no time and saw Elaine in the distance. She was standing at the bottom of the porch steps that led up into the pack house. Her eyes found me as I burst through the trees, and she waved me over.

"Hurry up, we are the last ones to go in" she hissed at me. I changed back and stood in front of her, buck-ass naked. She groaned and mumbled to herself as she stomped up the steps of the porch. She didn't go through the door though, instead, she turned and walked over to the railing. I saw what she was doing then, there were clothes lined up, draped over the railing. She grabbed some and came back to me and thrust them into my chest, all while groaning about horny males and that we can't be naked whenever we want anymore. She wouldn't admit it to my face, but I could already tell she was missing Luna Eclipse.

I pulled on the large grey shirt and black shorts and then we hurried into the pack house. I followed behind Elaine as she pushed open a large brown door. Once we stepped inside, the chattering and booming voices stopped, and all eyes turned to us. I looked around the room at all the Weres in attendance. The large room was packed to capacity. I picked up some Alpha auras, some Betas, and one or two Lunas.

"Beta Elaine, Lunaya, thank you for joining us" Cole boomed from the other side of the room.

"Please come and take a seat" he motioned to two empty chairs to his left, next to the Luna-mother and her Mate, the former Alpha. We slipped through the crowd of diplomats, and each set of eyes followed us closely as we made our way over to the empty chairs. We took our seats, and the room sat in uncomfortable silence.

"Where is Alpha Gunner and the Triple Goddess?" a muscular balding man asked from the other end of the table.

"The Alpha and Luna are not attending. I am holding an open line of communication with the Alpha. He can hear all and will answer your questions, within reason" Cole replied without hesitation. The same man then turned his eyes upon Elaine and I.

"Are the rumours true?" he announced, not exactly directing his question to us specifically,

"You have come from Luna Eclipse?" he asked eyeing Elaine curiously. The tattoo on her chin would be a dead giveaway. At least to the Weres that are familiar with the history and the stories. Luna Eclipse wasn't always in New Zealand, they have moved all over the country through the centuries. But tattooing or marking the higher ranked pack members has been a long held custom. Elaine took a deep breath and released it slowly, seemingly frustrated. She stood and placed her hands on the tabletop in front of her. A wave of her aura swept through the room. If anyone still had doubts about her position or her strength, they'd been gone now. She hadn't said a single word, yet she still commanded the attention of the entire room.

"Listen closely, as I am not in the habit of repeating myself" she said with her usual firm voice, only this time she let all of the power and authority she had seep into the words.

"Yes, I am Beta Elaine of the Luna Eclipse pack. We are very real and have existed in seclusion for decades. However, it was unanimously agreed that the arrival of the new Triple Goddess is worth revealing ourselves for. We are here for her protection and to assure an alliance between the Luna Eclipse and the Tri-Moon packs. Our loyalty is to that of the Goddess and only the Goddess. We will not entertain your notions of alliances or Mating or friendships with Luna Eclipse. So, save yourself the wasted time, and do not approach me with your futile requests. I will say no more on the matter. Now Beta Cole, if you'd please continue". With that, she sat back down, folded her hands on the table in front of her, and looked up at Cole expectantly. He, along with everyone else in the room, was watching Elaine with awe and caution. Her words were sharp, fast, and to the point. Messing about isn't really one of Elaine's personality traits. One Were, however, held a certain amount of lust and longing in his sceptical gaze.

The mammoth of a man stared at her intensely. His bald head shined under the light and his dark chocolatey skin glistened with a thin layer of sweat. Elaine either didn't notice or didn't care for his attention. I would assume the latter, Elaine notices everything. The Were sat at Cole's right, so he is of some importance in this pack or one of the others. The more I watched him, the more curious I became. Everything about his physical appearance should be daunting and intimidating. But there was something about him, something I couldn't put my finger on. He is different from the others, there is more to him, something magical.

I had gotten so caught up in studying the giant Were, that I had lost track of the back and forth conversation around the table. As I forced myself to concentrate again, I caught on to the fact that the visiting diplomats were upset that Tri-Moon didn't realize that their Luna was going into heat. They argued amongst themselves that they had no way of knowing and that she didn't show any signs. After someone asked why this was the first heat of such magnitude, my interest peeked, it was a question I had asked myself.

"That, we don't know" Cole answered him.

"How could you not know?" the older Were snapped back.

"She was in a coma for three fucking months, it's the first heat since then. We just didn't fucking know. How many more times can I say it" Cole roared and slammed his fists onto the table. A coma? How did we not hear of this already? I jumped to my feet and glared at Cole.

"Why was she in a coma?" I demanded. Elaine lifted her hand and took hold of my forearm.

"The Goddess was shot by a laced bullet in the attack against our pack" he admitted. By the hush that fell over the room, it became obvious that this was new information to everyone but Tri-Moon. This is why Astéri said that no one had heard anything more about her since the attack. Tri-Moon had kept it all under wraps.

"Her injuries were so bad that she was comatose for three months?" I asked. I tried to disguise the concern in my voice, but I don't think I succeeded fully.

"According to the doctor, her wounds were fully healed and the poison was out of her system after just two weeks. Besides the removal of the spleen, there was no remaining damage. The rest we don't know. By all accounts, she should have woken right away. The doctor couldn't give us answers to the questions as to why she hadn't" Cole answered, his eyes briefly looked around the room as he spoke but mostly stayed on my own. He knows about my personal stake in this, he knows why I care so much.

"So, you think this last heat is just a consequence of her coma? Because she was unconscious for her last three bouts?" a handsome Alpha said from the seat across from me. His white teeth shined through his perfectly shaped beard and his country twang filtered into his question. I have developed my own theories, but none that I am prepared to voice. So, I slowly sat back in my seat and turned to Cole for his answer.

"Artemis, you can answer these questions better than Gunner or I can. Will you take over please?" Cole asked as he turned to look at an old man standing in the far corner of the room. I hadn't even noticed him standing there. He stepped forward and walked around the table to stand next to Cole.

"Triple Goddess was sleeping, yes, three months with no heat. Is possible she feels it all now" he said slowly. His thick Greek accent was dominant in his voice.

"You don't sound convinced" Elaine spoke up from beside me. Artemis whipped his eyes to her, and he eyed her for a moment before his eyes shifted to me. His gaze was pointed and scrutinizing. He was looking into my soul, searching the inner corners of my eyes for my secrets. His eyes widened and he took in a sharp breath. There is something about him, something off.

"Artemis?" Cole said softly, looking at him with concern.

"I am not convinced" he said while keeping his eyes on mine. "Tell us then, what is your assumption, Prophet?" Elaine said firmly. Multiple gasps were heard from around the room at the term 'Prophet'. How could she possibly know if he was a Prophet? I understand that she has experience with Seer's, seeing as she lives with Pappi. But a Prophet? A Seer has natural power and ability, something that is tangible to the people around them, therefore not easily impersonated. A Prophet is not so easily recognized, as not all of them are powerful, and in most cases, the majority of them are frauds. Traditionally a Prophet is just a holy man, a disciple of the Goddess that claims to hold a direct line of contact. Weres have popped up all over the world claiming to speak to the Goddess and spread her word and prophecy. Whether this one is real or an imposter is anyone's guess.

"You're mistaken, Beta Elaine, Artemis here is a healer. A very powerful and talented healer, but he is not a Prophet" Roe's Mate said. I am still yet to get his name.

"You are?" Elaine asked him,

"Forgive me, I am Lupus, former Alpha of Tri-Moon" he said as he put his hand to his chest and tilted his head.

"Greetings, Alpha Lupus" Elaine responded with a tilt of her own head.

"Perhaps I am mistaken" Elaine bit out through clenched teeth. She's lying. She doesn't think she is wrong at all. I flipped my gaze between the two of them. At no point did Artemis deny the accusation, though he didn't confirm it either. After a moment all eyes were turned back to Artemis for his assumption.

"Artemis, you were about to tell us your theory" Elaine pushed.

"Yes. At ceremony, powerful magic was used. Moon Goddess came down, touched Triplí Theá. With extra magic and power from Moon Goddess, it has made her more" he said through his broken English.

"That's ridiculous" someone spat from the back of the room. More voices joined into the dispute of this theory until the room was alive with a mash of indistinguishable words. I looked around at the yelling and tense faces.

"Artemis" I spoke loudly to catch his attention, though it seemed I already had it. He was watching me still.

"You are sure about this? You think the Moon Goddess visited?" I asked him. The room slowly hushed again, to allow Artemis to answer my question.

"Yes" was all he said. That's a very 'Prophet' like theory.

"Alpha Gunner accepts and agrees with Artemis" Cole announced loudly.

"He said that during the ceremony the Luna told him she could feel the presence of the Moon Goddess" he continued.

"Alpha Gunner said this?" a strong and bulky looking Were with tattoos and curly hair asked from across the table. His aura was powerful, very powerful, and overtly dominating. He's a strong Alpha for sure.

"Yes, I told you, he is listening" Cole said as he tapped the side of his head.

"And did he feel it too? Did he feel her presence?" the same Were asked again.

"He is not sure, but would believe it if Artemis agrees". All eyes turned back to Artemis, who just nodded his head. I grabbed hold of Elaine's shoulder and pulled her across to my face. I pressed my cheek to hers and whispered softly into her ear,

"When we arrived at the border, I told Alyse that I could feel magic in the air".

"And you didn't think to mention this before" Elaine hissed back,

"I didn't think it was relevant before. It's not just that, I think she spoke to me. I heard a voice in the wind that was telling me to go to her. That was right before we ran to the village and found it in chaos. The Moon Goddess was there, she told me to find our daughter" I said with assurance. Elaine sat back and stared at me wide eyed. I couldn't tell if it was disbelief or admiration on her face.

"Ahem" a sound caught our attention. It was Cole, he was watching our exchange, as was Artemis and the giant bald Were.

"Care to fill us in?" Cole asked sarcastically.

"No" Elaine snipped back. Cole snarled before he turned to Artemis again.

"So, if the Goddess did visit the Luna, their bond, their shared bloodline, it could have affected her? That could be why the Luna went into heat so fast and so strongly?" Cole asked him.

"Yes" he replied bluntly. Artemis isn't much for words apparently, which is unusual for a Prophet.

"Well, that is good enough for me" Lupus bellowed as he stood,

"The Luna mother has arranged breakfast for everyone, it will be served outside shortly. Unless there is anything further, Beta Cole?" he asked, glancing at Cole.

"Actually, Beta Cole, I would like a private word if you please" the curly haired Alpha said as the rest of the room began to rise from their seats.

"Of course, Alpha Lace. Thank you all for your time. I know some of you are headed back to your own lands immediately, please seek me out before you depart. For the rest of you, if you need anything during the remainder of your stay, please let me or Delta Smith know" Cole called as the group of Weres began to filter out through the door. I followed behind Elaine as we exited through the door and continued outside onto the porch. The rest of the diplomats met with their waiting pack members and scurried off to the food tables spread out in the middle of the village clearing.

"Beta Elaine" a strong and velvety male voice called from behind us. We turned around to see the gigantic bald Were towering over us, staring intensely at Elaine.

"I just wish to introduce myself" he said smoothly,

"Very well" Elaine grumbled back.

"My name is Tobias, former Alpha of Blue Moon pack, now lead advisor of the Tri-Moon pack. It is an honour to meet you" he said smirking slightly at Elaine. He bowed low but kept his eyes on hers.

"Former Alpha?' Elaine questioned, curiously. Or as curiously as Elaine gets.

"Yes ma'am. I passed the role to my brother and joined Tri-Moon after the battle with the hunter clan" he told her. The amount of sexual tension and desire he was emitting was sickening, probably more so to a lesbian like myself. But that's fine because apparently, I have become invisible.

"You handed over the position? Why?" Elaine snapped. I have never seen her show so much interest in anyone who wasn't from her pack. Interesting.

"Yes ma'am. I needed to be closer to the Goddess" he answered, not at all put off by her harsh tone.

"Why would you need to do that?" I asked him. He looked at me as if only now seeing me for the first time. He smiled at me with a puzzled and questioning look.

"I am her guardian, of course" he said it like it was obvious, like it was common knowledge. I know the tale of the first daughter Selena having a guardian, appointed to her by the Moon Goddess. Only the story goes that they fell in love and became Mates. There has been only one other recorded Guardian throughout history, that was when the first clan of hunters became more of a cult with an actual following, and less of a nuisance to Were-kind. It was then that the first pack massacre happened by mere humans. The All Mother must have foreseen the danger because the guardian protected the Goddess and secured the continuation of the line. Well, obviously. Or I wouldn't be here.

Elaine looked to me for confirmation, and I just shrugged. How should I know if it's true? Though if it is, then this daughter must be the most powerful of them all. Or a harrowing danger is coming our way. Why else would the All Mother grant her a guardian?

"Her guardian?" I questioned him again, taking a small step closer.

"Yes Miss, selected by the Moon Goddess herself" he said proudly.

"It can't be" I whispered to myself,

"Sorry?" Tobias asked.

"Nothing, excuse me" I blurted out before rushing down the steps and off to our tent. Elaine's footsteps thundered behind me. I flopped down on the cot and flung my arm over my eyes.

"What is it?" Elaine asked firmly,

"Is it the guardian?"

"If it's true, if he was really selected to be her guardian, this whole arrival could be a bigger deal than we know" I told her.

"What do you mean?" Elaine demanded.

"The last chosen daughter to be appointed a guardian was when the first clan of hunters was formed. Before that, it was Selena. She has been the most powerful of all the past Triple Goddesses. If it's been decided that this girl needs a guardian too, then she is either just as powerful as Selena, if not more so. Or the Moon Goddess is anticipating trouble".

~

It was another day and a half until Alyse flashed to tell me that the Goddess was awake again and coming back to the village. We had maintained our rotation of guards at the hut the whole time. There was no trouble and no further signs or Ferals. Perhaps that one was just a random one-off. A lot of the diplomats chose to return to their homes. All except for Alpha Ambrose and his men from Lua Chei, the Alpha Lace and some of his men from Howlers, and Alpha Travis from Waning Wolf.

The novelty of members of the mythical Luna Eclipse being around didn't die off. The she-wolves were enthralled and constantly close by, trying to work up the courage to approach. Cleo quickly became known as a no-go-zone. With her almost constant wolf form and the growling and snarling at anyone who tried to talk to her, they all soon learned to keep clear. The guardian Tobias is an interesting creature. He is fiercely protective of the Goddess, this became evident after he nearly bit the head of a Howler for simply talking about what her scent made him want to do to her. But it has also become apparent that he holds no romantic connection to her. His eyes and desire appear to follow Elaine, wherever she goes. Elaine maintained an 'I'm not interested' stance, though I caught her eyeing him on more than one occasion. I could be reading it wrong, but I think there is interest on both sides.

The idea that the Goddess is ready to come back had my head spinning. I sat on the edge of my cot with my head in my hands. I wanted to rush out and meet her halfway, but I couldn't do that. I need to let her come to me. Gunner's sister is already too curious about me and hasn't let go of the fact that she thinks we have met before. Romeá is also starting to show more interest in me, encouraged by my initial run-in with Cole and his cryptic comment. My secret won't stay hidden for long. I just need a minute with her before it comes out. I need to know for sure that she is who I think she is, my lost child.

Alyse burst into the tent, breathing heavily with a wide smile on her face.

"What is it?" I asked her cautiously optimistic,

"We've been invited to dinner tonight at the pack house, to meet the Triple Goddess" she said excitedly. I swallowed the ball of vomit that rose in my throat and tried to brush off my nerves. Alyse came to sit beside me and wrapped her arm over my shoulder,

"This is a good thing. You will finally get to meet her after all these years" she said soothingly.

"What if the Seer was wrong, what if she isn't my child?"

"When have you ever known a Seer to be wrong?" she chuckled,

"I don't know, I'm sure it's not completely impossible".

"Nae, what are you so nervous about? You've waited all this time and now that it is finally coming to a head, you're acting like a cornered rabbit. Buck up. And get ready to meet your baby" Alyse said giving my shoulder a squeeze. Her encouragement was really all I needed. It's all I ever need. I don't know why I worked myself into such a stupor. I am excited. Really, I am. There is just so much to fear, so much that can go wrong.

We all showered and dressed nicely for dinner, even Cleo got into the spirit of it, donning one of her nicer looking blouses with a pair of tailor trousers. We headed to the house together and were led to a set of large double doors. I hung to the back to let the others go in first. Once the door opened a sweet voice called out Elaine's name. I listened to her greet each she-wolf and they offered their loyalties. Alyse gave my hand a quick squeeze before she stepped through the door.

"My Goddess" her angelic voice sang,

"Nice to see you again Alyse, please have a seat" the child replied. I stepped through the door and my eyes fell upon the most beautiful woman I have ever seen. Her dark ebony hair hung down from her ponytail and her pale silky skin shone under the light. She turned to me with a smile on her face and all I could see was Micha. She is him in every way. The hair, the skin, the smile, and the bright golden eyes. She is every bit her father's daughter. Our eyes connected and we stood still, staring intently at each other. A lifetime could have passed in that moment, and it would still not be enough. This is my child. She is my daughter. She is here, she is real. And she is mine.

"Hello" she said softly, stepping forward and holding her hand out for me.

"I'm Zelena" she smiled sweetly. I could feel the tears burning at the back of my eyes, threatening to fall down my face. Zelena. My Zelena. The name I gave to her, and she kept it all this time. Nearly eighteen years apart, but still, a part of me stayed with her. I pushed down the lump in my stomach and took a deep breath. Stepping forward I reached out my hand and wrapped my fingers around hers. Her body tensed, and her hand gripped mine incredibly tight. Her wide eyes lit up and shone a bright yellow before they rolled to the back of her head. She expelled a quick harsh breath, and her body dropped to the floor lifelessly.

Chapter Twenty-Three

Zelena

I feel warm. Not that the air is hot, it actually feels cool and calming against my skin. But on the inside, my chest, my stomach, my cheeks, they all feel wonderfully warm and cosy. I opened my eyes and sat upright. I was in the forest. But this is not the forest around the pack lands, it looks the same, but not. I was back in the white forest, the same one from my dream. As I slowly stood up, I looked down at myself. I was wearing the same clothes, the silk skirt and soft cami, only now they were crystal white and shimmering in the light, and my feet were bare. I started to walk through the trees. My body was on autopilot, going exactly where it needed to go. The field of white flowers came into view, and as before, the figure of the beautiful woman sat in the middle. I walked over and sat down beside her. All the while my eyes were completely entranced by her celestial beauty. She turned to look at me and smiled sweetly. I gasped audibly. I don't know if it was from her unnatural beauty or the feeling of peace that enveloped me. I stared at her perfectly symmetrical smile with perfectly white teeth. Her pure white eyes were daunting at first but the love she expressed through them was tangible. Her beautifully clear skin looked like it was alight with the shine of a thousand crystals. I don't know if it's just because she is dazzling to look at, but she seems to glow from within.

"Welcome back, daughter of mine" she sang, her voice like a symphony of the most glorious bells. Sensual and relaxing. She reached out her long thin fingers to gently stroke my cheek affectionately, her soft skin was unlike anything I had felt before.

"Back? I have been here before?" I asked her. I was a bit surprised by the sound of my own voice, it sounded like the softest velvet, delicate and alluring. It whispered around us like a gentle breeze.

"Many times, young one. I enjoy having you here" she said turning back to the flowers in front of her. I remember seeing this place in my dream, the strange white trees and all white flowers. Now that she is in front of me once again, I remember her too. But I don't remember many visits. I can only picture her face and this forest from one time, the time I dreamt of it in the bathtub with Gunner. But that's all I thought it was, a dream. She talks as if this is real, that it is actually happening. How could I have been here many times before and not remember it? How could I visit a place and not know about it? But her voice. The delicate ring of her angelic voice is so familiar to me.

"I'm sorry, I just... I can't... I don't remember it" I mumbled softly. She laughed and tossed her flowing white hair over her shoulder. The sound of her laughter was pure bliss, somehow it filled me with joy and happiness. I smiled broadly and gazed at her. I feel like I have heard the sound of her laughter before.

"No, you wouldn't". Her joyful expression soured for a moment and pain, or maybe guilt, crossed her face, but then she smiled and turned to me again.

"But look at you now. You are everything and more that I always knew you could be" she cooed as she brushed her fingers over my cheek again. The sensation of her soft skin against my own, made me want to melt into the ground in euphoric contentment. I know who she is, deep down, I know it. I can feel it. But still, I have to ask. I have to hear it out loud.

"You're Selene, aren't you? The Goddess of the Moon, the All Mother" I asked her, leaning my face into her hand.

"I am. But you, my sweet daughter, can call me Mother".
Mother. I mean, wow! I may not have been raised as a Were, but I still understand the significance of this interaction. The Moon Goddess herself, my ancestor, right here in front of me. In the flesh, and telling me to call her mother. Is that what she is though? In the flesh? Is this actually real or just another dream?
"Am I dreaming?" I asked,
"In a way, yes. But also, no" she answered me as she released my face and began to fiddle with the petal of a flower.
"I don't understand".
"This is the Ethereal Plane, my home. A mirror image of your own world. However, only myself, and those of my choosing, can visit. For a mortal, I suppose it would feel like a dream, but it is very real". Okay. So, I'm in another world? What the flipping heck! This is totally insane. I can see it and I can feel it, I know it's real and it's happening, but still, I don't think I can believe it. I have so many damn questions, but I don't know where to start. I pinched the bridge of my nose, a headache was starting to form.
"Okay" I said absentmindedly. Selene laughed again and pulled my hand into her lap.
"Don't think so hard, child, just let it be" she chuckled and stroked the back of my hand softly. Her tender show of affection reminded me of something, something rather important.
"Gunner, did you know about Gunner?" I asked her urgently. She giggled playfully and sighed,
"He is gorgeous, isn't he? I'm glad you're enjoying him" she said with a far-off dreamy look on her face. I was hit by a pang of jealousy, and a possessive growl bubbled in the back of my throat. I let her words sink in, and instantly I felt full of embarrassment. She said 'Enjoying him' like he is some kind of sex toy.
"You knew that Gunner and I were going to meet?" I asked while looking down at my lap,
"Of course, I did. He was the perfect choice to be your True Mate".
"Choice? You mean you chose him to be with me?"
"I did".

"Why Gunner? Not that I am complaining, I'm not. I love him with everything I have. I'm just curious" I mumbled quickly, trying not to sound ungrateful.

"Gunner is strong, kind, generous, loyal and I knew he would love you more than anything else in his life. You deserved that. And I knew that together you would both thrive".

"He is all of that, and more" I said dreamily. He is the perfect man. My man.

"You let him access your power, didn't you?" I asked, turning to look at her again.

"It is not my power, child, it is yours"

"But you gave it to me"

"I did"

"So, you did, you let him access it, through me". She smiled and turned her body to face me, still holding my hand firmly in her lap.

"I gave you the power, it was destined to be yours. Did I know that he would be able to use it through your bond? Yes. But the choice to let him access it, was always your own".

"You aren't mad?"

"Of course not, child" she smiled and squeezed my hand. I knew that Gunner and I were more than Mates, more than True Mates. We were destined. Made for each other. Even after all that, there was one thing that was bothering me. Something Selene said that has been repeating itself in my head.

"You said I've been here before?" I said while watching her large white eyes.

"I did, and you have" she answered without missing a beat,

"But why don't I remember it?"

"For some of your visits, you were very young, you brushed them off as just a wonderful dream, something you imagined. Other times, you were suffering and in pain. I brought you here to comfort you. But returning you back to your world with the memory of this place, it would only have caused you more pain".

"You took my memories?" I asked. Shock and betrayal filled my thoughts. That's why I don't remember it, because she stole my memories, she made me forget. How could she do that to me? Why would she do that to me? What else has she taken or hidden from me?

"I did" she answered without hesitation. I blanked for a moment, taken back by her straight up honesty. I expected her to deny it or maybe reason her way out of why she did it. But no. She just admitted it with no worry about my reaction. If I had been coming here since I was a child, then she knew how much I was suffering with Hank. I know that I would have begged to stay. I would have done or said anything for her to let me stay here, away from Hank. She would have seen or at least known about all my torture and my pain, and yet she did nothing. Is that why she stole my memories? To hide the fact that she left me to his devices. My chest tightened, and I could feel the tears threatening to fall. How could she just abandon me?

"Why?" I whimpered.

"Why would you sit by and let that animal beat me and torture me? How could you send me back to him knowing what he was doing to me?" Harsh sobs racked my body. I cried. I mourned. I felt all the pain of my youth. Cool tears flowed down my cheeks as I gasped for air between constricting sobs. Selene didn't answer. She only held my hand gently in hers and stroked her fingers across my skin. After a while, I slowly began to calm down. The tears eased and my breathing regulated. But the pain of feeling abandoned by the one who supposedly chose me is brutal. It was eating away inside me, forcing apart the existing cracks in my brutalized heart.

"Child" Selene whispered gently. I pulled my hand from hers and stood up abruptly.

"No! You call me your daughter and yet you did nothing to protect me. You let that monster break me, again and again and again. He crushed me, he took away every good part of me and you did nothing. Why? Tell me why!" I screamed and the sobs came back in full force.

Selene stood up. She didn't stand exactly, it was more like she floated upwards until she was at eye level with me. She placed her hands on either side of my face and a small smile graced her pale lips.

"Let me show you" she whispered. I scrunched my nose in confusion. Selene leaned in and pressed her lips to my forehead. My body felt like it lurched forward, spinning around while my feet were still planted firmly on the ground.

I was falling, yet not at the same time. I stopped spinning and opened my eyes. It was dark and I was in my old room, in my old house. Hank's house. Only it was different. There is a cot where my bed should be. Inside the cot is a screaming toddler. It couldn't be more than maybe two years old. I stepped forward to gaze at the child. Pale skin, deep black hair, and golden eyes. It's me. I gasped in shock and quickly stepped back. What is this?

The bedroom door flew open with a bang, and a younger, stronger, and healthier looking Hank stood in the doorway. He was glaring across at baby me.

"Shut up!" he roared,

"I would have killed you ten times over by now if it weren't for my fucking orders" he yelled down at the baby and roughly shook the cot by the railing. Baby me reared back and screamed in fear. Hank stormed back out the door, slamming it behind him. I walked to the edge of the crib and gazed down at myself. I reached forward to touch the baby, but my hand was not my hand. It was translucent, with a soft blue glow. I stepped away from the crib and raised my hands to my face to inspect my ghost-like limbs. As I did, a melodic soft humming filled the room. I looked up and saw that Selene was knelt beside the crib, her hand was rubbing slow circles on baby me's back. It was Selene who was humming, a beautiful soft, and internally calming song. The tune flowed around the small room, and as it once again hit my ears, a wave of memories washed through me.

The lullaby was like a catalyst, releasing all of my lost memories back into me. I remember her face smiling down on me. I remember being held to her chest as she rocked me to sleep. I remember the lullaby and the way it made me feel. I remember the calmness, the gentleness, the love. I remember her being there.

My body lurched forward again, and I reappeared in the lounge room. The sun was shining through the front window. Beer bottles and empty takeaway containers littered the floor. Sitting in the middle of the room was me, only now I was older, possibly five or six. I was holding a small dirty and raggedy looking doll to my face. Tears fell down my chubby cheeks as I cried, calling out for my Daddy to come back. This must have been one of the many times that Hank disappeared for days on end, leaving me without food or means to look after myself. Selene appeared in front of the little me and I stopped crying instantly, launching myself into her arms. "Mumma, I'm hungry" little me cried. I called her 'Mumma'. I don't remember that. I don't remember having a mother, or even thinking that I had a mother. Selene pulled me from her arms and sat me back on the ground. She waved her hands in front of her and a plate of meat and vegetables appeared. Little me squealed excitedly and dug into the food, basically inhaling it. Watching the scene, the way she smiled down at me as I accepted her food, another wave washed through me. I remember the taste of the food that she often brought me. I remember her playing with me, bathing me, brushing my hair. I remember her taking care of me when I needed her to. And I remember her disappearing again. But I remember her being there.

Another lurch forward and more spinning. When I stopped and opened my eyes, I was now standing in Selene's white garden. A few meters away is Selene sitting on the ground and in her arms is me. Only this time, I'm a young teen, perhaps around fourteen. Selene is slowly rocking me back and forth and combing her fingers through my matted and dirty hair. My thin and bruise covered arms were wrapped around her neck, while I wailed helplessly into her chest. The sight brought tears to my eyes. I remember being this girl. This scared and broken girl. I remember the fear and the pain, the hunger and the loneliness. This part of me, this life I was living, it really wasn't so long ago. It may feel like a lifetime, but it was less than a year. As Selene calmed and soothed me, she hummed the lullaby again. Once more the memories rush back in. She was there to calm me when I cried, to hold me when I was scared. She helped me through all the pain Hank caused me. So many times, I thought that I was alone in the world, and yet, now I remember her being there. With me. My tears rolled down my cheeks as I watched them together. As I watched us together. I had a mother all along. I just didn't remember it.

I closed my eyes tight as I began to spin again. When I opened my eyes, I was standing across the street from my old house, Hank's house. Walking towards me was Gunner, with Cole beside him. Gunner was carrying something carefully in his arms, but I couldn't quite see what it was. As they got closer, I saw it. He was carrying me. This was the night he rescued me from Hank. I looked down at my former self. Blood covering my face. Bruises covering my exposed legs. Both of my eyes were swollen shut. Hank's ripped t-shirt sat in tatters against my frail body, while burns covered my neck and chest. I was awfully thin and my bones were protruding through my skin. My skin was littered with bruises and scars. I had almost forgotten about all my scars. I wish sometimes that I still had them, as a reminder of what I survived. But in actuality, I am glad they're gone now.

"This was the night it all changed for you" Selene's voice came from beside me. I turned to look at her and she brushed a tear away from my cheek.

"This was the night your journey began" she said with a proud smile.

"You were here this night too. I remember you talked to me" I croaked as I watched Gunner carry me away.

"I was there every night, daughter of mine" she cooed and pulled me into her arms,

"You may not have seen me or felt me, but I was there. Every time".

"Why didn't you stop him? Why did you leave me to suffer through all that?" I whimpered as I pressed my face into her chest. Her scent filled my nose and I remember it. I remember how I loved her scent, how it always managed to calm me. I cried into her chest and she gently ran her hand over my back in slow smooth circles. I remember her doing this too, every time that she held me. After a moment, she answered my question,

"I could not interfere" she said softly.

"But you fed me, you bathed me, I mean you basically raised me. Isn't that interfering?"

"I cannot control the actions of others, nor can I take away the consequences of those actions. But you are mine. Feeding you, taking care of you, loving you, it had no direct impact on the lives of others and therefore not against the rules".

"There are rules?" I asked surprised,

"There are always rules" she chuckled and pulled me away from her chest and held me in front of her by my shoulders.

We were now standing back in the white flower field. Selene cupped my cheek and gazed lovingly at me.

"I was always with you, child. I may not have been able to save you from those atrocities, but I did not abandon you to suffer through them alone. I am sorry that I could not do more for you".

I reached up and grabbed hold of the hand she held against my face and nuzzled my head into her palm. I let out a long sigh and smiled.

"It's okay. You did more for me than I ever imagined. Thank you, Mother". She smiled back at me and pulled my face to hers to kiss the top of my head.

"But what happens now?" I asked, pulling back to look at her.

"Now you go back. There is someone very important that I'm excited for you to meet" she said with a higher pitch and a smile.

"Someone important, who?"

"Ah, that you will see in time" she said cryptically.

"Will I see you again?" I asked,

"Many more times".

"And my memories, will you take my memories again?"

"Not this time, no. They are now yours, forever".

"Why now though? Why did you bring me here and why did you show me all of that? Why not six months ago or two years ago?"

"There is something coming, Zelena. You will need these memories to guide you. I know your life has been hard, and the hard times are not over yet, but you are the daughter the world needs. You are my gift to them. Believe in yourself child, you are more than you think you are".

"I don't know what that means, and you didn't answer my question" I whined exasperatedly. Selene smiled and took a small step away from me.

"Time, daughter of mine. Just give it time. All will be revealed".

"This whole cryptic speech is giving me a headache" I groaned and pinched the bridge of my nose. Selene laughed and tossed her head back.

"You are never a bore, beautiful girl. I'll see you soon" she chuckled. I looked back up at her and she waved her hand.

Before I got to say 'stop', my body felt like it was flying backward, falling through time and space.
I hit the ground and flew upright with a loud gasp. The first thing I saw was Gunner, his worried face leaning over me. I whipped my head around and found Nat sitting behind me and Roe behind her. Then Lupus and Smith, using their bodies as a barricade to keep the very angry looking Luna Eclipse she-wolves back. An aggressive growl caught my attention, and I whipped my head around in the other direction. There I saw Tobias with his hand around the neck of one of the she-wolves, holding her firmly up against the wall. The growl I heard came from her, but Tobias was growling back just as aggressively. In fact, everyone was looking overly angry and aggressive. What the heck happened?
"What the fuck is going on?" I hissed.

Chapter Twenty-Four

Lunaya

Zelena was on the floor, unconscious. I was still holding her hand in mine, but everything else around me was a blur. Her skin tingled against mine. Warmth spread over my hand where we were still connected. I felt dizzy and nauseous. What the fuck just happened? Before I could gather my thoughts and get my bearings back, I was hauled off my feet and my back was slammed hard against the wall. I hit the wall so hard that could swear there was going to be an indent of my body in the plastering. A feral growl made the whole room shake and I was snapped back to reality. My airway was being blocked and my feet were no longer touching the ground. But that wasn't what concerned me. What did, was my child, lying comatose on the floor.

The room burst into a whirlwind of commotion. Gunner and his mother ran to the side of my daughter. Elaine, Alyse, and the others all prepared to attack. The sounds of growls and yelling echoed around the room until it all mixed together in one indecipherable sound. I tried to kick off the wall and rush to Zelena's side, but my movements were blocked. Let go, let go, let go. I screamed internally, frustration gnawing at my body and its lack of directional movement. I have to get to her.

I lifted my head to glare at the one holding me. It was Tobias, the colossal guardian. His wild black eyes bore into me furiously. His canines were fully extended, and a bead of saliva was dripping down his sharp fang, giving his expression a much more dangerous and feral look.

"What did you do?" he roared at me. I gripped hold of the hand on my neck and tried to lift myself, to get a little more air in through my constricted windpipe.

"Release her!" Elaine growled and took a menacing step towards where Tobias had me pinned to the wall. Lupus and a red-haired male that I didn't know, jumped in between us and kept them from getting any closer.

"Stay where you are" the young male demanded. Cleo stepped towards him and growled down at him ferociously. I could see the hair on the back of his neck stand up, his nature called for his wolf to come forward, to protect against the threat Cleo issued. But he didn't change instead he stood up taller and growled back. Brave lad. Stupid, but brave.

"Let her go, now" Alyse barked, I snapped my eyes to her and concern for her safety flooded my thoughts. If they hurt her, I will kill them all, regardless of if they are my daughter's pack. Tobias pulled my body forward and slammed it back into the wall, his way of bringing my attention back to him. My head hit the wall with a thud, and I turned my gaze back to the giant Were.

"What did you do to her?" he growled, leaning his face closer to mine, his canines bared and ready to rip my face off.

"I didn't do anything, I swear it" I gasped out from beneath his tightening grip.

"You're lying" he snarled and snapped his jaws at my face.

"I'm not. I would never hurt her". Gunner stood up from Zelena's side and stepped up beside Tobias. I now had the guardian and the Mate looking at me murderously.

"What have you done?" Gunner snarled, Tobias squeezed my throat and a gagged gasp left my mouth. Phoebe launched herself forward and collided with Tobias's side. I expected him to go down, to stumble, or to at least move. But nothing. Phoebe made no impact on his hold on me. Instead, Tobias grabbed the back of her neck with his other hand and threw her across the room in a very impressive show of strength. If it weren't for the fact that this monster was about to kill me,

I would probably be quite impressed by him. Phoebe hit the wall and a large crack appeared where she collided, and then she dropped to the floor. This had all the Luna Eclipse she-wolves, and Alyse, growling and snapping their teeth. They were ready to fight, and they wanted to.

"Stop!' I yelled and held my hand out to them. Alyse obeyed, and although she was still furious, she backed off and stopped growling. Venus retracted her canines, and her growls quieted down. Cleo and Elaine, however, were each a lethal weapon ready to be released. Cleo was flipping her gaze back and forth between the young male and Tobias. Her lips were curled back, and she was almost at the point of changing. Elaine completely ignored the large frame of Lupus in front of her and was staring directly at Tobias. If looks could kill, he would have been set on fire, covered in flesh eating spiders, soaked in a barrel of acid, and buried in a desolate swamp. I tapped on Tobias's hand in hopes that he would loosen his grip. He did, by the tiniest little bit, not enough for me to catch my breath though.

"I did not hurt her, I swear it. I don't know what happened" I choked, Gunner growled and leaned in close,

"Why should I believe you?" he snarled, his hot breath hitting my face like a hard slap. Tobias's grip tightened, again. and I felt myself gasp for air.

"You're killing her!" Alyse screamed, her pain and panic were evident in her voice.

"Then she dies" Gunner yelled, whipping around.

"If someone doesn't start talking soon, then you all fucking die" Gunner hissed at Alyse.

"We did not come all this way to just kill the Goddess" Venus screamed. The red haired male growled at her, leaning his body in her direction. She faced him and growled back louder. The male stood up straight and tilted his head, staring at Venus with unmistakable interest. My head began to feel quite heavy and black spots appeared across my vision. I was about to lose consciousness, I could feel the darkness lingering close at the edge of my mind.

"We had plenty of opportunities to kill her already. Why would we have wasted our time in protecting her if our plan was to kill her?" Elaine reasoned. She somehow managed to hold off her angry tone and evoke her diplomatic voice. If I wasn't seconds away from suffocating, I'd be proud of her restraint.

"Son, she can't talk to you if she is dead. Let her go" Romeá said from beside Gunner. He growled with his teeth bared, the sound vibrated around the room, shaking the furniture. The Alpha aura was strong and if I wasn't already being suffocated, I would have really choked on it. Just as my eyes began to flutter, I was released. I dropped to the floor and my lungs screamed for air. I lay on my back with my eyes closed, taking huge gulps of oxygen. After a minute I opened my eyes and looked over to my daughter. Her head was cradled in Gunner's sister's lap, and she looked completely peaceful, as if she was just sleeping soundly.

My shoulder was grabbed roughly, and I was pulled to my feet. Tobias held me against the wall once again, only this time his forearm was across my upper chest, instead of his hand around my neck. He and Gunner glared at me with the utmost hatred.

"Tell me what you did to her! Poison? A spell? What is it?" Gunner demanded.

"I promise you, Alpha Gunner, I have not harmed her. I would never harm her" I told him, letting all the truth and sincerity mix with my words. He looked unconvinced.

"As soon as you touched her, she passed out. That is not a coincidence" Tobias said accusingly. I dropped my eyes to Zelena, she was still lying on the floor, out cold. Maybe it isn't an accident. Maybe it has something to do with my being her mother. I don't know. Maybe it's a bloodline thing or a bond thing. I have no clue. But how am I meant to prove my innocence without revealing my secret? I looked at Alyse and Elaine, they were both watching me with careful eyes. Phoebe had now stood back up with the other she-wolves, looking a little angry or disappointed with herself. Alyse had wet tear stains down her cheeks and Elaine looked ready to kill. I have an idea, maybe a stupid one, but an idea nonetheless.

"Call your Beta" I requested. Both Tobias and Gunner raised their eyebrows, only Gunner looked more suspicious of me now.

"Excuse me?" Gunner blanked, Roe grabbed her son's shoulder and pulled him down to her level so that she could whisper in his ear. Luckily for me, they were close enough that I could still hear her,

"Cole said something the other day, about her, about who she really is, or something like that" she quickly whispered. Gunner reared his head back and gazed at his mother before his eyes flicked back to me. His suspicion had turned to anger once again, his eyebrows furrowed together, and the corner of his lips turned up in a snarl.

"Why wouldn't he come to me with this information?" Gunner hissed back at his mother quietly,

"You haven't exactly been on good terms, love. I think you need to call him in now. It's time, whether he is ready or not" she said softly, with a forlorn expression. I knew something was going on, I sensed a lot of animosity when I spoke to the Beta, Cole. He was grieving, but his grief had been fixed to anger, anger that he directed to the Triple Goddess. Perhaps that is the cause of the tension between the Alpha and his Beta. It was a long shot, hoping the Beta would vouch for me. And now that my suspicions of a rift between the two had been verified, my chances of Gunner taking Cole at his word had dropped significantly.

Gunner huffed and closed his eyes for a brief moment, before opening them again and glaring at me. In no time at all, Cole burst through the door with an annoyed look on his face. He froze in place and looked around the room, taking in the scene before him. He looked down at Zelena on the floor, and for just a quick flash, there was concern in his eyes. He quickly put back on his nonchalant mask and turned to Gunner.

"What is this about?" he asked as his eyes found mine. He stepped forward and glared at Tobias, a low growl bubbled from behind his clenched teeth.

"Release her. Now!" he demanded.

"I don't take orders from you, Beta" Tobias snapped back, spitting the word 'Beta'. Apparently, Cole has upset a lot of people around here.

"How do you know this she-wolf?" Gunner asked him as he pointed at me. His loud and firm voice bounced off the walls.

"I took the time to speak with her. Believe it or not, I take my role as Beta seriously, I'm not just going to let anyone roam around my pack" he quipped. Gunner stepped forward and pushed out his chest,

"You mean MY pack" he said condescendingly.

"Whatever" Cole huffed and crossed his arms over his chest.

"What do you know about her?" Gunner demanded. Cole stood tall, staring at his Alpha, but not answering him. His defiance must have hit a nerve in Gunner. Gunner leaped forward and grabbed Cole by the scruff of his neck. He marched them back with speed until Cole's back hit the opposite wall.

"You are the Beta of this pack" he roared,

"You may not have attended the ceremony, but you still made a vow. A vow to protect the pack, honour the rules and obey your Alpha. I am your Alpha, dammit!" Gunner screamed, his voice mixed with anger, pain, and frustration. Cole's hard face softened, just a little, but still, he didn't respond.

"Do you really hate us so much that you would threaten the safety of your Luna, of your pack mates?" Gunner asked him, his hard and violent voice was softer now, almost pleading with Cole.

"I would never" Cole snarled.

"Then why would you keep information from your Alpha, why would you allow the risk of danger?" Gunner yelled in his face.

"Because there is no danger here!" Cole yelled back, he grabbed hold of Gunner's wrist and pulled it off him, shoving him back a couple of steps. Cole stood up tall and stepped forward off the wall.

"I can see her laying there, I'm not fucking blind. I can also see the panic in your eyes, you're blinded by it, by her. I don't care if you don't trust me anymore, but I would never betray my pack". The room was silent, all of us watching the tense interaction between Alpha and Beta. Gunner dropped his head and let out a slow breath.

"Then now is your chance, prove it to me. Tell me what you know" Gunner said softly. Cole moved his eyes to mine, and I knew right away that he would talk. It was written all over his face, an apology. He was going to tell Gunner all that he knew.

"I know who she is, she told me so" Cole said quietly, his eyes still glued to mine.

"And! Who is she, is she here to hurt Zelena?" Gunner asked him urgently,

"You really think so low of me?" Cole asked as he moved his sorrowful eyes back to Gunner.

"I don't know anymore, Cole. You're not the Cole I used to know. You're not my best friend anymore. I don't know who you are now".

"I'm your Beta, your best friend since we were pups. I'm still Cole, and I'm just fucking grieving. It would have been nice to have my best mate around while that was happening". My heart broke for the boy in that moment. He was so broken and so hurt, and apparently, had been facing it all alone. It wasn't hard to guess that this was the boy he spoke about, the one he loved but didn't want him like that. How horribly tragic to fall for your best friend. I wanted to hold him and make it all better. But someone beat me to it. Alyse pushed passed the young male, who was too distracted by the scene to notice. She stepped up to Cole's side and slipped her small hand into his. Cole snapped his head to hers and paused for a moment, I guess trying to decide what to do about her show of affection. Cole lifted his eyes to mine, I smiled weakly and offered an encouraging nod. His fingers tightened around Alyse's hand, and he turned back to Gunner.

"I'm sorry" Gunner said softly.

"I'm sorry about Spartan, I loved him too. I'm sorry I left you to deal with it alone. But Cole, you can't do this anymore, you can't keep shutting us out. You can't keep stuff from me".

"I know" Cole said with a nod.

"And I would never willingly let someone hurt her, you have to know that". I knew he secretly liked her. He wanted to hate her or blame her, he tried to. But I saw it, he cares for Zelena. Gunner turned to look at his Mate, still lying unconscious on the floor.

"I didn't know that, I had no way of knowing that" Gunner's voice started to rise again. He was getting frustrated. I understood his frustration, all I wanted was to hold my child and make sure she was okay. But I couldn't, because they don't trust me.

"It's time to talk Cole" Gunner said firmly. Cole looked over to me once more and pulled Alyse's hand a little closer to his side.

"She's her mother" Cole said confidently.

"She's whose mother?" Gunner asked exasperatedly. Cole didn't answer him, instead, they stood quietly, staring at each other. Romeá snapped her head in my direction, her eyes bore into mine with keen interest. She was a bright woman, very smart and inquisitive. Which is probably where her daughter got it from. Her head was tilted to the side, and she had her bottom lip between her teeth. Her eyes widened and she paled. It took her all of a minute to put the pieces together. Her daughter stood just behind her, mirroring the expression of realization. Romeá gripped hold of her son's shirt and began to shake it roughly. Gunner shook off his mother and stepped closer to Cole.

"I'm running out of patience, Cole" Gunner growled. Romeá grabbed his shirt again and kept shaking him, all the while her eyes stayed fixed on me.

"Mum" Gunner snapped. He pulled himself from her grip and spun around to face her.

"What the fuck are you doing?" he growled. Romeá opened and closed her mouth a few times, trying unsuccessfully to voice the revelation she had made.

"Mum?" Gunner asked with a more worried tone. He stepped forward and grabbed her by the shoulders and tried to get her to look at him, but it was pointless, her gaze was pinned to mine. Gunner followed his mother's eyeline and caught me staring back at her.

"What did you do to my mother?" he snarled and let go of Romeá to step toward me again. Tobias moved his hand back to my neck and growled a warning, right up in my face. Behind Gunner, Romeá started to violently shake her head from side to side. She mumbled the word 'no' a few times before she grabbed Gunner's arm and pulled him back around to face her.

"Aren't you listening? Have you not heard a thing anyone has said?" she snapped at him. He seemed surprised by her harshness, everyone did.

"Use your brain, Gunner, I know it's in there. Think!" she snarled while tapping his forehead. Gunner stared at his mother blankly and then turned to look at his father who just offered him a shrug. He looked down at Zelena on the floor and held his gaze there. The room was silent as we waited for him to put it together. After a few moments, he turned to Cole and whispered,

"She's her mother?".

"That's what I said" Cole answered with a nod. Gunner's eyes finally turned to mine and he blanked.

"Her mother" he whispered to himself. Tobias had loosened his grip slightly, but he didn't release me. Zelena moaned from the floor, the first sign of life she has shown this whole time. Gunner dropped to her side and raked his eyes over her body. Zelena flew upright with a loud gasp and looked around the room. I tried to pull myself from Tobias's hands, to go to her, but he held me firm. I growled at him loudly, warning him to let me go. Instead, he leaned forward and growled back.

"What the fuck is going on?" Zelena spat.

"Babe, are you okay?" Gunner asked her urgently as he pulled her into his lap. She gently cupped his cheek and ran her thumb over his bottom lip before pressing her lips to his. She pulled back and rested her forehead against his.

"I'm fine" she answered him. Her voice held so much love and devotion for her Mate, it was hard not to soften at the sound of it. She pushed herself off him and stood up. She slowly looked around the room, carefully eyeing each Were present. She held her gaze on Cole for longer than any of the others, before finally settling on Tobias.

"Tobias, why are you strangling her?" Zelena asked as she placed her hand on his shoulder,

"I don't trust her" he snarled back, not looking away from me. But I paid him no mind, I was too busy staring at the beautiful creature that is my child. Her magnificent golden eyes looked like pools of warm honey. Her deep black hair made her skin look like porcelain. She is exquisite.

"That is no reason to kill her" Zelena cooed softly at her mammoth guardian. Tobias leaned closer and growled right in my face, I could feel his hot breath against my cheeks. I saw her hand squeeze his shoulder and she stepped closer to him again,

"Can you let her go, please" Zelena requested of him kindly. He growled in my face once more and then slowly peeled his hand from around my neck and stepped back next to the

Goddess. Alyse and Elaine rushed forward, and each of them held onto one of my arms for support.

"What happened?" Zelena asked turning to Elaine. Elaine was about to answer when Gunner cut her off,

"Cole, Smith, take the Luna Eclipse she-wolves to their tent and make sure that they are well guarded. They are not to leave and at no point are they to be left alone" he demanded,

"Son?" Romeá said softly, but he ignored her and pulled Zelena into his chest.

"The Luna and I need to talk".

Chapter
Twenty-Five

Zelena

The Luna Eclipse members were quickly ushered away, rather reluctantly I might add. The woman that Tobias was choking appeared to linger in protest the most. There was still a whole lot of tension in the room. A lot of things need to be said. We need to talk, that's what Gunner said. Talk about what though? About what happened to cause the fight that broke out? About why I passed out? Does he know somehow where I went and who I saw? Maybe I took him with me, like I can during a Drakos vision. Nah, not likely, if he knew he would surely be more excited for me. He knows how lonely I was growing up, we've talked about it a lot. And now I've learned this amazing thing. I had a mother. I want to tell him. I want him to know all about Selene, about the mother I never knew I had, about her raising me. I'm so excited for him to know all of it.

"Leave please" Gunner said abruptly to his parents and Tobias. What's with the attitude?

"You don't want us here for this?" Roe asked meekly,

"No, we need time alone" he answered just as roughly. There was some hesitation there, especially from Roe and Tobias. Both of them desperately wanted to stay, it was plainly obvious on their timid faces. But they left anyway. Lupus guided them out of the dining room, pushing them through the door. He looked back at Gunner with a nod, before closing the door behind him. What the heck happened here?

Gunner rested his cheek on the top of my head and sighed a deep long breath. His arms were wrapped tightly around my waist, it was like he was afraid I was going to slip away. I gently rubbed my hand in slow circles on his back, just like Selene used to do for me. I could feel his reluctance, he reeked of uncertainty. But it didn't put a damper on my joyous mood, it couldn't.

"Gunner?" I said softly, letting my smile spread across my face.

"Wait" he rushed out and tightened his grip around me.

"Just one more minute, let me hold you like this a little longer" he said and then followed it with a barely audible whisper,

"Before everything changes".

If I hadn't been working on honing my Were skills, I might have missed it, but I have been working with Artemis since I returned home from the hospital. The use of my Were abilities in human form comes naturally now. My hearing is better, I'm stronger and faster. My Goddess abilities are like second nature. I can not only levitate with ease but I can basically fly. Like Superman. The use of my gravitational power is tricky, but I'm really getting the hang of it. Making other things weightless is simple, the bigger the item the harder I have to concentrate, but I lifted one of the cars the other day. Making things heavy, is a little harder, it requires much more concentration, but still doable. Creating an impenetrable forcefield is definitely the easiest power. I can create one around myself, around others, even one flying in the air. We have tested it against guns, people, cars, wolves, everything, and nothing can get through it. The only downside, the more I use my powers, the more wiped out I feel. It takes a lot out of me.

"Okay" I said pulling away from Gunner slowly. I can't help but wonder what could be changing. It must be about Selene. He must have seen or felt her through me while I was unconscious. But remembering her and our relationship wouldn't change much, would it? I get it, she is a deity. All powerful and beloved by all Weres, but my relationship with her should have no impact. I mean we already share blood and a bond through my being the Triple Goddess, so how much more could a personal relationship change things.

"I have something to tell you". Both Gunner and I spoke at the same time. I laughed as I looked up at him, he smirked, but there was no joy or happiness there, just concern.

"What's wrong? You look like someone just killed your pet goldfish" I teased and shoved his shoulder. He took my hands and held them in between us, gripping them tightly.

"It's about your mother" he said softly. A wide smile broke across my face as I studied his beautiful blue eyes. I knew it.

"So you did see her, I thought you might have. This is wonderful, can you believe it?" I squealed and bounced on my feet.

"Wait, you already knew?" he asked shocked. He stood up straighter and tilted his head to the side.

"Knew what?" I questioned him,

"About your mother?"

"Well, no, I didn't know, I didn't remember. But then she showed it to me" I answered excitedly. Gunner stared at me blankly and blinked his eyes a few times. His blank face held no emotion, but I could see the question flicker in his eyes.

"What are you talking about?" he asked, trying to disguise the annoyance in his tone.

"My mother, what are you talking about?"

"Your mother".

"Then you saw it too? You came with me?" I asked again with confusion,

"Came with you where? And what do you think I saw? I think we're talking about two different things here, Babe" he groaned.

"How many damn mothers do you think I have?"

"At this point, I have no fucking clue" he said as he dropped my hands and took a small step back. He ran his hands through his hair and cursed to himself.

"What?" I huffed and screwed up my nose. He is losing his damn mind.

"Never mind, you go first. What are you talking about? Where did you go and what did I supposedly see?" he grunted and turned back to look at me. He perched on the table, crossed his arms over his chest, and watched me intently, waiting for my response.

"Just now, when I passed out, Selene took me to her home. The Ethereal Plane" I said slowly as I pointed to the ground where I collapsed not a few minutes ago. Gunner didn't respond, he just stared at me wide eyed.

"Gunner?" I whispered, stepping closer to him.

"I'm sorry, say that again" he mumbled with a shake of his head. I took a deep breath and smiled.

"I passed out, yes? Well, that happened because the Moon Goddess, Selene, called me to her home"

"The Ethereal Plane?" Gunner cut in,

"Yes, the Ethereal Plane. Turns out, I've been there hundreds of times. She has been watching over me all my life, taking care of me. She raised me, Gunner. She took my memories so that I wouldn't be hurt by not being with her, or something like that, but then she gave them back to me again" I spoke excitedly as I peered up at him.

"You've lost me again" he mumbled and rubbed his eyes.

"Selene, the Moon Goddess, she's my mother. She has been with me all my life" I said slowly, watching his face twitch as my words seeped into his ears. He nodded his head slowly and I continued,

"She lives in the Ethereal Plane, a mirror image of our world, and she takes me there, or she took me there. I'm not sure what context to use, seeing as I have only just remembered all the past visits, but still".

"When exactly?" Gunner interrupted my train of thought. He was trying to keep his voice level, but I could hear the confusion and frustration seeping into his words.

"Well just now for one. But I have been many times throughout my life. Every time Hank beat me, or every time something bad happened at school, she would call me to her and comfort me. When I was a baby, she brought me food, rocked me to sleep, and took care of me. And she sang to me, a lullaby, oh Gunner, it's the most beautiful song I have ever heard, and her voice is magnificent. Can you believe it? I had a mother this whole time! Gunner, I wasn't alone. Selene, or Mother, as I call her, she was there. My whole life. She was with me".

"Woah, woah, woah! Zee slow down! Are you telling me that the Moon Goddess has been visiting you, and you have been visiting her?" Gunner interrupted again as he stood up and waved his hands in front of me,

"Yes, what are you not getting?" I groaned back.

"Zelena, this doesn't happen. Selene doesn't show herself to people, the only Were that has been to the Ethereal Plane was Selena. Are you sure about this?"

"You don't believe me?" I said dejectedly. I dropped my head and my hands fell to my side. How could he not believe me? Why would he not believe me? I thought that he would be happy for me, or at least a little bit excited.

"Zelena" Gunner whispered as he stepped into me and slowly wrapped his arms around my body. He pulled my head to rest on his chest and I responded by gripping onto the sides of his shirt. Tears began to gather in the corners of my eyes. Just one second ago I was overjoyed and excited, full to the brim of happiness. But now, now I just feel rejected.

"I do believe you. This is just really huge. It's hard to take in, you know?" Gunner said softly as he nuzzled his cheek into my hair.

"I have a mother" I choked out, swallowing the sob that was about to come out of my mouth. My emotions were all over the place and I couldn't catch them long enough to fully experience each one. Joy, happiness, acceptance, love, sadness, abandonment, rejection. It was all whirling around inside me like an emotional tornado. I felt Gunner press his lips to the top of my head and hold them there for a little bit. After a minute he blew out a long breath and squeezed me tight.

"Yes, Little Wolf, you have a mother" he said quietly. Something in his voice tugged at me. The way he said it or the tone he used, it was a little concerning, like there was something else hidden under the words. Maybe he is just worried about having to share me now. I don't know. But there is something else going on there, I'm sure of it. Deciding to change the subject, in the hopes of gathering my thoughts, I lifted my head from his chest and peered up at him.

"Are you going to tell me what happened in here?" I asked while looking right into his eyes. His Adam's apple bobbed as he swallowed,

"What do you mean?" he mumbled,

"I mean why was Tobias about to tear the head off of that Luna Eclipse she-wolf?"

"Oh" Gunner replied. His eye twitched a little as he flew them around the room, looking at everything but me.

"Gunner?" I questioned more firmly.

"The moment she touched you, you hit the deck. We didn't know what happened to you, so of course our first thought was that she did something. I didn't know that you were with the Moon Goddess, I didn't know it was just a coincidence. I thought she stabbed you or something. Tobias was quick to grab her, you know how fast he is. By the time I realised you were fine, just unconscious, he already had her by the throat" he rushed out, his nerves and anxiety filtered through his skin, stinking up the room.

"Why are you so nervous right now? What's really going on?" I demanded of him. Gunner rubbed at the back of his neck, one of his nervous tells. He sighed and looked down at his feet. He stayed silent for a moment, until he finally looked back up at me, a new resolve and determined expression had taken over his face.

"It's nothing Zee. I was wrong and I'm sorry. I shouldn't have let Tobias attack her" he admitted,

"Okay, but shouldn't your apology be directed to the she-wolf?"

"Yeah probably" he answered me meekly.

"You will make it right, won't you?"

"I will. I have to".

"Good. How long are they staying for anyway?" I asked,

"I think they will be hanging around for a while, an estimated time hasn't been discussed. But they aren't going anywhere, I know that much" he said in frustration,

"Is that your choice or theirs?" I asked, watching his eyes carefully,

"Both, I think. They won't leave because of you. I don't want them to leave because I still have a lot of questions. Tonight didn't exactly go to plan".

"Yeah, I noticed" I mumbled. Gunner stepped forward and placed his hands on each side of my face, lifting my chin so that I was now looking at him.

"I'm sorry" he said earnestly.

"You've said that" I smiled up at him,

"Just making sure you heard it" he smiled and pressed his lips to mine. He stood back up and looked over my face, keeping his hands on my cheeks,

"Well, dinner was a bust, so how about we take some food and snuggle up in the movie room?" he asked me,

"That actually sounds amazing".

"Great, come on then" he said taking my hand and leading me to the kitchen through the door at the back of the dining room. The food was spread over the benches, and more was warming in the oven. Roe had really gone all out for dinner tonight. I feel kind of bad about it now. I didn't ask to pass out, but she clearly went to a lot of work to impress this pack. Gunner said that they were staying for a while, so I guess we'll get our chance to learn more about them eventually. Gunner can ask his questions, and I can find out why they came out of hiding just for me.

We piled up a huge serving tray with everything that was meant to be served at dinner, and then also grabbed some chocolates, sweets, and drinks. The both of us with our hands full, made our way to the movie room and we dropped it all down on the table by the large couch. The house seems more quiet than usual. Gunner told everyone to let us talk, but it seems like they have all just disappeared.

After we settled into the couch with a big blanket, lots of pillows, and the tray of food over our laps, Gunner put on an animated movie.

"A kid's movie, really?" I asked him, already feeling bored of it.

"It's one of my favourites, and it's a classic. Plus, you need to understand the reference I made the other day. So just shut up and watch it" he quipped and kissed my cheek before grabbing a handful of cooked meat. I watched him shove the strips of beef into his mouth and I started to drool. It looks too good. I grabbed a handful and began filling my gob. The meat was tender and juicy and perfectly cooked, but it tasted different than usual. It was way better.

"Oh my god" I moaned and piled more meat onto a little plate before sitting back and shovelling it into my mouth. I couldn't chew fast enough, and I couldn't get enough of it. I was ravenous. Gunner's laugh caught my attention, and I snapped my head up to see him watching me with an amused grin on his face.

"You hungry or something?" he laughed at me,

"Sorry" I mumbled through my stuffed mouth. I chewed and swallowed it down before turning back to Gunner.

"I'm starving. I honestly didn't realise how hungry I was" I giggled and shoved a spoonful of pasta into my mouth. The moment the smooth pasta hit my tongue, I regretted eating it. It is completely bland and boring compared to the sweet and juicy meat. I huffed and put the pasta bowl back down and picked up the plate with the marinated beef strips on it. The smell had me salivating. This whole Were thing has turned me into the ultimate carnivore. I settled back into Gunner's chest as a cowboy doll walked around on the TV screen.

As the movie progressed, my hunger did as well. I tried a bit of all of the food that we brought in with us, but for some reason, all I had a taste for was the meat products. I guess that little trip to the Ethereal Plane has drained me a bit, now my body is demanding protein to make up for it. I happily snacked away on the sausages and chicken skewers, but the marinated beef strips were heavenly above all else. As Gunner reached around my shoulder to grab a piece of the meat, I felt a growl bubble in my throat. As his fingers got closer to the beef, I snapped my teeth at his hand and growled.

"What the shit, Zee?" he gasped and flung his hand away from my face. What the shit indeed. I have no idea where that came from. I laughed awkwardly and lifted the plate to his face.

"Sorry, that was weird, I'm just kidding" I fake laughed as I tried to play it off as a joke.

"Oh" Gunner laughed at me and placed his arm back over my shoulder. He grabbed the meat and shoved it in his mouth. Watching him eat it, a strange possessiveness came over me. I wanted to snatch it from him, and I wanted to kiss him, to drag my tongue all over his mouth. What the actual fuck is wrong with me. I think I'm just tired. I obviously used up a lot of energy today with my little visit with my mother, and my body doesn't know what's going on. Yep, that's it. I just need to get some sleep.

"How long does this movie go for?" I asked Gunner, a little space man was arguing with the cowboy toy now.

"We're only like half an hour in, are you over it already?" he asked, sounding a little disappointed and surprised,

"No, no I like it. I was just thinking that I'm a little tired is all"

"We can go to bed if you want?"

"Nah, I want to watch the rest of it".

"Good cause this is my line, watch, watch" Gunner chuckled and squeezed me into his chest tighter. The little spaceman climbed onto the kid's bed, said 'To infinity and beyond' and then jumped off. Gunner laughed and shook my shoulder,

"See, you get it?" he laughed and pointed at the huge TV screen.

"I get it" I chuckled,

"Though, I feel like I should be weirded out that you were using quotes from a kid's movie while I was sitting on your face?" I teased and elbowed his hip. Gunner purred and leaned down to press his lips to my ear,

"Well, you know we can replay the scene, the one where you ride my face to infinity and beyond" he said softly with a seductive undertone. Butterflies erupted in my stomach and my crotch pulsed with desire. But I'm not giving in that easily.

"Nope. Sorry spaceman, I'm too busy watching the movie" I smiled and pushed his head away. He grumbled a little but sat back on the couch. As the movie played, I became more invested, it was actually pretty good. I can see a lot of myself in the different characters. The spaceman had to come to terms with the reality of his life, much like me. The cowboy had to learn to share and make friends, much like me. And all of them leaned on and trusted each other, like I do with my new family. I can see why Gunner likes it so much. I caught him multiple times staring at me with a strange expression on his face. I let it go the first couple of times but began to get nervous the more I caught him. I wiped at my mouth to see if I had food on my face. Then I picked at my teeth to see if I had something stuck between them. As far as I could tell there was nothing embarrassing going on with my face, so what is with the weird looks.

"What?" I snapped as I turned to see him watching me again. "Nothing, I just… I just love you, that's all" he stumbled out. I would like to think that I know Gunner pretty well by this point. I'm used to the faces he makes and what his expressions usually mean. But this one I haven't seen on him before. It was a little worrying. He looks guilty and worried, all mixed with the 'I'm keeping a secret' look and 'there's something on my mind' look. Still gorgeous, but troubled.

"Is everything okay?" I asked him. He lifted me onto his lap and pulled me flush against his body. I snuggled into him and my whole body melted into his embrace.

"Everything is perfect" he whispered into my neck as he nuzzled his nose across my skin. We stayed like this as the movie played. I must have fallen asleep, because the next thing I knew, Gunner was lowering me into bed and tucking my legs under the blanket.

"Did the movie finish?" I groaned as I turned onto my side,

"It did" Gunner answered as he kicked off his shoes,

"I'm sorry I fell asleep"

"That's okay Little Wolf".

"We can watch it again tomorrow and I'll stay awake this time" I mumbled as he slid into the bed beside me,

"Actually, I was thinking tomorrow we could go to the beach" he replied and pulled my body across the bed so that my back was pressed into his chest.

"That sounds nice" I yawned and was out before I could hear his could reply.

Chapter Twenty-Six

Zelena

I woke up in the morning to an empty bed. Gunner's usual spot was cold, so he's been up for a while. I pulled the blanket off my body to see I was wearing one of Gunner's t-shirts and a lacey thong. He changed my clothes, how did I not wake up for that? I must have been more tired than I thought I was. I dragged my weary body off the bed and went into the bathroom. After I finished my business, I pulled on a pair of denim shorts and headed downstairs. I could hear talking coming from the kitchen, so I went there first. As I pushed open the door, my eyes immediately went to the large plate overflowing with crispy bacon. I rushed forward and grabbed a fistful of bacon and shoved it into my already salivating mouth.

"Yeah, sure, help yourself" a feminine voice teased from the breakfast nook. I turned around to see Gunner sitting with a smirking Nat and a red-faced Smith.

"Sorry" I mumbled with bits of bacon spitting from my mouth. Smith laughed out loud and smacked his hand on the table. Gunner chuckled and shook his head before putting more food in his mouth.

"Just kidding, girlfriend. I made extra for you guys" Nat mused and tossed her short blonde hair over her shoulder. I filled up a plate with more bacon, a couple of runny eggs, and a piece of toast, then went to sit at Gunner's side. He leaned over and pressed his lips to my cheek as I slid in next to him.

"Good morning, beautiful" he said softly.

"Morning" I mumbled back.

"So, boss man says we're headed to the beach?" Smith piped up,

"Yeah, that's what he said. I can finally try out my new bikini" I smiled and shuffled my bum on the seat to sit up straighter. Gunner growled and tightened his fingers around his fork.

"You're not wearing a bikini" he growled through clenched teeth,

"Wanna bet?" I quipped back,

"Zelena" he warned.

"Gunner" I snapped back. Nat laughed and clapped her hands, "You two are hilarious" she giggled and pushed at Smiths shoulder. They slid out of the booth and stood up by the table.

"We'll meet you out front in say... forty-five minutes?" Nat said, looking down at us.

"Yes" Gunner groaned. I could feel his eyes boring into the side of my face. I smiled at Nat and Smith, and they turned and walked out of the kitchen. Gunner's fingers slid their way across my neck and up to my jaw, he gripped the base of my throat, and turned my head to look at him.

"I am not letting you out in public with no clothes on" he said slowly and calmly with a sharp edge to his tone.

"Gunner, it's the beach" I grumbled and tried to pull out of his hold.

"I don't care. I'm the only one who should be seeing your body" he hissed and leaned in close,

"So what? I'm meant to go to the beach in jeans and a jumper?"

"If I have anything to say about it, yes"

"Well, it's a good thing you don't have anything to say about it then" I teased and jerked my head back, freeing myself from his grip.

"Don't test me Zelena" he warned,

"Don't be stupid, now can I eat my breakfast please?" I snapped back. He didn't answer and I didn't care. I dug into my food, letting the delicious bacon wash away all the worries of the world. Gunner's eyes remained fixed on my face as I ate everything on my plate. When I was done, I got up and put my plate in the dishwasher before heading up the stairs, leaving Gunner in the kitchen by himself.

I quickly rummaged through my drawer and found the green bikini that I bought on my first shopping trip. I pulled off Gunner's shirt and tied the bikini around my neck and back. The little green triangles of fabric sat over my perky boobs. I turned to the mirror and looked at my chest. I didn't think it was at all possible, but they looked bigger in this tiny swimsuit. I pulled the same shirt back on and then stripped off my shorts and underwear. I was just tying the string at my hip when Gunner burst through the bedroom door.

He stopped as his eyes fell on me and a purr like growl bubbled up from his chest. In a flash, he was standing behind me with his chest flush against my back. One hand was under my shirt and stroking my stomach, the other was gliding up and down my thigh. I arched my back and pushed my ass into his crotch, his hard member pushed back. His fingers grabbed at the string of the bikini bottoms and pulled. The tie came undone, and they slowly slid down my legs. Gunner's fingers tickled their way across my hip and came to rest cupping my hot pussy. His middle finger ran along the moist slit, teasing me. I leaned my head back and moaned softly. Gunner leaned down and ran his tongue over my neck and jaw. He pushed one of his fingers inside me and I instinctually moved my legs apart.

I moved my hand behind my back and found the bulge in Gunner's jeans. I rubbed at the hard lump and moved my hips against his hand. I managed to undo the button and pull down the zip of his jeans when Gunner lifted me by the waist and carried me to the desk in the corner. He put me back on my feet and grabbed my wrist.

"Hands on the desk" he growled into my ear, and I obeyed without hesitation. He stepped away from me and I whimpered at the loss of contact. A second later I felt his hand grip onto the inside of my thigh. I turned my head to look over my shoulder. Gunner was on his knees, his face at my bent over backside, staring at my dripping pussy. His hands glided up the inside of my thighs and to my ass cheeks. He squeezed tight and spread my cheeks apart. I tried to pull away, but his grip tightened, and he growled.

"Don't. Move" he demanded. His hands massaged and rounded my ass cheeks, while his eyes were fixed on the sensitive flesh that sat between them. Without warning, he slammed his mouth against my wet lips and pushed his tongue inside me. I squealed in surprise and jumped forward before he pulled me back against him. His mouth worked wonders on my responsive flower, eliciting loud moans and cries of pleasure. He moved his mouth higher until his tongue found the soft flesh of my asshole. I cried out more as his mouth worked against the small button. I could feel my stomach constricting and the throbbing in my core intensify. "Gunner!" I screamed as the orgasm flooded through me. My arms gave out and I fell forward onto the desk. I rested my cheek on the cool wood and huffed out a spent breath. My moment of rest didn't last, Gunner stood up and was stroking the head of his dick over my slick pussy. I pushed my hips back onto him and his cock slid between my lips. In one long stroke, he pushed himself inside of me, all the way to the hilt. He groaned and gripped my hip tightly. He began to pull out and thrust forward again, slapping his hips into my ass. He continued like this, pulling back slowly and thrusting forward in a hard fast stroke. Slowly Gunner increased his pace, and the sensation was stirring up another orgasm inside of me. A sharp slap hit against my right butt cheek, only it didn't hurt, it made me moan. Another followed it immediately after, and then another. I screamed out and pushed myself back, hoping to increase the force of his thrusts. I could feel it building in the pit of my stomach. I wasn't far away from falling off the cliff.

"Gunner" I groaned out, pushing myself back against him more. His hand came to my lower back and slid down further. I could feel him pushing at my back entrance. It was everything that I needed. His hips moved faster and harder as his thumb slid into my asshole. The feeling of fullness and the pressure it created, sent my eyes rolling back. The damn broke and the pleasure spilled out of me. I continued to ride my orgasm with each of Gunner's thrusts. He groaned out as he found his own release. I collapsed back onto the desk as Gunner huffed behind me.

"Fuck yeah" he breathed out harshly. I chuckled and my legs gave out from under me, I began to fall to the floor, but

Gunner caught me. He scooped me up and deposited me on the edge of the bed. I flopped back and heaved for breath. I never understood how you can get so out of breath from just standing still.

"Come on, get changed, Nat will come looking for us soon" Gunner said as he walked off to the bathroom. I groaned and sat back up again, he could at least let me catch my breath again. He came back out with a wet face washer and tossed it to me.

"I can't shower?" I asked,

"You can never shower after I have put my scent all over you like that" he teased.

"Funny" I huffed.

"We're going swimming remember, the beach will wash it away enough as it is" he said as he pulled on a pair of boardies and a t-shirt.

"You know you're really gross right? A girl likes to be clean". Gunner stepped between my legs and leaned forward, placing one arm on either side of my body. Something about him felt different. He's been acting weird and possessive, well more possessive than usual, for a while now. The way he's staring at me now as he leaned over me, forcing me to lean back as he came closer, it was slightly terrifying. Not that I'm scared of Gunner, I could never be. But this wild look in his eye, it was a little daunting.

"And a man likes the smell of himself all over his woman" he murmured as his face was only an inch from mine. He kissed my nose and stood up again. 'Possessive prick' I thought to myself.

~

The sky was a clear crystal blue and the bright sunlight twinkled on the top of the water. Coming to the beach was a fantastic idea. I wanted time to just relax and hang out with my friends, even if Cole was still a no show. The soft white sand felt great under my feet. I curled my toes and dug them under the sand. I'd never really been given the chance to enjoy hanging at the beach. Before now I'd never had 'free time'. Any minute that I wasn't at school, or suffering through one of Hank's tough love lessons, I was cooking and cleaning, and doing everything else a common house slave does. Personal time or free time wasn't a thing under Hank's roof.

Smith and Nat dropped the esky and picnic basket and laid out some towels. I sat down on the edge of a towel and buried my feet into the sand. Smith stripped down to his swim shorts and Nat slid her dress down her body and let it drop at her feet. She was wearing a skimpy black string bikini that sat high up on her hips and barely covered her breasts. But hot damn does she have a banging body. Watching her I felt a little self-conscious. She is gorgeous, like a swimsuit model. Her body has never been covered in scars and bruises. Even if mine no longer is either, I can still see them in my mind sometimes. Gunner stood at my side and pulled his shirt over his head before dropping it on the towel behind me.

"You coming in?" he asked looking down at me,

"Not yet, I want to sunbake for a bit" I answered and pulled off Gunner's t-shirt that I was still wearing. I dropped it behind me and began to unbutton my denim shorts. Gunner's growl snapped my attention back to his angry face.

"I thought I said you were not going to wear that" he growled at me while tracing his hungry eyes over my exposed stomach and chest.

"It's a bikini Gunner, not lingerie, you need to chill out" I snapped at him,

"You're pushing it Zelena" he snapped back.

"Can you please not start. I really want to just enjoy this day in the sunshine, don't ruin it for me".

His hard expression softened slightly. I could tell he was still not happy, but I could also tell that he wasn't going to argue any further. He leaned down and kissed my forehead before jogging off to the water where Nat and Smith were already splashing each other. He tackled Smith into an oncoming wave before quickly getting up and running away again. Smith stood up and coughed out a mouthful of water before he shook his shaggy red hair and darted off after Gunner. They looked like they were having a lot of fun, and the water looked very inviting. I hadn't told anyone that I can't swim. I never learned how. Hank wasn't one to teach his pretend daughter the pleasures of life, like how to swim or ride a bike. But I wasn't going to let that tiny detail ruin this gorgeous beach day.

I unbuttoned my shorts and pulled them down my hips, lifting my butt I dragged them off and discarded them on the towel with my shirt. I pushed my sunglasses up my nose, laid back down on the towel, and splayed my arms out at my sides. The sun danced across my exposed skin and warmed my body from the outside in. The screams and laughing of the others got quieter the further out in the water they went until I could barely hear them.

I was lying with my eyes closed when I felt an unknown presence close by. I perched myself up on my elbows and looked down along the water's edge. We had walked a fair way away from the car park, any other people visiting the beach wouldn't come down this far. As I turned my head from side to side, scanning the horizon, I knew I was right, there was no one else to be seen on the beach. I looked over my shoulder at the tree line. At first, I saw no one, but then a figure stepped out from behind a tree. I gasped and shot upright, turning my body to face the figure. I ripped off my glasses and studied the person closer. It was a man, a man that looked familiar somehow. He raised his hand and motioned for me to come to him. I looked back to where Gunner and the others were swimming, completely oblivious of me or the mystery man. Looking back to the man, he had taken another step forward, the sun now illuminated his face, and I knew who he was right away. I stood up slowly, letting my eyes scan the trees around him but I saw no one else.

I took a step, and then another and another. Slowly, so very slowly, I walked to him. My eyes never stopped looking for signs of others, whilst still glancing back to Gunner. This could be a terrible idea, I know that, I'm not stupid. But I have to know what he wants, why he came here. If Gunner notices, if he sees him, I won't get another chance. As I got closer, he began to back away, back into the shadows of the trees. I froze, hesitant to follow him. My gut told me to turn back, but my head told me to keep going, to get answers. I looked back at the water, Gunner's handsome face smiling and laughing in the sunlight, had still not noticed my movements. I stepped into the shadows, walking further into the trees, my bikini clad body immediately missed the warmth of the sunlight. I looked around the forest, only he was now nowhere to be seen, the man was gone. I lifted my nose and breathed in hard, sniffing at the air.

"You don't need to sniff me out, Beauty, I'm right here" his accented voice spoke. I turned to the sound as he stepped out from behind a tree. I knew it was him. He's the man from the mall.

"What are you doing here?" I demanded of him. He smirked at me and stepped forward,

"I wanted to meet you, Cousin, properly this time" he mused.

"Cousin?" I blurted. My eyes blew wide and a ball clogged my throat. I don't have cousins.

"You are the descendant of Selena, are you not?" he asked, tilting his head to the side. I quickly regained my composure and placed a look of non-interest back on my face. The way he looked at me made me shiver. Like he was a ravenous lion, and I, his prey. I should flash Gunner, this is a bad idea.

"I am" I answered him. I crossed my arms over my chest, trying and failing to block his view of my overly exposed body. Maybe Gunner was right about this swimsuit.

"And who are you?" I asked.

"I am Alpha Galterio, of Origin Wolf. Descended from Gill, the first son born to Lycaon" he said proudly before lowering his eyes and smiling at me wickedly.

"See? We are cousins. You, a daughter of Selena, and I, a son of Gill" he said watching me with interested narrowed eyes, He tossed his head and chuckled, the sound making goosebumps appear on my arms.

"Well, distant cousins" he mused.

"You are not my cousin" I said firmly. He chuckled again and ran his hand through his slicked back dark hair. He stepped closer and smiled back at me.

"I suppose not, but isn't it nice to think so? We did come from the same Were, many generations ago, so we share blood all the same" he said smoothly, full of confidence and charisma.

"Why are you here, really? It's not just to meet me, is it?" I said taking a small step backward,

"Of course it is, we're family" he almost sang. It was all fake, the smoothness, the joy, he was putting on a show,

"If you're not going to tell the truth then there is no point continuing this conversation" I snapped and turned to walk away. Quicker than possible, he moved to stand in front of me, blocking my path. My hands fell to my sides and I nearly fell back at the surprise of him just appearing in front of me, like magic.

"How, how did you do that?" I mumbled,

"Do what, Beauty?"

"How did you move so fast?"

"You have your gifts, and I have mine" he said in a smug way that came off rather threatening.

"You have powers?" I asked. Fear bubbled in the pit of my stomach, with how close he was standing, I'm sure he could smell it on me. He tsked and moved his finger from side to side.

"You have been asking all the questions, why not let me ask one?" he smirked and stepped even closer to me, now only inches away. His tall and muscular frame was intimidating, the scent of cologne was strong, but above all, he made me feel a little sick. Nervous actually.

"You haven't answered any of my questions" I said, trying to keep my voice strong and level.

"That's not fair, you asked who I was, and I told you" he chuckled as he lifted his hand to my face. Just like before, at the shopping mall, I froze. I was unable to move or to think as the tip of his finger gently slid down my cheek, my neck, and between the valley of my breasts. He was staring down at my chest hungrily, I could smell his desire and it made me want to puke. He hesitated for a moment, his hand just hung there between my boobs. An awkward silence filled the space between us before he pulled his hand away. I released a shaky breath and crossed my arms over my chest.

"You haven't called for your Mate?" he questioned as he took a step back. The word 'Mate' coming from his mouth sounded dirty, disgusting even. The fear in my stomach was making me incapable of speaking, so instead I slowly shook my head. "Good" he announced.

"That Alpha is very frustrating, always around, never leaving you alone" he growled and turned away. The statement caught me off guard. How would he know something like that, that Gunner and I are always together? Unless he has been watching us. Or... The traitor has been relaying information. My stomach fell and I could feel a lump of vomit form in my throat. Shit. This was a really, really bad idea.

"You trust me, don't you? That's why you haven't called for him? You can feel safe with me" he said somewhat seductively. I snapped myself out of my little terror trance and glared at the Alpha in front of me. I lifted my hand and let the power flow through me. My skin burned and hot pins danced across my arm. I let it push against his skin, just enough for him to feel the pressure of gravity pulling him down. Little blue sparks sprung from my fingertips before quickly crackling out again.

"I can take care of myself" I told him in warning, he smirked at me before he disappeared in a blur, too fast for my eyes to follow. He almost instantly reappeared at my back. He slid his arm around my waist and spread his fingers out across the skin of my stomach. His other hand wrapped around my neck, not hard or constricting, but sensual. His hold on me was one of passion, not malice. He pressed his nose to the crook of my neck and inhaled deeply.

"So can I" he whispered lowly. His tongue poked out from between his lips and he dragged it up the sensitive skin of my neck. My stomach rolled and the anger I was already toying with erupted. That was the last straw. I flung my arm back, and using my power, I sent him flying deeper into the forest. I spun around to watch him land over forty meters away. The furthest I have thrown someone. He jumped to his feet and growled at me with his teeth bared. He took off running into the trees, but I couldn't see him move, he was too fast. The fastest I have ever seen a Were move. I tried to follow him with my eyes but I lost sight of him almost immediately. He reappeared in front of me with a smile on his face and his hands up in surrender.

"Truce. I admit, I deserved that, I just wanted to see how you'd respond" he chuckled. I raised my hand, ready to wrap my power around his throat when he stopped me,

"Wait, wait, wait" he rushed out,

"I'm sorry, I just want to talk to you, I promise. No more funny business, hands to myself, I swear" he chuckled, in that same flirtatious way that is starting to get on my nerves. He then put his hands behind his back and smiled at me with full white teeth. I hesitated and eyed him carefully. His large brown eyes were pleading with me, his face looked sincere enough. I nodded but kept my hand out at the ready. Alpha

Galterio leaned back against a tree and crossed his arms over his chest. He waited for me to do the same, but that wasn't going to happen, I'm not letting down my guard. Once he realised that, he started talking,

"I need your help" he told me like it was the simplest of explanations.

"With what?" I responded, trying not to give away any idea of my thoughts or feelings.

"With something big, something very important" he answered with a smirk.

"And how could I possibly help?" I sneered.

"You are the Triple Goddess, favourite daughter of the mighty Moon Goddess. The whole Were world knows about your arrival by now. That in itself is enough".

"So, you want me for my power and my status, not because you need my help" I said accusingly.

"No Beauty, you are the one we have been waiting for, you are the one we need. Without you, I'm afraid our cause is lost". I stared at him pondering his words. He spoke with passion and a hint of desperation. This isn't what I expected. Especially not from his flirting and skeevy behaviour.

"And what cause is that?" I asked, my curiosity rising,

"To bring freedom to all of Were-kind".

Chapter Twenty-Seven

Lunaya

"Touch me again and it will be the last time you have hands" Cleo growled at the young redhead. We were escorted back to the tent where we were right away surrounded on all sides. We could fight our way out, but that wouldn't solve anything and where would we go once we're out? Fighting at this point would complicate everything.

"What happened?" hissed Elaine quietly,

"I don't know" I whisper yelled back. I don't know why we are whispering, the guards outside could all hear us anyway. Alyse came to my side and pulled me down to sit beside her on a cot. She wrapped an arm around my waist and lifted one of my hands to lay on her lap. It was a good attempt at comforting me but had no impact. Elaine's furious frame loomed over me as she stood in front of Alyse and I. Cleo was standing in the far corner of the tent, watching on as usual. Venus and Phoebe sat on a cot opposite us. Venus checked the cut to the back of Phoebe's head, but both of them kept pretty quiet.

"Why did she collapse? Something must have happened" Elaine whispered harshly again,

"I told you I don't know" I growled lowly.

"Did you feel anything? You're her mother, perhaps she was affected by some kind of cosmic bond between the two of you" offered Venus,

"That's pushing it" Elaine snapped and glared back at her. Venus lowered her head and went quiet. That response from Elaine was completely unnecessary. For all we know Venus could be spot on, I too had the same thought for a second there.

"All I felt was nauseous, but that could have been nerves. I really don't know what happened. I wish I did. But, I will find out one way or the other" I told them.

"Well, her Mate knows who you are now, and he said they needed to talk. It's only a matter of time until he tells her and I'm sure she will seek you out after that" Alyse said comfortingly. She's right. The look on his face when he stared at me and whispered 'her mother' has been playing constantly in my head. It screamed realisation. He knew it, and he was going to tell her. As much as I wanted it to come from me, she may take the news better coming from her lover. Now I just have to wait. Wait for her to come to me.

Hours passed since we were ushered away and confined to the tent. What little semblance remained of my patience, had long since shrivelled and died. I was ready to tear this tent apart and hunt my daughter down. Why did she not come straight to me? Does she not believe him, or is this the first stage of her rejecting our relationship? The not knowing is killing me. Voices outside the tent came just in time to stop me from my rampage. I recognised two of them, one was Beta Cole and the other was Alpha Gunner, another voice was there as well, but I couldn't place it.

"You can't do that" Cole's voice hissed,

"I can do whatever the fuck I want, this is my pack" Gunner's voice growled back at him.

"Gunner, you're being unreasonable" the third voice commented.

"I just got her back, I'm not just going to hand her over to them, regardless of who she claims to be" Gunner grumbled,

"Just fucking talk to the she-wolf before you make any rash decisions. You don't even know if that's her plan" Cole spoke again,

"He's right Gunner, you're not thinking clearly. Try to let up on the possessive Alpha and think more like her friend, her Mate. You know it will hurt her if she finds out any other way" the unknown voice pleaded. I may just like that boy, he is the voice of reason. There was silence. By this point, all of us inside the tent were standing at the door and listening to the conversation.

"I don't like it" Gunner growled,

"I know mate, but this can't be your decision to make. It's hers, and I think you know that" Cole said strongly. There was silence again and after what felt like an eternity, Gunner stepped through the door of the tent, followed by Cole and the redhead from the dinner. He must be the voice of reason. Another Were, a warrior by the looks of him, stood just outside the door. Gunner came to stand right in front of me, a deadpan expression plastered across his firm face. His hands were placed on his hips and the position of his stance was all Alpha. He is actually quite impressive. Tall, broad shouldered, well built, and his aura was strong. For such a young Alpha, it's important to hold these qualities.

"If you lie to me, I will kill you" he said firmly, Cleo, Elaine, and Venus all growled softly at his threat. Gunner glared at them before averting his gaze back to my own.

"If you try to hide anything from me, I will kill you". I didn't respond, only stood tall and nodded my head.

"Speak she-wolf" he barked,

"Tell me you understand" he growled.

"I understand, Alpha Gunner" I answered him, my voice just as hard and firm.

"Very well, let's start slow. Who are you?" he demanded,

"I am Lunaya, formerly of the Moon Light pack" I answered him. The redhead turned his gaze to the side of his Alpha's head and his eyes blanked, he was flashing. Gunner blinked once and focused on me again.

"Moon Light, the pack from Alaska?" he asked,

"Yes"

"They were destroyed years ago"

"They were".

"There were no survivors, hunters killed everyone"

"Well not everyone, clearly, I am standing before you, aren't I? You are also Mated to another survivor" I said matter-offactly. Alpha Gunner didn't appreciate my reply as he leaned forward with his teeth bared and growled.

"Careful" he warned. Cole placed his hand on Gunner's shoulder and carefully pulled him back slightly.

"How did you survive?" he growled,

"I almost didn't. I was shot multiple times, trying to escape with my baby. But the bullets were laced with Aconite. They thought I was dead, that's why they left. With her" I whispered the last two words, trying desperately to swallow the grief that was rolling through my chest. Gunner was quiet as he digested my words.

"How do we know you are telling the truth?" he asked.

"I suppose you don't. I have no proof, only this". I grabbed the necklace from around my neck and opened the locket before handing it to Gunner. He studied the picture inside for a while before turning it to me. I looked over the photo once again, as I have done thousands of times before. Micha and I standing side by side with his large hand placed gingerly on my swollen belly.

"This is her father?" he said pointing at Micha.

"It is" I said as I took the locket from his hand. I traced my finger over the beautiful pale face of Micha as a tear rolled down my cheek.

"May I see?" Cole asked, stepping closer. I smiled and held the locket out for him to take. He looked at the photo and breathed in harshly.

"Gunner, she looks exactly like him" he said softly.

"I know" Gunner grumbled back. Cole passed the locket to the redhead, who had the same reaction. Gunner's eyes searched me, burning into my face. He was looking for any signs of threat or dishonesty, for something to prove that I was lying. However, he would find nothing. I am just a mother looking for her stolen daughter. After a while, the scent of anger from the Alpha was increasing steadily.

"Why now? Why are you only coming to her now? She was taken as a baby, so you've had what, eighteen years to track her down? Why are you only coming to her now that she has risen as the Triple Goddess? Is this some kind of power grab? What do you want with her?" Gunner demanded. I stared at him blankly, confused about his question. What do I want with her? What does he think I want with her? He actually thinks I'm here to hurt her, my own child.

"Excuse me?" I snarled,

"I'm not going to repeat myself" he snapped back,

"You think I want her for her power?" I asked dumbly,

"Why else would you wait this long?"

My chest exploded in a fiery burst of fury. The nerve of this damn boy. I don't care who's Mate he is, I don't care if he's an Alpha. I want his blood.

Nae, be calm

Alyse flashed me and stepped forward reaching for my hand. But it was already too late. I saw red and I was ready to kill.

"Because I thought she was dead!" I screamed, standing to my full height, only inches from his face.

"I looked! I searched for years, for any kind of sign that she was alive. I looked at each and every corpse of my fallen pack mates. I searched every burned-out house and every pile of bodies. I looked!" I was screaming in his face. My body was alive with emotions, grief, guilt, and rage.

"They were hunters! How was I meant to know that they kept her alive? How dare you accuse me of giving up, how dare you accuse me of coming after her power. She is my child. I never gave up. I mourned for my family every single day".

I hadn't realised that I was being held back by Alyse and Elaine. If it weren't for them, I would have lunged at the kid. My claws were out and my teeth had descended. He watched me with a stoic expression, but his eyes held the truth, he was surprised by my outburst. Tears streamed down my face in hot waves of painful memories. The thought that I had given up the search too soon has plagued my every dream. I heard the screaming of my child and saw the blood of my pack every time I closed my eyes. Was he right? Did I give up too easily?

"Okay, okay, okay" Cole rushed out and stood slightly in front of Gunner.

"That was a dick thing to say" he said pointedly looking back at Gunner as he spoke,

"But he needed to ask, for his own sanity" he added.

"Let's all take a nice big breath and calm ourselves. Then, we can talk calmly and rationally".

I wanted to rage, to hurt him for insinuating such things, but he is still my daughter's Mate. Going against him will only hurt my chances of reconnecting with her. I shook off Elaine and Alyse's hold on me and crossed my arms over my chest. With a large breath, I felt my canines return and my claws retract.

"Okay" I said firmly, eying Gunner. He nodded his head and also crossed his arms over his chest.

"Okay then, Lunaya, how did you find Zelena, after all these years?" Cole asked, he was now acting as a mediator.

"We had only just arrived at Luna Eclipse when the news of the Triple Goddess came from their scouts. Upon our arrival, I told the Luna Eclipse Alpha that I was descended from Rhea, the first female Alpha. If you know your history well, you will know that Rhea was a descended daughter of Selene. The Alpha took me to the pack Seer, it was her that said she was alive and that she was my child" I answered him while maintaining eye contact with Gunner.

"A Seer, really?" Cole asked, the surprise was evident in his voice. Seers are rare, very rare.

"Yes, our Seer has been a part of the pack for nearly eighty years" Elaine interjected.

"And she told you where we are? The Seer?" Gunner questioned,

"Not exactly no, she told us that we needed to come to Canada" I answered.

"Canada is a big place" Gunner snarled,

"Don't I know it" I huffed in response.

"You arrived with the daughter of Alpha Ambrose, from Lua Chei. Did they tell you where she was?" Cole asked. I hesitated, if I answer that question will they retaliate against Lua Chei? Will they see the deal they struck with Elaine as a betrayal? I looked at Elaine, asking with my eyes if I could answer the question. She very slightly shook her head. I think she is wondering the same thing.

"I don't think I will answer that question" I said looking back to Cole,

"I warned you" Gunner growled.

"I will not put an innocent pack in harm's way" I snapped at him,

"I take that as a yes then" Gunner growled lowly.

"Bring me Alpha Ambrose and his daughter" Gunner turned and snapped at the redhead. He hesitated before rushing out of the tent.

"Alpha Gunner, you can see that we mean her no harm, punishing Lua Chei will not accomplish anything" Alyse pleaded. Gunner turned and growled down at her. I moved to stand in front of Alyse, placing myself between them, and growled back protectively. Gunner's eyes blanked as did Cole's, they were flashing again. Gunner blinked and looked back at Cole before glancing between Alyse and me.

"Are you Mated?" he asked me,

"What does that have to do with anything?" I growled at him,

"Answer the question" he growled back,

"Yes, we are Mated" I snapped.

"With no male?" he asked, his voice, more curious than angry now.

"With no male" I mimicked. He didn't say anything further, and I couldn't read his face or his scent enough to figure out if he was going to accept our Mating with no issue. Cole had the same reaction when he learned of our same sex relationship. Curious and invested. I figured out why Cole was curious, but why is Gunner? After a few minutes, Alpha Ambrose, Analah, and the redhead returned. I really need to ask what this guy's name is, I can't keep calling him 'The Redhead'.

"What is the meaning of this?" Alpha Ambrose asked, clearly not thrilled about being pulled from his bed in the middle of the night.

"Did you or your pack offer up the location of the Triple Goddess to these she-wolves?" Gunner asked, cutting straight to the point. The alpha reared back, eyes wide and brows furrowed. I don't think he was expecting the interrogation. And I also don't think he is too impressed with it either.

"And what if I did?" he asked firmly staring Gunner down,

"You knowingly endangered the Triple Goddess" Gunner growled,

"Listen here boy, I have known you since you were a pup. Our packs have been allies since long before you were born. You want to stand here and accuse me of betraying our alliance, of endangering the Triple Goddess? Because, if that is the avenue you wish to take, I strongly suggest you rethink your strategy. You may be the Alpha now, but you are still a greenhorn. Watch yourself young one and don't test me" Alpha Ambrose spoke firmly and with authority. I wanted to clap my hands at his speech. Gunner dropped his hands and stood quietly glaring at the Lua Chei Alpha.

"We knew there was no threat from these Weres. At no point were they left unaccompanied or unsupervised. They were searched, properly questioned, and vetted before being escorted to your pack. We invited no danger and no risk to the Goddess. Now if that is all, you have interrupted my sleep, and I wish to return to bed".

Analah stood at her father's side, smirking. They both knew they were in the clear, they had done nothing wrong. I don't know the inside and out of their pack alliance, but on more than one occasion we have witnessed the history between them. Before Gunner got the chance to argue any further with Alpha Ambrose, he turned and stormed out of the tent. Analah winked at me before following behind her father.

Gunner was furious, he stunk of it. He was about to follow Alpha Ambrose out of the tent when Cole stopped him.

"He's right Gunner. You know he is. Lua Chei is one of our most trusted allies. They would never betray us" he said calmly with a hand on his shoulder.

"Plus, your mum will spit if you jeopardise the bond with her birth pack" Cole added. So, Lua Chei is Romeá's birthplace. That could explain the relationship between her and the Alpha, they probably dated before she left for Tri-Moon.

Gunner growled and pushed Cole's hand from his shoulder. He spun around and stood in my face.

"Why have you come?" he roared,

"To find my daughter" I answered calmly.

"She is mine, you're not taking her anywhere" he yelled, his hot breath hitting my face as he screamed.

"I never said I wanted to take her away" I told him.

"Then why are you here, if you're not here to recruit her to Luna Eclipse, why did you all come?" he demanded. His anger makes so much more sense now. He thinks I am a member of Luna Eclipse. He thinks I want to take her away. And if his Mate's long-lost mother is part of an all-female pack, what if she decides to leave him to go with me. He is just scared of losing her. His whole body was trembling. His eyes were wide and dark, he appeared to be on the verge of changing. The fear I can understand, he truly loves her. But this level of uncontrolled emotion is surprising.

"Alpha Gunner. I think you may have misunderstood. My Mate and I are Omega wolves, we were not initiated into Luna Eclipse. We have not come to take her away. We have come to be with her, here, in her home".

"You're not from Luna Eclipse?" he asked, stepping back from me,

"They are, yes. Alyse and I are not" I said as I pointed behind me to the others.

"Then why have you come?" he asked, now looking to Elaine.

"She is the Triple Goddess, we support women in power. We have come to offer our loyalty and arrange an alliance between our packs" Elaine answered without hesitation.

"You're not here to recruit her?"

"We are not. If she chose to come with us, we would allow it, but we are not here to sway her".

Gunner went silent as he stood staring at us. His mind was alive with activity, I could see him going through the motions. Will he be big enough to admit he overreacted, or will he remain on the defence? He couldn't possibly still believe that we are dangerous, not after learning the full truth.

"Okay" he finally spoke.

"I will let you stay, but for the time being, you are to keep your distance from Zelena".

"You can't expect me to do that. And what if she wants to talk to me, I'm not just going to run in the other direction. Now she knows that I'm her mother, you can't keep us apart" I yelled,

"She doesn't know about you" he yelled back. My anger slipped away instantly. She doesn't know. So, he didn't tell her? I'm confused, why would he keep something like this from her?

"What do you mean she doesn't know?" Alyse asked him. She was as angry and confused as I was.

"I… I didn't tell her" Gunner said, his firm tone turned to have a more meek and guilty feeling to it. He isn't sure of his decision to not tell her.

"Why not?" demanded Elaine,

"There were uh… something came up, something unexpected" he mumbled.

"What kind of something?" I came back strong, my anger burning again in full force. What could possibly be more important than telling her about me?

"I can't talk about it yet" he answered me,

"Like hell you can't! You want me to keep my distance, you had better have a damn good reason as to why" I yelled.

"It's hard to explain" Gunner rushed out,

"I'm sure we can keep up" Elaine growled.

"This isn't something I'm ready to announce yet" Gunner growled,

"We're good at keeping secrets" Cleo added from the back of the tent.

"We've noticed" Gunner snapped while flicking his eyes to Cole who stood very silent during this interaction. The frown on his face was one of frustration. From what we heard before they entered the tent, I think he is against Gunner's decision not to tell her, the Redhead too.

"I will see her" I snared angrily.

"She has been visiting with Selene" Gunner yelled. My anger dissipated. We all froze in silence, staring at the Alpha dumbly. Visiting? That's not possible.

"That's why she passed out at dinner, Selene called to her. I'm sorry Lunaya, but Zelena believes that Selene is her mother".

"What are you talking about?" I asked, I could feel my panic rising.

"Zelena told me that she has been going to the Ethereal Plane her whole life, that Selene has been taking her there. And apparently, Selene has been visiting with her here on Earth as well".

"No. No, no, no. That doesn't happen" I mumbled, my chest tightened, and my breathing quickened. A panic attack was coming.

"Zelena doesn't lie. If she said it happened, I believe her. She said that Selene raised her, and she sees her as her mother. I can't rock that boat right now. I need to let her have this, a least for a little while. Throwing you, her birth mother, into the mix will just overwhelm her. I promise this won't be forever, I will tell her about you" Gunner stepped close to me as he spoke. He jerked his hand, like he wanted to reach out for me but changed his mind. Instead, he just gazed at me apologetically.

"No" I said softly,

"Pardon?" Gunner answered,

"No, don't tell her" I croaked,

"Nae, are you sure?" Alyse whispered as she slid her hand into mine. I squeezed her hand tight and nodded my head.

"She has a mother" I croaked and a sob fell from my lips.

Chapter Twenty-Eight

Lunaya

"I think you're being irrational" Alyse snapped at me. We had been going around in circles having the same argument all morning.

"I'm not being irrational, I'm trying to do the right thing" I groaned once again.

"How is that the right thing?" Alyse yelled. She was pacing back and forth in front of me as I sat on the same fallen tree where I had my chat with the Beta, Cole. After our talk with Gunner last night and the revelation about Zelena and her relationship with Selene, I agreed to keep my distance. Alyse however thinks I'm being stupid and that I'm just scared of her rejecting me in favour of Selene. I mean, she's not wrong, but she isn't totally right either. Gunner told me very little about her upbringing at the hands of that filthy hunter. I don't know the details, but enough to know that her childhood was hell. She deserves this time, to bask in the newfound joyous relationship. Even if I am jealous, even if I wish it was me that was making her this happy. She deserves the time to enjoy these memories before I drop another bomb in her life.

"Alyse, this isn't easy for me. I know that you know this. I'm not going anywhere, I'm never leaving her again. If I stay in her life as nothing more than a friend or a pack mate, then that will have to be enough. If the time comes that she is ready to know the truth, then and only then will I tell her" I told her once again.

"This isn't right" Alyse whispered while looking down at her feet.

"My love, please, I just need your support. I appreciate your thoughts and feelings, but this is how it has to be. At least for now" I said reaching out for her. She stepped between my legs and placed her hands on my shoulders. I snaked my arms around her waist and rested my forehead on her stomach.

"I support you" Alyse said softly,

"Thank you" I whispered. We stayed like that for a while. Enjoying the moment together. At least Gunner decided to let us out of the tent. It shows that he has some kind of trust for us. The Tri-Moon pack has some beautiful landscapes. The forest is thick and lush and all different shades of green. The air holds so many different scents. Damp earth, tree bark, forest animals, and the distant scent of seawater. There could be worse places to call home.

"Can you smell that?" Alyse asked. I lifted my head from her stomach and looked up to her face. She had her nose scrunched up and her eyes were scanning the trees. I lifted my nose and sniffed. I caught the scent and shot to my feet. I sniffed again and turned on my heels, tracking the direction of the scent.

"What is it?" Alyse asked with concern,

"A Feral" I snarled back,

"Another one?" she questioned,

"No. The same one".

"But we're on pack land".

"Then it is either really stupid or it's up to something". I scoured the forest for signs of the Feral, but I couldn't see it. The scent is strong, so it has to be close. I lifted my nose and kept my eyes focused. I could feel my claws pushing at the tips of my fingers. The potential threat was calling forth my wolf. The breeze picked up and I caught the full force of the Feral's scent. A growl rumbled through my chest as I pushed myself forward.

"East" I growled as I took off. I changed into my wolf mid stride and charged through the trees. Alyse was at my side, keeping up with ease. Some backup would have been good right now. Having a pack to flash with is essential when calling for back up though. We ran through the forest towards the scent. It was moving, and moving fast.

There's only one

I flashed Alyse. She may not have a wolf, but her human is just as fast and strong as I am in my wolf form. As we pushed on, the scent got stronger and I could see the tracks the Feral was leaving behind.

It's up ahead, I can see it

I looked to where Alyse was looking, and I saw a small flash of dirt brown fur dash behind a tree.

Take the left and we'll close in together

We're nearing the edge of the territory

I pushed forward and veered right as Alyse did the same to the left. This Feral is weak, it is fast but not fast enough. I dug in my paws and lurched forward, pushing my legs as much as I could. I was closing in on the tail of the feral, I looked to the left and Alyse was gliding through the forest parallel to me.

Push in, now, before it gets to the border.

Alyse and I closed the distance until we were running at its side. The Feral panicked and lunged at Alyse. I pushed off hard and flew myself through the air, landing on its back. I hit it hard enough that it just missed Alyse. We rolled along the ground as I dug in my claws, I tried to get a grip on its neck with my teeth but couldn't get the right angle. We hit hard against a wide tree trunk, dislodging my hold on the Feral's back. We bounced apart and I jumped back up to my feet. I growled and barked, snapping my jaws threateningly at the small wolf. The Feral stood, holding its front left paw off the ground. It snarled and growled with its teeth bared. I flashed my sharp canines and stalked towards it. Alyse appeared at my side, her claws ready and growling ferociously. Her growl rumbled through the forest, echoing loudly through the trees. The Feral eyed her and barked out a snarl. It had chosen her as the weaker link, as its first point of attack, and it lunged for her.

I jumped forward, placing my body in front of Alyse's. The Feral hit against my side, its teeth sinking into the thick fur at the top of my shoulder. I howled and tried to thrash it off.

Alyse grabbed the Feral by the scruff of the neck and pulled it back. It ripped its teeth from my neck, taking with it a chunk of flesh. Alyse then swung the Feral around, flinging it into a tree. The tree crunched under the impact of the Feral's body, but still stood in one piece. The Feral howled and whimpered but got back up. I could feel my blood soaking through my coat from the wound to my shoulder, but I still got to my feet and growled at the filthy wolf. It was hurt, and I could see in its petrified gaze that it knew it was caught. It came down to fight or flight, and seeing as it couldn't fly, fight was the only thing left to do. Alyse and I bared down on the small Feral readying for the attack.

Just as we were about to lunge, a large tan wolf came from nowhere and landed on top of the Feral. It pinned the wolf to the ground with its teeth wrapped around its neck. More wolves appeared and surrounded the Feral and their leader. They must be warriors from Tri-Moon, maybe the border patrol. They must have heard the commotion. I tried to walk forward but stumbled, I had lost more blood than I realised.

"Nae" Alyse called as she rushed to my side. Her fingers brushed through my fur as she inspected the wound on my shoulder. It must be worse than I originally thought, I can feel myself getting weaker.

We need to question it, find out why it's here

I told Alyse. She nodded at me and stood to walk over to the wolves that were holding down the Feral. Upon her approach, they closed their circle around it, restricting Alyse from getting close.

"It needs to be questioned. A Feral has been spotted hanging around the pack lands, we need to know if this is that Feral" Alyse spoke with authority. The wolves snarled at her as she spoke, but none changed back in order to speak with her.

"Do you have a cell? It needs to be locked up until it can be questioned by the Alpha" she asked them. But still, no one changed form to answer. Something doesn't feel right about this. I lifted my nose slightly and breathed in the scent. They aren't Ferals, that much was obvious. But their scents aren't familiar either. I glanced around us and frowned. We're still on pack land. If these wolves aren't from Tri-Moon, the warriors will be aware of it by now.

Alyse, something is wrong

What do you mean?
I don't think they are from Tri-Moon
Alyse and I looked at each of the wolves, five of them, all stood around the Feral, blocking our view of it. Alyse stepped back to my side, keeping her eyes on the pack of Weres with the Feral. My head began to feel airy and my legs started to shake. The blood loss was affecting me at the worst time. I can't change back, not yet, I need to stay in my wolf form for protection. I don't like these Weres, I don't trust them.
"The cell? You will take it there? I need to get her back to the pack house" Alyse said, maintaining her firm tone and giving away none of our suspicions. Once again, none of them changed form. One of the wolves nodded its head slowly and that was the only sign of recognition that we got. I took the chance and struggled to my feet.
Play it cool, we have to get out of here
Alyse rested her hand on my neck and together we backed away. I walked forward with my ears focused behind us, listening for any signs of their pursuit. I heard rustling and quick movement but it wasn't coming our way.
They're taking it away
Which way?
Toward the border
I don't think they were Tri-Moon warriors
I think you're right
We need to alert the Alpha
Why would they take a Feral and not just kill it?
I don't know, but we need to find out. Run ahead and find the Beta
I'm not leaving you like this, you're hurt Nae
I'll be fine, I'm already healing. But we can't take the risk of letting them get too far away
It's not happening
Alyse, we don't have the time, go
I said no!
I growled lowly. She is always so damn stubborn. I stopped walking and shook out my fur, trying to get a feel of my body. My shoulder is in a bad way, the loss of blood has made me very weak. But I can run, not for long, but long enough to get back to the village.
Fine. Let's go

I slowly started to run in the direction of the pack house. Pain shot through my body with each impact of my paw to the ground, but I kept on. Alyse didn't say anything further, she just ran at my side, watching me closely the whole way. As soon as we reached the edge of the village, she took off. I hadn't realised how slowly I was actually running. I made it about four paces past the tree line when I collapsed. I had no energy left and my body radiated pain. Without warning, I shifted back and let out a loud scream. Changing when injured is always ten times more painful. Once the fur was gone, I could see the full extent of the wound to my shoulder. It sat at the joining point between the base of my neck and my collarbone. Because of its placement, I could only see part of it, but the part I could see wasn't pretty. A piece of flesh had been ripped away, leaving behind a large and bloody gaping hole. Blood coated my entire arm and chest. How the Feral had missed my jugular is a complete mystery.

I lay in the dirt on my back, butt naked. I pressed my hand to the wound, hoping to curve the blood flow. But with my thick fur gone, I could feel the blood trickling through my fingers and down my bare skin. I had my eyes closed and my breathing was becoming harsh.

"Lunaya, Lunaya can you hear me?" Romeá's voice called to me. I felt her hands on my skin but everything else was slowly becoming hazy.

"Get her up and someone get Artemis" Romeá demanded. I felt myself being lifted from the ground, but after that, there was nothing.

~

My eyes fluttered open and I flew upright on the bed. I'm in a bedroom, not the tent, and I'm alone. I grabbed my neck but the wound was gone, completely healed over. Meaning I have been here for at least a few hours. I was dressed in a large black t-shirt and a pair of grey sweatpants. I stood up and walked out of the bedroom door and headed down a hallway and to a large staircase. At the bottom of the staircase was the foyer, the only part of this huge house that I recognised. I focused my hearing and heard a scurry of voices coming from a door on the left, Alyse's voice was one of them. I pushed the door open, and all eyes turned to me. Beta Cole, Alyse, Elaine, Phoebe, Romeá, her Mate Lupus, the she-wolf

Faylene, and a warrior whose name I hadn't learned yet, all stood looking at me.

"Hello" I said awkwardly,

"Nae, you're alright?" Alyse asked as she stepped forward and placed her small hands on my cheeks. I put my hands over hers and smiled,

"Good as new" I said with a smile as I tilted my head to the side to show her my healed wound. She exhaled a deep breath and nodded. I took her hand and looked up at the others,

"What's going on? Did you find the Feral and the other Weres?" I asked, directing my question to Cole.

"No. They were gone by the time we got there, and they covered their tracks and disguised their scent" Cole answered me.

"They weren't from Tri-Moon then?" I asked him,

"Absolutely not" Cole barked.

"So what? Are they just gone? No clue as to where or why they took the Feral?"

"Correct" he answered again.

"Lunaya, Darling, we were just discussing the possibility that the other wolves were Ferals as well" Romeá said to me.

"No, they weren't. They didn't have the scent and they were too calm… too in control" I told them,

"I told you that already" Alyse grumbled.

"None of this makes sense" Lupus growled and slammed his fists onto the table,

"How the fuck did they get past the border?" he snarled over at the warrior.

"I don't know, the patrols were meant to be there like they always are" the warrior answered in a calm and collected voice.

"Who is in charge of those patrols?" Elaine asked, stepping forward.

"Why does that matter?" Cole asked her,

"Have you considered the fact that perhaps they had help getting onto your land?" Elaine said like it was the most obvious thing.

"Are you accusing my warriors of betraying their Alpha?" Cole snapped,

"No Beta, simply offering a possibility" she replied smugly.

"Felix, who was running patrol in that section of the forest?" Cole asked the warrior, whose name I now know is Felix.

"Jackson" he answered without hesitation. A growl rumbled in Lupus's chest, but he didn't let it out. Cole huffed and averted his eyes. Okay, so there is something up with this Jackson guy, something that has the others on edge.

"Bring him in. Now!" Cole barked his order. Felix bowed his head and he and Faylene left the room.

"Cole, what are you thinking?" Romeá asked him, gently placing her hand on his forearm.

"I think Beta Elaine is right, it was too easy for them to get onto the pack grounds, and then get out again without anyone raising the alarm. Our security is tight, our patrols are constant and thorough. The likelihood that they just slipped in and slipped out again is near zero".

"Traitors" Lupus growled. His anger stunk up the room and his powerful aura was suffocating. I would have liked to meet him in his younger years. I have no doubt he would have been a spectacular Alpha. Speaking of Alphas,

"Where is Gunner and Zelena?" I asked. Lupus snapped his angry gaze to me and huffed. Romeá placed her hand on his chest and murmured something into his ear. He calmed down and his pinched face relaxed, somewhat.

"They're at the beach. We haven't told them yet, we wanted to let them have a break, Goddess knows they need it" Romeá answered.

"The Alpha didn't feel the unwelcome visitors when they crossed?" I asked.

"We believe not, he hasn't contacted anyone about it. It's possible with the visiting Weres still here, and the fact they were so close to the border's edge, he may have dismissed the feeling as one of them"

"It makes for good cover" Alyse said pensively.

"Okay, that's fine, we can do this ourselves. Where are you at with it?" I asked turning back to Cole.

"Felix and his patrol went to the area and found nothing. Whoever these Weres are, they're smart. Not just smart, they're crafty" he answered me,

"And are you sure this Felix can be trusted?" Phoebe interjected. Cole stood tall and growled at her a warning,

"Felix is our highest-ranking Commander. He is loyal beyond compare, yes I trust him" Cole snarled. Lupus pulled Cole back by his shoulder, which Cole shrugged off.

"Calm down, she had to ask, you would have done the same in her place" Lupus said to him quietly.

"This is the second time we've come across a Feral on your land in the short time we've been here" I began but was interrupted by Cole,

"What! Why is this the first time I'm hearing of it?" Cole shouted,

"Because the first time we thought it was random, and it disappeared as quickly as it arrived" I answered him with a roll of my eyes.

"I still should have been notified. If I'm going to stick my neck out for you, I expect a little respect in return". That hit true, dammit. He's right, unfortunately. We should have told them. But in our defence, we still weren't sure who we could trust at that point.

"I'm sorry, Beta Cole, we should have told you".

"Yeah, you should have, clearly this is not random"

"Obviously" Lupus grunted.

"Alright, alright, everyone calm down. We're not going to accomplish anything by snapping at each other" Romeá called out and waved her hands above her head.

"Sorry love" Lupus said as he wrapped his arm around her hip and pulled her back to his chest. Romeá smiled shyly and sunk into his hold.

"So what's our next move?" Alyse asked,

"I think the first step is alerting the Alpha and Luna of what is going on. This is no small matter and they need to be here" I said firmly. Elaine and Phoebe had been unusually quiet during this entire conversation. I looked at Elaine and she was watching me. I pulled a face, trying to ask her 'What's up'. She raised a brow but said nothing in return.

"I think she's right Roe. They've had a couple of hours, that will have to do" Cole said, looking down at Romeá. She mumbled quietly to herself before giving in and nodding her head.

"Are we going to wait for Felix to get back with Jackson? So we at least have something to tell them" Lupus asked no one in particular, but his eyes were on Cole.

"I don't think…" Cole began to answer but was cut off by the door flying open. I turned to the doorway, as did everyone else, standing there was an enraged Felix.

"Felix, what the fuck?" Cole growled and stepped forward. My stomach dropped, I already knew this was bad. All you had to do was look at his face to know it.

"He's gone" Felix growled,

"Who's gone?" Cole demanded.

"Fucking Jackson" Felix answered, spitting the name Jackson like it burned his tongue.

"How did that happen!?" roared Lupus. The tension in the room skyrocketed. Anger was flowing out of everyone.

"He ripped out one of his warrior's throats and slashed apart another". With the news from Felix, screaming erupted from the Tri-Moon members, along with deathly growls from Elaine and Phoebe.

"Fuck!"

"WHAT!"

"Oh no! No, no, no"

"How? When?" Cole demanded,

"The bodies are still warm and his scent is fresh, couldn't have been more than half an hour".

"Call Gunner. Call him right fucking now" Lupus roared again. Elaine and Phoebe were whispering behind me and Alyse clung to my arm, but my focus was on Cole and his flash with Gunner. He had his eyes closed but an uncomfortable look on his face.

"What is it?" I asked,

"I can't reach him" Cole answered. He kept his eyes closed, still trying to get the connection. After a second his eyes flew open and he stared at me wide eyed. Just like he did on the road the night we arrived. He pushed passed Felix and rushed out the door. We all followed him as he continued through the front door and outside.

"Cole, where the fuck are you going?" Lupus screamed at him, but Cole didn't answer. We followed him around the side of the house to a driveway. A large black SUV was parked to the side with its doors open. The redhead Were was reaching into the backseat when Cole ran up to his side. Together they worked to pull something out of the car, then they turned around. Draped in between them, with one arm over each shoulder was an unconscious Gunner.

"My boy!" Romeá cried and rushed over to him, she grabbed his face in her hands and began inspecting every inch of her son's face and body.

"What happened?" she demanded of the redhead. My thoughts went straight to the Were Jackson and his disappearance. Did he attack Gunner and Zelena before he ran? Is that why he ran? I looked through the dark tinted windows of the SUV, trying to spot Zelena's body, but they were too dark.

The redhead hesitated, not wanting to answer. His cheeks were flushed and his hair was still wet. His eyes were wide and full of fear or worry, maybe dread. Whatever this look is, it's bad.

"Smith! Answer me!" Romeá growled at the young Were,

"It was Zelena" he said meekly. I stood tall and stepped toward them, my full attention now on the redhead called Smith.

"What do you mean it was Zelena?" Romeá hissed.

"She uh, she did something to him, I don't know what" he mumbled,

"Why would Zelena hurt her Mate?" I interjected. The Were looked at me and hesitated once again. The uncertainty was written all over his face.

"Speak boy!" I yelled at him,

"Because he attacked her" he answered.

Chapter Twenty-Nine

Zelena

I stood still in the shade of the forest, basically naked, and stared at Alpha Galterio. He is quite handsome. Thick dark hair and large brown eyes, creamy tanned skin that stretched over his taunt muscles. He's a big Were, a little intimidating as well, but I don't know if that is because of his size or the power that he exudes. Freedom to all Were-kind. That's what he said. How are we not already free? Is he talking about the scourge of the hunters? They are and always will be a threat to the Weres, but their numbers are unknown. How could we defeat them if we don't know where they are, or how many of them are out there? He stood watching me as I tried to understand the message behind his statement. I don't want to like him, he is cocky and arrogant, and he creeps me out. But there is something else there. Something that seems genuine, maybe. I really don't know about this. I don't want to trust him, but my damn stomach, it is reaching out for him.

"What does that mean?" I asked him cautiously.

"What's that, Beauty?" he answered with a sly smirk,

"Freedom to all of Were-kind. Freedom from what, from who? And how does that happen?"

"That happens through you. The Triple Goddess, standing at my side, supporting my cause and calling forth all the Weres of the world to join with us" he said smirking. He stood up from the tree and stepped towards me.

"You are the gift that the Moon Goddess promised us, you are the one that is meant to lead us. She has given you to us for a reason. I believe this, this cause, our cause, this is that reason. You will free us, Beauty. With my help, Were-kind will thrive in this world once more".

He is quite the motivational speaker, and even if I didn't want to believe in him, he had me on the ropes. What he says makes a lot of sense. Selene said that I was a gift, that I was the daughter the world needed. She also said that something big was coming, this must be it. This must be what she was talking about. A fight to free Were-kind.

"Thrive?" I said to myself softly,

"Thrive. Unbridled, unshackled, and free" he said encouragingly.

"By defeating the hunters?" I asked, looking deep into his big eyes,

"Among others" he smirked.

Zelena!

Gunner's panicked voice filled my head. I snapped my head back towards the beach, but I couldn't see the sand through the trees.

"I have to go" I said looking back to Galterio,

"We need to discuss this" he replied, the edge in his voice hardened.

Zelena, where are you?

"I'm sorry, Gunner is calling and if he sees you right now, he'll kill you on the spot"

"He can try" Galterio growled. His brown eyes darkened and a deadly look came over his face.

I'm coming

Where the fuck are you?

"We will talk more, let me calm this situation first" I said trying to ease his anger or rage, or whatever that look in his eye was.

"Don't make me wait too long, Beauty, time is of the essence" he snarled,

"I won't".

"I'll be waiting" he said as he turned to leave,

"Wait, how do I find you?" I asked him,

"I'll be watching" he offered a crooked smirk over his shoulder before he took off in a blur. He'll be watching, creepy. The way he snaps between personalities is like a roller coaster ride. Seductive, then sweet, threatening, then genuine, nice then creepy. Who the heck is this guy? But irregardless, I want to know more about this cause. Defeating the hunters, the monsters that stole my life, it would be such sweet candy. Ending their threat to Were-kind would bring all of us peace, and in a way, freedom.

Zelena!

I gazed in the direction that Galterio had run, but he was long gone. I huffed and turned around to jog back towards the beach. As I got to the edge of the trees, I picked up my pace. I wasn't looking ahead as I burst through the last of the tree line and I collided with Gunner's chest.

"Ouch" I mumbled as I steadied my feet and rubbed my nose. Gunner gripped the top of my arms hard, really hard. His fingertips dug into my skin. He held me close, but not pressed up against his body like usual. He was holding me at a distance.

"Ow Gunner, you're hurting me" I hissed as I tried to break out of his hold. I grabbed at one of his hands and pulled at his fingers, but he didn't relent. I looked up to his face and felt instant dread. I have never seen him look at me like this. His eyes are murderous, dark, and narrow. His jaw is clenched tight and his neck muscles are tensed and strained. The corner of his top lip was curled up and exposed one of his sharp canines.

"Where were you?" he snarled harshly,

"I went for a walk" I lied. I tried to pull his hand from my arm but he wouldn't budge.

"Gunner stop, you're hurting me" I snapped. A low growl came through his clenched teeth and he leaned down to me. He ran his nose over my shoulder and up my neck. Oh no. I forgot.

"I can smell him on you" he growled dangerously.

"Gunner, listen to me, please. Let me go and we can talk" I pleaded. I tried to wriggle from his grip but he was not letting go. Tears pooled in my eyes and panic began to set in.

"Who is he?" he asked. His voice was calm, but the threat behind it was anything but.

"Gunner, let me go!" I screamed as the first tear slid from my eye.

"WHO IS HE!?" he roared. The sound of his voice echoed across the beach and through the air. The anger he was exuding washed over me like a hot wave, burning deep into my skin. I remember what happened last time I gave over to it, what I did to him. I don't ever want to do that or feel that again. More tears began to fall from my eyes and roll down my cheeks as I fought against the urge to give in to his rage. I struggled angrily against his grip, but he only pressed his fingers into me harder. He's too big and much stronger than I am. I have no hope of overpowering him this way. The tips of his claws pressed into my flesh, piercing the skin. I cried out in pain and looked up to meet Gunner's eyes. Fear overwhelmed my body as I took in his dangerous and uncaring expression. The fact that he was causing me pain didn't register, he was more than angry, he looked crazed and bloodthirsty. He is fully engulfed in his rage, and I don't know how to stop it. He's going to hurt me. For the first time ever, I am afraid of Gunner.

"Please" I cried, continuing to wiggle around. He didn't answer me, just watched me cry and thrash in his deathly grip. This wasn't my Gunner. My Gunner was loving, caring, and gentle. Whoever this Were is, he's rough and callous, and downright terrifying. His anger danced through my veins, trying to seduce me to the darkness, but I fought against it. The growl that rumbled through his chest was enough to put a stop to my thrashing. I looked up to his dark and dangerous eyes. Tears blurred my vision, but the rage on his face was clear.

"Gunner, stop it, please" I pleaded. But it was no use. There was no getting through to him, not like this. Tobias is too far away to flash for help, and Gunner is the only other person I have flashed with. I don't know what to do, I can't use my powers on him. Not again. Not after the last time. I looked over Gunner's shoulder and saw Smith and Nat standing together further down the beach, they were too far away to be able to hear us. They were watching Gunner and me, but still totally unaware of the situation. And then it dawned on me. I have become close with both of them. Nat is like my sister, and Smith is my bestest friend. We are meant to be able to flash with the ones we have a special bond with, that's why I can flash with Tobias. In a last-ditch effort, I called for them, reaching out with my mind.

Help me!

No response. Gunner tightened his hold and shook my body. I looked back at him, and his canines were now fully extended. I sobbed and tried to kick him, but my bare feet hitting his shin had no effect.

"Stop it" he growled and lifted me off the ground so that my face was in line with his.

"Who is he, Zelena?" he demanded. His hot breath slapped against my face, his claws buried into my skin. I looked back to Smith and Nat and they were walking slowly through the water towards us.

Smith!

I flashed. With all the power I could, calling on every tiny aspect of our bond. He stopped in his tracks and looked up at me with a tilt of his head.

Zelena?

Smith's voice echoed in my mind. I cried out a sob and struggled in Gunner's hands. He caught where I was looking, seeing my eyes on Smith and it only enraged him further.

Smith, help me!

I screamed through my flash. He took off running just as Gunner tipped his head back and roared. The sudden burst to my eardrums startled me and I screamed out loud. As Gunner's head came back down, he glared at me and growled. His head came forward and before I had a chance to react, his teeth sank into the side of my neck. The pain was excruciating, worse than anything I had felt before. The other times that Gunner had bitten me was during an intimate moment, and that pain was pleasurable. But this... this was all pain. Uninvited, unwanted, and completely torturous. I felt like my body was on fire and my insides were trying to tear their way out.

I screamed so loud, the sound disappeared. Instincts took over and I lifted my hand. Gunner and his grip on me went flying away. I dropped to my knees and grabbed my neck, as I pulled my hand back to my face, it was covered in blood. Gunner landed in the sand at the feet of Nat and Smith. He quickly snapped back to his feet in a crouched position and growled with his full canines bared.

"Gunner, what the fuck are you doing?" Nat screeched and grabbed at his shoulder. He snatched her hand away and used it to throw her across the beach. She screamed as she flew through the air before thumping back onto the sand, her head hitting the ground first. That was all it took, that was enough to knock her unconscious. Smith ran to Nat's side as Gunner charged back towards me again. Just as he was about to reach me, I put up my force field. Gunner hit it at full speed and bounced backward. This did nothing to snap him out of his rage, if anything it made it worse. He roared and yelled as he smashed his fists against the invisible wall. Smith was approaching him from behind with his mouth moving, he was trying to talk him down. But when Gunner turned around to swipe at Smith with his claws, I snapped.

I dropped the wall and wrapped my power around Gunner's body. I lifted him into the air, and he screamed for me to release him. He growled and barked and tried desperately to thrash about, but my hold was unbreakable.

"What the fuck happened?" yelled Smith from the other side of where Gunner was hovering. He shifted his gaze from Gunner to me and then his eyes went wide. He ran to me and dropped down at my side, he went to touch my neck but I pushed his hand away.

"What happened Zelena?" he asked urgently,

"He attacked me" I snarled up at Gunner. Smith looked from me to Gunner and back again,

"He would never" Smith said with a deep breath.

Gunner roared again and tried to fight against my hold. His rage was getting worse, and it was getting harder to push it back. If I didn't get him to calm down, if I couldn't bring my Gunner back, we could both get lost in the darkness. I struggled to my feet, keeping my eyes on Gunner. The pain in my neck and arms was drowned out by the hot anger crushing against my flesh. I twitched and contracted my fingers and the power around Gunner tightened. He screamed out in pain and frustration. I moved the power further up to his neck and I let it tighten around his throat, I held it there until his screaming stopped.

"Zelena! Zelena, stop!" Smith yelled and tried to grab my hand. I pushed his hand away and hissed at him.
"Zelena, your eyes are glowing. Please stop, you're killing him" Smith begged me.
"I'm not going to kill him" I snapped.
I just wanted to knock him out, a minute without air should put him on his ass. Gunner growled and coughed for a little longer than I expected, then he was quiet. As I lowered him to the ground, I felt sick to my stomach. My body felt weak and tired. Smith rushed to Gunner's side and checked his pulse. He looked back at me and nodded his head, indicating that Gunner was okay. Pain erupted through my body, constricting my very breath, My head began to spin and my vision went blurry. I was falling, slowly heading face first into the sand, when my body was flung upwards, and I landed against a hard chest.
"Put her down" I heard Smith growl. I tried to refocus my eyes and look at the face above me, but I was just too tired and I didn't have the energy. My body went limp in the arms of the one holding me. I took in a deep breath before I passed out, cologne and wet earth filled my nose.

~

My stomach was in knots and I felt weak and nauseous. I ached all over. Everything hurt. I groaned and rolled over on the bed, reaching for Gunner. What a terrible dream. I pressed my face into his chest and inhaled deeply. I quickly flew upright and stared at the person I was just cuddling into. Galterio smirked back at me. It wasn't a dream.
"I prefer to be the big spoon" he mused with a cheeky twitch of his lip. He sat on the bed with his back leaning against the headboard and his hands behind his head, his legs were laid out along the bed with his ankles crossed. I quickly looked down at myself and saw that I was now draped in a baggy white t-shirt. I flicked my eyes over the room we were in, confirming that we were alone in here.
"Where am I?" I snapped back at Galterio,
"Is that the welcome I get after rescuing you?" he teased, still smirking. I closed my eyes and pinched the bridge of my nose, hoping to ward off my headache. What the fuck happened? Gunner was angry, he was hurting me. I looked at my arms where Gunner had been holding me, staring back were large

angry bruises and angry red cuts where his claws penetrated the skin. Then I remembered he bit me, I whipped my hand to my neck and felt a bandage on the place that he bit. He attacked me. Gunner. How could he do that to me? Tears began to fall from my eyes and my breathing quickened. He said he would never hurt me. He knows what I went through with Hank. Why would he do this to me? Broken sobs burst from within me and I felt like my heart was being ripped from my chest. He hurt me. He hurt me. He hurt me.

"It's alright, you're alright" Galterio said softly as he pulled me into his lap and forced my head to his chest.

"I got you Beauty, you're okay" he said with a smooth tone while he brushed his hand over my head and hair. I slapped his hand away and pushed myself off of his lap. He looked hurt or angry at my rejection, but quickly brushed over it with a charming smile.

"What am I doing here Alpha Galterio? Where are we and why aren't I healing?" I asked, letting him hear the anger in my voice.

"So many questions, can't we just lay back down and cuddle?" he chuckled and tried to grab my hand,

"It's not funny Alpha Galterio, where did you take me?" I growled lowly.

"Firstly, we're family so it's just Galterio, or Teri, to you. But if you play your cards right, I might even let you call me Gilly" he winked and blew me a kiss. I growled and flashed my teeth.

"Ugh, you're no fun. Fine! You're here because your Mate nearly ripped your throat out and you needed my help. And here is my temporary residence" he answered with a slight frown and a wave of his hand to the room.

"I had that handled, my packmate could have helped me" I snapped. Galterio jumped to his feet and using his extreme speed, he dashed to the side of the bed that I was sitting on. He placed one hand on either side of my body and leaned forward, forcing me to lean back.

"The same packmate that let his Alpha nearly kill you" he growled down at me,

"That wasn't Gunner, something was wrong with him. And besides if you hadn't put your greasy hands all over me, he wouldn't have been able to smell you, and then he wouldn't have gotten so angry" I growled back just as furiously. Galterio scoffed and stood up straight. I moved to slide off the bed when a tight cramp pulled at my insides. I clutched at my stomach and winced with a hiss.

"What's wrong?" he asked. He tried to remain firm but the worry in his voice seeped through.

"My stomach hurts, my arms hurt, I have a hole in my neck, I'm tired, I was kidnapped, and my Mate tried to hurt me. Take your pick" I groaned.

"I'll get you something to eat and drink" he mumbled before walking out the door. The lock clicked behind him and as much as it hurt me, I jumped to my feet and ran to the door. Locked. I thumped my back against the door and slid down to the floor. For the first time, I took a proper look around the room. It had soft white walls, and the furnishings were pretty and modern. The bedspread was light grey with teal and there was a matching teal armchair in the corner by a window. A window. I curled my arm around my stomach and jumped to my feet again, then dashed to the window, pulling apart the curtains. Nothing. There was a board or something blocking it from the outside. He has me locked up in here like a prisoner. I turned around feeling defeated and went back to the bed. As I sat down, a sharp pain burst through my stomach and I cried out from the unexpected feeling. I fell onto my side, clutched at my stomach, and curled myself into a ball. It felt like something inside me was trying to claw its way out.

"Zelena" Galterio called as he burst through the door. He placed a plate and bottle of water on the bedside table and came to my side. He grabbed my face between his large hands and turned it so that I was looking at him.

"What is it? What's wrong?" he asked me urgently while searching my eyes,

"It's my… my stomach" I strained to talk through the pain. Galterio grabbed the water and quickly opened the cap. He lifted me so that I sat leaning against his chest and pressed the bottle head to my lips.

"Drink" he said softly and I did as he asked. I took a large gulp and then another. The cool liquid slid down my throat and a chill ran through my chest. As I swallowed the water, I breathed in through my nose and caught the most mouth-watering scent. I pushed off Galterio's chest and sat upright with my nose in the air. I sniffed and followed the smell to the plate sitting on the bedside table. I crawled over the bed and reached for the plate. Picking up the large steak in my fist, I shoved it into my mouth and took a very large bite. The tender meat rolled around inside my mouth and a low growl rumbled up from my chest. I took another large bite, the biggest I could manage, and chewed slowly, letting the taste fill my mouth. I opened my eyes and saw Galterio standing beside the bed staring down at me with wide eyes. I must look like a total savage, with a piece of meat in my hand and steak juice running down my chin. I was immediately filled with shame and quickly looked away from him. I placed the steak back on the plate and swallowed the large chunk of meat in my mouth.

"I um… I'm sorry, I didn't realise how hungry I was" I mumbled full of embarrassment. He didn't respond, just stared at me with huge eyes and his mouth slightly open. I waited for him to speak but he didn't, which only made me feel more embarrassed.

"Galterio?" I said softly. He shook his head, blinked his eyes, and cleared his throat. He looked uncomfortable and unsure. He shifted from foot to foot, not something I had noticed him do before. He always stood strong and still and full of confidence. Now he looked about ready to run away.

"Galterio?" I said again,

"Yes, sorry. No need to apologise. Do you feel better now?" he asked quirking one of his eyebrows,

"Yes, weirdly I do. I guess I was just hungry" I said with an awkward smile. Galterio picked up the plate and handed it back to me,

"Well, eat up then" he said with a smile. The smile didn't reach his eyes though. He is a good actor and a smooth talker, but somehow, I can see right through him. And right now, I see hidden intentions and dark excitement. Despite that, I was starving, so I ate it all. I had to force myself not to lick the plate clean of the steak juice. Galterio watched me the entire time. Once I was done, he took my plate and was about to leave the room again.

"Wait" I called to him,

"Yes Beauty?" he asked as he turned back around.

"Where are you going? Can I come with you?" I asked, trying to make my voice as sweet and innocent as possible. But in truth, I just needed to find a way out of here and back to Tri-Moon. Galterio looked me over for a minute, studying my face closely.

"Will you behave?" he asked with a smirk. That smirk is really starting to get on my nerves.

"What exactly does 'behaving' entail?" I asked as I crossed my arms over my chest.

"You don't hurt anyone. You listen with an open mind when I talk to you about the cause. And most importantly, you don't run" he said back, mimicking my stance with his arms crossed.

"Don't run? So, I'm a prisoner?" I sneered,

"No Beauty, you are a guest. A very important and protected guest. It will be hard to protect you if you are running from me and my guards" he mused with a teasing grin.

"Fine, whatever. But I want to know more about this cause. Like now" I demanded. Galterio laughed and opened the door of the bedroom.

"As much as I like seeing you on that bed, Beauty, I think we should have this chat somewhere else. Especially if you want to keep my attention on the cause and not those legs of yours".

I shuffled uncomfortably in place and tried to pull the t-shirt further down my exposed legs. Galterio stepped through the door and stood holding it open for me. I slowly got up off the bed and went to the door. I slid through the frame, putting as much space between the two of us as I could manage. He watched me with hungry eyes as I moved, which made my skin crawl. He headed down a hallway, passing closed doors on both sides before it opened up into a large open-plan living space. For a temporary residence, this place is nice! Everything is so shiny and modern, with sharp edges and clean colours everywhere.

First, Galterio led me to a very big and open kitchen with huge white marble benchtops and lots of floor to ceiling cupboards. He went to the fridge and pulled out a blue container and then handed it to me with a smile. I took the container but didn't get to open it because he began walking away again. He stopped at the front door and placed his hand on the handle, then turned to look at me.

"You will behave?" he questioned. I didn't respond just nodded my head. This is it. My chance to escape. Galterio opened the door and stepped through. As soon as I followed him, a flurry of noise invaded my ears. The space around the large white house was alive with activity. Weres and wolves all moving about busily. I hadn't realised that I had stopped walking to stare at the commotion until I felt a hand on my back, gently guiding me forward. Galterio led us to a small table and chairs that were sitting under a pergola. He sat down and indicated for me to do the same.

"What is all this?" I asked him as I kept watching all the movement.

"First, eat" he replied and pointed to the container in my hands. I popped open the lid and pulled out a cold lamb chop. I took a bite and swallowed it quickly,

"Okay, now explain, what this is" I said, waiving the lamb chop in the air.

"This is the cause. My pack, a couple of other packs, even a few roamers and Omega's. All united under one dream" he said with pride.

"To defeat the hunters?" I said turning my gaze to him.

"That, among other things" he chuckled and kicked his legs up onto the edge of the table and crossed his arms behind his head. The bottom of his shirt rode up, exposing a set of smooth and creamy and perfectly defined abdominal muscles. He caught my staring and laughed again as he grabbed the hem of his shirt and pulled it up to the top of his chest, exposing his entire abdomen. He ran his hand over his defined muscles and chuckled.

"Do you like what you see, Beauty?" he asked as he watched me with an amused grin,

"You're no Gunner" I quipped back. I put the container up on the table and smirked at Galterio. He frowned and lowered his shirt again.

"That Alpha..." he began to growl with a harsh and hateful tone, but I quickly cut him off,

"Don't! Don't you dare talk about him. If you want me to listen to this plan of yours, then you leave him out of it" I snapped. Galterio growled and his lips turned up into a snarl.

After a second, he dropped the angry look and huffed out a short harsh breath.

"Fine" he conceded.

"So, go on then. Your plan?" I pushed him to start his spiel. The quicker he gets this over with, the quicker I can get out of here, hopefully.

"With you and I leading the charge, the last two remaining direct descendants of the children of Lycaon, no Were could turn us away. We will be able to rally together Weres from across the world, they will all want to join our fight" he began,

"To defeat the hunters" I interjected,

"Yes Beauty, to put an end to the hunters and more" he replied,

"What is the 'more' part you're talking about?" I asked him cautiously, I don't quite like where this is heading.

"Once the hunters are gone, Were-kind will have one less thing to fear. But in order for us to truly become free, we need to come out of the shadows".

"What does that mean exactly?"

"It means that us Weres are the apex predators. We are the strongest, fastest, and the best in every way. Why should we live in secret? Why should we be forced to hide away from the world? Weres are the higher beings, we should be ruling" he spoke with conviction and pride. He was sure of every word that came from his mouth. But I was still confused as to what he was trying to get at.

"Galterio, I don't understand. You want me to help you rule over the Weres?" I asked with my nose scrunched up. He chuckled and leaned back in his chair.

"No Beauty, I want the Weres to rule over everyone" he answered with a cocky grin,

"Everyone, as in..."

"The humans, Zelena. I'm talking about the filthy fucking humans! They kill each other for fun, half of them are too fat and the other half are dying of hunger. They are stupid and selfish creatures, and they are beneath us in every possible way! They should be the ones hiding in the shadows. They should be scared of us hunting and killing them! Not the other way around" Galterio's voice slowly raised in volume and anger as he spoke, until he was screaming at me with his hands on the table and his body leaning forward. All this time he was talking about defeating all humans, not just the hunters. The amount of hatred in his voice was disarming. What could possibly have happened to him for his hatred to go so deep?

Galterio was fuming. He sat glaring at me with his chest heaving up and down in ragged breaths. His face was red and his dark eyes were watching me through thin slits. As I tried to wrap my head around this new revelation, a commotion in the yard caught my attention. A small group of wolves came running into the space in front of the house, barking and growling at everyone to get out of their way. Galterio shot to his feet and walked to the edge of the pergola,

"Stay" he growled back at me before walking over to the group of wolves. Stay. Like I am a dog at his command. I don't think so. I stood up and watched him as he approached them. I noticed one of the wolves, a large tan coloured wolf, was carrying another smaller brown wolf in its mouth. The tan wolf dropped the small wolf on the ground at Galterio's feet. The little wolf jumped to its feet and snapped its jaws at the tan wolf. Something about the dirty brown wolf rang familiar in my mind, but I'm not sure why. Galterio grabbed the brown wolf by the neck, one hand holding the front and one holding the back. He lifted the wolf to his eye level, displaying an incredible amount of strength. The wolf was bigger than Galterio in his human form, but still small for a Were. The fact that he could lift it with ease, was a show of power if nothing else. Galterio had his canines fully extended and on show. He pulled the wolf close to his face and growled at it,

"Shift" he commanded of it. I have never seen an Alpha demand a Were to change form. I didn't even know it was possible. The small brown wolf howled and shook in Galterio's hold, but it looked like it was struggling to change. After another minute of the wolf shaking, its bones snapped out and then back in again, but it didn't turn back. Watching it was horrendous. The little wolf was in an incredible amount of pain. It was gruesome.

"SHIFT!" Galterio roared. The wolf howled, throwing its head back at an impossible angle. And then, it changed. The human left dangling in Galterio's hands was thin, gauntly, and covered in dirt. I recognised who it was right away. The bitch that wanted me gone. Fucking Zoe.

Chapter Thirty

Lunaya

"WHAT DO YOU MEAN HE ATTACKED HER?!" I bellowed. My furious voice echoed around the entire pack land. I'm sure every Were in the vicinity heard me. Elaine jumped forward and wrapped her massive arms around my upper body. I suppose she assumed I was going to attack. She wasn't wrong. I wanted to kill the Were called Smith, I don't care that he is just the messenger. I really wish that I could shoot lasers from my eyes at this moment. I glared at my daughter's Mate's limp body. I wanted blood for what he did to her. I looked behind where Smith and Cole were holding the unconscious Gunner, waiting for Zelena to exit the car. But she wasn't there. Roe was crying hysterically while running her hands over Gunner's face, and Lupus was pacing back and forth, swearing to himself. Phoebe stood close to Elaine and me, ready to help Elaine restrain me should it be needed. Alyse was cautiously moving closer to where the boys were holding Gunner, taking slow steps so as to not make it too obvious. And Zelena was missing.

"Where is my daughter?" I hissed angrily. Lupus snapped his eyes to me and stomped a few steps in my direction,

"She isn't just your daughter, she's our daughter too. She's our Luna! We love her too!" he yelled. He held his hands in tight fists at his side and his whole body was shaking. I could see he was hurting and scared, but all I could focus on was my own anger and concern. I went to step toward the two males holding up Gunner, but couldn't move under Elaine's hold.

"Before we do anything, we need to restrain Gunner. I don't know what he is going to be like when he comes too again" Smith groaned under the weight of the Alpha hanging from his shoulder.

"Felix is busy, and he has taken two other patrol groups with him" Cole addressed the group of us that had gathered in the driveway,

"Wait, busy with what? And why does he need that many fighters?" Smith asked, angling his neck forward to see over Gunner's drooping head.

"I'll explain after" Cole replied to him.

"I've called Mazz and Julien, they will take Gunner to the cabin and keep him there until we know what's going on" Lupus said, his voice now sounding much calmer. All this talk and still no one has told me where the heck my daughter is. A growl slowly bubbled in my chest, growing steadily, until it came bursting out through my clenched teeth and waved over everyone. Elaine's hold on me tightened as the growl vibrated through my body.

"Where is Zelena?" I demanded. My voice was low and threatening. Two men came around the side of the house. One short with no hair and the other tall with long grey hair. I had noticed them both around the village over the past couple of days, they were each respected and high ranking. They nodded to Lupus and carefully pulled Gunner from Roe's grip and took him from Smith and Cole, as they turned to leave, I screamed,

"Stop! What has he done with my daughter?". The two men turned to Lupus, who nodded his head once. I struggled in Elaine's arms but was forced to watch them walk away with my child's Mate. Once they were out of sight, we all collectively turned back to Smith. Alyse had made her way over to Roe's side and took her hand, lifting it to her chest and gripping it with both hands. Roe smiled gratefully at Alyse and pressed herself into her side.

"What happened?" Alyse asked Smith in a cool and gentle tone,

"I don't know exactly. Nat and I were in the water a bit further down the beach from them, we thought they were just arguing because Zelena went for a walk without telling him. The water was drowning out the sound of their conversation" he paused and looked at Roe. He cares for her, not just because she is his former Luna, there's more to it than that. It seemed like whatever he was going to say would hurt her.

"Go on" Roe nodded.

"He had her by the upper arms. She flashed me, screaming for help, but before we could get the them..." he hesitated,

"What?" I pressed,

"He bit her. He tore into the side of her throat. We never thought he would actually hurt her" Smith pleaded. I felt my knees buckle, but with Elaine's support, I didn't fall. He bit her. He actually bit her. And against her will. Sorrow, anger, and pain squeezed at my heart.

"And where is Nat now?" Roe cut in,

"She's still at the beach. Gunner tossed her across the sand, she hit her head pretty bad and is seriously fucking scared of him right about now. She wouldn't get back in the car with him in it. So, she stayed to look for Zelena"

"What do you mean she's looking for Zelena? Where the fuck is my daughter?" I yelled again and struggled under Elaine's hold.

"Fuck! Will you just let me talk, all of you, please" Smith yelled back, shaking his fists in front of his face. Alyse looked over at me and mouthed the word 'stop'. I snarled and thrashed in Elaine's arms but didn't say anything more.

"Smith, where is Zelena?" Alyse asked, maintaining her smooth calm tone. Alyse, always the level-headed one. Forever dependable and willing to be the mediator.

"I... I don't know" he mumbled,

"Excuse me?" I snapped,

"I said I don't know. After Gunner bit her, she suspended him in the air and cut off his oxygen. She was bleeding a lot, and using her power to hold him off just seemed to make her even weaker. I was checking that Gunner was still breathing when she passed out, but before she even hit the ground, some guy just appeared out of nowhere and grabbed her. I warned him to let her go, but before I could stop him, he just disappeared again" he muttered as his hands ran through his shaggy hair and pulled on the ends. The further he got in his story, the more I wanted to kill. Her Mate attacked her so badly that she was suffering from blood loss! How could he do this to her? Why the fuck would he do this to her? If Gunner doesn't have some kind of magically brilliant, beyond brilliant, reason behind his actions, I will end him.

"What guy?" Lupus growled,

"I had never seen him before. He just sort of appeared there, he wasn't on the beach, and he wasn't anywhere nearby. I don't know how he got there, or how they vanished" he groaned.

"Hunter?" Lupus growled,

"No, he was definitely not human" Smith answered. He was frustrated. His face was pale, his green eyes were blown wide, and his breaths were short and sharp. He was on the verge of a full blown panic attack. I would know, as I've had them for seventeen years. But still, he let some unknown man kidnap my child. I was burning with anger, my blood boiled from it.

"You let someone take her" I growled.

"I didn't let him take her, he just did. How the fuck am I meant to stop an enigma" Smith snarled back.

"Where is her guardian?" Phoebe spoke for the first time,

"He's at his former pack, his younger brother just had his Alpha ascension ceremony. He is due back today though" Roe answered the question.

"Good fucking use he is then, isn't he?" Phoebe cursed quietly.

"When are we going to stop pulling on each other's dicks, and go and actually find my fucking daughter?" I growled and struggled again to break free of Elaine. Damn this she-wolf and her unnatural strength. Elaine growled lowly and moved her mouth to my ear,

"Calm the fuck down, or I will lock you up alongside the Alpha" she warned me.

"You wouldn't dare" I hissed back,

"Try me, Lunaya". I growled at her, and she growled back at me. We stood there, me struggling to get my arms free of her iron grip, her holding onto me in a bear hug, and the both of us growling like feral animals.

"Enough you two" Alyse shouted. I snapped my eyes to her and frowned.

"We won't get anything accomplished with you two at each other's throats as well. Lunaya, you need to chill the fuck out. I get it. This is your daughter, and you're scared. But we need to work together now more than ever if we are going to find her".

This woman and her common sense. I both love it and hate it about her. I tried taking a deep breath to calm my erratic heartbeat. After a few more breaths I could feel the heat slowly leaving my body. The fear didn't budge though. I had only just gotten her back, and now someone has taken her from me once again. My stomach had collapsed in on itself with fear and dread. I won't wait another seventeen years to find her again.

"Beta Elaine, you can let me go now" I said calmly. Very slowly Elaine loosened her hold until I was able to step out of her arms.

"I'm sorry" I said to Roe and Lupus,

"No need to be, I'm worried too" Roe squeaked.

"First, we need to wake up Gunner. If he is in his right mind, he may be able to tell us more about the man who took her" Cole said to the group,

"And why he attacked the Triple Goddess" Elaine inserted. No one answered her, but it was evident that we all wanted an answer to that question. Cole turned to Smith, and they began a conversation about fighters, commanders, and gathering a small pack together. Lupus had pulled Roe into his arms and was trying to soothe her and calm her weeping. Elaine and Phoebe were whispering about gathering the other she-wolves and preparing them for a fight. It looks like both Luna Eclipse and Tri-Moon are expecting this to get violent. I already know it will. I will personally rip off the arms from the Were that took her.

Finally, Elaine, Cleo, Lupus, myself, and Cole, all headed for the cabin. The same little hut that they took Zelena to during her heat. We all changed into our wolves and ran through the forest at top speed. As we neared the cabin, I could hear roaring. I guess Gunner is awake.

We came up to the front door and changed back, all except Cleo who elected to wait outside. The outside of the small hut shook under the force of Gunner's roaring and banging on the walls. Lupus led the way inside and down a narrow staircase. The two men that brought Gunner here were positioned on either side of the large steel door.

"How long has he been awake?" Lupus asked,

"He started screaming about five minutes ago" the tall one answered.

"Have you spoken with him?" Cole questioned,

"Are you fucking kidding? I'm not opening that door, not when there is an out of control Alpha on the other side" the tall one huffed and walked past us and stood at the bottom of the staircase. The short one smirked and stood beside him and motioned for us to open the door.

Lupus gripped the handle and pulled the heavy door open. We were met with a ferocious growl and a body slamming against the steel bars that separated us from him. Gunner looked crazy. Dark wild eyes bursting from their sockets and red flushed skin. His claws and canines were out and sprouts of hair were bursting through the skin on his arms and exposed chest. Gunner's eyes found Cole first and he roared and shook the steel bars.

"You fucking traitor!" Gunner screamed at the top of his lungs while glaring at Cole. Where did that come from?

"Gunner!" Lupus bellowed. Gunner snapped his head to his father and his face fell. A look of confusion and hurt came over him and he stopped shaking the bars.

"Dad?" Gunner said softly,

"What did you do, son?" Lupus asked him firmly,

"I... I didn't do anything. What's happening? You're with Cole?" Gunner mumbled, moving his eyes from his father to Cole and back again.

"Gunner, what do you remember?" Cole asked stepping closer to the cell door. Gunner growled and threw his arms through the gap in the bars and tried to swipe at Cole. When he missed, he grabbed the vertical bars and shook the door with all his might.

"Don't you fucking speak to me you filthy fucking traitor! I'll kill you for this you bastard" Gunner roared. I am completely lost now. What is it that Cole has done? Either way, my patience was starting to run thin.

"Gunner! Enough!" Lupus yelled,

"How could you, my own father! How could you side with him?" he half yelled half sobbed.

"Son, I don't know what it is you think he has done, but I'm still on your side" Lupus replied calmly.

"He locked me in this fucking cell so he could take over the pack, that's what. You've been the traitor the whole time, haven't you?"

"Gunner, what the fuck are you talking about?" Lupus asked exasperatedly.

"He's the one that's been working with Origin Wolf. He betrayed me, he betrayed this pack. And all for what? So that he could take over" Gunner hissed back with venom dripping from his words. Lupus looked at Cole for an answer, but Cole didn't give him one. He dropped his head and his shoulders fell. Oh no. Cole said he did something bad, did he really betray his Alpha, his pack?

"You aren't even going to deny it" Gunner grunted.

"Gunner, I..." Cole began,

"Don't bother" snapped Gunner.

"Is it true?" Lupus asked, turning his full body to face Cole.

"No. Not all of it" Cole answered meekly,

"Explain" rumbled Lupus.

"The Alpha from Origin Wolf called the pack house about three weeks after the battle. I was still reeling from Dad's death, and I was angry, you know that. He asked if the rumour was true, if we had the Triple Goddess. I wasn't thinking, I just had a fight with Gunner, I was just so damn mad. I didn't mean to tell him, it just slipped out" Cole spoke very quickly.

"You told Origin Wolf she was here?" Lupus repeated back to him,

"Not intentionally. I swear I didn't mean to. He kept going on and on about what a gift this would be, and if we had her he had to know. I just couldn't hear anymore more praise for her. All I said was that she's nothing special. I didn't think they would come here and demand to see her. I promise I haven't had any other contact with them, not since that one phone call. I swear on my father's grave" Cole rushed out.

"Your father's grave!" Lupus bellowed. He stepped up to Cole and wrapped his large hand around Cole's neck. I rushed over to them and tried to pull Lupus's hand away, but he didn't even register my presence.

"Your father would be rolling in his grave if he knew what you had done! You betrayed her. You betrayed this pack!" Lupus screamed as he lifted Cole off the ground.

"I didn't mean to" Cole spluttered.

"Lupus! Let him go" I ordered, but he ignored me. I looked to Elaine for help, but she stood with her arms crossed, watching the show unfold with keen interest. Gunner was growling and shaking the bars once again. The whole lot of them were going crazy, and none of this shit is going to help find my daughter.

"LUPUS!" I roared. I finally caught his attention, and he turned his murderous gaze to me.

"We have more pressing matters right now, remember?" I growled and pulled at his hand once more. Lupus growled at me and then turned and pulled Cole close to his face and growled again.

"We will talk about this more later. In the meantime, she's right. We have more important things to worry about". Lupus threw Cole away from him and slowly turned back around to face his son. I could feel his anger rolling off him. This subject is definitely not over with yet. Cole got back to his feet and rubbed at his throat.

"Are you okay?" I asked him as I helped him to his feet, he shoved me off and huffed,

"I'm fine" he ground out.

"Gunner" Lupus snapped to get Gunner's attention off Cole and back on him,

"Gunner, what do you remember from the beach?" Lupus asked him.

"The beach, why are you asking me about the beach?" Gunner muttered with deep frown lines running across his forehead.

"Answer the damn question" Lupus growled. He has definitely lost his patience now.

"I uh... I don't know. I was in the water with Smith and Nat, but I couldn't stop thinking about Zelena. I wanted to be with her, so I went back to the shore. After that it's kinda blank". He was looking down as he spoke, recounting the memory in his mind. But as he finished talking, he looked up and around the space where we were all standing. He was looking for her.

"Where is she, what did you do with her?" he asked, concern and urgency filtered through his words.

"That's it, that's all you remember?" Cole asked him,

"I don't answer to you, traitor" Gunner snarled at Cole.

"Son!" Lupus roared, recapturing Gunner's attention once more.

"That's all I remember" Gunner said with a nod. His fingers squeezed around the bars tight, until his knuckles turned white.

"Son, she isn't here. She's gone" Lupus said, cutting right to the point. Gunner reared back and his eyes went wide.

"Gone? Gone where? Tell me what the fuck is going on, what has gotten you all so fucking spooked?" he demanded and pressed his face right up to the bars of the cell.

"You happened, you attacked her. You tried to tear her fucking throat open!" Cole burst out. His own anger was now shining through. I knew he cared about her.

"Liar!" Gunner hissed venomously.

"You want to hate me for taking a phone call, well at least I didn't try to kill her" Cole growled,

"Stop it" Gunner spat,

"You don't fucking believe me? See for yourself" Cole snapped back. He closed his eyes and then Gunner's eyes went blank. They were flashing, which means Smith had already shown Cole everything that he saw at the beach. After a few seconds, Gunner's body began to shake. He stumbled on his feet, blinking his eyes rapidly, and then dropped to the ground on his knees.

"No. No, I couldn't. I wouldn't" he mumbled to himself while shaking his head.

"What happened Alpha Gunner? Why did you do it?" I asked, stepping up to the cell door.

"I... I don't know, I don't remember. How could I do this to her? I love her" he mumbled as a few tears rolled down his face.

"Julien! Bring Artemis" Lupus yelled over his shoulder. I heard the door open upstairs and the stomping of feet. Gunner had curled his legs to his chest and had his head resting on his knees. I felt terrible for him. Which was surprising to me. I wanted to kill him earlier, and now I just want to hold him. How could he not remember something like this? There has to be more to it, it's the only explanation.

"Whether you remember it or not, you did it. Now we need to figure out why" Lupus said with a low grumble.

"I wouldn't Dad! I would never hurt her, not intentionally" Gunner cried out from his slumped over body on the floor.

"But you still did, didn't you? We need to know why, and if you can't fucking remember attacking your own damn Mate, then something else has to be going on" Lupus yelled back. Gunner lifted his head and looked up to his father. His eyes were red and raw, and his cheeks were stained with tears.

"Something else?" Gunner asked softly. No one replied to his question. All of us were now deep in thought. Gunner was damn sure that Cole was a traitor, that he betrayed him. Why did his mind go there if he wasn't already thinking about it? Could Tri-Moon really have a traitor? And if they did, could whoever it is possibly be responsible for Gunner's violent behaviour?

I have no idea how long we all stood in silence for. Lupus stood against the wall with his arms crossed and his head down. Cole sat on the bottom step with his head in his hands. Elaine was at my side, also silently thinking. Gunner didn't move. His arms were wrapped around his legs and his face was buried in his knees. Every so often he would sniffle or curse to himself, but he didn't move from his spot. The door upstairs opened, and footsteps slowly made their way downstairs. Artemis appeared at the bottom step, next to where Cole was sitting, and he moved his eyes around the room. He looked at each of us carefully, before his eyes met mine and he held them there. He lifted one of his large bushy eyebrows, and he looked at me with a knowing look, a look that made me feel extremely uncomfortable.

"Artemis" Lupus said stepping forward.

"Yes?" Artemis replied and finally moved his eyes away from me.

"Something may be wrong with Gunner, can you run some tests?"

"What wrong?" Artemis asked as he peered through the cell bars and down at Gunner. Though I couldn't help but notice, he didn't look very concerned or like he cared for the Alpha at all.

"He's overly aggressive. And has been experiencing memory loss" Lupus replied,

"He is Alpha. Alpha always aggressive" Artemis said with frustration, his eyes once again finding mine.

"This is different. It's… excessive" Lupus said trying to recapture his attention. Artemis was staring into my eyes, looking deep inside me. Elaine stepped forward and moved slightly in front of me, blocking his view of me, and growled lowly at the healer.

"Artemis!" Lupus snapped. Artemis turned back to Lupus without a word.

"Can you test him for something?" Lupus growled with annoyance,

"No" Artemis quipped,

"NO?" Lupus repeated. His anger boiled through his words and his chest puffed out as he stood up tall and straight.

"What the fuck do you mean, no?" he rumbled. Artemis didn't respond he just turned on his heels and went for the stairs. Cole jumped to his feet and blocked the stairwell, keeping Artemis in the small space in front of the cell.

"Are you refusing to serve your Alpha?" Cole growled down at him,

"No" Artemis snapped back and pushed past Cole and went up the stairs. It became apparent that neither Lupus nor Cole was going to follow him, so I did. I rushed up the stairs and ran out the front door. Cleo's wolf was standing by the door, looking at Artemis. Artemis was about thirty meters into the thick of the trees, standing still, just looking out into the forest. It was like he was waiting.

"Wait here" I said to Cleo with a flick of my hand,

"Artemis, please, we need your help" I said as I jogged over to stand in front of him. He looked at me and once again quirked his eyebrow. His lips twitched like he was going to say something, but he didn't, and instead pressed them into a firm straight line.

"Please, can you help?" I asked him with a tilt of my head,

"I know your secret" he said ominously. I reared back and stared at the healer. How could he know I'm Zelena's mother? Only those of us who were at the dinner should know. I didn't think he was in the inner circle of Tri-Moon, privileged to that kind of knowledge. Or maybe... Could Elaine's assumption be true?

"You're a Prophet?" I said quietly. His lip twitched and a sly smirk spread across his face. My stomach turned, and at that moment, I knew I needed to be wary of this Were.

"What do you know?" I asked him. He stepped towards me and leaned in closer. His eyes rolled back and then he spoke in an eerie monotone voice,

"Spawned by the one who gave us breath. Vanished from life but spared from death. The Ethereal one gives she who is promised. To wield the power of the Triple Goddess. Where the moon is three, two will come. Once the seal is made, destiny is done. With one comes death, pain, and destruction. The other comes life, love, and devotion. Peril will end and the wolf will thrive. But for peace to reign, only one can survive".

Chapter Thirty-One

Zelena

Zoe. The whore that took Gunner's virginity. His only other lover. Why the heck is she still around? After being banished, she was meant to leave. She should be far away from Tri-Moon by now, Gunner can and will kill her if he catches her near his land. Wait, Zoe is a Were, I've seen her change before, she did it right in front of me. Why then did she struggle so much this time around? Also, what the fuck is she doing with Galterio's pack?!

Galterio was talking quietly to Zoe, quiet enough that I couldn't pick up what they were saying. I strained my hearing to try and make out the words, but I could only hear parts of it. The words 'failed me' and 'useless' and 'no longer needed' stood out above the rest. I remember Zoe being kind of pretty, big boobs, nice hair, and a face full of makeup. But this Zoe was wretched. Skin and bones with a feral look in her eye. I watched her closely as she talked with Galterio. Her mouth twitched a lot, especially when she spoke. Her eyes darted all around the place, like they were too hyper to stay in one spot. Her fingers twitched and scrunched and her foot bounced non-stop. She looks high as a kite. The longer they spoke, the crazier she started to look. After a few more seconds, Zoe seemed to snap. Her lips curled up and her forehead creased with deep frown lines.

 Zoe turned her gaze around the yard, she found my eyes and her frowning face hardened. Her mouth opened into a hiss, with her canines fully extended. Her body started to shake, and I thought she was having some kind of seizure. In a split second, she charged towards me. I was so shocked by her sudden burst of speed and surprised by her attack, that my brain didn't allow me the time to defend myself. She screeched out a high pitched deafening scream as her hand swung out at me. Just in the nick of time, I reared back. But not far enough. Her claws missed my throat, but instead caught my chest and left shoulder. I screamed and fell backward to the ground. Zoe flung herself towards me again and I crossed my arms over my face, readying myself to feel the pain she was about to inflict. But it didn't come. I looked back up and Zoe's body was now hanging above me. Her legs were kicking around wildly, and she was screaming and roaring into the air. One of Galterio's hands was holding the back of her neck, and his other hand was holding her wrist, keeping her claws away from his face. His growl shook the ground and echoed around the yard, catching the attention of everyone nearby.

"She is not yours to touch" Galterio roared at her. Zoe screeched again and tried to claw at Galterio. He did a weird flick thing with his arm and wrist. A sickening crack followed by a crunching sound came from Zoe, and then she was quiet. Her body was dropped limp in front of me, hitting the ground with a thump. My eyes immediately found her lifeless grey eyes. Her mouth was hanging open, but there was no air coming in or out of it. My gaze then moved to the bone sticking out of her neck. My stomach spoke before my mind did, I turned to the side and vomited all over the ground.

I was on my hands and knees, emptying my stomach when gentle hands gripped hold of my hips. My hair was pulled from my face and a hand moved from my hip to rub a soothing circle on my back. Once I stopped heaving, a cloth was pushed to my face so that I could wipe my mouth. I took the cloth and cleaned off the corners of my mouth. I looked back at Zoe's dead body and stared blankly into her barren eyes. I should feel something. Sad, scared, repulsed. Something. But

I feel nothing when I look at her. She wanted me gone, she tried to kill me. And now she is the one that's gone. I feel nothing.

"My apologies, Beauty, I shouldn't have done that in front of you, especially in your fragile state" Galterio's smooth voice came from beside me. He carefully placed his hand on my cheek and turned my head away from Zoe's body. I looked up to glare at him, but instead, I moved back out of his touch after realising he was now shirtless. I looked at the cloth in my hands and held it out in front of me, it was his shirt. He gave me his shirt to wipe the sick from my face. That's kind of sweet, I guess. But it doesn't take away from the fact that he just murdered someone right in front of me.

"Why did you do that?" I choked out as I began to struggle to my feet. Galterio jumped forward, gripped my arm, and helped to slowly pull me upright. Using one hand, he held my forearm, and the other he wrapped around my waist to hold me up. He carried me back to the table and chairs and carefully lowered me into my seat.

"She hurt you" he hissed while looking at my chest. Oh, I forgot about that. I looked down at my chest where she struck me. The white shirt I was wearing had been ripped from the neck hole to the left sleeve. I had four deep slash marks from the middle of my chest, to up and over my collarbone and shoulder. My blood dripped down my chest and soaked through the fabric of the shirt. I felt it in the moment, the pain, but then it was quickly forgotten after seeing Zoe's dead body. But now that I can see the aftermath of her claws, the pain is all too real.

"Oh my god, oh my god" I gasped and started to panic. It's nothing serious, I told myself. You suffered worse, you just need to clean it. Like muscle memory kicking in. Like a trained and seasoned professional, I knew what to do. I searched around me for something to use to clean the wound. I couldn't wipe the blood with the shirt in my hand because it had my throw up on it. I pushed Galterio back and stood up. I ripped off the t-shirt that I had on and began to press it against the open wound. A low growl rumbled from behind me, I whipped around to see that Galterio had stepped back close to me. Only he wasn't facing me, he was growling at the other Weres. His arms were slightly outstretched beside him, like he was trying to stop them from seeing my bikini clad body. Is he jealous or is this protective? I moved the shirt from my chest, but the blood still hadn't stopped.

"I'm not healing, why aren't I healing?" I cried.

"Zelena, will you please put your clothes back on" Galterio hissed angrily, completely ignoring my question.

"Alpha Galterio, why aren't I healing?" I asked again, my voice was a mixture of panic and anger. What did that stupid cow do to me? I looked down at my chest and back up to him. Why isn't he more worried about this? As I moved my eyes between us again, a figure in the yard caught my attention. I snapped my head up and zeroed in on the person. That can't be right. Is that... Artemis? No. I stepped forward and was about to call out to him when Galterio growled lowly. Using his speed, he hit the back of my knees with one arm and my upper body with the other. It was so damn fast that I didn't get the chance to prepare for it. He had me in his arms bridal style, and in a flash, we zoomed back into the house and back to the same bedroom that I woke up in. He placed me on the edge of the bed and went to step back. The exceptionally fast movement made my stomach turn. Galterio must have picked up on my nausea because he dashed away and was back in a blink with a bucket held under my chin. Once again, I emptied whatever was left of the contents of my stomach into the bucket. All my thoughts of pain from the claw marks to my chest were erased by the endless stream of dry reaching. I hate vomiting.

I have seen far more gruesome things than a broken neck. I have inflicted far worse things on others and had less lethal but still just as brutal things done to me. And I run, I run as my wolf and my human, I can use my Were speed with no repercussions. Why now am I suddenly vomiting at the sight of a broken neck, and getting sick from quick movements? This isn't right. I don't get sick. The food! It must have been the food. Oh shit, the fucker poisoned me! I glared up at Galterio and snarled,

"What did you do to me?" I growled. He tilted his head to the side and frowned,

"Unfortunately, Beauty, it was not me that did this to you" he grumbled.

"Bull shit" I hissed and pushed his hand away from the bucket that I hugged to my chest. He smiled at me. A full wide smile. He is actually quite beautiful when he smiles. But something behind it made me want to vomit again.

"Trust me Zelena, if it was I that put you in this position, you would have remembered it" he mused with a cocky gleam in his eye.

"What the fuck is that supposed to mean? I am so over all the cryptic talk" I groaned and dropped my head. The smell of my vomit hit my nose and I quickly shot my head back up again. Galterio was still watching me intently.

"You poisoned me, didn't you?" I questioned him firmly. My eyes held his, and my lip lifted into a snarl. His smile dropped and he took a step away from me. After a brief moment, he placed his hand over his heart and smirked,

"You think so little of me, dear cousin" he feigned a hurt face and pouted his plump lips.

"I'm not playing with you Galterio, why else would I be so sick after eating your food? If you didn't do it then someone from your pack did".

"If you think that I have such little control over my pack, if you think that any of them would dare defy me, then little girl, you don't know me in the slightest" he snapped in a hard voice.

"Don't call me that" I hissed and dry reached.

"Don't call you what?" he chuckled,

"Don't call me a little girl. I may be small, but I could do a hell of a lot worse to you than just snap your neck".

Galterio kneeled in front of me so that he was at eye level with where I sat on the bed. His teasing smile was gone, as was his flirtatious behaviour. His eyes were dark and the muscle in his jaw was tensed tight. He was past the point of angry. I poked the bear, and now I was going to see if he would bite back.

"Are you threatening me, Triple Goddess?" he asked in a deadly yet calm voice. It is the first time I have heard him refer to me as Triple Goddess. Yet somehow, the way he said it didn't feel like a term of endearment.

"Not threatening, just warning" I answered him. Keeping my face even and my tone level. He glared at me, and I glared back at him. We held each other's gaze for I don't know how long. But after a while, he winked at me and smiled. He stood up, took the bucket from my grip, and then held out his hand for me.

"Come on, I bet you're hungry again after all that" he said as he waved his hand towards the bucket. How can he do that? Just switch between emotions like flicking on a light switch. It's giving me whiplash. I moved my eyes from his outstretched hand, up and over his thick bicep to his bare chest. A smattering of dark hair coated his chest, leading down to the top of his pants. This man is fit. Smooth skin pulled tightly over perfectly defined abs. Galterio cleared his throat and I flicked my gaze up to meet his big brown eyes.

"I'm not eating your food again" I said shocked. I know he just tried to poison me. I mean, I called him out on it, right to his face. And yet he still thinks I would trust him to give me food. This Alpha is full on crazy town.

"And why not? You seemed to really enjoy it the first time around" he teased me,

"Yeah, but that was before I realised you poisoned it. I'm not stupid enough to trust you again after that" I sneered. Galterio huffed and crossed his arms over his chest.

"You're impossible. I'm starting to see why your Mate tried to kill you". I didn't expect his words to cut so deep. But they did, down to the bone. My heart clenched and pain rang through my body. Could Gunner have hurt me on purpose? He promised that he never would, and until now, he lived up to that promise. I don't believe that was really Gunner, I can't believe it. He wasn't in his right mind, he didn't know what he was doing. I can't believe it. If I lose him, I will have nothing left.

A tear rolled down my cheek and I very quickly wiped it away. Galterio already saw it though, he let his arms fall at his side and looked down at me with pity in his gaze.

"I'm sorry, that wasn't fair to say" he said softly and moved closer. He was about to sit down next to me on the bed when I jumped up. I don't want his pity, I don't want anything from him. I heard him out, I listened to his rant about the horrible humans. I even considered helping in his cause. Freedom from the hunters is something I can be passionate about. But now I'm done.

"Don't bother" I snapped at him,

"I'd like to leave now, I'm not staying around Weres that tried to kill me" I hissed at him venomously, he stood up slowly and ran his hand through his hair.

"Didn't we just cover this? I didn't poison you, Zelena. Why would I bring you to my home, take care of you, ask you to help with the cause, and then poison you?" he asked frustrated. I suppose I didn't think of it like that. When he lays it all out on the line like that, it actually doesn't make any sense. But still, I'm not the type of person to get sick spontaneously. I know there is more going on. He may not have done it, but I'm not ruling out the possibility that someone here did. Especially after learning that they had Zoe hanging around.

"I don't get sick. Not like this" I ground out.

"Maybe you didn't before, but you do now, apparently" he said with a smile and followed it with a chuckle,

"Why is this such a joke to you, what do you know that I don't?" I yelled and stomped my foot. I could feel my anger rising inside me. The power danced through my veins under my skin.

"You'll figure it out in your own time" he teased and winked again. His attitude was rubbing up against my last nerve. The weightlessness in my chest told me that my power was ready to be released.

"Now let's go and feed the little monster before I decide to make you beg". He held out his hand, but I refused to take it. If I moved my arm at this moment, I may just send him flying through the wall.

"Galterio" I growled. He smirked and turned for the door. As he was about to grab the handle, I lifted my arm and flexed my fingers. I grabbed hold of him, wrapping him in my force field. I squeezed and forced his arms to his chest, and then turned him around to face me. He growled out a growl that shook the room.

"I will say this once, you hear me?" he hissed at me, and I smirked,

"I am not your little pup of a Mate. I will not be so forgiving when you use your power against me. I have been patient and gracious with you up until this point. But if you try this with me, if you force your power onto me, then I will just simply take what I want from you" he snarled.

"Sorry to break it to you, Alpha, but there is nothing you can do about it" I sneered with my own cocky grin spreading across my face.

"Are you sure about that?" Galterio asked me. I admit, I was a little caught off guard by his assuredness. I thought he would have been at least a little bit panicked by being pinned in my hold. But he was calm, angry, but still in total control. "I can lift you high into the air and let the force of gravity bring you back to the ground. I can increase the gravity around you so that you can't move. I can twist and contort your body until it is nothing more than a lump of flesh and broken bone. This force field has never been broken or penetrated, by anything or anyone. So yes, Alpha Galterio, I'm sure" I said confidently. Just to prove my point I tightened the hold around his body. He hissed and curled his lip back into a snarl.

"You're too confident" he grunted,

"I think I have a reason to be, don't you?" I squeezed again and Galterio growled.

"You're sure you want to play this game with me, Beauty?"

"There's no game. Can't you see that? I'm in control now, and I'll let you go once you tell me what I want to know. If you don't then I will just keep squeezing" I growled out the last few words as I tightened my hold on him once again. Galterio threw his head back and hissed, but he didn't scream.

"Did you or one of your packmates poison me?" I demanded,

"No" he groaned,

"Then what has made me so sick?" Galterio didn't answer, he just smirked at me with a knowing look. I squeezed my power, tightening the hold on him more. I heard the snapping of a bone and a grunt from Galterio.

"You're lying" I growled,

"Let me go Zelena".

"Tell me what you did to me!" I yelled. The tables by the bed began to rise off the floor and the cupboard doors rattled. The chair in the corner creaked and groaned.

"I did nothing to you, you need to ask your Mate what he did to you" he grunted and strained to talk through the pressure.

"Gunner did nothing. That wasn't him, he didn't mean to" I screamed. I could feel my emotions getting out of hand. The teal chair in the corner split into pieces and then split again into even smaller pieces, until it was just a floating warping ball of wood and cotton.

"I'm not talking about the bite to your neck" he growled, his eyes moved down my body and stopped on my lower abdomen. Now I know he is crazy.

"What are you talking about then?" I demanded. I don't think I want to know the answer, but how could I not? Surely he doesn't think what I think he does. He couldn't be. I can't be.

"You're pregnant, Beauty" he half smiled. No. I'm not pregnant, I can't be pregnant. I'm only nineteen, I can't be a mother. No, he must be lying. It's just a trick to distract me from the truth. I'm not pregnant. He would say anything in this moment to get me to release him. I glared at him and twitched my fingers,

"Liar!" I screamed. I pushed my power the furthest it would go without killing him, he growled and thrashed his head. I heard a crunching sound as more of his bones broke. He yelled and growled over at me. The look in his eye was terrifying.

"Enough of this" he snarled. He tilted his head back and to the side and then back again. It looked like he was trying to bring forth his wolf. I kept my hold on him, but I could feel him pushing against me. This feeling was different from everything else I have tested my power against. I could actually feel him pulling at the edges of my power, like he was peeling sticky tape from my skin. He roared loudly and threw his arms out from his chest. My power, the hold I had on him, it burst like a balloon. As Galterio broke the hold, my body felt weak. It felt like he sucked out all of my energy like some kind of energy vampire. I stumbled slightly on my feet, I thought I was going to fall backward. As I began to tip back, Galterio appeared behind me and wrapped his large arms around my body. My arms were pinned to my side and my back was pressed flush up against his chest.

"I warned you, Beauty" he said with a low deep voice,

"I told you not to try me, and now it's my turn".

Galterio gripped my heavy and bobbing head and pulled it back to rest it on his shoulder. He brushed the hair away from my face and neck and leaned in. His nose caressed the back of my neck as he inhaled deeply, sliding his nose and lips along my skin.

"You smell delicious" he said softly. A purr like growl rumbled through his chest and vibrated through my body. I wanted to push him off, fight him back. But I could barely lift my arm. His grip was too firm, and I was too weak now. How did he do it? It shouldn't have been possible, so how could he break free?

My knees buckled but Galterio was holding me up, his hard arms took all of my weight. My eyes started to droop, and I could feel myself slowly losing consciousness. Galterio moved to sit on the edge of the bed, keeping me in his arms so that I sat on his lap. I could be half dead and still feel the monster in his pants. Galterio's huge erection pressed into my backside as I was held in his lap. I tried to push myself away, to get up and run, but all I managed was a bobble of my head.

"Stop" I mumbled out drowsily.

"Shh" Galterio whispered as he took hold of my chin and pulled my head back to his chest. He peeled the bandage from my neck and tossed it away. His hand returned to grip at the top of my neck, angling my face back by my jaw. I felt his tongue slide along the top of my shoulder and up my neck and around the still stinging would.

"You had your fun, now I get mine" he breathed into my ear. His hips moved forward as he ground himself against me. I wanted to die in that moment. Please, Mother, I begged silently. Don't let this happen to me.

Chapter Thirty-Two

Lunaya

"Spawned by the one who gave us breath. Vanished from life but spared from death. The Ethereal one gives she who is promised. To wield the power of the Triple Goddess. Where the moon is three, two will come. Once the seal is made, destiny is done. With one comes death, pain, and destruction. The other comes life, love, and devotion. Peril will end and the wolf will thrive. But for peace to reign, only one can survive".

I stared into the healer's wide eyes and watched as they slowly rolled back and refocused. It can't be possible. It shouldn't be possible. I heard that same riddle one time before, nearly twenty years ago. I did everything that I could do to stop it from coming to fruition. And I thought that I had succeeded. That prophecy should have died with me and my family seventeen years ago. How and why is he reciting it again now? It shouldn't be possible.

Twenty years ago.

"Child, it was never your destiny to wield the power" the older woman spoke softly as she sat across from me in the library in a big armchair. I was sitting on the floor with the book of my lineage in my lap. Elder Maxine is a Prophet. She basically raised me after my parents were murdered by hunters when I was nine. She has taught me everything there is to know about Were-kind and my history. Though it seems she has gotten crazier in her older years, always muttering about 'the turn of the tides' and 'the evil one comes'. She is quite fascinating to sit and listen to. I've never met an Elder as old as she is. But I've also never been out of Alaska.

"Why not? Why am I not worthy?" I asked her.

I have finally Mated with the love of my life. Micha. Oh, Goddess is he dreamy. That dark hair and those smooth bulging muscles. I don't want to ever stop licking him. He knows who I am, or what I am. The whole pack does. In fact, everyone has been anxiously waiting for me to choose a Mate. Which was hard, I had a lot to pick from. Almost every unmated male in the pack had tried to win me over. All except Micha. Maybe that was why I was so drawn to him. He didn't care about my possible status, or what being my Mate could do for him. He cared only for the pack and keeping it safe. He is the perfect choice.

Hmm, our night of passionate lovemaking was more than I ever dreamed it would be. I had given myself orgasms before, so the feeling wasn't foreign to me. But holy fucking shit, when he does it to me, I see fireworks.

After a few hours and multiple orgasms, I checked my wrists. No mark. Micha checked the back of my neck. Again, no mark. We checked over every inch of my body. Nothing. To say that I was beyond disappointed, was an understatement. I don't know why, but I always thought my destiny was to be the next chosen daughter. I have always felt that I was meant to do something important. We gave it a few more days and went at it like rabbits in the meantime. Not that I'm complaining. If I could live in bed with Micha forever, I would. But even after all that, still no mark appeared, I guess I'm not meant for greatness after all.

"It is not about being worthy, for that child, I know you are. It is the will of the Moon Goddess. We don't get to choose, and we don't get to question her choices" Elder Maxine said smoothly. Her old voice was crackly but still soothing.

"I don't understand, she hasn't blessed us with a daughter for over two hundred years. What is she waiting for?" I complained. I know I shouldn't, it's not my place to question the will of the All Mother. Maybe there won't be another, maybe none of us are worthy anymore. But if I'm wrong, what could she be waiting for?

"I can't give you the answers you seek, Dear" Maxine said with a kind smile.

"I know, I just... I really thought it would be me" I said dejectedly.

"Come here" Elder Maxine requested as she held her hands out for me. I placed the heavy book on the table and sat up on my knees, then I crawled across the floor to kneel in front of her. I placed my hands in hers and waited for her to give me one of her crazy yet exciting pep talks. But she didn't. Instead, her hands tightened around mine and her eyes turned a pitch black. She sat up straight, took a deep breath, and then spoke in a shudder inducing echoey tone.

"Spawned by the one who gave us breath. Vanished from life but spared from death. The Ethereal one gives she who is promised. To wield the power of the Triple Goddess. Where the moon is three, two will come. Once the seal is made, destiny is done. With one comes death, pain, and destruction. The other comes life, love, and devotion. Peril will end and the wolf will thrive. But for peace to reign, only one can survive".

Maxine let go of my hands and gasped loudly. I jumped up and took a large step away from her. What the heck was that about? If not me, then who is the Triple Goddess? And what does it mean about the three moons and two will come, come where? I don't understand. Elder Maxine's eyes returned to their normal crystal blue and her eyebrows furrowed together.

"What does that mean? The three moons, two will come and only one can survive. Maxine, what's happening?" I asked her with a shaky panicked tone.

She looked at me inquisitively and tilted her head to the side. After a moment her eyes widened, and she slowly stood. On wobbly legs, she stepped closer to me, and I fought the urge to run. She took another step and reached out her hand. I thought she was going to take my hand again, like heck I want that to happen again. I pulled my hand back, but she didn't go for my hand, her hand went straight to my stomach.

She spread her fingers out over my lower abdomen and hummed.

"Ahh" she said excitedly,

"There is the Goddess".

I was frozen in place. Not sure if this is just more of her crazy talk, or if she is actually saying what I think she is. I couldn't be pregnant already. Micha and I have only been sleeping together for less than a week. Can it happen that quickly? Also, I haven't even had my first heat. I thought I had to be in heat to get pregnant.

"Elder Maxine, are you saying that I'm pregnant?" I asked her, watching her face closely.

"Yes, Dear" she said with a wide smile,

"And it's a girl? She's going to be the next Triple Goddess?" I asked, my voice raising an octave or two. My excitement exploded inside me like a burst of joy and happiness. I was never meant to be the next daughter, I was simply meant to birth her, raise her, and train her.

"She could be" Maxine said, her smile faltered, and fear filled her eyes. She quickly masked it over, but I still saw it there. She could be. What is that supposed to mean? Either she is or she isn't. Oh, my Goddess, I have to go tell Micha. I hope he is happy. Oh... what if he isn't happy? What if he doesn't want to be a father? We haven't talked about having children, it was just always assumed that I would. So that I can continue the line. What if he rejects me? Tears flooded my eyes as fear and panic flooded my mind. Maxine noticed my shift in emotions and wrapped her arms around my shoulders.

"Come now dear, it will be okay. You will make sure it all turns out okay. I have taught you well, you have the ability to turn the tides".

"Enough of the crazy prophecies Maxine. Can't you see that I'm scared. I don't need to hear another story about turning the tides and the Evil Were. I just need a little reassurance that my Mate isn't going to leave me" I said and burst into tears. I sobbed and covered my face with my hands. Maxine grabbed my wrists and pulled them down, away from my face. Then she slapped me. A good smack across my cheek. That definitely made me stop crying. I grabbed my cheek and looked at her in shock.

"What was that for?" I asked,

"You are a daughter of the moon. Pull yourself together and go find your Mate to tell him the good news" she grunted at me. She turned around, picked up the book that I was reading, then took it back over to her seat, sat down, and began reading it quietly. With that, I turned and went to find Micha. I'm sure he'll be happy. How could he not be?

Present Day.

"How… how do you know about that?" I asked Artemis, still reeling from the shock of hearing that prophecy again. Artemis didn't respond he just stared at me with his intense searching gaze.

"This prophecy is void. If you really are a Prophet, you would know that" I snapped at him. Again, he didn't respond. The corner of his lip turned up into a smirk. I snapped my hand forward and gripped hold of his neck.

"What do you know?" I growled and squeezed my fingers around his neck tighter. He growled back and reached his arms behind his back. I stepped closer and showed him my fangs. I suppose I don't really need answers from him. I can just kill him. His death would have little to no impact. I lifted my jaw and moved my head forward, then his hand flew up and he jabbed something into my neck. Fire erupted under my skin. It crawled through my veins, slowly moving from my neck to my arms, chest, abdomen, and legs. My hand fell from Artemis's neck, and I dropped to my knees. I grasped at my neck where he stuck me. Fucking Aconite. Cleo's loud howl rang through the forest like a battle cry. I glared up at Artemis one last time. He smirked at me and turned on his heels. I dropped to the ground, my face pressing against the dry leaves and dirt. Cleo's paws thumped past me after Artemis, followed closely by another set and then another.

"Lunaya" Phoebe called as her hands grabbed at my body. The poison was moving through my veins, burning me from the inside out.

"Lunaya, what happened?" Phoebe asked me,

"Artemis… Aconite" I groaned out. I wanted to scream, my entire body was alive with pain. But I couldn't do it, it was hard enough to just speak two words, let alone scream my lungs out.

"That fucking traitor!" Lupus bellowed.

My eyes closed and I heard more howling and more heavy footsteps. The pain was excruciating, flowing through me like waves of hot lava. My muscles spasmed and contracted, over and over, each time my heart pumped another round of blood through my veins. As the darkness of my pain clouded over my senses, I reached out for the Moon Goddess in my mind, I prayed to the All Mother with everything that I had left.

"I don't know if you can hear me, but please let me survive this, I need more time. I need to tell Zelena who I am, and where she came from. There is so much more that I have to tell her. Let me survive this. Just one last chance. I won't squander it. I acknowledge you as her rightful mother, I thank you for doing what I failed to do. But please Selene, let me live".

~

I flew upright in the bed and looked around the room. Alyse was lying beside me, and Cleo was asleep in a chair by the window. I'm getting tired of waking up in this room after nearly dying. I really thought I was a goner this time. I was caught off guard the first time I was poisoned with Aconite, and it cost me my family. I was never going to let that happen again. If I hadn't been building up my tolerance to it over the past seventeen years, it would have killed me for sure this time around.

Alyse sat up a moment after I did, Cleo's eyes flew open and she shifted herself to the edge of the seat, her eyes studying me like usual.

"Nae, Babe, you're okay?" Alyse asked as she ran her hand through my hair.

"I feel like I have been hit by a truck, but I'm alive, apparently" I groaned and took Alyse's hand. I pulled it to my mouth and pressed my lips to the back of her hand.

"Did you catch him? Artemis, did you get him?" I asked looking over to Cleo. She leaned back in the chair and growled.

"The fucker got away" she said venomously,

"How?" I asked. I was angry and frustrated, but I couldn't blame anyone for this. This is on me, I let him jab me with the syringe. I wasn't ready or prepared, I wasn't good enough. This is my own fault.

"We don't know, I was on his trail with the Beta Cole and one of the former Alpha's men. We had him surrounded and were closing in, but he vanished. No tracks, no scent, just gone" she snarled and curled her lips up to expose her fangs. I guess I'm not the only one with some self-deprecating thoughts and feelings.

"So what now then?" I asked her,

"Nae, let them handle it, you need to rest" Alyse urged me,

"Like hell I do. My daughter has been kidnapped, AGAIN, her Mate has gone off the deep end, and the pack healer turned Prophet, tried to fucking kill me. I need to get the fuck out of this room and find her, maybe rip apart a few Weres along the way" I said angrily as I moved my body to the edge of the bed. Cleo growled excitedly and stood from her chair.

"I'm with you" she grunted. Alyse quickly moved to my side and placed an arm around my shoulder.

"Lunaya, you need more time to heel, there is still Aconite in your system. You almost died for fucks sake. Can you just slow it down for a minute" she pleaded desperately. I shrugged off her arm and stood up. I would never admit it, but she's right. My legs felt like jelly under my body weight and my arms hung at my side like weighted down spaghetti. My head is pounding, and I feel like I could down the entire contents of the Nile River. I am in no position to fight, but I won't give up on her again. Never again. Alyse jumped off the bed and stood in front of me, bracing me with her arms on both my shoulders.

"Nae, please" she said softly,

"I have already lost her once, I'm not going to lose her again. Get on board or get the fuck out of my way" I snapped at her. I didn't mean for it to come out so harsh. But it did, like a kick to the guts. Her face fell and she stepped to the side.

"Okay" she whispered softly. I should have sucked it up and apologised for acting like a raging bitch. I should have held her and told her that I love her. I did none of those things. Instead, I trudged past her and back down the hallway and the stairs, with Cleo in toe. I burst through the door of the war room and glared at Beta Cole. The room was full of Weres. Beta Elaine, Lupus, the guardian Tobias, and a Were that looked like a smaller version of him. The warriors Felix and Faylene, as well as Alpha Ambrose, the Howlers Alpha

Lace, and the Alpha from Waning Wolf, all were in the room, and all were glaring at me for interrupting. I looked around the room at each furious face, but one was missing.

"Where is the Alpha?" I snarled and flicked my eyes back to Cole.

"Until we know more about what has happened to him, and if he can be trusted to control his anger, he will remain in the cell" Cole answered without hesitation and full of authority.

"We don't need him to control his anger, we need him to let it the fuck out. We need him to let loose and kill the fuckers that took my child" I growled back at him. Beta Elaine stepped forward and stood in all her tall and broad, boss-bitch glory, arms crossed over her chest and a scowl on her face.

"I get that you're angry, we all are, but either pull it together or get the fuck out and let us do this without you" she snarled down at me. I stood to my fullest height and hissed,

"Like fuck, I am not going anywhere" I snapped,

"Then shut the fuck up and take your place, quietly!" Elaine growled. I hissed again as she turned to stand back at Cole's right. All eyes were on me as I moved to stand at the table, placing myself between Tobias and Lupus. The table was full of maps and pictures of farmhouses and large properties. I wanted to ask about them, I wanted to be caught up on what was going on, but I knew better than to go against Elaine. She is not the type to not follow through on her word. One sound from me and she will toss me out on my ass.

"Scouts have searched all the larger properties around the pack land. They went as far north as Capstick and as far south as Sydney and Inverness. If it is Origin Wolf, then we can expect the pack to have joined their Alpha. So there will be a lot of them, especially if they have allied with other packs. These are the only possible places to maintain the large numbers and remain inconspicuous". Cole talked and everyone listened. He commanded the room, just like an Alpha would. And they all paid attention, following his lead in every way. He wasn't their Alpha, but they showed him the same level of respect.

"Have any of you even tried to flash the Triple Goddess?" the Howler's Alpha asked, his deep gruff voice was full of frustration.

"Don't test me, Alpha Lace! Of course we have tried to reach her. Only Gunner, Tobias, and Smith have links with her, and none of them can get through to her" Cole snarled at the burly tattooed Alpha.

"Is she blocking you, or is something blocking her?" asked the Waning Wolf Alpha, Travis,

"The little Goddess has only had her wolf for a short time, as she didn't grow up with Weres, there is a lot that she doesn't know. She trains daily, but her skills are still limited" Tobias chimed in,

"And you're telling us this why?" Alpha Lace sneered at him,

"Because she has not mastered the skill of blocking yet. She can't block out her feelings and emotions nor can she stop herself from projecting them. Which means she also can't hold off an open link" Tobias snarled back.

"So then something is blocking her, either they have drugged her, or she is unconscious" Alpha Travis concluded. A deathly growl rumbled through my body at hearing what they could possibly be doing to her. I want that Origin Wolf Alpha's head on a platter and his limbs scattered across the corners of the world. I, myself have never encountered a descendant of Gill, thank the Goddess. But our lines have crossed paths far too many times.

"And your scouts have found nothing? There have been no signs, anywhere, of anything?" asked the Alpha Lace,

"Not as yet" Cole answered him,

"So, we're chasing ghosts? How the fuck are we meant to prepare for a fight, when we don't know who or what we are fighting against?" he shouted.

"If you're too fucking scared to stick around, then head on back to your pack of mutts" Tobias yelled across the table at him,

"Howlers are scared of nothing!" he screamed back,

"Then why is your tail between your legs?" Tobias sneered. The amount of tension in the room was gagging. Four current Alpha's, two former Alpha's, a couple of Beta's, and some warriors, all of which are on edge. I'm surprised that no one has lost an arm... or a throat, yet.

"Enough!" Lupus's loud and firm voice bellowed around the room. The shouting stopped and all eyes turned to Lupus.

"We all want her back. We are all here to get her back. Ripping each other apart is not going to help. Settle down and listen up" he demanded of the room.

"We have five packs ready to go to war against whoever has taken the Triple Goddess" Cole began,

"Six" Elaine interjected. All eyes now turned in her direction.

"Excuse me?" Cole asked with a curious yet annoyed tone,

"Myself and my she-wolves will fight, plus, more Luna Eclipse warriors are on the way" she said in an uncaring manner.

"They are?" I asked her. She turned to me with a frown and nodded her head.

"When?" Cole asked,

"The Alpha and fifteen warriors will arrive either through the night, or first thing in the morning" she answered him. I watched Elaine as I processed what she was saying. I have made that journey, on average it took nearly three days. This means she called for them before Artemis revealed himself, it would have been right after Zelena was taken, if not before. If it was after, then she knew a fight was coming to get her back. If it was before, the night of the dinner maybe, what would have possessed her to call for backup? She wouldn't... She wasn't going to... Was she planning on attacking Tri-Moon?

The door burst open once again and a breathless Smith, with two other Weres behind him, filled the doorway.

"We found them" he huffed out. The aura of the room exploded into a mix of fury, excitement, rage, and anticipation.

"How?" Lupus grunted angrily,

"We picked up Jackson's scent not far out of Inverness, followed him to the Mabou harbour mouth before we lost him in the water. But then we found them all".

"Where?" growled Cole,

"They've taken over a farm near Little Mabou, but Cole, that's not all" Smith said, with concern written all over his face.

"What is it?" Cole asked,

"It's not just Origin Wolf, there has to be at least three other packs with him. It was hard to see all of the land without getting seen, but there has to be around one fifty, maybe two hundred of them".

"They're gearing up to fight then?" the Alpha from Waning Wolf spoke.

"It appears that way" Smith nodded to him.

"It's settled then. We gather our warriors and go fetch the Little Goddess" the Alpha said as he crossed his arms over his chest. Growls of agreement from the other Weres filled the room.

"Howlers will fight" Alpha Lace growled with excitement.

"Blue Moon is with the Goddess" the smaller version of Tobias inserted, I'm assuming he's his brother, the one Tobias handed the role of Alpha to. Elaine grunted and nodded her head, indicating that Luna Eclipse was in for the battle too. All eyes then turned to Alpha Ambrose of Lua Chei. He had been watching and listening quietly without adding any input. I have no idea where he stands on this. He folded his arms in front of him and lowered his head. We all stood silent, waiting for him to speak. After a brief pause, he lifted his head and turned his gaze to mine.

"My eldest son will join us with three commanders and their patrols" he told us,

"Lua Chei is south of Little Mabou. If your warriors are coming from your pack lands, then they too will be travelling from the south. I think it is best that they join together and converge on the farm from the opposite direction to us. With Tri-Moon, Blue Moon, and what other warriors we have here already, we will come from the north, cutting them off and getting them surrounded. Leaving no room for escape" Alpha Ambrose spoke confidently. He directed his eyes first to the Alphas from Howlers and Waning Wolf, as neither of their packs are in Nova Scotia, they will join us from the south. He then turned to Tobias and his brother, as their fighters were already here. As he finished verbalising his plan, he was looking at Cole. All this time he wasn't being indecisive, he already decided they would fight and had moved on to battle plans. We all stood and contemplated his plan. It is a good one, makes a lot of sense, and leaves little room for surprises.

"Alpha Travis, Alpha Lace, how long will it take to organise your packs?" Cole asked the two Alpha's across from him.

"Howlers are ready and will move out tonight" Alpha Lace replied instantly.

"Waning Wolf can also be ready to go by tonight" Alpha Travis answered.

"Good, organise together where to get them to meet up before crossing onto the island. Alpha Ambrose?" Cole said as he turned to face him,

"Yes?" the Alpha replied,

"You can get your son and his men to wait at the Causeway, then you will all cross together?" Cole requested more than he did ask. Alpha Ambrose nodded his head and smiled,

"That was my thinking as well" he said proudly. He is a very smart Were, a good Alpha. Ares has definitely had a good teacher. I hope he follows in his father's footsteps.

"And how many in total will that give us? Will it be enough?" asked Lupus, to no one in particular.

"Waning Wolf will bring four patrols, roughly sixty-five" answered Alpha Travis,

"Seventy from Howlers" Alpha Lace answered,

"Blue Moon have brought forty-nine" Tobias's younger brother spoke, I should find out what his name is.

"With the additional fifteen from Luna Eclipse and the hundred and twenty we have ready to fight, then we should outnumber them easily. That is if Smith has estimated their numbers correctly" Lupus said with are more confident tone.

"Like I said, it was hard to tell for sure, but I'm pretty confident" Smith told everyone.

"Okay, go and make your final preparations. We will meet again to go over finer details in two hours" Cole said with finality. The groups broke apart and began to head out of the room. Cole, Lupus, and I stayed behind. Cole looked me over before looking to Lupus,

"He isn't going to be okay with being left behind" Cole said cautiously.

"We can't Cole. We still don't know what is going on with him. If Artemis poisoned this one, he may have been doing the same to Gunner. If we take him, and if we get her back, what if he attacks her again?" Lupus said annoyed,

"When" I said in a low voice. They looked at me with unsaid questions,

"You said 'if' we get her back, you should have said 'when' we get her back" I reiterated.
"And so we will" Lupus said as he placed his hand on my shoulder,
"I promise you" he nodded.

Chapter

Thirty-Three

Lunaya

Alyse was avoiding me. I tried to talk to her, to apologise, but she just said it was fine and then walked away again. Three times I've tried to get her alone. Three times she has brushed me off. I was too harsh with her, I knew that. But fuck, I just wish that she'd let me apologise. The idea that I have hurt her is killing me. There may be a lot going on right now, and a lot still to come. I just don't like the thought of going into a fight with our relationship the way it is. I need to make it right, preferably before we leave.

Night fell not two hours ago, and the Tri-Moon village is a constant stream of activity. After the second meeting, a more thorough battle plan was arranged and communicated to the incoming fighters. Elaine confirmed that Luna Eclipse had landed and was on the road. The other packs had begun their journey to the Causeway. Alpha Ambrose has proven himself to be a very capable strategist, his mind for war and planning is both incredibly admirable, and terrifying. However, I have noticed the amount of tension and hostility shown between him and Lupus. I think it has something to do with the flirting and sexual chemistry I picked up on between Roe and Alpha Ambrose. I'm about eighty-five percent sure that my theory is correct, that they dated in their youth. It's not my place, but hot damn am I curious to know what happened there.

For the time being, Gunner is to stay in the cell while we go south to Origin Wolf. I don't like it. I probably should be happy that he is locked in a cell. After all, he did hurt my daughter. But I'm not convinced that was all on Gunner. Artemis made himself quite popular at Tri-Moon. He didn't talk a lot, but he had his hand in almost everything. He was involved with almost all of Zelena's training, something that really bugs me. Training her was supposed to be up to me. But Lupus, Roe, and Cole have all confirmed that Artemis made sure that he was close with Gunner. He had his ear and Gunner trusted him enough to ask for his council. I can only imagine what the bastard was putting in his head. Above all, something Lupus said has stuck with me. Artemis had access to Aconite. He tried to kill me with it. If he had been giving non-lethal doses of it to Gunner, over a long period of time, it could have been affecting him, like his emotions and control. It's just a theory, but it's a theory I am willing to bet on. I can't even imagine him dosing Zelena as well. I know intimately the kind of pain it causes, and I don't want her to know it too.

I was sitting silently with Cleo on a log by the fire pit in the middle of the village, watching Alyse ignore me as she chatted with Roe. If circumstances were different, this would have been a really nice and relaxing setting. But there's a war coming, the atmosphere is a little tense. Cleo has been sticking close to my side a lot lately, it escalated tenfold after Artemis's attempt on my life. I think she is blaming herself for not stopping him. She was there, not thirty meters from us, but she couldn't stop him and didn't catch him. For a Were like Cleo, with what she told me of her past, I can imagine that would be playing on her mind a lot. I was ready to tell her to let it go, that it was my fault for not seeing him better. I had my doubts about him, but I did nothing to act on them. I was going to tell Cleo not to beat herself up about it, but before I did, she stood up and stretched her arms over her head.

"Come" she said firmly,

"Come where?" I asked as I stood up also,

"Alpha is here" she replied. Hina. The Luna Eclipse warriors made better time than I expected. I followed Cleo to the driveway where Elaine and the others were already waiting. Cole, Lupus, and Roe came around to greet them also. We all stood in the driveway quietly waiting. The sounds of a vehicle in the distance filtered through the trees, and a few moments later two large Humvees and two smaller sedans pulled into the driveway. I spotted Alpha Hina immediately. Her intimidating yet beautiful figure sat in the front passenger seat of the first sedan. The warriors began to pile out of the Humvees and stretched their arms and legs. Elaine went to Hina's door and opened it for her. Hina stepped out and embraced Elaine, they pulled back and stood with their foreheads pressed together. After they broke apart, Alpha Hina walked around the car towards the rest of us with Elaine close behind. Her eyes scanned over Cole, Roe, and Lupus before they settled on me. Her lip twitched as a small flash of a smile broke through her hard façade, she quickly covered it again and walked over to stand in front of me. She grabbed my face with both hands and pulled me to her, pressing her lips firmly against my own. Surprised by her show of affection, I stood there unmoving as her lips connected with mine. She pulled back and moved her hands down to my shoulders.

"Hello Lunaya" she half smiled,

"Alpha Hina, thank you for coming" I said back to her with a smile and a nod,

"Where is your beautiful Mate?" she asked as she looked around at the gathered group, all of which were watching our interaction with interest.

"She's..." I began,

"I'm here" Alyse called from behind me. She walked over, wrapped her arms around Hina's neck, and kissed her cheek. My jealousy flared and I could feel a growl bubble in my chest. The fact that she has been avoiding me made it all that much worse. I swallowed my growl and tried hard to keep my facial expression blank.

"It is so nice to see you both again, regardless of the circumstances. Elaine tells me the girl doesn't know who you are" Hina said as she turned to face me again. Wow, right to it huh? I glared at Elaine before looking back at Hina.

"No" I grunted,

"Why didn't you tell her?" she asked me firmly, if I didn't know better, I would say she sounded disappointed.

"There were other factors at play"

"Ahh, yes, Elaine told me about that too. Visiting with the Moon Goddess. Your child must be very important". The way she said it didn't sit right. Like she was overly excited or interested in this piece of information. Is that why she came? Because she believes Zelena is more than just the Triple Goddess? Does she think that there is more going on here?

"Is that why you came?" I asked her with a tilt of my head. Her jaw twitched and her face hardened,

"I came to help rescue the Goddess, your child" she answered with an irritated tone,

"That's not completely true though, is it? You had to have left New Zealand before she was taken, for you to get here so quickly. You left days ago, right?" I asked her sceptically,

"Are we no longer trusting each other Lunaya?" Hina asked in a hard voice, a voice that said she would cut me if I pressed her.

"That all depends" I answered,

"On what?"

"On your intentions"

"What do you think my intentions are, Lunaya?"

"I'm still trying to figure that out" I said, my eyes roaming her face for answers. I could feel other bodies closing in on us, watching and listening. But I paid them no mind.

"For you to be here now, you would have left the pack before, or, on the night of the dinner… the night we found out Selene had been visiting her" I mumbled as the pieces clicked into place in my head. She wasn't just here to help rescue Zelena, she was here to recruit her.

"You want to take her back to Luna Eclipse, don't you?" I asked her with wide eyes. Threatening growls began to rumble around us. I finally looked up and noticed that many of the Tri-Moon pack had come out to meet the elusive Luna Eclipse she-wolves. And after hearing me verbalise my assumption on the intentions of Alpha Hina, they took it as a threat against their Luna. The Luna Eclipse warriors surrounded their Alpha and growled back, readying themselves into attacking stances. Fuck, what have I done?

Alpha Hina stood firm with her gaze piercing into mine. I have questioned her intentions, in front of everyone. This can't possibly end well. Then all of a sudden, Hina began to laugh. A full and happy belly laugh. I can safely say, that was not the kind of reaction I thought she was going to have. I expected growling, snarling, and even violence. Not this.

"I have missed your crazy imagination" she cackled and wiped an imaginary tear from her eye.

"We are not here to steal your child, Lunaya. After hearing that she had seen, spoken to, and even visited the home of the Moon Goddess, I knew that she was beyond special. I had to meet her for myself. And just as well too. We have come right on time to help you get her back" she said with an amount of humour and joy in her voice that I had never heard from her before. It was actually quite weird and uncomfortable.

"You swear it?" I asked her,

"You doubt me?" she quipped back,

"Do I have reason to?"

"I'm glad to see you haven't lost your spunk. I promise Lunaya, I only want to meet the child. If she wants to come with us, I will take her. If not, then okay" Alpha Hina chuckled as she patted my shoulder. I turned to look around at the rest of Luna Eclipse and the surrounding Tri-Moon pack. Cole and Lupus pushed their way forward through the warriors. One of Hina's warriors growled at Lupus as a warning to stop. Lupus stopped and turned his head to glare at the she-wolf, he growled back at her, ten times as powerful and vicious. The warrior twitched and fought against the urge to drop her head, but she let him pass. I've got to give her props for just attempting to dominate a Were like Lupus.

"Alpha Hina, this is Beta Cole and the former Alpha, Lupus, of Tri-Moon" I said as I gestured to each of the men.

"It's a pleasure to meet you both, and thank you for housing us on your land" Hina offered them. She extended her hand to Cole first, he took it and she pulled him in close for Sevasmo. After they broke apart, she did the same to Lupus.

"We appreciate your assistance in getting back our Luna, and may I offer my apologies for the hostile greeting" Cole spoke with firmness and authority well beyond his years.

"I'm happy to let it all go, start fresh over a big feed" Hina said with a wave of her hand,

"Of course, my wife and the she-wolves have been hard at work in the kitchen for hours. The food will be out shortly. In the meantime, shall we fill you in on the plan so far?" Lupus said with his loud voice booming like always.

"Sounds good, but first, where is the Alpha?" she asked. Just like Alpha Hina to not hold her punches. I do not doubt that Elaine has filled her in on what Gunner has done, and where he is being held. But this is just her, testing them, just like she did with Alyse and me after we arrived at Luna Eclipse.

"The Alpha is currently unavailable" Cole grunted in reply,

"Oh, I am very aware of that" Hina said condescendingly,

"I am curious though, why he is still breathing after threatening the life of the Goddess?"

Lupus growled and stepped forward, standing only an inch away from Hina and towering over her. His lips curled over his teeth and his canine slowly extended. It was a truly terrifying face. Not a look I have seen on the former Alpha before, and not an expression I want to be on the receiving side of.

"Are you threatening my son?" he growled at Alpha Hina.

"Not at all, simply asking a question. I assumed any person that dared threaten the Triple Goddess would be given a swift death" she quipped back as she placed her hands on her hips.

"Not when it's her Mate" Lupus snarled,

"Oh, so if she meets her death at the hands of her Mate, it's okay, just not if it's done by anyone else" Hina said sarcastically. Cole and Lupus both growled at her, to which Elaine growled back.

"Alpha Hina" I hissed. Is she trying to start a fight? What could she possibly gain out of stirring them up?

"I think it's a fair question. I am fairly surprised that you, her own mother, didn't end his life yourself" she smirked at me and I rolled my eyes.

"We don't believe he attacked her knowingly, he doesn't even remember it. But irrespective of that, even if execution was an option, which let me make clear it is not, it wouldn't matter anyway, he can't be killed" Cole told her.

"Everyone can be killed" Alpha Hina sneered at him,

"Not if you want her to stay alive" he snapped back. Hina looked at him curiously, evaluating what he just said. Her face hardened and she crossed her arms over her chest,

"Explain" she demanded.

"They are True Mates. You weren't aware of this?" Cole said with a smirk of his own. True Mates? How did I not know this? If this is right, she's the most powerful Triple Goddess since Selena, and the Moon Goddess has opened a way for her Mate to access her power. This can't be right. Would she really allow a male, and one not from her direct line, to use her power? This could change everything. Gunner has to come with us to Little Mabou. If he can use her power without consequence, we need him.

"You're telling the truth?" I asked, my full attention now on Cole. He looked at me and his smirk dropped.

"You didn't already know?" he asked back,

"Of course I didn't know".

"I'm sorry Lunaya, I thought you knew already" Cole said softly.

"It doesn't matter. You kill him then you inevitably kill her. End of discussion" Lupus grunted roughly. I grabbed Cole's shoulder and turned him to face me.

"Has he used her power?" I asked him urgently, Hina was now watching our conversation closely and with keen interest.

"A few times yes" he answered quickly,

"Incredible" Hina whispered.

"He has to come with us, to Origin Wolf, to the fight. If he has her access to her power, we could use him" I rushed out.

"They have only ever shared the power when in close proximity. We don't even know if he can access it when they aren't next to each other. Plus, with whatever is going on with him, the risk is too great. I'm sorry, but no" Cole grunted firmly.

"Well, I'm sorry, Cole. But if you don't let him out, I will. Gunner has to come, he has to fight. If he can use the power of the Goddess, he can almost guarantee our success" I told him defiantly. Alpha Hina seemed to agree with me as she grunted and nodded her head. Cole and Lupus looked at each other and back to me, and then at each other again. A silent conversation went on between their lingering gazes. After a few moments, Lupus nodded his head and Cole puffed out a harsh breath.

"Fine" he huffed.

~

It was almost time to leave. Three large buses waited in the driveway to take the warriors part of the way there. Hina offered the use of the two Humvees as well. With the five vehicles, it will be a very tight fit, but we will all squeeze in. The plan was to leave the vehicles around the Glendyer area, and then go in wolf form the rest of the way. We are to converge on the farm an hour before dawn, at the same time as the packs coming in from the south. That gives us a little over three hours to get there and get into position. Surprisingly, there was no fight and no pushback from Alyse when I asked her to stay here. For her to agree so easily, to not even try to convince me she should come, she must be really upset with me. I've really fucked up this time, I just hope that I get the chance to make it right again when we return with Zelena.

Tri-Moon began to say their goodbyes and the rest of the warriors started to pile into the buses. A tight fit was an understatement. Every space on the busses was filled, some sitting, some standing, some sitting on top of others. It's going to be an uncomfortable drive. I was standing by one of the Humvees watching Gunner say goodbye to his mother. He looked calm. His skin was back to its usual colour and he wasn't twitching and shaking any longer. Whatever it was that had him all bent out of shape, it appears to have passed. Gunner leaned down and pressed his forehead to his mother's while she cupped his cheeks. Her thumb rubbed affectionately over his cheek, as a tear rolled down hers. Their bond is beautiful, and if I'm being honest, I'm envious. The moment that I learned I was pregnant, I dreamed of sharing moments like this. I saw myself as the loving and doting mother who would move heaven and Earth to see my pup's smile. I saw our shared giggles and hugs while I brushed hair. I saw cooking in the kitchen with matching aprons. I saw dancing in the living room as we sang into hairbrushes. I saw a first crush, a first date, and a first heartbreak. I saw our futures. And then I lost it all.

Gunner left his mother with his father and came to stand beside me. He and his Beta were to ride in the Humvee with Hina, myself, and as many others that would fit. Gunner leaned against the car at my side and pushed his hands into his pockets.

"You convinced them to let me out" he said without looking at me.

"I did" I answered him. He was quiet for a moment, just watching the last of the goodbyes.

"Why? After I hurt her, you should want me gone" he asked, not looking at me. Cole hung close by, giving us space to speak, but not enough that Gunner could attack again.

"You're her True Mate. Besides me, I trust no one else to put her safety above anything and everything else".

"Thank you" he said quietly.

"Don't mistake my intentions, Alpha. I trust that you will do anything to save her. But if you hurt her again, I will put you down personally" I said as I turned my body to face him completely.

"If I hurt her again, I will end it myself" he said with conviction. I didn't respond. I didn't need to. We both know why I fought for him to come. We would both do absolutely anything to get her back. Or we'd die trying.

As the last of the Tri-Moon boarded the bus, we gathered into the Humvee. The engine vibrated through the vehicle as it came to life and started to drive off. The drive was relatively quiet. A few hushed conversations between some of the Luna Eclipse she-wolves, but not much else. We were all too lost to our own minds, getting ourselves ready for the fight ahead. Taking a life is never easy. In the moment, maybe. The desire and the urge leading up to it can blanket the fact. But it's the after that's hard. The memory of it, the reliving it in your mind. No matter how noble or important the reason, killing does not come easily.

The first Humvee pulled off onto a rough track and drove for a few more minutes before coming to a stop. The three buses, followed by the other Humvee, pulled in behind us and everyone began to file out. The feeling in the air was anticipation mixed with excitement. The warriors were riled up after the cramped drive and ready to let loose. Impatient growls and wild looking eyes bounced around the large group of warriors, all ready to kill to get back their beloved Luna and Triple Goddess. Lupus came to stand with Cole and Gunner as Alpha Ambrose, the other Alphas, and Tobias all gathered around.

"Are your packs in place?" Gunner asked while looking at Alpha Travis,

"They are, they have been waiting for over an hour" he responded with a nod.

"Tell them to move in, spread out wide while keeping the lines thick. They are to wait for each of you to give the word before they attack. We have to do this as one, or else we lose the element of surprise" Gunner spoke while moving his eyes to each Alpha.

"Get your wolves to sniff each other out first. Commit the scents of the other packs to memory, so that they all know who not to attack". Everyone listened closely as Gunner delivered his final preparations.

"Cole has filled me in on the plan you have all arranged, thank you for doing that in my absence. However, if the winds pick up, if our scents are blown in and our cover is compromised, don't hold back. Don't wait, don't hesitate. Call out the warning and then attack".

"Tobias, I want you with me. I need your help to find her and get her out" Gunner said now looking at the giant Were. For an Alpha to admit to needing help is no small thing. It takes courage. Some could see him as weak, others could deem his request as brave. Either way, with Gunner asking for help in front of his strongest allies, it could go either way.

"Of course Alpha" Tobias replied.

"I'm with you as well Alpha Gunner" Hina piped up. I was surprised by her outburst, I thought she would stick with her she-wolves. But if she's going, I am too.

"As am I" I said firmly, leaving no room for argument,

"And me" Cleo's hard voice grunted from behind me. Now her, I did expect.

"Very well" Gunner said as he gazed around at the gathered group. His eyes studied each Alpha, each Beta, and every other Were in the tight circle. He had in front of him the head of each of his allied packs. He's by no means in this alone.

"Let's move out" he called loudly for all to hear. As the army began to move, so did we.

Chapter Thirty-Four

Zelena

Galterio's mouth slid along the skin of my neck. Goosebumps covered my skin, but not the good kind. I felt like I was flying above my body, watching the situation unfold. I could barely move a muscle, my energy had been completely depleted. But I fought desperately to stay awake. I couldn't pass out. My mind flooded with images of my past. Of Hank beating me to the point of oblivion. How I fought to stay awake, each time. Always afraid of what else he may do to me if I was unconscious. I never thought I would be back in this position. Completely defenceless against an animal that could do whatever they wanted to me.

I don't understand it. I don't know how he did it. However Galterio managed to break through my power, it did some serious damage to me. I was a limp noodle on his lap. Unable to fight back, unable to defend myself, completely vulnerable, and his for the taking. I closed my eyes tight and tried to focus on my body. Everything was numb and fuzzy. I knew he was there, and he was touching me, but I couldn't feel it. I tried to summon my power, I tried to pull it to the surface. But the warmth it usually brings, the feeling of heaviness in my feet when it fills me, it never came.

Galterio's fingers squeezed my neck as he moved his mouth over the top of my shoulder. His slimy tongue dragged across my skin, making me want to scream, or vomit, or both. He stopped when his lips came to Gunner's mark. His first mark, my favourite of his marks. A deathly growl spilled from Galterio's mouth. His grip tightened on my neck, making it nearly impossible to get a breath.

"Please" I rasped out. I wanted to say more, to tell him to stop, to let me go. But please was all I could manage. My eyelids started to close as my breathing got more difficult.

"It'll be over in a minute, Beauty" he whispered into my neck. I felt his teeth drag along my skin, and dread filled my dazed body. No. No, he can't. I fought it, I tried to stay awake, I tried to access my power, I tried to push him away. I tried everything that I could think of. And I accomplished nothing. I no longer had control over my body. I could feel the tears falling down my cheeks. I knew what was coming next, I knew what he wanted to do with me now. It was never about raping me or using my body for his pleasure. But it was still about ravishing my skin. Taking what he wanted by force. It was always his sick plan to make me his, just not in the way I thought.

Galterio's teeth pierced my skin, burying deeply into the spot on the top of my shoulder. Gunner's spot. The place where his mark sat. I screamed. I closed my eyes tight and screamed out a piercing shriek. The pain was unfathomable. Worse than anything I have ever experienced before. Worse than what Gunner had done on the beach. Worse than what Hank had done in that basement. Death would be better than this. My stomach twisted and turned. An intense pressure in my chest exploded through my body sending waves of fire through my bloodstream. My scream was so loud that it rang in my ears. I heard glass shattering and a deep rumbling in the walls around us. I could feel a surge erupting out of my body, and Galterio's teeth were ripped from my skin. I fell back onto the bed, completely motionless. I prayed for respite to the pain, I prayed out to Mother to save me. Please let this end. The sounds of creaking, rumbling, and shaking, slowly died out as I lost myself to unconsciousness.

~

My skin was burning. Fire danced across my body, leaving my skin aching and itching in its wake. Everything hurt. Everything. I have never felt in so much pain before. Even my heat on the night of the party wasn't this bad. I lifted my arm and it felt like I had a ten-kilo weight attached to my wrist. I moved my hand to the top of my shoulder. My fingers brushed over the place Gunner's mark sat, just like they had affectionately done so many times before. This time, when my fingers came in contact with the spot, it stung. I hissed and pulled my hand back. That fucking bastard marked me. And he did it over the top of Gunner's first mark. How dare he! I will kill him for this. I was about to get up off the bed and find a mirror when voices on the other side of the door made me freeze. I laid still and listened quietly.

"It worked" Galterio's voice came first,

"Just like you said it would".

"Told you, you have same blood, power is weaker against you" a heavily accented voice came next, a voice I felt was very familiar.

"And the mark, will it stick, will it remove the effects of the other one?" Galterio asked. My stomach dropped and I felt sick. Could he really overpower my bond with Gunner? Please no, it can't be possible. We are destined for each other, Selene said so. That can't change. Surely a bond like ours can't be wiped away by force. Oh god, please don't let this happen.

"Not clear. If normal Mate, yes. True Mate, don't know" the other voice answered. I know that voice. A loud growl shook the door and made me jump a little.

"You said I was her True Mate. You told me I was called forth, I was destined for her!" Galterio hissed angrily

"Yes, this true" the other person answered meekly.

"How can there be two? This is all pointless if it doesn't work!". This can't be happening. Does he think we're True Mates? I felt nothing when I saw him that first time in the dress shop. I felt the Earth move beneath me when I met Gunner. He consumed my thoughts. I was drawn to him. I didn't even think of Galterio when I was back with Gunner. He must have it all wrong.

"And the pup? Can we get rid of the pup without putting her at risk?" Galterio growled. His voice dripped with venom and disgust. He wants to kill my baby. The way he spat the word 'pup' like that, he truly hates it. I moved my hands to my stomach and cradled it. There's really a baby in there? Gunner's baby. My baby. I'm going to have a baby. And Galterio wants it gone. He wants to be my Mate, and he wants to kill my unborn child. That was it, that was all I needed to hear. The fact that I'm scared no longer matters. I don't care if I think I'm not ready for this. It doesn't matter that I don't know anything about being a mother, or a parent. It doesn't matter if I'm too young, if I haven't had time to figure out who I am, as a person, a partner, a sister, a Luna. None of that matters now. As unplanned and unexpected as this may be, he will not touch my baby. Gunner's baby. This little thing inside me is all that matters now. Galterio won't hurt it. I won't let that happen. Ever.

But how do I get out of here? Wherever here is. If he is immune to my power like they said, how the fuck am I meant to fight him off? If I even can. I still feel so weak and so drained, can I really fight my way out of here like this?

"How will we know if the mark has taken?" Galterio's voice asked angrily,

"When she wake, she will feel for you. Want you. If not, other bond too strong". That voice. That dammed voice. I have to be wrong, it can't be who I think it is. There is more than one person in the world who talks in an accent. Galterio for fucks sake has an accent. But this one. This voice. I have been listening to this voice nearly every day for weeks. I know who it belongs to. I just hope that I'm wrong.

"Let's test that theory then" Galterio sneered threateningly. I turned my head and closed my eyes. I tried to steady my breathing and calm my heart. Is playing unconscious the right play here? I don't know. We will see. The door slowly creaked open and two pairs of footsteps entered the room. The bed dipped near my upper body as Galterio sat down. I could smell him. His scent overpowered everything else in the room. It filled my nostrils and I found myself trying to breathe in more of it. But still, I didn't move, I didn't open my eyes. My composure nearly broke when his finger brushed across my cheek. I expected to feel nothing. I expected to want to turn away from his touch or hit his hand away. I was wrong. I didn't hate the feel of his skin against mine, in fact, it was cooling and soothed the fire burning underneath it. I didn't want to push him away, in fact, I wanted to feel more of it.

"Wake up now, Beauty" Galterio cooed down at me. I don't want to open my eyes. I don't want to know if seeing him will change things. I like his touch, does that mean his mark took? I'm not ready to find out for sure. I'm not ready to say goodbye to Gunner.

Galterio moved his hand to the back of my neck and turned my head to face upwards. Still, I kept my eyes closed. His hot breath brushed against my face. He was close to me, really close. My first kiss with Gunner, that's when everything changed for us. That's when I knew for sure how I truly felt about him. Is Galterio about to kiss me? Would the same kind of thing happen if I didn't kiss him back? I felt his face hovering just above my own. His presence was hard to ignore. He moved his head to the crook of my neck and inhaled deeply. He groaned, a deep and pleasure filled groan, and then buried his face into my hair and neck.

"You smell delectable" he breathed heavily. His mouth found the skin of my neck, and he began to nibble and suck at the tender flesh. The feel of his skin on mine was relieving the burning sensation. But the internal feeling that ensued in my stomach, was far from the kind of feeling a Mate should have for their partner. The thought of him greedily devouring my skin, it made me want to hurl. I still hate him. I can feel it deep inside of me. But my body seems to have a mind of its own. Maybe it is just because I feel so hot. Maybe it's just my burning skin aching for something to cool it down. Doesn't matter, I hate him. Can you be mated to someone that you hate? I don't know. But either way, I really don't like being in two minds about this. There is only one way to know for sure if he has truly taken Gunner from me.

I blinked my eyes open and stared up at the ceiling. The room was lit up by the hanging light on the roof, it shone in my eyes brightly, forcing me to turn them away. Galterio's head was still at my neck. One of his hands held the back of my neck and the other was on the bed by my head. His tongue and lips moved their way across my neck and to his new mark. He licked kissed and sucked at the mark. Out of everything that I feared I would feel from him, none of it came. His lips on the mark didn't make me quiver and shake the way Gunner's did. The thought of him ravishing my body the way Gunner does didn't bring moisture to my panties. In fact, I was drier than a saltine cracker. My skin liked the cooling effect he gave me, but nothing more. I don't want him. Gunner is still at the forefront of my mind. So, does that mean it didn't work? We aren't Mates, I still belong to Gunner. I groaned out loud in happiness, unable to hide my joy. Unfortunately, Galterio heard the happy noise come from me. Fortunately though, he thought it was caused by something else.

"You like that, don't you, Beauty?" he mumbled into my skin. He thinks I groaned out of pleasure. Maybe that's a good thing, maybe I can work with that. I have a plan. A dumb, gross, horrible plan. But it's still a plan.

"Galterio" I moaned, putting on the most erotic, sex filled voice I could muster. It worked. He growled sensually and shifted so that his whole body was now hovering over me. He used his knees to part my legs and lowered himself between them. He pushed his hips forward, pressing his erection into my groin. Thank fuck for the clothing between us. My insides were spinning, I could taste the bile in the back of my throat. With a hell of a lot of reluctance, I lifted my leg and hooked it around his waist. Galterio growled with excitement and began to slowly move his hips back and forth, grinding his groin into mine. My god, I hate this. Dry humping the Were that wants to kill my pup. But I really don't have any other options.

A rough cough came from behind Galterio. I forgot the second voice, the other pair of footsteps. There's another person in the room and he was watching Galterio rub himself all over me. This couldn't get any worse.

"Fuck off" Galterio grunted without moving from his position on top of me.

"Alpha, we have work" the voice called with annoyance.

"Later, first I need to enjoy my new little Mate" Galterio chuffed and pushed his hips hard into mine. I grunted from the force of it, but Galterio seemed to like that. Fuck, fuck, fuck, fuck, fuck. How do I get out of this now? I'm so stupid. Of course, he would want to mate the first chance he could.

He has been all over me from the first time we met. Why didn't I think of that before?

"Galterio?" I said softly as I moved my hands to his chest and pushed slightly. I hope this works.

"Yes, my little Mate?" he muttered into my ear.

"What is this, you called me your Mate?" I said with a breathy tone. Play dumb. He already thinks of me as an object for him to use as he pleases. It makes sense that he would believe I am nothing more than a bitch to stand at his side, look pretty and smile.

"Yes, Beauty. You are mine now, as you should be" he growled playfully as his tongue swiped across my collarbone.

"Yours" I sighed deeply and lifted my other leg to wrap around his waist. I hate this. I hate this so fucking much. I want to cry. I feel like I have, or I am, betraying Gunner. Would he forgive me for this? For playing along and leading Galterio on. Would he understand? He can hate me if he needs to, as long as I find my way back to him. I will spend the rest of my life showing Gunner how sorry I am for entertaining the thought of being with another man, whether it's fake or not. As long as I have the chance to do so, the rest doesn't matter.

"Alpha" the voice called again. I took the chance and pushed at Galterio's chest. As I pushed him back, I sat up so that he couldn't just pin me down again. My eyes met with those of the other Were in the room. He stood with his back against the wall and his dark scrutinising eyes pinned on me. I really wanted to be wrong. I hoped I was. This time, I'm not so lucky. His messy greying hair sat down past his shoulders, and his long grey beard made him look like an evil wizard.

"Artemis" I said disheartened.

"Triplí Theá" he said looking down his nose at me.

"What are you doing here?" I asked harshly. Galterio laughed and spun around on the bed so that he sat next to me, then he slid his arm around my waist.

"She already has my fire in her, see" he chuckled and pressed his lips to my temple.

"I here for you, Theá" he answered me.

"You betrayed… Tri-Moon?" I stuttered. I nearly said Gunner, I almost said his name out loud. If I do that, it may ruin this whole charade.

"No little Mate, he did his duty. He interpreted the prophecy, found you, and brought you to me. Just as he was supposed to" Galterio answered my question as he stroked his finger affectionately down my cheek. The prophecy, what prophecy? And how in the hell did he find me? He didn't find me, Gunner did. But now he is taking credit for that, seriously. Something in the way Galterio talks, makes it sound like these two have known each other for a long time. Not just since Galterio kidnapped me. Could Artemis have been working with Origin Wolf, working against Tri-Moon, this whole time. Was Artemis the traitor all along?
"You look confused, Beauty" Galterio said smoothly, though my eyes stared unseeing at Artemis. I nodded my head, blinked my eyes, and forced forward a smile.
"I am a little" I said with a fake grin,
"What is a prophecy?" I asked him in my sweet and innocent voice.
"The prophecy talks of Selene, and how she will provide us with a Triple Goddess, and how that Goddess will have to choose between two Mates. One good and one bad" Galterio spoke as he looked deeply into my eyes, like he was trying to hypnotise me or something. I wanted to look away from his intense stare, but I knew that if I did, he could see it as rejection. I need him to believe I am all in with him, and him alone.
"Two Mates?" I said dumbly, using a breathy delirious voice.
"You don't need to worry about that now, my little Mate. I am the only one you will ever need" he leaned in close and breathed deeply into my ear,
"I will please you like never before, and you will be my devoted queen" he said in a low rumbled voice. He's trying to seduce me. But nothing he could do would ever be able to pull that kind of effect from me. But fuck. If he is to believe that we are Mates, he would expect to be able to draw those sorts of reactions out of me effortlessly. Okay. Time to act. I leaned my head to the side so that Galterio had more access to my neck. I closed my eyes and thought of Gunner. His smooth creamy skin pulled tight over broad shoulders and rippling abs. Firm muscular arms that wrap around my waist perfectly. His magical fingers and the delicious things they do to my body. I could feel the desire pulsating through my

body, and the wetness seeped into my underwear. Galterio seemed to notice too.

"I can smell you" he growled sexually into my hair. I huffed and breathed out a deep sigh. Thank fuck.

"Soon Beauty. I will give you everything you want, but not just yet" he whispered and slid his tongue over my cheek to the corner of my mouth. I swallowed down a dry reach and pushed out a choked groan. Galterio laughed and sat up straight again.

"But why me? You can have anyone that you want, why would you want me?" I asked him as I curled my hands around his bicep.

"Because it was prophesized. Because you and I are the highest beings, the apex predators in a world full of predators. We are the purest of all the Weres. The blood of the Moon Goddess flows thick in our veins, it makes us stronger, it powers us. We are absolute in ways that no other Were can achieve. You and I are the future of our race. We are fucking royalty. And the pups you will bear me, they will be treated like Gods on Earth". This dude has taken the train past Crazy Town and gone all the way to Bonkersvill. He thinks I will have his pups. He is truly mad. I need to get the fuck out of this place, and fast. Galterio stood up and offered me his hand.

"Come, you need to eat" he said firmly,

"But Alpha" Artemis began to argue. Galterio roared at him and flashed his fangs,

"She eats first" he growled at him.

"We need to check her" Artemis said with a slight shake to his voice.

"We are Mated, you saw her reaction to me, smelt her desire. It's done!" he snapped and pulled me to my feet. He dragged me from the bed and out the door, slamming it hard behind him. Thank God his ego was too big to ever believe someone could fake affection with him, that there could ever be a woman immune to his charm. Thank God I am one of those women.

"Disobedience!" Galterio roared and slammed his fist into the wall. His whole arm went through the wall as plaster, bricks, and dust tumbled to the ground. He grabbed my shoulder roughly and slammed my back against the wall. My head bobbed back and hit against the wall hard, sending a ringing through my ears.

"You will never disobey me, will you Beauty?" he snarled at me. I was tiny in his presence. His huge frame was twice my size and it was intimidating. He loomed over me, blocking out the light around me. He was huffing harshly and his eyes were wide and held a wild edge. How does he do this, flip between moods so swiftly? I should be used to it by now, but each time it still surprises me.

"Never" I said softly. Galterio leaned forward and pressed his forehead to mine.

"I will give you the world, I will have you rule at my side. But when I am angry, I will not play nice. It is in your best interest to keep me happy" he said slowly and with a deep-seated threat threaded through his words. I would be an idiot to not be afraid. And I am. I'm terrified. I took in a slow deep breath and lifted my hands to wrap them around his waist. I pulled his body closer to mine so that my head was pressed against his chest.

"I'll make you happy" I said as confidently as I could. I held my breath and waited to see if he believed me. After a minute, Galterio's hand moved to the back of my neck and he gripped it tightly. He pulled my head back so that I was looking up at him.

"I know you will" he said coldly. He stared into my eyes and I thought he was going to kiss me. But he didn't, he just stood still, staring at me. After a moment he huffed and let me go before stepping out of my arms.

"Come, you still need to eat" he snapped and strode off down the hallway. I watched him take long heavy strides away from me, and finally released the breath I had been holding. I noticed that I was at the other end of the hallway compared to last time. The room he had me in originally is on the other side of the house. I peered past Galterio's retreating figure and gazed down the darkened hallway. I could just make out the door, or what was left of the door, now in pieces on the ground. There was a stack of other broken furniture, dirt, and rubble, all swept into a pile in the hallway. What happened there, I wonder?

"Now Zelena!" Galterio yelled and I quickly jumped forward to follow after him.

We came to the kitchen and Galterio flicked on the lights. The night sky outside was dark and made the situation that much scarier. Galterio pulled out a chair at the large glass table and gestured for me to sit down. I sat down slowly and watched as he then went to the fridge and pulled out a rather large plate. He put it in the microwave and beeped a few buttons. He didn't look up or turn around, just stood facing the microwave until it sounded its finished beeping song. He carried the plate over and slid it in front of me. A mountain of steaming beef, pork, and steak, filled the plate to the brim. Upon seeing it, it was like a switch went off in my brain and I became a ravenous beast. I lurched forward and began shovelling the meat into my open mouth. I grunted and moaned and growled as the delicious flesh filled my gob. I was a literal never ending pit of hunger, but hot damn, I will try my best to fill this hole with juicy meat. The plate was half empty by the time I looked up again. Galterio was watching me with deep frown lines across his forehead. He looks really unhappy. I had meat residue all over my hands and halfway up my forearms. I could feel the blood and juice dripping down my chin. Reluctantly I dropped the meat from my hand and tried to compose myself again.

"I'm sorry" I mumbled as I tried to swallow my mouthful of chewed up beef.

"No need to apologise. I know how it is for you during this stage. For now, you need this to keep you strong, and because of that, I will allow it. But know this, it won't last little Mate. That pup doesn't belong in there and its days are numbered. Your body is mine now, and only my seed shall give you offspring".

Chapter Thirty-Five

Zelena

I stared at Galterio as he stared back at me. He was waiting to see my reaction after saying outright that he was going to kill my pup. He doesn't know that I heard him say it earlier. But I still wasn't expecting such an upfront admission. I kept my gaze firmly placed on his. But in the corners of my vision, I was searching for a way out. I kept coming back to the large floor to ceiling glass doors that led to the backyard. I couldn't see beyond the doors, it was too dark outside. I have no idea what could be waiting for me out there if that's the path I choose. But at this point, it is either through the glass doors to the backyard, or try my luck back through the house. At least now I have eaten and have my strength back. I can summon my power to fly the fuck out of here.

"Did you hear me, Beauty?" Galterio said smoothly, drawing my attention back onto his watchful face,

"That uninvited guest has worn out its welcome. Your womb is for me, for my offspring. You don't want to upset your Mate, now do you love?" his calm and smooth tone was bating me. He didn't let Artemis test our supposed bond, but he has found a way to do it himself. Threaten my child. See if I will choose him and his happiness, over the life of my pup. He made a smart play. But for me, after hearing his plan spoken out loud and to my face, the game is over. I'm not hanging around to give him the chance to follow through on his word.

I let the power flow through my veins and tingle at the tips of my fingers. I smirked at Galterio with a wicked glint in my eye. I waved my hand over the table in a quick swiping motion. The glass table and the chairs all flew at high speed towards Galterio. I may not be able to hold him, but I can still use my power on everything else around him. The weight of the table forced Galterio to fall backward out of his chair. I didn't hang around to see the rest of it crush him. I jumped to my feet and bolted for the glass doors. Using my power, I picked up a coffee table and thrust it through the glass. The panes of glass shattered and rained down over the ground, creating a pool of shards in my way. As I was running to the door, I lessened the gravity around my body and flew myself over the pieces of glass and out the now open doors. A smile broke across my face as I felt my freedom in reach. Far in the distance, the sun was starting to make its appearance, settling a soft grey over the distant horizon. I was home free.

I screamed into the air as something latched onto my ankle. I looked down and saw Galterio's half changed face glaring back at me. His mouth had started elongating into a snout and his cheeks were sprouting dark grey fur. I had never seen a Were hold onto a partial shift. It was horrifying. The pain in my ankle intensified and I saw his claws were dug deep into the skin, with blood pouring out of the slash marks. We were hovering in the air, maybe ten meters above the ground. I tried to kick at Galterio's hand to dislodge his grip. It didn't work. He only dug his claws in deeper and I swear he was about to rip my foot off. On instinct, I threw my head back and screamed, only that scream melded into a long pain filled howl.

I wrapped my power around Galterio's throat and tightened. I held it so tight that if it was anyone else, their head would have popped right off. But the effect it had on him was weak enough that he could ignore it. Galterio's pack and the other Weres on his property started to appear on the ground beneath us. All of them wanted to check out the commotion and all of them watching us with wide and surprised eyes. I continued to kick at Galterio as I tried to shake myself free.

"YOU ARE MINE!" he roared. His deep animalistic voice shook me to the core. He sounds like a demon. Galterio swiped his other arm up and dug his claws into the flesh of my thigh. I screamed in agony as we began to fall back to the ground. Somehow, Galterio managed to land on his feet first, and then rolled onto his back as I came down on top of him. He quickly rolled us over so that I was under him. His elongated snout and long sharp canines were mere millimetres from my face. A blob of drool dripped from his long fang and landed on my cheek as he growled at me.

"You are mine" he snarled dangerously. He wrapped his fingers around my throat and squeezed. I coughed and hit at his hand, trying to get him to loosen his grip. I can't breathe. He has completely constricted my windpipe. I spluttered and kicked my legs wildly. Galterio lifted his head back with his jaw open, he was going for my throat. But just as he was about to bring his sharp teeth back down, an echoed howl filled the dawn air. He snapped his head in the direction of the howl, then came another and another until we were surrounded by howls. A battle cry. One call stood out above the rest. One howl called to every part of me, pulling forward the will I need to fight, pulling forward the will I need to live. Gunner. Gunner is here.

I turned my hands around and used all the force I could to push Galterio away from me. He went flying through the air across the yard. I sat up and watched as he completed his change mid air before he landed back on four awfully large grey paws. He is big, really big. His wolf is the same size as Tobias's. And Tobias is by far the biggest Were I had ever seen. He jerked his head to one side and then the other, but before I could register what he was doing, I was grabbed. Two hard hands on one arm and another two on the other. Big mistake. I sent one of the Weres flying off into a tree and the other high up into the air, only to crash back down again with a sickening thud. Galterio barked and growled over at me. I replied with a smirk, and I wrapped my power around the neck of another of his pack-mates, one that was trying to sneak up on me. I flexed my hand to the side and his neck snapped. The Weres body dropped to the ground and Galterio's eyes followed. I guess he knew that Were, perhaps closely. He snarled back up at me and growled. He's mad.

Good. He should be mad, because now I'm going to kill the bastard.

The howling in the distance was closing in. By the sounds of it, Gunner has brought backup. Maybe even all of the packs that remained after the party. That would be a lot of fighters. I haven't seen much of Galterio's camp, but I don't think he had that many Weres. Wolves and Weres were running all around the yard, scattering to their battle positions. But I was only focused on Galterio. He kidnapped me, violated my flesh, threatened my bond with Gunner, threatened our pup and he is straight up coo-coo balls. He dies today. Galterio crouched down, readying himself to charge. I twitched and stretched my fingers, feeling the power twirl around my flexed fingers. More of his men came for me, teeth bared, claws out, and ready to kill. I lifted my forcefield to hold them back, but one slipped through before I could. I dodged backward, narrowly avoiding the extended claws of the angry Were. As I was distracted by him, Galterio made his move. He charged forward, lowered his shoulder, and barged into the shield. I felt it shudder under his attack. The Were inside my shield went for my neck, but I moved again, ducking under his arms. I felt another shudder ram into me and then a snapping sensation sounded in the back of my consciousness. I turned in time to see Galterio's wolf charge right for me, the force field now completely gone. He tackled me down with full force. I fell onto my back and Galterio pinned me down with his paw on my shoulder. The other Were quickly threw his body across my legs, restricting my movements. I tried to push Galterio back but he dug his claws into my collarbone. I screamed out in pain. For a Were that claims he wants to be my Mate, he sure isn't too worried about hurting me.

I struggled under the weight of his paw. Knowing my power was near useless against him, made fighting him off that much more challenging. I kicked at my legs wildly, trying to kick off the Were holding them down. Galterio shifted so that he was now standing over my head. I looked up at his furry stomach as he moved his face toward my belly. He opened his massive jaws wide and held it above my stomach. His long sharp fangs were only centimetres from my abdomen. I kicked and hit and punched like my life depended on it, because let's face it, it does. Galterio growled and leaned down further so that the tips of his teeth pressed against my stomach. Right at the place where my pup would be.

"No, please! Stop! Don't hurt him" I screamed and begged him. Galterio's wolf scraped his teeth over my stomach again as a rumbling growl vibrated through him. He was toying with me. Showing me how easy it would be for him to kill both my pup and me. I thrashed under his paw and ripped out a fistful of his fur. Galterio pressed his teeth harder against my stomach, piercing the skin. I could feel the constricting pressure in my lower abdomen. Galterio growled and shook his head. His teeth against my flesh pressed and tore deeper into my skin. Once again, I screamed. Not because it hurt, because it really did, But I screamed out of fear. I was scared for my baby. Galterio was warning me. Giving me a chance to stop fighting before he does actually rip the baby from my stomach. There's no guarantee that if I quit fighting, that if I give up, he will honestly spare my baby's life. I could keep fighting. Try to use more of my power and risk draining my energy. But there's no guarantee that that will work either. What choice do I have, when he has his teeth pressed at my pup's neck.

"Okay" I huffed,

"I'll stop fighting, I'll stay. Just let him go. Please. Spare my baby" I sobbed and let my body go limp. Galterio withdrew his teeth from my stomach and stood up straight, also pulling his claws from my chest. I winced at the pain but held in the urge to scream again. Galterio's wolf huffed and growled and jerked his head. The Were that was lying on my legs mumbled a quick 'yes Alpha' and then scrambled off of me. He picked me up by the arm and began to drag me back to the house. Now that I was standing once again, I got a better look at my surroundings. All the Weres from before had disappeared, but the loud sounds of fighting were coming from close by. Really close by. How did I not hear that before? I looked around the yard and out through the trees. With the sun now just a little bit higher in the sky, it was starting to lighten up and I could see further into the forest. I caught sight of a large group of wolves fighting. They're here. I looked to the other side and again saw more wolves fighting. They're all here.

I was only a few steps away from Galterio's wolf when a thunderous growl rumbled through the yard. I turned my head just in time to see a large brown wolf tackle Galterio to the ground. The Were pulling me to the house became rougher and more urgent with his dragging. The torn skin of my chest was stretching and stinging at the angle at which he was pulling my arm, and my ankle was impossible to stand on. But still, I fought to watch the wolf tackle Galterio. They rolled across the ground and both quickly got back onto their feet. As they began to circle each other, I got a better look at the brown wolf. I've seen that wolf before. It's Cole.

"COLE!" I screamed at the top of my lungs as I tried to rip my arms free of the other Were. When I couldn't get free, I turned to him and held up my hand. I increased the gravity around him, and inside him as well. He screamed and let go of my arm. But just to be sure, using both my hands, I flew them towards each other and clapped them together loudly. The Weres body compacted in on itself in a horrible array of scrunching and squelching. Done. I quickly turned back around to see Galterio and Cole going for each other's necks. The roaring, barking, and growling was deafening, and the blood, fur, and saliva flying everywhere made me want to vomit. I have to do something. I have to help him. I waited, watching nervously. I finally saw an opening, Galterio reared back in order to lunge forward with more power. Before he got the chance to, I flew him to the side and slammed him into a tree, then again into another tree. But he still got back up, so, I sent him high into the air and then pulled him crashing back down again. This time he didn't get up. Cole's wolf limped over to me and shook out his fur. He stood up in his human form, in all his naked glory. He was covered in blood and deep slash marks. Three really bad slashes ran parallel up the side of his neck and over his cheek.

"Oh Cole" I said weakly as I eyed all of his wounds. I went to touch his cheek but stopped. The last time I saw Cole, he still hated me. Has that changed or is this just Cole doing his Beta duties? Cole grabbed my shoulders and turned me around in his grip, looking over my body at my wounds.

"Are you okay? Did he do this to you?" Cole asked urgently as he spotted the blood on my shirt. Without hesitation, he grabbed the hem of my shirt and lifted it up to see the bite marks on my stomach. Cole growled and gently ran his hand over the small puncture wounds.

"What happened?" He asked me roughly,

"Galterio" I answered softly. I swallowed hard and tried not to let myself cry at Cole's show of concern, I've really missed him.

"He, uh, he got mad when I tried to escape" I stuttered.

"Can you walk?" he asked as his eyes moved down to my mangled ankle,

"Maybe, not far though" I said quickly. Cole didn't waste any time in sweeping out my knees and lifting me into his arms,

"Cole no, you're hurt too" I argued and tried to wriggle out of his hold.

"I'll be fine, but we need to get you out of here" he answered and began to jog awkwardly away from the house.

"No wait, Artemis is inside. It was him, he was working with Galterio" I said and pointed back to the house. Cole looked at the house and then at me, then out into the forest before looking back at the house once more. He closed his eyes for a second and opened them a gain.

"Others are on the way to apprehend Artemis. But you are the most important, we have to get you to safety first" he said and kept jogging. He was struggling to run, I could tell he was in pain. But he would never admit it. I tried to lean my head on his chest, but he was covered in blood. Plus, the bobbing around from the running would probably make me sick… again. The sound of battle was echoing around us, from all directions. How we hadn't come across anyone yet was amazing. Cole stopped running and ducked behind a large tree, just in time to avoid three wolves running towards the house. As we hid behind the tree, Cole leaned down and sniffed at me.

"You smell different" he whispered quietly. My cheeks burned with embarrassment, I couldn't tell Cole what I had to do with Galterio to get out. I think he already hates me enough, I don't need to pile on more reasons for him to justify his hatred.

"It's Galterio, I think" I whispered back. Cole sniffed again and his eyebrows furrowed together.

"It's not that, you don't smell like a male, you smell sweeter". Cole looked out from around the tree but quickly ducked

behind again as two more wolves ran past. Does your scent change when you are pregnant? No. I don't think so, if so, Gunner would have smelt it already. Unless it only happens when you become further along. I don't even know how far along I am. Couldn't be more than maybe two weeks. But people don't have morning sickness at two weeks pregnant. That can't be right. I should tell Cole. Gunner should have been the first to know. But that has already been blown apart by Galterio and Artemis, and their knowledge of my little situation. Should I tell Cole? Maybe it's vital he knows while he is trying to get us out of here. Maybe it will help him stop hating me so much. Maybe it will do the opposite. Ah, fuck it.
"Uh… Cole" I whispered,
"Yeah?" he said as he brought his head back around to me,
"I um… I'm… I'm pregnant" I said softly, so softly I don't think he even heard me. Cole stared at me blankly, eyes wide, not blinking. He quickly shook his head and cleared his throat,
"You're sure?" he asked while looking back around the tree and out into the forest.
"Yes, very sure" I whispered,
"Well, that explains a lot" he said quietly as he ran forward a bit before crouching down behind a large bush.
"What…" I started to ask, but he quickly pressed his hand to my mouth. We heard rustling in the forest brush and low growls. They were getting closer to us, and by the look on Cole's face, I don't think he knows if they are friendly or not. Cole squatted behind the bush with me across his lap, and the both of us remained deathly silent. After a few minutes, the rustling died down and the growling went away. Cole grabbed my chin and turned my head to look at him. He did the 'zip your lip' gesture and then pointed to his ear, he then spun his finger around in the air. I think I got what he is saying. Be quiet, they can hear us. I nodded my head and pressed myself into his chest. Cole slowly stood up and took careful steps toward another large tree. We got to the tree and Cole pressed me into it, shielding the rest of my body with his own. We stayed there for a brief minute while he looked around some more, and then we started moving again. Cole was taking slow and cautious steps, his eyes moving all over the forest as he went. I was looking up at Cole's face,

studying the three deep open slashes on his cheek. His head suddenly flew back in twisted agony, and his grip on my legs and waist tightened to the point that it hurt. Cole looked like he was screaming, but no sound was coming out. Panic exploded inside my chest, my heartbeat quickened and my breathing got harsh. I looked all over his face, searching for an answer to the problem. It took me a second to move my eyes down. When I did, the world around me stopped. Cole's hold on me disappeared as his arms dropped, and I fell to the ground. I sat at his feet and stared up at his contorted face. I screamed out, a scream I had never felt before. A scream that shook me to the core. The ground beneath me shook and the trees around me creaked and cracked and splintered to pieces. All matter of forest brush lifted off the ground and began to circle around us in its own little tornado. My gaze stayed on Cole's face. His head bobbled down and his eyes found mine. His glassy, tear filled, scared eyes. His lips twitched up into a weak smile and his eyes fluttered closed. My head went back, my arms spread open wide, and a burst of energy exploded out of me. It sent everything flying outward in one giant wave. Tears streamed down my face as I looked up at Cole. Right in the middle of his chest was a bloodied fist, forced through his body from the other side. And held in grip of that bloodied fist, Cole's heart.

Cole's body was lifted off the ground and then hurled through the air away from me. I watched as his lifeless body hit the ground hard, rolled for a bit, and then stopped. He didn't get up. He didn't move. He just laid there, dead. Cole is dead. A deep and dark rage ignited in every corner of my being. The darkness that I have fought so hard to keep away, managed to burst through the cracks, disintegrating all the walls I have built to contain it. Only this time, I welcomed it. I moved my eyes back to the one responsible. Galterio. He stood with a proud and evil smirk plastered across his face. Cole's blood was smeared over his arm, all the way up to his elbow. Galterio clicked his tongue and shook his head slowly from side to side.

"I told you, Beauty, you are mine now" he said with a wicked grin.

Chapter Thirty-Six

Lunaya

Alpha Ambrose had already broken off from the group to cover the East. His son, Ares, and their warriors would head up to meet him and then their pack would cut them off from there. Alpha Lace took his men, and at the request of Alpha Marius, half of the Blue Moon warriors, to the coastline on the West. I can understand now why Tobias so easily handed his brother the Alpha title. Marius is a smart Were, very capable and wise beyond his years. He is cocky as all hell, but the devotion and loyalty he has is strong. I'm glad Zelena has such a strong alliance with that pack. With Alpha Travis's warriors from Waning Wolf coming from the South, and Tri-Moon and Luna Eclipse coming from the North. Plus, the addition of the remaining Blue Moon warriors spreading out to pick off the stragglers. We will have them completely blocked off and surrounded. The sun was not far from rising, meaning the battle was imminent. We were all now in position. Before the Alphas broke apart, they made a blood bond. All six of them, even Hina, slit their palms and mixed their blood. Blood bonds are an outdated alliance ritual. But it allows the Alphas to flash, so in this instance, totally necessary.

My black and white wolf stood between Hina's snow white wolf and Gunner's massive silver wolf. Cleo stood just behind me, and Cole and Lupus were right behind Gunner. Unsurprisingly, Tobias has the biggest wolf I have ever seen. It's no wonder he was picked as the guardian. He is a tank on legs. Gunner handed out his orders to his pack. Let no one escape, kill or be killed, and of course, call him at the first sign of Zelena. Hina didn't need to voice her orders. Her she-wolves were extremely well trained and prepared. They knew where to go and what to do. The first sign of sunrise began to sparkle over the horizon. Gunner was ready to sound the charge order when a howl rang out through the dawn air. It was filled with pain and fear, and it struck me through the heart. The pain shot through me like ice in my veins. It's Zelena. Gunner and the other Tri-Moon pack members knew it too. They all perked their ears forward and their shackles raised. Gunner threw his head back and howled in response, followed closely by Cole, Lupus, and the rest of the wolves. Hina, Elaine, and I joined in. And all at once, in one collaborative movement, we charged.

We got a lot further in than I was expecting before we came across the first enemy wolf. I guess the great and almighty Origin Alpha didn't expect us to attack. Idiot. The enemy came at us in dribs and drabs. A few at a time and easily taken out. But the closer we got to the farmhouse, the more we came across. Soon we hit a tight line of warriors and could no longer push forward. Tri-Moon pack are good fighters. Skilled and quick on their paws. The Luna Eclipse she-wolves, however, were like slick blades, slicing through the Weres like butter. I had never seen them in action. And they most definitely lived up to their reputation.

I had the neck of one Were in my jaw when I spotted a large group of reinforcements closing in. I dropped the dead wolf and barked at Gunner. He ripped open a small tan wolf's neck and looked over at me, his muzzle was covered in blood, and he looked terrifying. I nodded my head in the direction of the wolves heading for us. Gunner snarled and barked over to Cole. Cole and Gunner snarled and growled as they flashed, and then Cole quickly turned and ran for a tree. With impressive agility and ease, Cole bounded up the tree and jumped across the branches effortlessly. I was so completely transfixed by his graceful movements that I didn't see the Were coming for me. Cole disappeared through the trees in the direction of the farmhouse just as I was tackled to the ground. The Were managed to quickly get their jaws around my neck and squeeze. Right when I thought that I was done, a large set of snow white jaws ripped the Were from me and then threw it across the ground. Hina growled and snapped her teeth, scolding me for losing focus.

I got back up and pushed off the ground, jumping over Hina's back, and landing on a wolf that was charging up behind her. I grabbed the wolf's ear between my teeth as I jumped, and ripped it clean off as I dragged it to the ground. The wolf howled and charged at me again. I reared up onto my back legs and swiped my paw across its neck. My claws ripped open the soft flesh and blood poured out of it. The wolf stumbled and fell to the ground. I turned to Hina with a wolf version of a cheeky grin. She huffed and grunted and then leaped onto another wolf.

Quickly enough the large battalion was brought down, with minimal casualties on our side. The pack began to push through the trees once more when Gunner stopped running and growled. He was flashing. He looked at Hina as they began flashing with each other. Fuck me, I wish I could hear them.

Beta Cole has found your daughter

A voice popped into my head. I looked around and found Cleo staring directly at me. Cleo? Cleo and I can flash?

Cleo?

I asked her and her wolf nodded,

When did this happen?

I pledged to help you avenge your family. I gave you my loyalty, and with it, our bond was made.

Well, I suppose I can't be too surprised. We have gotten very well acquainted. I would even call her my friend. This is great, Hina can fill her in on what's going on and then she can relay it to me. Finally, a little clarity.

You said Cole has her?

Yes

Where?

He is trying to get her to the coastline and then North from there

Excellent, let's go then

Wait, he said that Artemis is at the farmhouse. He has been helping the Origin Alpha

A growl bubbled through my exposed teeth at the mention of that traitorous Prophet. I would love nothing more than to sink my teeth into his neck. Kill that bastard and that damned prophecy along with him. Fuck. Do I go to her, or go find him? Gunner started off again, but this time he was headed West, towards the coast with Tobias in toe. Lupus was leading the Tri-Moon warriors towards the farmhouse.

Is she safe?

I asked Cleo. She didn't respond right away, so I assume she is confirming with Hina.

They said she has some bad looking slashes and a fucked-up ankle, but nothing life threatening.

Artemis it is then.

With both Gunner and Tobias going for Zelena, it's safe to say that I can go after Artemis, and trust that they will take care of her. It's their job, after all, both of them. We kept running towards the farmhouse but were stopped when we came to another battalion. This one, however, is much bigger than the last. Without a pause, we all dived in and fought. Blood was splattering everywhere and pained whimpers and dying howls echoed around us. It was a gruesome bloody scene. Not one that I ever wanted to see again. Not after Moon Light, not after what the hunters did to my pack. I've never liked killing. Hunter or Were. A life is a life.

I saw a large dark brown and red wolf, rip the head off one of the Luna Eclipse she-wolves. With Cleo at my side, we both bounded for the large wolf. I leaped forward and landed myself half on its back, while Cleo got hold of one of its hind legs. I was snapping my jaws at its neck, trying to get a good hold on it, when it bucked me off. The wolf whipped around and slashed its claws over Cleo's shoulder. She growled in pain but didn't let go of its leg. As the wolf went for her again, I charged forward and got its front paw between my teeth.

Pull Cleo!

I screamed through our flash. At the same time, we each pulled as hard as we could. Cleo ripped the back leg from its body, as I did with its front. The large wolf howled out and fell to the ground. With only two legs it could no longer stand, but it also wasn't dead. Cleo stalked over and pressed her paw to the wolf's neck. And with one swift swipe, she tore open its throat. Blood spurted from the open gashes and then settled into a steady stream, slowly watering the earth beneath it with its thick red blood. With a nod to Cleo, we each jumped onto our next target. We stayed close to each other, helping each other when we needed. Cleo is a fantastic fighter and a brilliant battle partner. We can read each other and anticipate each other's movements without needing to talk.

The last of the battalion was finally brought down, our side this time taking a heavier hit. There were still a lot of us, but many of the warriors were looking a little worse for wear. Some bore large slashes and patches of missing fur, others with missing ears and blood-soaked fur. We had taken a beating. Finally, I could see parts of the farmhouse through the trees now. We are getting really close. As we began to move in again, a shudder inducing chill ran up my spine. My fur stood up straight and electricity danced across my body. A second later, a hard wind slammed against us all. The force of it was like a large wave of water. But it wasn't just any kind of wind, it was pure energy. It pulled at us, all of us, dragging our bodies to the ground. My body felt heavy, I felt compelled to drop to my stomach. But I didn't. I managed to stay on my feet. Everyone else, however, they were all laid flat on their bellies, whimpering and whining. It's from Zelena. Her power. This can't be good.

What the fuck is this?

Cleo growled through our flash. I looked over at her, and she was on her side, burying her nose into the dirt. Hina was not far beyond her, on her belly and scratching at her head with her paw.

It's Zelena. Her power. She must be in trouble.

She can do this at such a distance?

Clearly. Tell Hina to flash Gunner, he has to find her now!

I struggled on my paws but was able to walk over to Cleo and nudge her with my muzzle. She whined and pushed her head into mine. The weight of the power was strong, I can only imagine what Cleo and the others must be feeling. I was taught as a child, by the Elder Maxine, that a Triple Goddess cannot use her power over her family. It was deemed so by The Moon Goddess after the children of Lycaon began to turn on each other. Most of those tales have been lost to time, but it is told that a war broke out between them. Selena on one side and the eldest son, Gill, on the other.

After a few minutes, the heaviness dissipated, and the wolves began to stand up again. I went to Hina and nudged her side.

Did Gunner find her yet?

I asked Cleo, expecting her to be the middleman between Hina and myself.

Yes.

That was it, just 'yes'. I don't know if the simple answer should please me or concern me. Lupus's wideset grey wolf walked over to us, growled and shook his head, and then awkwardly trotted off towards the farmhouse, with the remaining Tri-Moon warriors following. Tri-Moon have been hit hard. They have already lost many fighters, and we haven't even breached the house yet. Lupus himself is covered in blood and slashes. Luna Eclipse have only lost two. But those two will hit them hard. We came to the edge of the tree line before the area opened up into the large clearing that was the front of the property. The Tri-Moon and Luna Eclipse warriors spread out through the trees. Off to the left is where Lua Chei was meant to be coming in from. But so far, no sign of them. Over to the right is where Howlers and the rest of Blue Moon are coming in from. As I was watching the tree line, I spotted a big dark grey wolf standing beside a large tan wolf. Alpha Lace and Alpha Marius.

The house was teeming with wolves. Some walking around the building, others stationed at the doors, some even on the roof. Whatever or whoever they are guarding, they must be important. As we stood watching the house, the sounds of more fighting was filtering through the air. This isn't over. Not by a long shot. A figure in the upstairs window caught my eye. Brown coat, grey beard, dark beady eyes. Artemis. Finally. I threw my head back and howled into the air, giving the signal to attack. It wasn't for me to make the call. But I was done waiting. The signal was returned on all sides, and then a stampede of wolves charged for the farmhouse.

We were met with more wolves, a lot more of them, filing out of the house and lining themselves up as a barricade. I hit the wall of wolves' head on, taking the leg of a smaller brown wolf between my jaws and throwing my head to the side. The leg ripped away effortlessly, and as the little wolf lifted its head to howl, I slashed my claws across its throat. A sharp pain erupted down my back, and I turned to see a grey wolf with its claws buried into my fur. I tossed myself to the ground in a rolling motion, dislodging the wolf's hold on me. I turned and jumped around as the wolf was getting back up off the ground, lunging myself forward, I grabbed the soft of its neck between my teeth and ripped the flesh away. A large gaping hole was left, seeping blood down the front of its body. The wolf fell to the ground, and I spat the chunk of meat from my mouth. As I turned to the next, I was tackled to the ground. A black wolf was on top of me with its teeth digging into the tender spot between my hip and stomach. I growled and kicked at the black wolf, but it didn't budge. I could feel my flesh starting to rip at the sharpness of its fangs. Lupus's large grey wolf appeared over me, and he grabbed the black wolf by its neck, tossing it away like garbage. I got back to my feet and immediately saw an opening in the enemy line. I pushed off hard from my paws, sending myself leaping through the air over a tan wolf, and landing on the ground behind the rest of their line. The tan wolf watched me as I went, but before it got the chance to alert the others, Lupus sliced his claws through its throat. Lupus nodded to me and turned to his next target.

I quickly dashed through the yard towards a Were standing by the door facing in the other direction. I leaped onto his back and buried my teeth into the soft flesh of his human form. He coughed and spluttered and dropped to the ground. The noise he made alerted another Were, who came charging towards me. He dived for my legs, and I jumped, kicking him to the ground with my back legs as I leaped over him. He rolled over at the same time that I turned around. He started to change form, so I quickly bit down into his upper thigh, piercing the femoral artery. He screamed out and his semi changed face reverted back to human. Moving as quickly as I could, I lunged for his neck and wrapped my jaws around his throat. I cut off his scream as I ripped the front of his neck away. By this point, the white of my fur was now red with blood. I got to the building and ran along the side until I came to a door. I snapped my head up and to the side and shook out my fur, then slowly stood up in my human form.

As I stepped to the door, a sharp pain in my hip made me wince. I looked down and saw the deep seeping bite wound. I pressed my hand over it and grabbed the door handle. Locked. Of course, it wasn't going to be that easy. I moved along, keeping to the side of the house. As I approached the corner, two men walked around it. They both spotted me at the same time, and I jumped into action. I pushed my body into a front handspring and wrapped my knees around the head of the Were on the right. Maintaining the rounding motion, the top half of my body kept flying forward, with my hands connecting with the ground. Keeping my knees locked on his neck, I activated my leg muscles, pulled the Were off his feet, and tossed him to the ground a few meters away. I must have been moving too fast as the other Were hadn't even turned around yet. I jumped up and enclosed my arm around his neck and gave a hard twist. His neck snapped cleanly and his body dropped to the ground. I turned back around to the other Were and met his hand connecting with my throat. His large strong hand gripped my neck as he growled angrily. I lifted both my arms up and thrust them down on top of his wrist, forcing his hand away from my throat. With my elbow bent, I then snapped it back upwards, connecting it with his chin. He fell backward, landing on his ass. I stepped over him with one leg on either side of his. He reached out to grab at me, but I grasped hold of his hand. I twisted it harshly and his arm snapped loudly. This made him yell. I quickly dropped his arm and grabbed his head, thrusting my knee up, I slammed it into his nose. Now he was out.

I peeked around the corner of the house. Three more Weres were standing a bit away, facing away from me. They were watching our warriors fighting. It was the Howlers group and they were decimating the enemy. A few meters away from where I was standing, is a medium size window. I could go for the window, break it, and jump through before they turn around. But, I don't know who might be on the other side. I looked back behind me. Lupus, Hina, and the warriors were doing okay, but I couldn't see Cleo. I would appreciate the backup right now.

I decided to go for the window, I can't risk standing around out here in the open, waiting to be seen or captured. I looked down at myself, I'm naked, what was I going to use to break this window. I looked at the unconscious Were lying on the ground. That will work. I ripped the shoe off his foot and scrunched up my nose as I pushed my hand into the warm running shoe. I quickly checked around the corner again, they were still watching the fighting. I ran to the window, fisted my hand inside the shoe, and thrust my arm forward. The glass shattered and fell to the ground. I pushed out the large shards left in the windowsill and then climbed through. I was in a bedroom. It was empty, but the lingering scent told me it hadn't been empty for long. Which means they could come back at any moment. On the floor by the bed was a grey t-shirt dress, I picked it up and pulled it over my head.

I pressed my ear to the closed door and listened. I can't hear anything, but that doesn't mean there isn't anyone out there. I pulled open the door, the tiniest bit, and peered through the crack. I can't see anyone. I opened the door a little wider and slipped through it, then began to tiptoe down the small hallway. I passed another bedroom with the door wide open, and a fancy looking bathroom. The hallway came to an end and it opened up into a large kitchen. The kitchen was a total mess. Like a bomb had gone off in there. Glass everywhere and furniture thrown all about. These guys are not too keen on housekeeping, apparently. The kitchen area was empty, but on the other side of that was a living space, and I could see four Weres in there. I waited a few seconds and then dashed past the wide walkway and to the other side of the hallway. The first door I stopped at looked a little ominous and out of place in this fancy house. A large and heavy looking wooden door with a padlock on it. It stood taunting me, my mind filling with the possibilities of what could be behind it. Is this what they are guarding? All thoughts of Artemis were pushed to the back of my mind as curiosity took over.

I gripped hold of the padlock and tried to muffle the sounds of it with my other hand. I pulled hard and twisted at the same time. The metal creaked and groaned at the force, and with one final pull, it snapped off. I looked behind me and listened, it seemed like no one heard that. When I was sure that no one was coming, I threaded the rest of the broken lock through the hole and then flicked open the latch. I cracked open the door and angled my ear to listen. It was quiet. Next, I put my nose to the slightly ajar door and sniffed. I can smell a few different scents, some fresh and some aging. I checked behind me once again, and then I looked through the crack to make sure that there was no one standing there either. Once I was satisfied that the coast was clear, I slipped through the door and pushed it closed behind me.

It was pitch black, but I could tell that I was standing at the top of a staircase. I blinked my eyes a few times to help them get accustomed to the darkness. When I could make out more details of the narrow stairwell, I slowly walked down the steps. At the last step, I stuck my head out and peered around the wall. On one side was a dead end, just a brick wall. On the other side though, were two Weres. One was sitting with his head leaned back and his eyes closed. And the other sat scrolling on his phone. This guy is actually sleeping, in the middle of a battle. Seriously, what the fuck? In between the two Weres was another door. A big metal door with a little bit of rust in the corners, held together by steel plates and bolts. By the looks of it, I really don't think they want anyone in there. If I can quietly take out the Were that is awake first, and then move on to the sleeping one, I might actually be able to break in without being detected. And then I'll figure out what's behind the door. I lifted my hand in front of my face and let my claws come forth. The long sharp black nails were still stained with blood. I crouched down low, took a deep breath, and rushed around the corner. The first Were looked up at the same moment my claws swiped across his neck. The slicing sensation of skin under my nails is always something that I have found pleasing. But it's still killing. My nails tore into the neck of the sleeping Were before he even got the chance to wake up properly. His eyes flew open wide in fear but quickly faded away again.

Once they were dealt with, I stood back up and examined the door. Two more larger padlocks were latched onto this one. I searched the two bodies for keys and found a small gold key hooked on a chain around the once sleeping Weres neck. I ripped it off and tried the first padlock. Bingo. The lock clicked open, and I pulled it off. The second one was a combination lock. Shit. It was a big chunky lock, and I don't think I'll be able to snap it like I did the other one. These guys aren't so bright so let's try the obvious. I put in 000. Nothing. 111 next, still nothing. 123 maybe. The lock clicked open, and I smiled to myself. Fucking dipshits. I threw the lock to the ground and pulled open the door. The smell that hit me was horrendous. I gagged and covered my mouth. My word! Are they hiding dead bodies in here? I pushed the door open all the way and let the dim light shine in. There, huddled in the far corner of the tiny little windowless room, was a filthy and scrawny looking woman. And under her arms, was a small boy, maybe three or four years old. They were both Weres, I could pick up a hint of their scent through the stench of their own filth. But who the fuck are they, and why are they locked in a cell?

Chapter Thirty-Seven

Lunaya

I stared at the dirty woman, who looked like she had been through her own version of hell. The little boy in her arms was digging himself as far into her embrace as he could. I imagine they'd both reek of fear if I could stand to smell them over the grotesque stench of human filth.

"Who are you?" I hissed quietly. The woman shielded the boy from my view, pulled her lips back over her teeth, and growled at me.

"Why are you here?" I whisper-yelled. Still no response, just more growling. Can this chick even speak? Ah fuck it, I don't have the time right now.

"I'll be back" I said firmly before closing the door and putting the locks back in place. I put the chain around my neck and made my way back up the stairs. I pressed my ear to the door and listened. I could hear shouting. One male voice was yelling for someone to come back, while another male voice was yelling about backup. I guess things have progressed in the ten minutes I've been down here. I pushed open the door and snuck a peak through the small crack. I can't see anyone, and the yelling is coming from the kitchen area. I stepped through the door and pushed it closed behind me. The sound of glass shattering and more yelling and screaming filled the house, followed closely by growling barking, and snapping bones. I ran to the walkway where the hallway opens to the kitchen and living space. The scene here had definitely changed. The Weres that I saw in there earlier were now dead, and their blood covered the walls. Alpha Hina was standing over one of the bodies in her human form. She was drenched in blood, but if it was at all possible, I don't think she had a scratch on her.

"You made quick work of them" I said as I stepped into the room. Cleo's wolf dropped a human arm and growled at me. I don't need to hear her speak to understand that she's mad I came in here without her. Hina turned around and smirked wickedly.

"They are weak" she hissed. Two more Luna Eclipse wolves were in the living space with them, one of which I think is Phoebe.

"Did you find the Prophet?" Hina asked as she stepped over a body,

"I found something" I quipped back with a roll of my eyes. She crossed her arms, which made her bare breasts lift and push together. I'm not blind, and I'm still part human. I licked my lips as I gazed at her perked nipples. Not the time Lunaya. I scolded myself as I shook my head and looked back up to Hina's dark eyes. She was smirking at me with a raised eyebrow.

"I'll show you after, but first, Artemis. I think he is upstairs" I said feeling a little flushed. Hina motioned her hand and turned her body, allowing me to take the lead. I stepped around her as her eyes remained firmly on mine. We headed towards the back of the house, looking for a staircase. More bodies were splayed out on the floor, with more blood covering the walls and hardwood floors. They really did work quickly in here. We got to a large stairwell, and I went to head up. Hina grabbed my arm and pulled me back, then waved her hand for Cleo and the other two wolves to go first. She held me there for a minute as we listened. There was a loud crash, then a yell, then silence. Another crash, more yelling, some barking, and then silence again.

"Okay" Hina said and let go of my arm. I ran up the stairs and went to the right first. A few dead Weres were spread out here and there. But no Artemis. One of the rooms was interesting though. No door, no glass on the windows, and deep cracks etched into the brick walls. Looks like something big went down in here.

"Lunaya" Hina's voiced called out. I left the room and followed her voice to a room at the other end of the house. She was standing by the door, leaving me enough room to step in. As soon as I did, I spotted the Were I came here for.

"Artemis" I growled as my anger ignited. He sat in an armchair in the corner of the room. Cleo stood beside him in her human form with a firm grip on his shoulder. The other two wolves surrounded him as well. But he didn't look like he wanted to run or fight. He looks like he is right where he wants to be. I walked over to him, swung my arm back, and then flew it forward, connecting my fist with his jaw. He grunted and his head snapped to the side. I have no doubt that if it weren't for Cleo holding him, he would have gone flying off his seat.

"Traitor" I growled down at him. He lifted his head and smirked.

"I not betray, I help, I guide" he said with a cocky confidence.

"You turned on the Goddess and aided in her kidnapping. How is that not a betrayal?" I yelled.

"I do as prophecy foretold. Deliver her to the right Mate" he snapped back.

"The right Mate?" I mumbled confused,

"Gunner is child. He weak, soft. Alpha Galterio is strong. He ready to lead, he ready to dominate. Wolf need this. Wolf need king, not boy". I watched Artemis as he spoke. I can hear him, and although his accent is thick, I understand what he is saying. But what does this have to do with the prophecy?

"You took her from her True Mate, to do what? Mate with another?" Alpha Hina asked him as she stepped up to my side. Artemis didn't answer, just smiled wickedly. He thinks that she could take another Mate, even after meeting and mating with her destined Mate? Why would he think that is at all possible? What am I missing here?

"A True Mate can never take another. What kind of Prophet doesn't know that?" Hina snapped at him, taking the question right out of my mouth.

"Prophecy foretold it" he said back, with the utmost belief and conviction in his words.

"You keep saying that, but I am starting to wonder if you even know what the prophecy is" I said with a tilt of my head. "Spawned by the one who gave us breath. Vanished from life but spared from death. The Ethereal one gives she who is promised. To wield the power of the Triple Goddess..."

"Yes, yes, yes. Where the moon is three, two will come, blah, blah, blah. We've already done this" I snapped at him, becoming more and more frustrated.

"Yes, two will come. Two Mates. One weak, that Gunner. One strong, that Galterio. Triplí Theá must choose one and kill the other". Cleo growled and looked up over at me. Hina also turned to look at me now. All of them waiting and watching for me to react. Two Mates. Kill Gunner. This idiot has been hitting that Kool-Aid too hard. I blinked my eyes and laughed.

I laughed hard. Artemis frowned and shuffled uncomfortably in his seat. This fucking idiot. He has no idea. All this time I have been stressing and worrying over what he knows and who he has told. He knows fucking nothing. I rested my hands on my knees and continued to laugh. Letting all my pent-up stress flow out of me.

"Are you done?" Hina growled lowly. I stood up straight and sighed. A dramatic and overly exaggerated sigh.

"Oh, Artemis. You're not a Prophet at all, are you? I chuckled. He frowned and clenched his fists.

"You know nothing, you see nothing, and you sure as shit aren't special enough for the All Mother to convey her will through you. You aren't a Prophet. You're just a fool" I sneered. He growled and leaned forward, only to be slammed back into the chair again by Cleo.

"I know this" he snapped at me.

"You think Gunner is weak, and yet the Moon Goddess herself picked him to be with her chosen daughter. You thought that you could replace her True Mate with that pretender? Please. Origin Wolf is a joke. They are egotistical and self-important douchebags. They have been since that first idiot, Gill" I snapped. My voice getting louder and harder as I spoke. I stepped forward and leaned down, placing each of my hands on the armrests, forcing Artemis to lean back further. I moved my head to his ear and growled.

"You think the prophecy speaks of two Mates. Well, you're wrong. Very, very wrong. And now, you'll never live long enough to learn the truth" I hissed into his ear. I heard him gasp in shock, but before he got the chance to question me, I slammed my fist into his chest. Punching through his ribcage and hitting his heart. I felt his heart rip apart from the force of my fist. Blood spurted from his mouth and dribbled down his chin. His eyes rolled back, and his head flopped to the side. I withdrew my hand from his chest, and stood up straight, flicking the blood from my fingers. Cleo and Hina both looked at me with proud expressions.

"Come, I'll show you what I found in the basement" I said as I walked out of the room. Leaving Artemis and the dead prophecy behind me, hopefully for good this time.

~

Neither Alpha Hina nor Phoebe could get a word out of the mystery woman. Though I think we all had our theories on who they might be. Phoebe tried to coax her out of the tiny dark room. She offered her food, water, and blankets, but nothing worked. I can't help but wonder how long they have been in there. We checked over the house once more, confirming that there was no one else left inside, and then we went back out to the yard. The battalion that I left Alpha Hina and Lupus to deal with, had been killed. Bodies littered the ground, both in wolf and human forms. The grass was stained with blood. We jogged around to the other side of the house where the Howlers had been fighting. They had moved on now too, leaving more bodies in their wake. We eventually found the rest of our allies. Taking out what looks to be the last of the Origin Wolf pack warriors and their allies.

Before we left Tri-Moon, the leaders briefly discussed the possibility of them surrendering and taking prisoners. It is not in the nature of a Were to be forgiving, a trait that I have always disliked in our kind. The majority of the pack leaders were against leaving survivors. And they haven't. I was just glad that I could not see the bodies of children among the dead. Meaning the young, the elderly, and the unfit to fight, had been left in another camp somewhere away from here. The battle was brutal and very bloody. But we came out on top. As the last enemy wolf fell to the ground dead, the remaining fighters howled into the air to signal their victory.

Hina, myself, and the others howled along as well and then broke apart to hug each other. Cleo wrapped her massive arms around my body and squeezed. A gesture I was not expecting from her. She is usually so reserved and sullen. Joy is a strange emotion on her fierce face.

"You fought well" she said firmly. She let me go and tapped my cheek lightly before turning to hug one of her pack mates. Hina grabbed my shoulders and rested her head against my forehead. She moved her hands up to cup my neck and I held onto her waist.

"Thank you for coming" I said softly,

"You're welcome" she said back.

"I don't know if we would have had the same outcome without you and your warriors".

"I came for you too, not just the Goddess. You are very special Lunaya" she said as she moved her head forward, pressing her lips against mine. I kissed her back, just slightly, then we broke apart. Lupus walked over, with a very obvious limp. His wide thigh had a cloth tied around it tightly, but his blood had still soaked it through. Behind Lupus stood the redhead Smith, the warriors Felix and Faylene, and the tall Were with the long hair, Julien, I think. They were all covered in blood, Smith wore a few scratches across his chiselled chest. The she-wolf, Faylene, had a single slash from the top of her forehead, over her left eye, and halfway down her cheek. She had tied a piece of cloth over her eye like a pirate's patch. Felix looked untouched, just like Hina. He must be an excellent fighter.

"Glad to see you're alive" Lupus said roughly as he stopped in front of me,

"Is that sarcasm?" I asked with a smirk,

"Not at all, it would be a damned shame if you died before Zelena got to know who you really are" he said as he extended me his hand. I gazed at him wide eyed and took his hand. I had gotten the impression that he and Roe were not happy I had arrived, that maybe they thought I was going to replace them as her parental figures. Hearing a compliment from the brutish Lupus was a right shock. Lupus pulled me forward and pressed his forehead to mine, initiating Sevasmo. As his emotions and feelings washed through me, I felt that he was tired and weak from fighting. He wants to go home and kiss his wife. So do I, Alyse that is, if she'll let me. Lupus pulled back and tipped his head to the side while continuing to hold my forearm.

"Where is Artemis?" he asked me,

"He's dead" I answered bluntly, Lupus snarled and squeezed my arm,

"Was that by your hand?" he questioned harshly,

"It was. Is that a problem?" I asked back, just as hard. I could feel that Cleo, Hina, and Phoebe had come to stand behind me.

"He was not yours to kill" Lupus growled and dropped my arm.

"It was our pack that he betrayed, our Luna, our Alpha. His punishment was ours to hand down" Smith spoke up as he stepped forward slightly. He has shown on multiple occasions that he has guts to spare. I admire that about him. But he was wrong this time, he and Lupus.

"The Prophet made an attempt on 'my' life, aided in the kidnapping of 'my' daughter, and recited 'my' family prophecy. He was mine and mine alone to kill". Lupus, Smith, and the other Tri-Moon Weres began to growl at my defiance. Alpha Hina stepped between us and raised her hands.

"What's done is done, the traitor has been dealt with. Let's take the win and move on. Besides, we still need to figure out who is in the basement" she said using her diplomatic Alpha voice. Lupus perked up at the mention of the mystery woman.

"Who's in the basement?" he asked,

"Yes, that's what I said" Hina quipped back. Lupus growled and huffed,

"No, are you saying that you found someone in the basement?" he asked annoyed.

"Yes, that's what I just said" Hina teased him. I know she can handle herself, but she is playing with fire here. Lupus growled and stepped closer. This made all of the Luna Eclipse she-wolves growl and close in. Smith moved in front of Lupus and pushed him back.

"Show me" Smith demanded as he turned to face me fully. I shrugged and nodded my head and then turned to go back into the farmhouse. Smith and Faylene followed behind me, while the others stayed with Lupus and Hina. We descended the steps, and I unlocked the two padlocks. I figured that Origin Wolf has kept them locked up for a reason, and seeing as we don't know what that reason is, it's best we keep them under lock and key as well. At least for now. I pushed the door wide open and let the light shine in. The woman was still in the corner with the boy tucked away behind her. She was facing us with her canines extended and on full display. Smith stepped into the doorway and the woman growled and hissed at him.

"I wouldn't get too close. She already took a swipe at Phoebe" I told him.

"Who is she?" he asked while studying the woman.

"Were you not listening when we said we didn't know that yet" I answered sarcastically. Smith crouched down and extended his hand towards her. She growled and snapped her hand out, nearly clawing his arm. He jumped back and came to stand beside me by the door again.

"You have a theory though, I can see it on your face" he snipped.

"Yeah, I have an idea" I said as I looked over the small boy. The girl was young, even through the grot caked to her face and her emaciated frame, I could see the young features. I would guess she was not far out of her teen years. If she wasn't covered in dirt and grime, and she didn't smell like a sewerage, I would also guess that she was quite attractive. The kind of attractive that would lure in a cocky young Alpha.

"Are you going to share it?" he grumbled. I crouched down and looked into the woman's bright green eyes.

"I think this is the Origin Wolf Luna, or at least the Alpha's plaything. Which I would have to guess, makes that that boy the Alpha-son. Meaning he is a descendant of Gill. My rival. Zelena's rival". As soon as I said the word 'Gill' the woman began to snarl and bark. Her body was shaking, like she was having trouble changing form. I would bet my right arm that she is near on Feral. Without her Alpha here to help with the change, one more shift and I would guess she'll be stuck. It sure as shit explains the aggression and lack of talking.

Smith was quiet, probably letting my thoughts digest through his mind as he watched the dirty pair. After a minute he huffed, turned around, and began to go back up the stairs.

"I'm sending someone down for them. We're taking them back to Tri-Moon" he grumbled over his shoulder,
"Isn't that for your Alpha to decide?" I shouted back to him. Speaking of, where the fuck is he? And where is Zelena?
"The Alpha isn't here" Smith yelled as he stomped away. I looked back over to the woman and chuckled.
"Looks like you're getting a new home, little lady" I chided and shut the door again. I went back up the stairs and as I got to the living area, Felix, Faylene and four others marched past me.
"You'll need this" I called and tossed the key to Faylene. She caught it, nodded, and continued on their way. I got back outside as a bit of a commotion began to break out. I heard some sobbing and a few pained screams. Oh no, what happened now? I pushed through the gathered crowd but was grabbed by Elaine. Where did she come from? I frowned at her and tried to pull myself from her grip.
"Don't' Lunaya" she growled at me.
"Don't what?" I snapped back. The way she looked at me sent a shiver down my spine. Something is very, very wrong here.
"What is it?" I asked her urgently. My mind immediately went to Zelena. Was she hurt? Was she worse than hurt? I can't lose her, I have only just found her again. Elain didn't answer me, she just looked at me with a deeply strained and concerned expression. Oh Goddess, not Zelena. I yanked my arm from her grip and shoved my way through the crowd of shocked onlookers. I got through the wall of people and found Gunner and Tobias each holding a body. I saw the long black hair hanging from Tobias's arm and ran to him. Zelena's unmoving body was cradled gently in his arms, with her head hanging back. My fear exploded and tears flooded my eyes. She was covered in blood, her blood. And under all that blood, she was so pale. She looked dead.
"My baby" I sobbed and touched her cheek. She was cold, but there was still some warmth under her skin.
"She'll be okay" Tobias said sullenly. I brushed the back of my fingers over her cheek and nodded my head. I then turned to Gunner and watched as he slowly lowered the body he was holding to the ground. I walked up behind him at the same time as Lupus and Smith approached from the front. Lupus ran his hand through his hair roughly and Smith dropped to

his knees, all colour drained from his face. Lupus threw his head back and roared into the air. The sound shook the trees and made everyone close by take a few steps back. He fell to the ground as his large grey wolf and howled. I stepped closer and looked down at the body that Gunner was leaning over. Gunner had his arms wrapped around the top of the body, lifting the head to his chest. Gunner's silent sobs broke me. I looked over the body and fell to my knees at his side. I picked up Cole's hand and held it to my cheek. He was like ice. I hadn't known him long, but there was something between us. He trusted me, and I cared deeply for him. He was motherless, and I had every intention of filling that role for him.

As Lupus howled into the sky, the rest of Tri-Moon that had gathered around, changed into their wolves and cried into the air with their former Alpha. Felix came barging through the crowd and stopped just shy of Cole's dead body. Behind him came Faylene carrying the screaming child, and three others struggling with the erratic she-wolf.

"Take her away" I snarled up at them. Faylene nodded and went to leave again,

"Wait" Gunner's voice growled. He lifted his head and looked up at the she-wolf fighting to get free. His eyes were dark, and his expression was one of anger and hatred. Right then, he looked dangerous, evil even. Gunner slowly stood up and walked to stand in front of the she-wolf.

"Who is she?" he demanded.

"We don't know for sure, she's basically feral and isn't talking. But we think she is the Origin Luna" Felix answered as he came to stand at his Alpha's side. Gunner growled. A deep and ferocious growl that made my hair stand on end. He stepped forward and wrapped his hand around her neck. The she-wolf fought against his hold. She barked and growled and snapped her teeth. With a flick of his wrist, Gunner snapped her neck, and her fight was gone. The fighters dropped her body and stared blankly up at Gunner. Apparently, I was not the only one surprised by his callousness. He then turned to Faylene and the child in her arms. Faylene looked terrified. She can't refuse her Alpha, but I don't think she wants the blood of a child on her hands.

"And him?" Gunner snarled,

"He uh... he's... he was her son" Felix answered. It was the first time I had ever seen the strong warrior show any kind of weakness or uncertainty. Gunner stepped forward and reached for the child, but Faylene stepped back, a look of horror on her face.
"Gunner" I snapped and jumped to my feet,
"He's just a baby" I growled at him. Gunner grabbed the child from Faylene's arms with a loud growl.
"I don't care what he is, only who he is. Galterio does not get an heir, his line doesn't deserve to survive. This ends here and now" Gunner snarled hatefully. The amount of venom and darkness in his voice was shudder inducing. What happened to him? Gunner tucked the boy under his arm and grabbed hold of his head. The little boy wailed and thrashed his arms about. Gunner jerked his arm and hand in opposite directions and the sound of the pup's neck snapping rolled over the crowd. Faylene screamed but quickly covered her mouth with both her hands. Shocked gasps bounced around the pack and harsh whispers began to fly. He killed a child. A pup. He didn't even hesitate. This goes far beyond uncontrollable aggression, regardless of who sired the pup, he was still an innocent. I don't know how Gunner is meant to come back from this.

Chapter Thirty-Eight

Zelena

The blood in my veins bubbled under my skin. I could feel my light dying out, and the cold darkness rose to take its place. My power ignited and the electric sparks caused my hair to stand up. My narrowed eyes burned holes into Galterio's face, while he stood smirking down at me.

"I will kill you" I hissed through my clenched teeth. Using his unnatural speed, he appeared in front of me and grabbed my jaw roughly. Cole's still warm blood smeared over my chin, where Galterio's fingertips pressed into my face.

"You will love me" he hissed back. He pulled my face forward and crashed his lips hard against my own. I tried to push him away, but his other hand came around and grabbed the back of my neck, holding me in place. Galterio pushed his tongue into my mouth and swirled it around. I would rather gouge my eyes out with hot spoons than feel his slimy tongue roll around in my mouth. I chomped my teeth down, biting into his tongue hard. So hard that I could feel his warm blood fill my mouth. He grunted and jumped backward. His hand flew up to his face and he wiped the blood from his lips. I spat out the blood and saliva that had gathered in my mouth, hoping it would also get rid of the taste he left behind. I laughed and the rest of his blood dribbled down my chin. I laughed at the stupid look on his face, he thought I wasn't going to fight back. He thought I was just going to lay back and take it, like the weak little girl that he thinks I am. I'm not that girl anymore. I haven't been that girl for some time now. I will never not fight back, ever again.

"You're a fucking idiot if you ever think I will have you. I will never be yours" I cackled evilly. The darkness in my heart sent a shiver down my spine that lit me up with pleasurable power. I was burning with rage, but my blood ran cold. The ice slipped through my veins, chilling me to the core.

"Now, now, Beauty. You don't want to hurt my feelings, do you?" he sneered and stepped up closer to me again.

"Fuck you and your feelings" I snapped up at him. He crouched down and leaned his elbows on his knees.

"You will either give yourself to me willingly, or I will take you by force. Either way, that mut you are carrying will die, and then you will bear my heir" he hissed venomously. I dug my fingertips into the earth, if I didn't, I would swipe out and slap his stupid smug face. I lowered my head, narrowed my eyes, and smiled. Galterio seemed confused by my smile, his head tipped to the side and the corner of his lip quirked up.

"In your fucking dreams" I snickered. With that I flung my arm out, sending Galterio flying back and colliding with a tree. He jumped back to his feet, with one hand on the ground and his canines extended. I let the power flow through my body and made myself weightless. I lifted myself up and stayed hanging just inches from the ground. I moved my hands and positioned them in front of me, with my fingers directed at Galterio. The blue sparks that have recently been appearing with the use of my power were now gone. In their place, black whisps of smoke twisted and twirled around my fingers, like alien tentacles. The darkness now has control over my power, not just my heart. Good. Let's see how he likes this.

I pictured myself stabbing Galterio through the heart. Like he did to Cole. I saw the long sharp blade in my hand and felt myself driving it into his flesh. The smoke at the end of my hands reformed into jagged pike like shapes. I wrapped my fingers around them, and they felt like cold ice. Hard and rigid, but cold to the touch. I looked back up to Galterio who was watching my hands curiously. I flung my right hand out and the little dagger flew through the air towards Galterio. He rolled to the side and the crystalized smoke hit the tree behind him, it burst into smoke again and then dissipated. I flung another and this time he jumped over it. I curled my teeth back and growled. Fine. I moved my arms in a continuous motion, throwing dagger after dagger at Galterio. The fucker was too fast. He ducked and weaved, rolled, and jumped, avoiding all of them. If I can't throw it where he is, then I need to throw it to where he will be. I took a deep breath, letting the air fill my body. The power swelled inside me, pushing at the seams and ready to burst out. I threw both of my arms out to the side and multiple daggers shot out of me. They flew from my hands, arms, chest, and stomach, shooting in all directions.

Galterio screamed and grabbed at his shoulder. The sharp little edge that had lodged into his skin, puffed into smoke and disappeared. The point where it stabbed into Galterio's skin had turned black and little veins began to spread out from the black oozing mark.

"What is this?" he roared,

"This is me, dear Mate. You said you wanted me to give myself to you. Well here I am, take it" I shouted and threw more pikes in his direction. He was just a little slower now. This new dark magic could affect him, unlike my usual power. Why? I don't know. But I will use it to my advantage. Another one hit him in the side between his hip and ribs. He yelled and doubled over, holding his side.

"Stop it Zelena, I'm warning you" he growled and glared at me.

"This is what you wanted, remember" I sneered,

"I'm not playing with you"

"You only want to play when you are winning, that's no fun" I chuckled,

"Enough!" he roared. He ran forward and grabbed me around the neck. He was talking as a way to distract me. And stupid me, I fell for it. My feet touched back down on the ground and my ankle screamed at the added weight. I lifted my hand, but again he was too quick, he grabbed it before I got the chance to wiggle a finger. I growled and tried to pull my arm free. Galterio rolled his lips back and showed his fully extended canines. He jerked his hand to the side and my wrist snapped. I screamed out loud as my legs gave way. Galterio didn't let me fall, instead he held all of my weight by my broken wrist and compressed throat.

The darkness within me was anything but weak, and I could feel the fight brewing steadily. It powered my rage, giving me the energy to keep fighting. It made me bloodthirsty. And after watching Galterio punch his arm through Cole's chest, I thirsted for his blood above all else. The cold crept along my skin, leaving goosebumps as it went. I felt it twist its way along my arm and slowly wrap around my wrist. Galterio hissed and quickly dropped my hand, he moved his eyes to my broken wrist, and they widened in shock.

"What are you doing?" he snarled at me. I felt the blood in my fingers and hand turn to ice, and then came the audible crack of my bone snapping back into place. The pain was incredible, but for some reason, I liked it. It made me feel indestructible. Galterio may have been holding me up by the throat, but he was in no way dominating this current situation. I was in control here. He just didn't know it yet. I lifted my now healed hand and rested it on his shoulder. The cool darkness slipped from my fingers and caressed his bare skin. His face contorted with the pain, but he was unable to move. His mouth opened and he roared into the sky. I smirked at the pain written all over his face, it pleased me that I was the cause of it. I let my claws extend through the tips of my fingers and pressed them into his skin. The black smoke that was my darkened soul, slithered its way into his bloodstream, causing him to roar once again. One second, I was getting pleasure out of the pain on his face, and the next he was gone from my sight.

I was spun around through the air and large firm arms were wrapped around me. A ferocious growl echoed through the trees, a growl I recognised. I looked up over my shoulder, to see Tobias's dark and angry eyes looking down at me. Deep frown lines ran across his forehead and his long fangs were out and ready to rip into some flesh. I turned to look forward again and the sight that greeted me sent chills of pleasure and excitement through my stomach. Any previous thoughts of fear of him, or betrayal for his angered attack were all gone. I was just happy to see him again. Gunner stood completely naked, with his hand around Galterio's neck, holding him a few inches off the ground. Galterio is no small Were, neither is Gunner, but the way his muscles tensed and flexed as he growled up at the murderous bastard, had my pussy clenching.

"Gunner" I breathed out softly. He snapped his dark eyes to mine and I shuddered. His normally bright blue eyes were narrowed into slits and extremely dark. His lips were curled back to expose his fully extended and blood-soaked canines. Dried blood coated his chin, neck, and chest, and my first instinct was to lick it off him. The moment our eyes met, I felt the anger and rage flowing through him. It was intoxicating and seductive. I like it. Gunner growled as his eyes raked down my body and back up again, lingering briefly on each wound and each patch of blood on my body.

You're hurt?

I'm fine

As Gunner was watching me, Galterio lifted his hand, claws extended, and went to swipe at Gunner's throat.

"Gunner!" I screamed and jerked my body forward, but Tobias's firm hold kept me in place. Gunner's arm flew up, blocking Galterio's blow. The black whisps of smoke twirled around his arm, shielding him from the sharp claws. Galterio screamed out and yanked his hand away from the dark power. I huffed a sigh of relief, glad that Gunner wasn't burnt by the smoke in the way that Galterio was. Gunner examined the odd substance coating his arm, and then the smoke reformed into a long sword like shape. That was not my doing, but his. He has control of the darkness. If Gunner can access the black magic too, then things just got much more exciting.

"Where's Cole?" he grumbled. His question wasn't aimed at Galterio, even though his murderous gaze was. I froze. Unable to answer. With the darkness swirling through my body and my rage at the forefront of my mind, for a moment I had forgotten why I let the darkness in in the first place. My head whipped to the body lying in the brush twenty meters away. Tobias followed my line of sight and a growl rumbled through his chest as he saw what I saw. I could feel the anger and sadness expel from him as he took in the sight. Gunner turned to look at me and asked again,

"Where's Cole?"

When I didn't answer, he too looked to the place where Cole's body was lying. The sword thing in his hand dissipated and he froze, staring at his best friend's body. He turned back to me with the question in his eyes. Is he okay? I shook my head as a sob broke out of my mouth. Tears fell down my cheeks and I relaxed into Tobias's hold, letting him hold me up. Gunner roared into the air and threw Galterio across the small space. Galterio's back hit hard against a tree, and he fell to the ground. Even with the effects of the darkness slowing him down, Galterio was still quicker on his feet than the rest of us. He jumped back up and charged towards Gunner. I noticed it before Gunner did, and raised the shield, making Galterio run face first into the invisible wall. I pushed Tobias's arm from around my waist and went to step forward. "No" Tobias growled at me and grabbed my arm. I turned around and glared at him. He reared back and his mouth fell open.

"What have you done?" he asked blankly whilst still gripping my arm.

"Nothing. Yet" I snarled back. I tried to pull my arm from him again, but his grip wouldn't budge.

"This is not the way Zelena. You don't belong in the dark, you are the light, you are the love. Don't give yourself over to it, please Little One" he pleaded with me. I wanted to listen. I really did. But until Galterio was dead, and Cole was avenged, the darkness is where I will roam.

I lifted myself from the ground and hovered to Gunner's side. Galterio was pacing back and forth in front of the shield. Running his fingers along the wall. The shield was different too. No longer was it clear impenetrable space, but now swirls of black and jagged edges. The darkness was replacing all aspects of my magic, and I welcomed it all. The sparks that tingled through my body with the contact Galterio made against the shield, urged me on. The spot on his shoulder that was pierced by the black smoke, was now looking like a funky tattoo. Deep black protruding veins had begun to spread out from the point of impact. The same thing was happening at the spot near his hip. The darkness was in him now too. Gunner looked at me as I reached him. His eyes were nearly black and he looked ready to kill. My darkness, or maybe it was his darkness, whoever it originated from didn't matter, but it was cursing through him. I could see it in his eyes, and feel it in this aura. I reached my hand out for him and he took it. His eyes began to shine a bright silver, but dark swirls could be seen in the depths of his gaze. Gunner lifted off the ground at my side and we both turned to Galterio. We don't need words. We didn't need to speak to know what needs to be done. Galterio will die. Slowly. Painfully. And by our hands.

I lifted my outside hand and let the dark power seep from my skin. Gunner did the same with his hand. I thought about the daggers, about them piercing Galterio's skin. And just like before, the smoke morphed into a sharp jagged blade. In Gunner's hand, a longer blade appeared. Galterio eyed the black weapons in our hands and took a step back. I dropped the wall and smiled wickedly at him.

"Last warning, Zelena. Kill this bastard and come with me now. Or I will kill you all" Galterio growled. He truly believed he still stood a chance, his ego knows no bounds. His anger was thick and palpable. I could feel it in the air. But it didn't scare me. In fact, I fed off it. Or more like, my darkness did. Gunner's hand squeezed mine and I turned to gaze at the side of his dangerously handsome face. He was glaring at Galterio, ready and itching to kill him. There was no question for him, Gunner knew where he stood, where we stood. He didn't need the reassurance that Galterio's demand was never a possibility.

"You still think I will be yours?" I mused and smirked back at Galterio,

"Look at him, look at us. This is what pure and powerful looks like. You never came close. You wanted a Were king, well here he is". With that, Galterio lunged. I'd pushed just the right button. I played on his ego, and he snapped, just like I knew he would. Galterio got a hand on my collarbone and growled. Gunner flicked his hand around and tensed his fingers. The dark smoke wrapped around Galterio's wrist and lifted it off me. Galterio growled with pain as the darkness caressed his skin. Gunner flicked his wrist again and sent Galterio flying sideways through the air. He laughed and squeezed my hand. Galterio jumped back to his feet with a roar and charged again. This time, I stopped him. I wrapped my power around his body and flung him up into the air. He came crashing back down hard but still, the fucker managed to jump to his feet. He crouched on the ground, moving his eyes from me to Gunner and back again. He stood slowly and growled. As he growled his face began to morph. His nose pushed forward, and his mouth widened, making way for his teeth to sharpen and grow. His eyebrows thickened and his ears pointed. A brush of dark grey fur sprouted down his neck and along his jaw. He looked like something out of a scary story. The monster in the dark that you tell kids about when you want to scare them.

He stalked forward, eyes pinned on me. Gunner let go of my hand and moved himself to hover in front of me, blocking Galterio's forward attack. If I didn't know any better, I would say that Galterio just smiled. He was there one second and gone the next. I was snatched from the air with sharp claws pressed to my neck and a hard body pressed to my back. I turned my head to the side, to relieve the pressure of his claws on my jugular. And that's when I realised that Tobias was gone. He was no longer standing where I left him. Did he abandon us? Leave us to fight alone. He was mad about me accepting the darkness, I know that, but I didn't think he would leave me. Gunner roared and went to lunge forward. Galterio clicked his tongue and moved his other hand to my stomach. He pushed his claws into the skin, and I winced.

"You don't want to do that Alpha, one slice, that's all it will take" Galterio sneered. His vicious menacing voice sounded wilder and deeper than before. Gunner paused, he looked at the hand at my neck, and then the hand at my stomach. His dark eyes snapped to my face, and I could see the confusion.

Are you pregnant?

I'm sorry, I didn't know

"Ahh... the True Mate doesn't know, does he?" Galterio's rumbling voice teased. I tried to shift my body so that I could reach up and grab his face. I managed to lift my hand and was just about to make contact with the side of his face, when Galterio growled.

"No Zelena!" Gunner yelled.

The pain in my stomach intensified. I scrunched my eyes closed, lifted my chin, and I screamed. Galterio had pushed his fingers deeper into my stomach, ripping their way through the muscle. Just a little further and he will be able to tear my pup right out of me. Gunner growled and stepped closer again.

"Tsk, tsk, tsk. No, no. Stop right there, or your little pup will join you earlier than planned" Galterio sneered. He pushed his face against mine, nuzzling his nose into my cheek. I felt his cool wet tongue slide along my jaw to my ear. Gunner growled, a loud and rumbling growl that echoed through the trees. I opened my eyes and looked at him. He was looking at the hand on my stomach, and thankfully not the slippery tongue on my face. The dark smoke was swirling around his body, wrapping around his legs and slithering up and down his arms. I could feel his anger, it was crawling over my skin, penetrating my mind. But I felt his fear too. Fear for his pup. Well, Gunner knows now. He's going to be a dad. Maybe. Galterio tensed the fingers he had buried in my stomach, and I screamed again. Tears ran down my face and I felt completely helpless. I have a way to fight him now, he is powerless against the darkness, but he still has his speed. I'm caught. I can't risk moving or fighting, not with his claws so close to my pup.

"I can see now, Beauty. You can never be mine while you have a piece of him inside you" Galterio whispered into my ear. He nuzzled against my neck and inhaled my scent. Gunner's growl rumbled across the space between us. He was now looking directly into my eyes. Seeing Galterio rub himself against me was sending him crazy.

"I'll fix that" he growled and pushed his fingers into my stomach. This is it, no more playing and no more threats. He's going to kill my baby. I can't let that happen. I screamed from the pain and my arms shot out to the sides. The darkness shot out of my body like a wave, fully engulfing Galterio. I focused on my stomach, letting all my power be directed there. I surrounded my womb with my forcefield of darkness. Nothing was getting near him now. I heard snapping and crunching and Galterio shouted. He lifted his hand from my stomach and held it in front of his face, which was in front of my face. His fingers were bent and broken, sitting at horribly impossible angles. They had compacted in on themselves, shattering all the bones. Blood dripped from the exposed bones and torn apart skin. Galterio pressed the claws at my neck harder into the skin, his desperate attempt to finish me off. With my pup now safe, I can fight back.

I gripped his hand and pulled it from my throat. As I felt my warm blood roll down the cool skin of my neck, I let the cold shards of my black magic enter his skin. He screamed and stepped back so that his body was no longer pressed up against mine. Keeping hold of his hand, I turned around to face him with a deadly expression plastered across my face. I pushed out with my power, forcing it to roll over him. He growled and hissed and dropped to his knees. The black smoke whirled around us both, like my own personal tornado. The thick black mist shrouded us in darkness, blocking out everything else. I could no longer see the trees and the shrub, or Cole's lifeless body. It was just me and him. But there was one missing, someone that needed to be here for this.

Gunner

I flashed, calling him to me. A second later the smoke parted, and Gunner's worried face stepped into the whirlwind of darkness. His eyes found mine and the worried look morphed back into one of anger. He stepped to my side and gently slid his hand over my lower stomach. I winced as his fingers brushed against the gaping wounds left by Galterio's claws. What was meant to be a tender moment, was ruined by the pain on my face. The pain caused by the monster in front of us. Gunner growled and snapped his dark eyes to Galterio. He moved slowly, shifting his stance so that he was behind me, his body pressed flush against mine. The tingles and sparks caused by his skin on mine made my pussy clench. Keeping one hand resting protectively over my stomach, Gunner stroked his other hand down my arm, to the hand that was still holding Galterio's. He wrapped his fingers around mine and tensed them. Galterio grunted and dropped his head. The black whisps of smoke flowed freely from Gunner's and my connected hands, it covered Galterio's hand and slowly spread up his arm.

"You take my Mate, you hurt her. You try to kill my pup, you murder my Beta!" Gunner's voice started out level with a deadly tone but escalated to a deep rumbling roar. Galterio was looking up at Gunner, the cockiness and confidence was all but gone. He could see his fate now. I could see it too. His death was written in his evil dark brown eyes.

"That was a mistake" Gunner hissed. The darkness covering Galterio's hand began to turn and swirl faster around his deformed fingers. Gunner's fingers tensed over mine and the black smoke whipped out. Galterio's wrist snapped to the side with a loud crunch. He screamed through clenched teeth but didn't move to fight back or run away. Movement at his feet caught my eye and I focused on it closer. The whirls of dark smoke had wrapped around his legs, keeping him planted in place. The darkness had a mind of its own, and it was helping us, encouraging us. Gunner and my fingers flexed, and the smoke travelled further up Galterio's arm. The smoke tentacles spread out over his bicep, down to his elbow, and up to his shoulder, and then it seemed to tighten. With a flick of Gunner's wrist, the smoke jerked in a hard quick movement, and Galterio's arm was ripped away from his body. His mouth opened into a scream and his head went back. Blood poured from the stump that was now his shoulder. If it was anyone else, it would have made me sick. But it was Galterio. The man who stole me away from my family. The man who forced himself on me, who tried to take away my love and my baby. Seeing his suffering, his pain, it made me feel alive. His sharp canines came back down on his lips, piercing them through. His own blood covered his mouth and dripped down his chin, giving him even more of a psycho-killer look.

I felt Gunner's chest shake behind me. I looked over my shoulder and was surprised to find him smiling, laughing even. Was this reaction caused by the darkness within him? Gunner never seemed to enjoy hurting people before. But this time, he was loving it. The joy on his face made me smile. Regardless of the reason it was there, his smile is breathtaking.

"You will... will never be... p-pure" Galterio mumbled through his obvious pain. I leaned forward a little and smirked.

"I never cared about that anyway" I said with a wink.

"You will... you'll kill th-them. All. Of. Them" he said slowly, "You let it... it in. You can't... come b-back now" he groaned with a smirk playing at his lips. I tilted my head to the side as I studied him. What is he going on about? I think he's actually lost it now. If he ever really had it to begin with.

What's he talking about?

I have no idea

I lifted my hand and extended it towards Galterio. I promised to make this painful, I'm not one to break a promise. I let the smoke pour from my fingers and brought forth the shape of a blade. I like the feeling of it in my hand, I like the roughness of the cool ice. I looked over the sharp black weapon and then lifted my eyes to Galterio. Without giving myself a second to think about it, I thrust my hand forward. The tip of the hard ice pierced the skin of Galterio's chest. As I pushed it deeper into his body, his head flew back and he howled. I twisted the blade into his flesh and slowly pushed it deeper. Galterio's howl turned from one of pain to something different, something final. His head came down and he peered at me through glassy eyes. This was the second time today that I looked into a pair of eyes as the life left them.

"Beauty" Galterio said softly. His eyes rolled back into his head, and his body slumped to the side. The swirl of darkness melted away and Gunner and I stood looking down on Galterio's body. I listened carefully as his heart thumped its last beat. He exhaled his final breath, and as the air left him, with it went my anger. It's over. He's gone. And I killed him. I turned around and threw myself into Gunner's arms, pressing my face into his chest. My rage had burnt out, but the darkness still lingers inside me, I can feel its icy sting flowing through my veins. I don't think there is any chance of keeping it out now. I let it in, and now I fear it's here to stay.

Zelena

Gunner's large arms held me tightly. Soothing me. The warm skin of his chest pressed against my wet cheek, and I found myself nuzzling into him. I was rubbing my face against him like an affectionate cat. Gunner kissed the top of my head and then moved to my forehead, cheek, corner of my mouth, and neck. His tongue ran over the puncture wounds on my neck, cleaning the skin of my blood. Then he continued with his soft kisses, over my collarbone and the claw marks on my chest. His lips moved down my body until he was on his knees in front of me. His ear pressed against my stomach as his large hands cupped my lower abdomen. I ran my hands slowly through his hair as he listened to his pup.

"You have a bump" he said softly and turned to press his forehead to my stomach, being careful to avoid the open wounds from Galterio's claws.

"I can't have a bump, it's only been a couple of weeks" I chuckled,

"Women don't start to show until they're like three months or something" I told him. He looked up and smirked at me.

"Not Weres, my love. A she-wolf's pregnancy only lasts three months". My heart stopped and I thought I was going to chuck. Three months? He can't be serious. How am I meant to get myself ready for parenthood in just three months? Well less than that now.

"Are you joking?" I asked dumbly,

"Not at all" he smiled and kissed my belly. He gently ran his tongue over the ripped flesh of my stomach. I was about to argue, thinking it was gross. But the second his tongue made contact with the wound, I felt soft tingles. Like little bubbles popping around the bloody flesh. What is this? I watched as Gunner swiped his tongue carefully over each wound. And unlike anything I had ever seen before, it looked like they were healing magically. The skin became less red and inflamed, and the large holes seemed to shrink.

"How did you do that?" I asked him, astounded,

"I helped heal you. Your body is working hard growing and protecting our pup, so your healing ability has slowed. I just gave you a boost" he said, like it was totally obvious. He gently pressed his lips to my stomach before he stood up again.

"All this time, that's why I was feeling so crazy" he laughed to himself with a shake of his head.

"What are you talking about?" I snapped, sounding slightly harsher than I intended.

"I've been so wild, so possessive and dominant"

"I noticed" I quipped, but he ignored my little jab,

"I can't believe I didn't realise it. I could sense my pup, that's why I was so possessive. Plus, I bet you've been craving hardcore. I would have picked up on that too. Fuck, I'm so stupid. How didn't I see it?"

"Craving?" I questioned. Has he completely forgotten that I'm new to all this? Were anatomy, pups, and she-wolf pregnancies. It's all foreign to me.

"Yeah, pregnant she-wolves go nuts for meat. If you don't keep up a steady intake of raw or cooked meat, you'll get sick. You'll get violent and aggressive too". I thought about what Gunner was saying. All the little remarks and snide comments that Galterio made over the last few days made sense now. He knew why I was acting like a ravenous animal. I wasn't losing my mind, my pup was just starving is all.

"I can't believe I didn't feel how ravenous you were. Babe, I'm so sorry. Shit! I nearly bit your head off for just smelling like another male for fucks sake" he grumbled and wrapped his arms around my waist,

"Don't remind me" I mumbled quietly. Gunner grabbed my chin and lifted my head to look at him.

"I will never be able to apologise enough for that Zelena. I swear I will spend the rest of our lives showing you how sorry I am" he said earnestly while staring deeply into my eyes. His dark eyes were showing hints of his normal blue, but they were still so dark. Are mine the same I wonder?

"I forgive you" I whispered, while looking at the black whisps swirling around in his iris. It's only been a short time, but holy crap have I missed him. His scent, his warmth, his taste, all of him.

"Don't. Not that easily" he said firmly. A rush of anger swept through me, it made me shiver. It wasn't mine though, it was from Gunner. He was angry with himself. Maybe me too, I don't know.

"Don't forgive me! I don't deserve it" Gunner growled and pushed me out of his arms.

"Look at you Zelena! You're fucking covered in blood. That fucker nearly killed you, the both of you. None of that would have happened if I had just fucking realised what was going on" Gunner stomped back and forth in front of me. His rage was clear, I could almost taste it. It tingled over my skin, and the darkness inside me shuddered back awake. I shook my head, trying to clear the dark haze away. We can't do this, get mad at each other, we have to think about the pup now. But boy do I love the way it makes my skin crawl.

"Gunner" I growled lowly. He glared at me and stopped marching.

"Why are you so weak? Why can't you hate me?" he yelled. His anger flew over me like a wave of icy water.

"I am not weak" I growled back. His lips curled back, and he snarled. The black whisps of smoke slithered from the tips of his fingers and began to crawl up his arms. I let go of my hold on the darkness and let it flow through me. Just like Gunner, it curled up around my arms. Kissing my skin with sharp icy sparks of electricity. I felt my body lift off the ground as the dark magic filled my chest.

"STOP!" a loud and echoed voice rang out. It sounded like it came from inside me, as well as all around me. The voice was full of pain and anger, it hit against my chest, shaking me to the core. It rang through the forest and seemed to hang in the air for a long time. I didn't just hear it, I felt it. I turned my eyes to the side, as did Gunner, both of us searching for the source of the powerful voice. My eyes found it almost instantly. I mean, it was hard to miss. My feet touched back down on the ground, and I felt all the anger get sucked out of me.

Tobias stood before us, tall and strong. His gigantic muscular arms folded over his chest and his dark eyes glared at me. Where the heck has he been? His powerful aura seemed to glow. He has always been strong and powerful, but this was something else. His normal dark chocolaty skin glistened under the early morning sunlight. It was the figure standing next to him that caught me off guard. Now this I was not expecting. Her usual serene face was pinched with concern and her beautiful eyes were narrowed and angry.

"Mother?" I said meekly.

"Yes, daughter of mine" Selene answered me.

"You're Selene, the Moon Goddess?" Gunner stated obviously. She turned her angry eyes to him and nodded. Gunner dropped to the ground on his hands and knees with his head pressed into the dirt. Tobias huffed and shook his head.

"Too late for that, don't you think? You've already insulted and disrespected her" he grumbled.

"Stand up boy" Selene snapped. Gunner shot back up to his feet immediately. He stood with his hands at his side and his head facing down.

"Mother, what are you doing here?" I asked her, stepping forward.

"I had no choice. I won't stand back and watch you destroy yourselves. You are meant for more than that" she hissed harshly. I lowered my head as I filled with shame. She's mad. I made her mad.

"I... I'm sorry" I said softly. A tear ran down my cheek as I looked back up at her. Her pale white eyes gazed back at me sadly. She wasn't just mad, she was disappointed. I've never had to worry about the whole 'I'm not mad, I'm just disappointed' speech from parents. Hank was always just mad. But seeing the look on Selene's face. I didn't need to hear the speech to understand it. I felt it through her sorrowful stare.

"You chose the darkness. You wanted for it, called for it in fact" she said in a monotone.

"I didn't have a choice" I whispered hissed.

"There is always a choice" she quipped harshly.

"What was I meant to do? Let him kill me? Let him kill my pup?" I yelled. If she was really watching over me like she said she was, then she would have known. She would have seen him. I had no other way of beating him. I had no other choice. Gunner growled and moved to my side, then he placed his hand over my stomach. Just the mention of danger to his pup and his protective nature flares.

"No, my girl, you were supposed to fight against it" Selene answered with a deep exasperated breath.

"I did fight. And I won. See, there he is, dead and defeated" I yelled and pointed to Galterio's dead corpse. The anger in me blazed to life. This life has thrown me challenge after challenge my way. Each time I wanted to give up, and each time I pushed forward. When will it be enough? How much more am I expected to endure? What else do I have to give? I could feel the dark haze moving back in, slowly taking back over.

"I'm not speaking of him, Dear One" Selene said slowly.

"Then what are you talking about? What do I have to do to be good enough? When will I be enough to be the great and powerful Triple Goddess?" I screamed. The dark tentacles sprung from my fingers and curled themselves around my hands. The darkness slithered through my chest and wrapped itself around my heart. I was lost to it. I could feel that now.

"You were meant to fight the dark. You were my gift. You were meant to be the light in the world" Selene's voice raised in volume and power as it rang through my head. Her ethereal glow increased until it surrounded her in a bright white light. She is the light the world needs, she always has been. And me, I can never measure up to her. I clasped my hands over my ears, trying to block out the painful ringing sound. Her voice bounced around inside my head. Holy fuck it hurt. I dropped to my knees and screamed. Gunner growled and ran towards Selene, but she didn't even blink. Tobias leaped forward and grabbed hold of Gunner. With speed I hadn't seen in him before, Tobias managed to lock Gunner's arms behind his head. He held him in place with ease, even as Gunner growled and thrashed in his arms. Selene ignored him as she slowly walked towards me. She extended her hand forward and lifted it. My body followed suit, rising off the ground and floating in front of her. I couldn't move. My legs, my arms, my head, everything was completely immobilized. So, this is what this feels like, to be frozen in place at the will of someone else. Not fun.

"No daughter of mine will be lost to the dark side of the moon" she said slowly. She placed her hand on my chest softly, but it felt like I had been punched. My whole body lurched, yet I remained completely still. It was like the wind had been knocked out of me. I shivered, and my skin turned to ice. I felt like claws were being scraped through my veins, like something was being ripped out of me. I screamed out. My voice echoed through the air in a painful wail.

"STOP!" I begged her. I looked down at her hand and saw the black whisps of smoke being sucked from my chest. It snapped out in all directions, slicing through the air like a whip. But each whisp and tendril was pulled back into her hand, like water down a drain. The darkness poured from the canter of my chest like an open faucet, but it didn't go quietly. It really did have a mind of its own, it fought, it tried to fly off into the sky, and it clawed at me, trying desperately to hold on. The longer Selene held her hand to my chest, the lighter I felt. I felt the darkness slipping from me. But it was still fighting. Holding on to any part of me that it could. The immense pain made way for cold numbness. The anger and rage that I felt so strongly before, it was gone now. My legs and arms went numb, as if they were completely weightless. I felt dizzy. My eyes became blurry, and if I could move, I imagined my head would wobble like a bobblehead toy. Gunner's growl was the last thing I heard as my heavy eyelids closed and everything was pushed out.

~

My sore eyelids wouldn't budge, it was too hard to open them. I breathed in through my nose, taking in all of the familiar scents of home. I was in my and Gunner's room, back at the pack house. Gunner's scent was strong in here as well, I could take a safe guess that he was here with me. My body was weak and weighted. Everything hurt. I took a deep breath and focused on moving my body. I managed to straighten one of my legs, that was it. My stirring must have caught Gunner's attention. His arm which was around my waist, pulled me in closer to his chest. His entire body was pressed flush against my back. My head rested on his shoulder, while the rest of his arm was tucked over my chest, his hand cupping my breast. One of his legs was wrapped over mine, with his face buried into my hair. I was in a vice grip. He had himself tangled all around me like a choker vine. But I like it. I've missed this, I've missed him.

If I stay like this, I will drift off again, I could feel the exhaustion clawing at the back of my eyes. Wait, Selene was there. She did... something. I don't know what she did. But whatever it was, it knocked me out. How long was I out for? Goddess, it wasn't another three months, was it? And my baby, Galterio tried to kill my pup. Is he okay? Is everyone else okay? I could hear all the fighting when Cole was trying to get me out. How bad was the fight? Oh, Cole. Cole was dead. I saw him die. He's dead and we never got to fix this whole thing between us. Those glassy eyes and that weak smile, his dying face will haunt my memories for the rest of my life. Tears pooled behind my closed eyes and began to leak through. My chest tightened and my heart ached. Cole died. He died because of me, just like his father. A sob burst through my dry cracked lips and shook my body. I tried to scrunch my eyes closed tighter. I don't want to see his dying eyes anymore.

"Hey. Hey now, you're okay. You're home, you're safe. I've got you, Zee. You're okay" Gunner soothed as he squeezed my body into his. He nuzzled his nose into the back of my head and lifted the hand from my waist to wipe the hair away from my face.

"You're okay, Little Wolf" he said as he pressed his lips into my hair.

"Cole" I choked out in a strangled sob. Gunner's body tensed behind me. His every muscle constricted and his breathing halted. Another sob shook my body and Gunner seemed to snap out of it.

"I know" Gunner said quietly. He tried to keep his voice even, but I could hear the sadness in it.

"It's all my fault" I mumbled through my tears. Gunner was quiet. His tight grip on me stayed firm, but he didn't respond. After a minute I calmed my tears and quieted my sobs. Only then did I hear the sound of Gunner's crying. As much as my body protested, and as painful and difficult as it was, I turned around in Gunner's arms so that I was facing him. His eyes were red and puffy, meaning he had been crying off and on for a while. His usual creamy smooth skin was pale and blotchy, and his face was wet with tears. I lifted my hands to cup his face and gently ran my thumbs across his wet cheeks. "It's not your fault" Gunner's croaky voice broke out. He closed his eyes tight and his face scrunched together, it was a kind of pained look that I had never seen on him before.

"Talk to me Gunner" I pleaded with him as I swiped my thumb over his bottom lip.

"I was so fucking mad at him, for calling Origin Wolf" Gunner began. I held my expression in place, but it almost broke at the revelation. Cole called Galterio? I can't believe that. Cole was angry, but he wouldn't go against Tri-Moon. He loved this pack. I thought Artemis was the traitor. He and Zoe, working together. How did Cole fit into that?

"I sent him off on his own. I knew it was a bad move, I knew he should have had backup. I was just so angry. I didn't want to look at him anymore, so I gave him an impossible task".

Fresh tears flowed from Gunner's eyes as a strained sob wracked his large body. I dragged myself up higher on the bed and pulled his head to my chest. Gunner's arms squeezed around me so damn tightly. I stroked my hand through his hair and the other held him against me. I could feel all of it. All of his guilt and sorrow. He was in so much pain, and my heart ached from it. My own tears fell freely down my face. My pain and sadness mixed with Gunner's, and we were both tied together in an emotional mess.

"It's my fault. I sent my brother to die" Gunner cried and squeezed his arms. My chest constricted under his hold, and I couldn't take a full breath. But my concern was for my pup. His arms were crushing me under the weight of his guilt, and our pup along with it. I tapped on his head to let me go but my signal didn't register.

Gunner, you're crushing our baby

I flashed him in a strained tone. He immediately shot himself back, flying his body off the bed and across the room. He held his hands out in front of him, trying to show me he wouldn't hurt me. The same way he did on the day I first changed. I know he won't hurt me on purpose. What is this about?

"I'm sorry, I'm sorry. I didn't mean to, I swear it" he rushed out as his eyes swept down my body. A look of shame and disgust filled his eyes. But I could still feel him, his emotions and thoughts. He wasn't disgusted with me, he was disgusted with himself, with the fact that he could have possibly hurt me... Again.

"I'm okay, you didn't hurt me. It was just a little tight" I said soothingly and held out my hand for him to come back to the bed. He stared at my hand and pressed himself into the wall. Hurt flashed across my face at his rejection. And Gunner caught it before I could wipe it away.

"I'm sorry, I shouldn't be here. I should be far away from you" he mumbled painfully.

"What? What is that supposed to mean?" I snapped. Why would he need to stay away from me? Was it because of the thing that happened on the beach? We sorted that out though, I just need to eat to ward off the violent hunger urges. Gunner eyed me warily, uncertainty was written all over his face. Uncertain of what though? Of having a baby?

"Gunner, what's going on?" I asked him softly, my own fear and panic started to rise. He doesn't want a baby, he's going to kick me out, kick 'us' out. Oh, Goddess. He's rejecting me, isn't he?

"Don't think like that" Gunner growled, his eyes turning a little darker.

"Think what?" I asked him. He clenched his fists and his jaw clicked together tightly. Was this the darkness? I can't feel it in me anymore. It's just gone. I can feel his anger, but nothing more than that. It's not rage or fury, it's just anger. How is that possible?

"Don't think that I don't love you. That I don't want you, want this, a family. I want all of that. You're just not safe with me anymore" Gunner's hard voice rumbled around the room.

"This doesn't make any sense Gunner, what is going on?" I pleaded with him. I dragged my tired and pained body to the edge of the bed and let my legs flop over the side. I was about to stand when Gunner rushed forward. He dropped to his knees in front of me and placed his arms gently on my lap.

"Don't, you still need to rest" he said quickly,

"Then tell me what's going on. Now!" I demanded. I placed my hands over his and squeezed. Gunner peered up at me. I could see his mind working hard. The bright blue of his eyes held a shade of black in their depths and it made me shiver. He huffed out a breath and dropped his head to my knees.

"Okay" he mumbled. I grabbed his head and lifted it up so that he was looking at me again.

"Okay?" I questioned,

"Tell me what you remember" Gunner said softly while looking into my eyes.

"I don't know, everything, nothing. I don't know what was real and what wasn't" I answered as I wracked my brain for what I could remember.

"Tell me what you think you remember, and then we can go from there". I nodded my head and cleared my throat.

"Cole died. Galterio punched a hole through his chest" I said first. The flash of his pained silent scream and then his weak smile flashed through my mind. Gunner tensed but nodded his head, indicating for me to go on.

"I was mad. It's like I filled with rage and everything went kind of hazy. Galterio and I fought. My power was useless against him, he could just suck it out of me or something". I flashed back to the bedroom when he snapped my hold and then bit me. A tear rolled down my cheek and I ran my fingers over the raised scar on my neck. Gunner pulled my hand away and pressed his lips to my knuckles. It's where his mark should be, not that monstrosity of a man's.

"What else?" Gunner encouraged.

"I realised that the dark power could hurt him. I heard him and Artemis talking about how he was pretty much immune to my normal power. They said it was because we are distantly related. Anyway, I was about to kill him, but then you showed up" I paused and looked down at Gunner. He was watching me intently. Listening carefully to my recollection.

"We... we killed him. I killed him. Using the dark magic". Gunner squeezed my hand as I choked out the words 'I killed him'. Galterio was a monster, there's no question there. But in some weird twisted and totally gross way, we were family. And I still killed him.

"Is that all?" he asked me gently,

"No. I remember Selene was there, with Tobias. Tobias was different though, it looked like he was glowing or something. Was Selene really there? Did you see her?" I asked. I couldn't help the excitement that filtered through my words. I would love for him to see her. For them to meet in person, my mother and my Mate. That would have been amazing. Gunner nodded his head slowly, but he wasn't excited about it. Then, of course, I remembered why. I did it again. We did it again.

"Oh" I said breathlessly.

"I was going to hurt you. I wanted to hurt you, and her. I wanted to hurt everyone. The darkness was inside me. It was so strong, and I couldn't see past it. It was controlling me, I guess. I don't really know what happened next. I was looking at Selene and the black smoke was all around her. Then nothing, I woke up here with you".

"That sounds about right" Gunner said slowly.

"Okay, then what happened? After I passed out or whatever, what did she do to me? How did we get back here? What happened during the fight? Is everyone else alright? Smith, your dad, Tobias?" I began to ramble, my voice going up an octave and speeding through my many questions. Gunner cupped one of my cheeks and ran his thumb over my lips to quieten me down.

"One question at a time, Little Wolf" he said smoothly, looking at me with all the love and adoration in the world. My heart swelled at the love in his gaze.

"What did Selene do to me?" I managed to ask breathlessly,

"She expelled the darkness, cast it out of you. You're back to yourself again now" he said with a soft smile.

"Really? No more rage, no more urges to kill?" I asked him, full of hopefulness.

"You will still feel anger, just like anyone. You will still get mad and sad, and sometimes you'll want to wring a neck. But that is just you, no more persuasion and temptation from the darkness" he answered me solemnly. For some reason, he doesn't look happy. If anything he looks scared, or maybe even a little sad. No more darkness, this should be a good thing, right? I gave the darkness to Gunner, through the bond, I shared it with him. So if it was my darkness to begin with, that would have to mean it is gone from him now too.

"This is great, right? We don't have to fight it anymore. It's gone. We can go back to living our lives" I asked him brightly. But he still didn't look too thrilled.

"This is very good. You'll be able to raise our pup with love and light" he smiled up at me,

"You mean we. We'll raise our pup, together" I said cautiously. Gunner was hinting at something, trying to be subtle about it. But I don't need him to spare my feelings right now, I just need to know what the fuck is going on.

"Right Gunner. WE!" I said harshly.

"No, Little Wolf" he said and dropped his hand from my cheek.

"Selene expelled the darkness from you. Only you". I stared at Gunner with wide eyes. Why would she save me and not him? That doesn't make any sense.

"Why would she do that?" I whispered, scared to hear the answer.

"Zelena, I failed her. I failed you. I didn't even try to save you from the dark, instead, I stepped into it with you willingly. She is unsure if I am strong enough to stand beside you. This... this is my test".

My head spun like a kids spinning top toy. She is testing him. Why? How could she do this to me? We are True Mates, I can't survive without him. She said he was the perfect choice, she said we would thrive together. And now she is changing her mind. She can't do that!

"Calm down Zelena, I can feel you getting all worked up" Gunner said soothingly as he ran his hands up and down my thighs.

"Calm down. Calm down! How can I calm down when she is threatening to take away my Mate, the father of my pup? That is what she is threatening, isn't it? She's going to kill you?" I asked as a hot angry tear fell down my cheek.

"Of course not Zelena. She is firm in her punishments, but she is not cruel" he answered with a forced chuckle.

"Explain" I growled through my clenched teeth.

"She has given me three weeks to let go of the darkness, to expel it on my own" he answered me,

"And at the end of those three weeks?" I snapped.

"If I haven't found a way to get rid of it on my own, she will take it away, along with my wolf".

"Can she do that?" I asked shocked. Would she actually strip him of his wolf? Our wolves are a part of us. A really big part of us. Who are we without our wolf?

"She is the Moon Goddess, she created us all. Yes, she can do it". Wow. I never thought this could be a possibility. Roe explained to me once, that once you're a Were, you can't go back. There is no cure or anything like that. Would Selene really do it though?

"Well, I mean that isn't so bad, is it? You can live without your wolf, right?" I said quietly. I was still reeling from the ultimatum handed down to him. If he can't expel the darkness, he will still be alive. We will still be together. I can still love him, even if he can't change form anymore.

"It's not that simple. Without a wolf, I can't be an Alpha. Without a wolf, I can't do and feel things like a normal Were can. Including having any kind of Mate bond"

"You mean we won't be Mates?"

"Correct".

"But we can still be together. I love you. And not just because of some stupid bond. I know I will love you, with or without it" I cried out. I gripped Gunner's shoulders as my body started to shake from fear. I can't lose him. Gunner is my everything. We are having a baby together for fucks sake. We can make it through anything. Gunner laid his head in my lap, his hands came up to rest over my stomach. He stayed like that, silently for what felt like hours. All the while, I sat and quietly panicked to myself about possibly losing the one person that showed me what love is.

"I promise, I am trying" Gunner eventually said as he lifted his head and looked up at me. His red rimmed eyes, tear stained cheeks, and pale skin proved just how hard this was going to be. I took a deep breath and nodded.

"I won't let this happen. We will figure this out together, you and me. The way that it should be. Okay? Together?"

"Together" Gunner nodded weakly.

"But first, you need to eat. I can already feel your hunger and it's making my teeth tingle". Gunner stood up and wrapped his arms around me. He lifted me up off the bed so that my legs locked around his waist and my arms around his neck. With one hand under my ass and the other around my back, he leaned forward and pressed his lips to mine. I leaned into the kiss, throwing myself into the delicious way it made me feel. Gunner's plump lips and warm breath tickled me. His tongue sought entrance into my mouth and I complied, parting my lips and letting him in. Before too long I found myself grinding my hips against him. My skin heated up, and that wanton ache throbbed between my legs. Gunner growled and took my bottom lip between his teeth. He pulled it out slightly before letting it go with a pop.

"Food first, we can finish this later" he growled seductively. Gunner is and always will be my favourite distraction.

Chapter Forty

Lunaya

The trip back to Tri-Moon was dismal. All of Lua Chei, apart from Analah, Ares, and four others, went back to their pack lands. Alpha Travis bid farewell and left for Waning Wolf with his warriors. Tobias insisted that his brother, Alpha Marius, went back home. They argued over it for a while, but Tobias won, and his brother went back to their pack. Alpha Lace, however, refused to go home. He sent his men and Beta back, keeping only three Weres with him. He was very insistent on coming back to Tri-Moon, and I am very curious as to why.

Tobias and Gunner were very tight-lipped about whatever happened out there. All they said was that the Origin Alpha murdered Cole, and then they killed him in return. As for Zelena and her unconscious state, they said that she depleted her energy fighting off the Alpha. I could tell they were lying. Zelena is a Triple Goddess. It would have weakened her, but not to this extent. Something else happened. And I'll be dammed if they are going to keep it from me.

The vehicles pulled into the long winding driveway that leads to the Tri-Moon pack village. The bus came to a harsh stop, and the beat up and blood soaked Weres slowly filed out. Romeá came running over with her daughter, and multiple other she-wolves in toe. Roe stopped and searched the crowd, her eyes found Lupus and her body relaxed. She ran to him and jumped into his arms, causing them both to fall to the ground. I looked out to the approaching she-wolves and searched for those brilliant green eyes. A body slammed into me, and I was enveloped in a firm hug. The scent hit me first. Cherries and dark chocolate. Alyse. I wrapped my arms around her and buried my face into the crook of her neck.

"I'm so sorry" she sobbed,

"I was so scared and so stupid. I do support you, I will always support you. I shouldn't have got so upset over it. I'm so sorry" she cried into my chest. Oh, my sweet Alyse.

"Hush now my love, you don't need to apologise, but I do. I shouldn't have yelled at you. I know that you were just looking out for me. I was scared is all, and I took it out on you. That was wrong of me. I am sorry" I cooed as I stroked her back in a soothing circle. She pushed herself out of my arms and looked around at the much smaller crowd of Weres.

"Did you find her? Where is she?" Alyse asked urgently. I should have never doubted her love. I knew she cared for Zelena, even though they never met, I knew she loved her as I did.

"We found her. Origin Wolf were defeated and Zelena is home" I told her. The sound of a high-pitched wail snapped our attention. Both Alyse and I turned our gaze to the source of the scream. Roe was kneeling on the ground, her hands gripping Cole's pale face. She was distraught, crying and gently rubbing his cheeks.

"Oh Goddess" Alyse gasped,

"Gunner?" she asked turning back to me. I shook my head and wiped a tear from the corner of my eye.

"Cole" I said softly. A strangled croak left Alyse's lips before she slapped both hands over her mouth. She turned back around and slowly walked over to where Roe was cradling Cole's head in her arms. The Alpha-daughter, Nat, was kneeling at her mother's side, sobbing as she brushed her fingers through Cole's hair. Lupus stood behind Roe, gripping her shoulders tightly. Alpha Lace appeared at Nat's side and gently picked her up off the ground. He turned her away from Cole and wiped the tears from her cheeks. There was too much noise around us, and I was still too far away to hear properly, but it looked like the rough and tough tattooed Were was comforting her. Smith popped up and quickly pulled Nat from Alpha Lace's arms, with his teeth bared he snarled at the Alpha. Nat wrapped her arms around Smith, and he carried her away. Tobias walked past me, with Zelena in his arms. He dodged the prying eyes of her pack and walked straight for the house. I looked over to Alyse, she had her arms around Roe's shoulders and was trying to get her to let him go.

Tobias is taking Zelena inside, I'm following them

I flashed Alyse as I ran after Tobias.

It's okay, I'll be there as soon as I can

She flashed me back. As I came around the side of the house, I saw that they had prepared beds and medical stations in the clearing. It was like a full blown first aid outpost. Shade sails to keep away the afternoon sun, carts full of gauze and saline, and even a male doctor wearing a long white coat was running between the injured Weres. Many of the she-wolves were tending to the less serious wounds. Luckily, most of these Weres will be completely healed in the next day or two. I ran into the house and lifted my nose. I followed the scent up the stairs and into a large bathroom. Tobias stood under the showerhead, still clothed, with Zelena in his arms. The water falling off them both was a mix of brown and red. With both of Tobias's arms carefully cradling Zelena, he wasn't able to wash the blood from her face. I walked into the large shower and went to brush away the wet hair that was stuck to Zelena's neck. Tobias growled and turned his body so that she was out of my reach.

"Please Tobias, let me help wash her. I won't hurt her, I promise" I begged him. His growl rumbled through the bathroom. It made my knees want to buckle. Something was very different about the guardian. His energy and aura had completely changed. Before the battle, he was calm and cheerful, fiercely protective over Zelena, but not aggressive. Now though, he didn't even have to say anything for me to feel the change. He felt powerful before, but this was unlike anything else I have felt. His air of power was stronger, more than even that of a strong Alpha. I felt like I needed to bow to him or lower my head. I have never had that urge around another Were before. What the heck happened in the forest?

"Tobias, I just want to help" I said softly as I took a very small step closer. He growled again and this time I was hit with a wave of energy, similar to that I felt when Zelena used her power. But Tobias is just a guardian, he doesn't have power. Does he?

"Okay" he grumbled, the sound echoed around the large bathroom. I didn't wait for him to change his mind again, I stepped forward and grabbed a loofah that was hanging from the tap. I pumped a squirt of soap onto the sponge and turned around. I ran the sponge over her arm. Her chest and stomach were covered by what I assume was once a white t-shirt, now in tatters and stained with blood. I picked at the ripped collar of the shirt and lifted it.

"May I take it off?" I asked Tobias, being careful to not anger him. He nodded his head silently. I extended one of my claws and dragged it along the length of the cloth. As it came away, I saw the extent of her wounds on her chest and stomach. A mix of a growl and a sob fell from my shocked and agape mouth. The wounds had already started to heal. But there is no denying that she was banged up pretty badly. I ran the soapy loofah over the skin that didn't have open wounds, which didn't leave a lot of other areas. I moved down her bruised legs to her mangled ankle. The skin was ripped and shredded. I carefully inspected the limb and found it wasn't broken, miraculously. But she's going to need a lot of stitches, or else it will heel incorrectly and her movements will be affected.

I continued to wash the copious amounts of dirt and blood from her body. Is it any wonder she's unconscious, she's has to be wearing at least a quarter of her blood. Slowly her soft pale skin, just like her father's, began to shine through again. Tobias moved so that just her hair was under the water, and the dried blood and dirt began to wash out. I got the shampoo and squeezed it onto my hands before lathering it into her long ebony hair. As I ran my fingers through her hair, I noticed the fresh mating mark on the top of her shoulder. Gunner wouldn't have marked her during the fight, would he?

"This is new?" I asked Tobias as I moved the hair out of the way to show him the mark. His eyes hardened and his brows drew together. A rumbling growl rattled the glass shower screen door.

"That does not belong to her Mate" Tobias's deep voice growled. How could that not belong to her Mate, it's a mating mark. Outdated and considered a possessive gesture. But they are True Mates, so what the hell. But if it's not Gunner's then who's is it?

"Gunner didn't mark her?" I asked him,

"He did, but that marking is not his. The Alpha's mark was healed. This mark is forced, aggressive, and messy" he answered me.

"But then who did this?" I didn't need to hear an answer to the question. As soon as I asked it, I knew what the answer was. That fucking Origin Alpha. He tried to force her to be his Mate. Not the first time a descendant of Gill has tried to blend the bloodlines. The fucker already had a Mate and heir, plus Zelena has a destined Mate. What idiot told him that it would work? Oh, let me guess that fool of a Prophet. Fucking bastards. Artemis thought she had to choose between two mates, and so they tried to force her hand. Those damned idiots! My anger flared and before I got the chance to compose myself, I slammed my fist into the tiled wall. The tiles cracked and shattered at the force of my punch and then clattered to the floor. Tobias looked at me with a quirked eyebrow,

"You already know?" he said.

"Yeah, I already know. The Origin Alpha, right? That fucking treacherous line of egotistical morons. Gill's descendants have been trying to snag a daughter of Selena for generations. Came close at one point, but they never succeeded in joining the lines" I snarled.

"Come, she is clean," Tobias said firmly before marching past me and out of the bathroom. It felt like an Alpha command only stronger. I have never been affected by an Alpha's order. But this time, I felt compelled to do as Tobias asked. I grabbed a towel for myself, wrapped it around my shoulders, and followed Tobias to a bedroom. By the strong scent of sex, and the mix of both Gunner and Zelena's scent, I'd say this is their room. Tobias laid Zelena on the bed with a towel covering her body. I stood back and watched as he carefully dried and dressed Zelena. Not once did his gaze linger on her exposed body too long, and not once did his hands touch her inappropriately. He loves her. That's plainly obvious for everyone to see. But he has no lust for her. And that made me feel overwhelmingly at ease with their special bond.

"What happened out there?" I asked him quietly. I don't know why I felt the need to whisper. She was unconscious and couldn't hear me anyway. It just felt weird to talk in a normal volume.

"It doesn't matter now" he answered as he pulled socks onto Zelena's feet. It's the middle of summer here, but he still put socks on her.

"I disagree, you've changed. And what Gunner did, to that child..." I shuddered at the memory.

"Something happened" I argued. Once Tobias was done dressing her, he tucked her into the bed, pulling the covers up to her chest. He peeled his own soaking t-shirt from his massive frame and sat on the edge of the bed. He gingerly placed his hand on her stomach, then he sat silently and stared at her. I watched her as she lay completely still, with only the small movement of her chest going up and down with each breath. After a few minutes, Tobias's deep voice whispered,

"She turned to the darkness. I could not stop her, and I could not bring her back. She was almost lost to it". I didn't respond, just listened as he explained.

"The black magic was consuming every part of her. Every part" Tobias whispered as his hand moved in a slow circle over her abdomen. I know of the darkness. It is a big part of the stories and training passed down from our ancestors. Throughout history, only one Triple Goddess has been completely lost to the dark side. She lost her Mate and went mad with grief. It took a lot to kill her, and along the way, she wreaked unimaginable havoc. That was generations ago.

"How did you get her back? You did get her back, didn't you?" I asked as I stood up from where I was leaning against the wall.

"We did" he said sullenly. I waited quietly for him to continue, after a few minutes of silence, he continued speaking once again,

"I had no other choice. We were losing her. There was nothing else that I could do, so I called for the Goddess, for

Selene. I begged her to help me. She heard my call, and she came" Tobias paused, and I swallowed the lump in my throat. Selene came. And apparently, she didn't just show herself to Zelena this time, but Tobias too. Maybe even Gunner. This is unheard of.

"She pulled the darkness from Zelena, that's why she's unconscious. Once the darkness was gone from her, she collapsed" Tobias said quietly after another moment of silence.

"And what did she do to you? This is why I can feel you have changed, isn't it? She has blessed you somehow" I asked him, taking another step forward. I have no idea if I'm right. The only other man to be given the power of the Goddess was her lover, Endymion. Before Gunner accessed the power through Zelena, no other male had ever been given the gifts of Selene.

"She said my loyalty and courage deserved rewarding. She said I was a good guardian, and it was not my fault she stepped into the dark. She blessed me with some of her power" he continued without looking away from Zelena.

"What power?" I asked him, keeping my voice smooth and level, to gently coax more information out of him,

"Heighten speed and strength, among other things" he trailed off. I want to know more, I'm desperate to know more. But I don't want to push him, I'm amazed he has told me this much so easily. One wrong question and this little conversation could end.

"And Gunner? He was affected by the darkness as well, did she pull it from him too?" I asked softly. Tobias stood to his full height, towering over me with an air of intimidation swirling around him.

"No" he growled then stomped out of the room. That was an abrupt exit. I guess I found my one wrong question. So, if Gunner is still under the influence of the darkness, that would explain the extreme actions taken against the Origin child. But why would the All-Mother help Zelena and not her Mate? That part doesn't make any sense. I sat on the edge of the bed that Tobias just vacated. I ran my finger over Zelena's cheek. She looks so much like Micha. Her nose tilts at the same angle his did. Her soft hair flows the same way his did. She is his daughter, his clone. And I want to tell her the truth. This whole second kidnapping has really made me realise how precious the time we have is. I don't want to spend any more of it as a stranger to her.

~

I left Zelena to rest and went in search of Alyse. No doubt she is tending to the injured Weres. As I made my way outside, I found the clearing filled with bandaged and bloodied Weres. Most of them were up and about, walking around or sitting and talking. Some, however, were laid out on stretcher beds, in far worse shape. A few tables had been set up with some she-wolves serving food to the warriors. I spotted Alyse flittering between two stretcher beds and made my way to her.

"Can I help?" I asked. I stepped up behind her as she was wiping the blood from a she-wolf's face. Alyse jumped with a squeak and turned around, I'd startled her. I smiled and she sighed.

"No love, you need to rest as well". She went to brush me off before her eyes landed at my side.

"Come and sit down" she ordered, leading me to an empty stretcher.

"Love, I'm fine" I protested,

"Don't be stupid, Lunaya. It needs to be cleaned or an infection will spread" Alyse scolded. Of course she's right, she usually is. I sat on the edge of one of the stretcher beds and let Alyse clean, treat, and bandage my wound.

"You'll live" she declared.

"Thank you, my Darling" I smiled and planted a kiss on her forehead.

"Now, how can I help?" I asked while surveying the makeshift infirmary.

"You can't, we have it handled" she answered with a sweet smile.

"You're sure?"

"Yes. Go get yourself something to eat, I will join you shortly". She squeezed my forearm with a soft smile on her beautiful face, before turning back to the other she-wolfs. I looked around and spotted Ares sitting with his sister on some large logs around an empty firepit. I headed over to them and sat down across from him. Analah nodded and offered a crooked smile. She had fought well. I saw her blonde wolf take down a much larger grey wolf during the fight near the farmhouse. She had a bandage around her upper right arm, and another holding a piece of gauze to her neck. All in all, she still looks perfectly fine. She will fit in well with Luna Eclipse if she ends up deciding to stay there. I nodded my head to Ares, who smiled and nodded back. He stood up and held out a large bowl with a spoon in it for me. I took the bowl and held it to my nose. Beef stew.

"Thank you" I said as I sniffed in the hot beefy scent.

"You're welcome. I'm glad to see you mostly unscathed. You're a great fighter. Lua Chei would be lucky to have a Were like yourself" he said confidently with a wide smile taking up most of his face. He wasn't trying at all to be subtle about his offer to join his pack.

"Thank you. You as well, both of you. You can really hold your own" I said as I raised my bowl in a cheers motion.

"Is that something you would consider?" Ares asked,

"What's that?" I replied, playing dumb,

"Joining us, at Lua Chei. You and your Mate of course" he smiled. The offer was very kind, and if I'm honest, a little sudden. As flattered as I am, and as lovely as the Lua Chei pack land was, it would never happen.

"I appreciate your offer, I really do. But I think we both know why I can't do that" I said kindly.

"Ahh, of course, the big secret" Ares chuckled,

"Are you ever going to tell her the truth?" he asked, turning his body to face me, giving me his full attention. I'm not at all surprised that he knows. He is a smart man. Plus, after the battle, I think a lot more people know about my terribly kept secret.

"I am, as soon as she is on her feet again" I said with conviction. And I was. I'm not going to live at her side as a stranger any longer.

"Good. That's good" Ares smiled.

"And you? Are you going to take your rightful place and let your father retire?" it wasn't my place to ask, but we were getting personal so why not. Ares huffed and slapped his thigh. A laugh burst through his plump pink lips, and he threw me a 'you're bold' kind of look. I lifted a shoulder and smirked.

"I am. The old geezer needs a break I reckon" Ares chuckled. This elicited a giggle from Analah also.

"What will he do with all that spare time?" Analah snickered. "Thankfully he and Mum are too old to keep reproducing. But I reckon they will keep up the vigorous practicing" Ares boomed and slapped his thigh again. I was glad to see they weren't as shy about their parent's very active sex life as their younger brother was.

As we sat and ate our food, the conversation flowed easily. More Weres joined us and also partook in the discussion. As the sun set, a fire was lit, and the warriors soon congregated around the heated flames. The sullen feeling of the battle and the heavy losses we all bore, was soon forgotten. Laughter, songs, and avid conversations filled the air. It was almost easy to forget about the dead in that moment. However, the good feeling didn't last for too long. The songs turned to dreary medleys and the conversation quietened to whispers. Tears fell and sadness took over those gathered. The warriors slowly broke off to go to their homes and loved ones, while the visiting Weres left for their temporary accommodations. I was left sitting alone on the log, staring at what remained of the fire. A soft hand snaked around my neck from behind, and I looked over my shoulder to see Alyse smiling down at me.

"Come on, time for bed" she said softly and pressed her lips to my temple. Her stomach growled loudly, and she giggled.

"Did you get to eat at all?" I asked her as I stood from the log and grabbed her hands. She smiled at me and shook her head.

"Nah, there was too much to do. The poor human couldn't keep up with it all" she chuckled,

"Human? What human?" I rushed out,

"The doctor. Apparently, he has a special deal in place with Gunner and Lupus. He keeps his mouth shut, and they fill his pockets" she said with a shrug of her shoulder.

"That doesn't sound exactly safe" I grumbled. I imagine if he is greedy enough to be taking money on the side for working with Weres, it probably wouldn't be too hard to turn him. I would hope that hunters didn't find out about this arrangement. They wouldn't be too forgiving with his healing of werewolves.

"Meh, not our concern. He agreed to it willingly" Alyse huffed and pulled me forward. We were heading for our tent when her stomach rumbled again.

"No. You need something to eat before bed. We'll go snoop through their kitchen" I mused as I pulled her towards the packhouse.

Chapter Forty-One

Lunaya

Alyse and I were huddled in the corner booth, stuffing our faces with bread and lukewarm stew. Alyse had her legs draped over mine so that she was nearly in my lap. I had a piece of bread hanging between my teeth as I waved it in front of Alyse's mouth. She chuckled and snapped her teeth at the bread, pulling it from my mouth. I laughed and grabbed either side of her face, I pulled her to me and pressed my lips to her cheek. The kitchen door flew open and in walked Gunner with Zelena in his arms. She had her arms and legs wrapped around him like a koala. Alyse and I went silent as we watched them enter. Gunner paused and flicked his eyes to mine. He quickly looked to Alyse and then down at the bowls in front of us, before continuing on into the kitchen. I sat up straight, expecting that he would put Zelena down so I could see her. But instead, he kept one arm under her backside and carried her with him to the fridge. Zelena had her head nuzzled into the crook of his neck, hiding her face. A whirlwind of questions flooded my mind. She had a wrap around her ankle, so it seems someone tended to what was left of her tattered skin. I wanted to ask if the rest of her wounds were healed, how was she feeling, is she holding up okay after the battle, so much I wanted to ask but I swallowed them all down. Alyse and I watched silently as Gunner prepared a bowl of stew, a large plate of steaks and some bread and butter. After he had finished heating it up and getting it ready, he made his way to the booth where Alyse and I were sat watching. Gunner deposited Zelena onto the booth bench and then slid in beside her. Zelena finally noticed our presence, and she jerked back with wide eyes before she offered a small smile.

"Oh hi, I didn't realise anyone else was in here" she said quietly, while smoothing down the wild strands of hair at the back of her head. Her eyes were sunk in and surrounded by dark circles. The whites of her eyes were stained with red, indicating she had been crying. She looked tired, more than tired actually, she looked weathered. I smiled back and nodded to the plate in front of her,

"Looks like we both had the same idea" I said with a forced chuckled. Zelena looked down at the plate of steaks in front of her and her eyes darkened. She snapped up a whole steak with her hand and shovelled it into her mouth near whole. The amount of meat in her mouth meant she couldn't close her lips as she chewed. She grumbled and moaned as the steak juices dribbled down her chin. The way she ate was like a wild animal. Was this because of her upbringing with the hunter? I know he treated her badly, is this the aftermath of that? Eating what you can, when you can, as fast as you can? It was odd behaviour in the least. Alyse and I, even Gunner, all stared at her wide eyed as she shoved another steak into her mouth. Alyse's hand found my thigh and she squeezed, pressing her fingernails into my skin. After a few moments, Zelena's rabid eating slowed and she looked at each of us shyly. She wiped the steak residue from her chin and chuckled awkwardly.

"Sorry, I was uh… starving" she mumbled as her cheeks flushed pink with embarrassment. Gunner wrapped his arm around her shoulders and pressed his lips to her temple.

"No I get it, sometimes you just can't chew fast enough" Alyse mused with a sly smile. She flicked her eyes between both Gunner and Zelena, the smile staying on her face.

"Eat" Gunner grumbled and handed her another steak. She blushed and eyed us both hesitantly before she took the steak and bit into it. Taking a much smaller mouthful this time round. We all ate in silence, none of us sure who should talk first or how to break the quiet.

"I'm glad you made it home safely, Goddess" Alyse finally spoke up,

"Thank you, and please, will you call me Zelena" she smiled kindly back at Alyse,

"As you wish, Zelena. I just have to say, I was so unbelievably sorry to hear about Cole. I had only met him a few times, but I could tell he was a special Were" Alyse said as she reached across the table and gently placed her hand over Zelena's. Gunner's eyes snapped down to where their hands met, and he glared at them. After a moment he shook his head and blinked his eyes a few times, then he lifted his gaze to me. I was frozen in place by what I saw in his eyes. Bright blue orbs with whisps of black dancing around within them, stared me down and had me shifting in my seat. The darkness had its claws buried into him deep. It's going to be hard, really bloody hard, to get him to let it go.

"That's kind of you" Zelena choked out with a sniffle, catching Gunner's attention once more. Without saying a word, he ran his hand down the length of her arm. He lifted her from the booth and placed her carefully in his lap. Zelena sighed and leaned into him, resting her head on his shoulder. His hand moved in slow soothing circles on her back, as she drew aimless patterns on his chest.

"Thank you for your assistance here, Alyse. I know my mother would have been lost without you" Gunner said in a deep gruff voice, a voice that sounded tired and overworked. Like he too had been crying a lot recently.

"Oh stop, it's the least I could do, especially as I could not fight" she cooed back.

"You can't fight? But from what everyone has told me, Luna Eclipse she-wolves are fierce terrifying warriors. Aren't you as well?" Zelena said as she lifted her head and looked to Alyse. Alyse chuckled and leaned back in her seat.

"You've been told right, Luna-Eclipse are the fiercest warriors you will ever come across. However I, we, are not from Luna Eclipse" Alyse said with confidence. It wasn't a secret anymore. I had already confessed this to Gunner. But I don't know if I'm ready for where this conversation is leading. I want to tell Zelena the truth, and I have every intention of doing so. But I had hope to have a little time to practice what I would say to her first.

"You're not?" Zelena asked, sitting up straight. Clearly Alyse had piqued her interest.

"Nope".

"So what pack are you from then?"

"We don't have a pack. We are Omega's"

"You are?" Zelena asked, her voice raising an octave,

"Yes, Zelena" Alyse giggled. Zelena thought for a moment, lowering her eyes to the table. She looked back up at Alyse and tilted her head to the side,

"Gunner told me about Omega's. They don't have a pack or an Alpha. So, where do you live then?" she asked slowly,

"We are roamers, we don't have a home in one place" Alyse answered with a curt nod.

"But then what do you do? Like, where do you sleep and all that?"

"Roamers, roam. We visit packs all over the world, and with their permission, we stay on their territory for a little while. Or we camp in the wilderness. Sometimes, not often, we seek out empty or abandoned houses" Alyse explained. I like that she is so comfortable talking with Zelena about this. I like that Zelena seems so interested in our lifestyle.

"Don't you get sad or lonely, not having a home?" Zelena questioned as she leaned back into Gunner's embrace,

"Roaming isn't for everyone. It can get tiresome, and it can be sad sometimes, not having a place to call home. But I am never lonely, not with Nae at my side" Alyse smiled up at me and squeezed my thigh again. I gazed at her beautiful green eyes and ran my finger down the tip of her nose.

"Aww, you're Mates" Zelena said with awe as she smiled at us adoringly.

"We are" I answered, while keeping my eyes on Alyse. I looked back to Zelena, who had her eyes closed and her head leaning back on Gunner's shoulder. Gunner held his arm around her waist with his hand spread across her stomach. The other one twirled a tendril of her hair around his finger. It filled my heart with love that they were okay again. After his crazy stint and attacking her, it seems like it is all in the past now. But this darkness inside Gunner will have to be eliminated. I will help him do it. I was trained for it.

"Did you eat enough?" Gunner whispered into Zelena's ear. I don't think he meant for us to hear, and I didn't mean to eavesdrop. Zelena placed her hand over his on her stomach and nodded. The way in which they both held their hands there, so gently and so protectively. It had me sitting up straighter in my seat. I snapped my eyes to their hands, then to Gunner, then Zelena, and back to their hands. Zelena scoffed down that steak like it was the greatest thing on Earth. She had an animalistic, wildness to her when she ate. I know that feeling, I experienced something just like many years ago. Gunner attacked her out of the blue, he had been acting overly possessive and protective, according to his family. I remember someone else once acting like that with me. Alyse sat forward and squeezed my thigh. I turned to her, and she had a knowing look on her face, she had already put the pieces together. I turned to Zelena and deadpanned,

"You're pregnant" I blurted out. Zelena choked and sat up straight. Her wide eyes finding mine immediately.

"Excuse me?" she squeaked. Gunner snaked his arm further around her waist and pulled her into him closer. A protective and possessive motion. Something I remember all too well with Micha. His protective instincts increased tenfold. He was a warrior, so he was already very protective. But the second he could sense his pup, he wouldn't let anyone get close to me without a warning growl. Gunner's an Alpha, so his instincts would be higher still.

"I said you're pregnant. Am I correct?" I asked her. My heart was thundering inside my chest, I was worried they would be able to see it beating against my chest cavity, or even hear the heavy drumming. Zelena was silent, while Gunner peered at me over Zelena's shoulder. He had his mouth and nose pressed into the back of her neck.

"I uh... I'm..." she stuttered, while her eyes flicked back and forth between mine and Alyse's anxious gazes. Zelena turned her head to look at Gunner. She didn't ask him out loud, and it didn't appear like they were flashing, the question was held in her stare. Gunner closed his eyes and very slowly nodded his head once, giving his permission for Zelena to continue. Zelena turned back to Alyse and I and shrugged her shoulders.

"I am, yes" she said softly. My smile split my face in two. I'm going to be a grandma! I had to dig my fingers into the cushion of the booth seat, just to stop myself from jumping up and embracing her in an all-consuming hug. I can't believe I'm going to be a grandma! I couldn't move, because I didn't trust my body. I couldn't talk, because I didn't trust my voice. All I could do was stare at my child with my ridiculously huge smile.

"Congratulations Alpha, Luna. We are so unbelievably overjoyed for you both" Alyse said, her voice thick with emotion.

"Thank you" Zelena breathed out and melted back into Gunner's chest.

"How far along are you, do you know?" Alyse asked,

"Uh not sure, I haven't seen a doctor yet. But I'd guess a couple of weeks" Zelena answered. Then her eyes went wide and she grasped her stomach.

"Gunner" she whispered as her head snapped around to look at him,

"I need to see a doctor. Galterio, he tried to hurt him, we need to make sure that he's okay" she rushed out. The panic in her voice was evident, as was it clear from the way her small body began to shake. My lips curled back into a snarl, and I could feel a growl starting to bubble in the pit of my stomach. That bastard tried to kill her pup, my grandpup. He is lucky that he's dead, because I want to resurrect him just so that I can murder him myself. My anger was on a steadily increasing burn. Alyse squeezed my thigh and pressed her lips to the side of my face and flashed me,

Calm down, love. He's dead now

I want to hurt him, really fucking hurt him

Well, you can't, he's already gone. Let go of the rage, she needs love right now, not anger

Gunner cupped Zelena's cheek and pulled her head to meet his lips. He kissed the tip of her nose and pressed his forehead to hers.

"The pup is fine, you still have your cravings, and your healing ability is still diminished. None of that would have been happening if he succeeded" Gunner told her in a soft soothing tone. The love her showed her was beautiful. In that moment it made me miss Micha. I have Alyse, and I'm grateful and appreciative of her. But my pregnancy and those experiences were shared with Micha, and I would give anything for him to be here to meet his grandpup. Zelena looked back over and caught me staring with my eyes starting to water. She averted her gazed and looked uncomfortable. Of course she is, a person that she doesn't know, a stranger, is staring at her in awe. I lowered my head and began to fiddle with the locket around my neck.

"You said 'he'. You wanted to make sure that 'he's' alright. You're having a boy?" Alyse spoke up, breaking the awkward silence that was currently sitting over all of us. Zelena chuckled and I lifted my gaze back to her face. She is even more beautiful when she smiles.

"I don't know for sure, it just feels like a 'he' you know" she said as she rubbed her hands over her stomach. Gunner growled lowly and buried his face into her hair. Such an Alpha male.

"Please don't say anything, we haven't told Gunner's parents yet. We haven't told anyone yet" Zelena pleaded looking up to meet Alyse's gaze.

"Of course, our lips are sealed" Alyse smiled at her,

"Roe is going to be so excited" Alyse said with a chuckle. To that Gunner groaned and Zelena laughed.

"Don't remind me, she's suffocating enough as it is. Now we're giving her a grandpup, she's going to be impossible to live with" Gunner grumbled with a roll of his eyes.

"Hey!" Zelena snapped as she hit his chest,

"Be grateful. She loves you. You should be more appreciative that you actually have a mother around to act all crazy and obsessive over you" she chastised him. Her words felt like a knife to the heart. I pressed my hand over my chest, my way of trying to hold the pieces of my heart together. I wish I could have been there to suffocate and obsess over her as she grew. But I'm here now, and I'm going to make damn sure that she knows how much I love her. I looked up to see Gunner's piercing gaze scrutinising my blank face. I looked to Zelena, and she had a crestfallen expression. She may have been able to hide her envy from Gunner, but I could see the sadness and longing all over her face.

"Zelena..." I whispered. I want to tell her, I need to tell her.

"I'm sorry, I'm sorry. I didn't mean to put a downer on the conversation" Zelena said as she waved her hands through the air and placed a forced smile on her face.

"I guess I'm just emotionally exhausted you know. That whole thing with Galterio and Artemis, being kidnapped and finding out I'm pregnant, and that weird ass prophecy stuff. I'm just drained, I'm sorry" she said dismissively. The prophecy, she knows about that. How?

"You know about the prophecy?" I barked out. I didn't mean for it to come out so harsh and abrupt, but she surprised me. I sat up straight and stared at Zelena intently.

"The thing about choosing between two Mates?" she asked me. She was wary of my hard face and curious expression, as she should be. Gunner growled possessively and pulled her into him.

"What are you talking about?" he growled at me, or her, I'm not sure who he was asking. Zelena looked to me, waiting to see if I was going to answer the question. I'm not. I want to hear what she thinks she knows first.

"Artemis was helping Galterio because of some kind of prophecy. Apparently, I am meant to choose between two mates, one good and one bad. Galterio thought that he was the other choice, besides you. That's why he..." Zelena paused, she had a faraway look in her eye, and her hand flew up to the mating mark on her shoulder,

"That's why he marked me. He was trying to get rid of our bond, so that I would have to pick him. But it didn't work".

Gunner lifted Zelena from his lap and stood up. He paced back and forth in front of the booth with his hands fisted at his sides. The anger coming off him was thick. It hung in the air, threatening to choke us. Zelena sat still and quiet, watching Gunner stomp back and forth. Without warning, Gunner roared and sent his fist flying through the wall. On instinct, I jumped to my feet and placed myself between Gunner and Zelena, knees bent and claws out, ready to attack. I growled a warning and eyed the angry Alpha. He turned to me and snarled, his blue eyes were gone, and black orbs had taken their place. This was no longer Gunner, this was the darkness in control.

"You knew about this?" he growled at me. I didn't respond just nodded my head slowly.

"There's a prophecy about her and you didn't think to fucking tell me!" he roared. Whisps of black smoke began to seep from his fingers, wrapping around his hands and crawling up his arms. I have read and heard so much about the darkness, about how it works and how it affects the being it controls. But I have never before seen it in action, and as incredible as it was to witness, I know just how dangerous it is. And how dangerous it can make the person wielding it.

"Gunner, please don't! Remember what she said Gunner! You have to let it go" Zelena screamed from behind me. I could feel her close to my back, peering at Gunner from over my shoulder. But I have no doubt that Alyse is keeping her there. I wondered what she meant by that, who said what? I can contemplate that later, first the Alpha. Gunner looked at Zelena and growled, his lips curled back and his canines extended. I stepped to my right, blocking his view of her and forcing his dark eyes to snap back to me.

"The prophecy is dead" I said with a level voice. Part of the training, speak slow and calm. Do not whisper and do not yell. The darkness feeds on fear and sorrow.

"Then why does she wear another male's mark, why did that fucker think he could Mate her?" he yelled and took a step closer. I stood to my full height and crossed my arms over my chest. Remain passive, do not attack and do not show violence.

"Artemis told me before I killed him, he thought the prophecy spoke of two Mates for the Goddess. He obviously conveyed this to the Origin Alpha" I answered him. My voice still level and even. The back whisps were slowly be drawn back down his arms and into his hands. His anger was still fresh and overbearing, but the darkness was withdrawing.

"And does it? Does she have two Mates?" Gunner growled,

"She does not. Once a True Mate bond is formed, neither Were can claim another, or in turn be claimed by anyone else. There is only you".

"How do you know all this?" Zelena's soft voice spoke from behind me. I looked over Gunner's arms, the black smoke was gone. His eyes still held darkness, but blue was the dominating colour. He is back. For now. I turned around, keeping my half my body still facing Gunner in case the darkness came back out. I looked over Zelena, Alyse had her arms wrapped around Zelena's shoulders, keeping her from going to Gunner. Just like I expected. Both the women were kneeling on the booth seats, directly behind me.

"I was taught this as a child and continued to learn about it until my early twenties" I told her. She looked at me with such curiosity and fascination. If she keeps looking at me like, I will tell her anything and everything. I will hand her the secrets of the world on a silver platter. I looked back over at Gunner, he was calm again. No signs of black smoke and the scent of anger had decreased significantly.

"You may go to your Mate, Goddess" I said as I stepped to the side. Alyse let her go and Zelena jumped off the seat in into Gunner's arms. He lifted her up and she wrapped herself around him, just like before. Gunner nuzzled his face into her neck and hair, while Zelena ran her fingers through his hair. They need each other, desperately, their connection is unlike anything I have ever seen before. He won't be able to dispel the darkness without her, I can see that now. After a moment of them embracing each other, Gunner placed Zelena back on her feet. He held her in front of him with his arms around her waist and hands on her stomach.

"You know about this prophecy?" Zelena asked me,

"I do" I answered.

"How do you know so much about all this, about me?" She looked at me intently, those bright golden eyes burning into me, eating away at my resolve. I shifted my eyes to Gunner, who was also watching me. I held his stare, silently asking if I could tell her the truth. He nodded his head and rested his chin on Zelena's head.

"It's time" he said.

"Time, time for what?" Zelena asked confused.

"Zelena, there is something I have been meaning to tell you" I said softly. Alyse came to my side and slipped her hand into mine. I was so relieved to feel her support, to have her at my side. I looked down at her and she was smiling back up at me. She nodded her head and gestured to Zelena. She is just as keen for her to learn the truth. I looked back to those beautiful eyes, their deep golden depths were staring at me, waiting.

"What do you know? Tell me please" Zelena rushed out, she was starting to panic.

"Zelena, I do know about this prophecy. I heard it for the first time when I myself was pregnant. I know all about you, your history, your ancestry line, and your Triple Goddess abilities. I know all of this, because a long time ago it was once my history too" I said slowly,
"I don't understand what you mean" she said as she tipped her head to the side,
"Zelena, Sweetheart, I'm your mother".

Epilogue

Zelena

My brain is ready to explode. Firstly, I found out that I'm pregnant, which of course I'm thrilled about now. Admittedly, I was terrified at first, but it's hard to be scared when so many people around you are happy and excited. Their excitement has rubbed off on me. Roe has already started arranging a Litter Party, which is apparently like a baby shower. She hasn't let me see it, but I know she is working on a nursery as well. Nat has been a constant at my side. Always happy to talk babies and throw ridiculous baby names at me. Something is going on with Nat, I can't put my finger on it yet. She has been avoiding talking about herself, which is weird and alarming all on its own. Each time I try to talk about her, she swings the topic back around to me or babies. Maybe she is just lonely, with Smith taking on most of the Beta duties, he is barely around. I understand if that's what is bothering her, I miss him too. Smith is my closest friend and he always knows how to cheer me up. But if it's not about Smith, then I don't know. I'll get it out of her eventually though.

Second, Cole died, along with forty-three of our fighters, plus another sixty-five from the allied packs. Tri-Moon took a huge hit. I feel each and every one of their deaths personally. I can't shake the feeling that it's all my fault. They went there for me, and they died trying to get me back. Their deaths are mine to carry. The funerals lasted a week and the whole village was in mourning. Another placard has been fitted to the stone in the memorial garden. But Cole got his own stone. A pure white marble rock, carved into the shape of a howling wolf's head. Dealing with his death has been really hard. Gunner has been shutting me out when I try to bring him up. That first night back, when we were in bed together, it was the only time he had let me see him cry over it. I can feel how torn he is. He still holds so much anger towards Cole, he feels betrayed by him. But the guilt and sadness he feels, it's eating away at him. I just wish he would allow himself to mourn. He lost his best friend, his chosen brother, and his Beta. Holding it all in is destroying him. Which is not helping with the whole darkness thing.

This brings me to the third thing, Gunner has been told to get rid of the darkness or else Selene will take away his wolf, and our True Mate bond along with it. I'd be lying if I said I wasn't terrified. But he has been working so damn hard, and I can see the toll it is having on him. He is tired and drained most days, but he never misses an opportunity to show me love and affection. He is constantly rubbing my steadily growing baby bump. Gunner hasn't been around me a whole lot lately, not as much as before the kidnapping anyway. I think he is still worried about accidentally hurting me again. I can't push him though. Apparently, I need to keep a calm and level head when he is around. Spiking emotions is what brings out the darkness. Or so I was told. Gunner has been spending a lot of time training and meditating with Lunaya. By all accounts, she appears to be helping him. I'll hand it to her, she knows a hell of a lot about all of this, and I'm thankful that she's here. But I have been actively keeping my distance from her.

Which takes me to fourth, Lunaya. The woman who claims to be my mother. After her little confession the night in the kitchen, I have kept away from her. I don't know how to process this. With Selene returning my memories, I see her as my mother. She was the one that was there as I grew up. But now, this she-wolf is here, and I am meant to just accept her? I don't know if I can do that. I often find myself on the porch swing, it's relaxing and the pup seems to enjoy it. When I'm swinging gently back and forth, I don't feel the need to spew. Each time I sit on the swing and look out over the village, I always seem to find Lunaya. I end up watching her as she talks with the Luna Eclipse she-wolves, or with her Mate Alyse. I don't even think I am doing it intentionally, my gaze just seems to gravitate to where she is. She is a beautiful woman. Tall with defined muscles, lightly tanned skin, and dark golden hair. I look absolutely nothing like her. But there are things that she does, the way she chews on her bottom lip when she thinks, she flexes her fingers when she is frustrated, and she lowers her chin when she's angry. These are the same things that I do. I have so many questions that I need her to answer, and I know I will need to sit down and have a conversation with her eventually. Just not yet.

And finally, fifth, Tobias. He stays close to me, like he always did, but this time I am never out of his sight. I think he feels guilty about not being there when Galterio took me. Our bond is as strong as ever. I feel myself craving his presence when I am feeling stressed or upset. And like the good guardian that he is, he comes to me. Like he knows when I need him. When I'm not with Nat or Gunner, I'm with Tobias. He is almost always sitting next to me on the swing. With his long legs, he can reach the ground and so he swings us. I haven't been able to pry the details from him yet, about what happened to him in the forest. He knows that I can feel the change in him, and he hasn't denied it. But he also hasn't admitted to it yet. He feels bigger, in every sense of the word. Not only has our bond gotten stronger, but he has too. I can see the power radiating around him. It's like a pale glow under his skin. However, I seem to be the only one that can physically see it. The others can only feel the difference. I suppose he will tell me when he is ready. Or at least he better. We've got only five more days until Gunner's time is up. I have every faith that he can do it, if he hasn't already. I can feel the change in him. He may be tired and exhausted all the time, but he is far less angry. I haven't seen the darkness spill from his fingers in almost a week now. I think we'll be fine, but time will tell I suppose.

"You are staring again" Tobias's gruff voice rumbled next to me. I snapped my eyes away from where Lunaya sat talking animatedly with the Alpha from Luna Eclipse. They both leaned in close as they laughed and smiled at each other. I've come to realise that they are very close.

"Huh?" I huffed up and Tobias,

"Why don't you talk to her? Ask her all those questions that you've got swirling around inside your head, maybe then you'll feel a little less... weighed down" he said while watching Lunaya.

"I don't know. How am I meant to approach this? Do I just be like 'Hey Mum glad you're back, it's okay that you left me in the hands of a hunter that tortured me my whole life, kisses'. I don't know what to say to her" I grumbled. Self-doubt and uncertainty flooded my mind. Tobias lifted his arm and rested it over my shoulders, he pulled me to his side so that I could lay my head on his massive pectoral. I lifted my hand and intertwined my fingers with his as they hung over my shoulder. A sense of calm instantly washed away all the negative thoughts and feelings, and I took a deep breath.

"Do you honestly think that she left you voluntarily, or is that just your own self-doubt talking?" he asked gently. His voice still came out in a deep rumble.

"I don't know. No. Maybe. Ugh! Why does this have to be so hard?' I groaned and banged my head against Tobias's chest. He laughed, which vibrated through his chest, making my head bounce.

"You are the one making this hard. All you have to do is walk over there and say 'Let's talk'. You know she is dying for you to reach out to her"

"Well, she could reach out to me first, why do I have to be the one to make the first move?"

"Little One, she is giving you your space. Letting you work through your thoughts and feelings until you are ready to talk. She will not approach you because she doesn't want to push you".

"What makes you so sure?" I asked sarcastically,

"Let's just say that I know, and then leave it at that, okay" he answered me bluntly,

"But how do you know?"

"Drop it Zelena" he grumbled.

"Argh! Fine. But you'll have to tell me sooner or later you know".

"Later it is then". We went back to silently swinging on the chair, watching the village life move on around us. With my head on Tobias's chest and the warmth of his body washing over me, his steady heartbeat was slowly lulling me to sleep. That peace was broken when a group of wolves came running through the village, stopping at the bottom of the porch steps. I stood up and walked to the railing, only for Tobias to push me behind him and growl down at the gathered wolves. The largest of the group, a brownish orange wolf, changed form and stood up. I recognise this guy, he's the same age as Gunner and me, and he's a friend of Gunner's. He had been making his way up in the ranks over the past few months. Daniel, I think his name is. I stepped around Tobias and looked down at the muscular Were. His blonde hair sat in a shaggy mess of curls atop his head, and his dark hazel eyes looked back up at me. He was quite tall, with a slim frame sporting a lot of defined muscles.

"You're Daniel, right?" I asked him. He bowed his head and placed his hand over his heart.

"Yes, Luna. We were briefly introduced once before. I am a scout, but I'm in training to become a commander" he said before he stood back up again,

"Yes, I remember you. What's going on?" I asked as I gestured to the rest of the wolves that also started to change back to their human form. We had attracted a lot of attention around the village, and a small crowd was beginning to form. Among those was Lunaya and the Alpha Hina.

"I bring important news, Luna. Where is the Alpha?" Daniel said quickly, a slight spark of panic filled his tone, though he tried to hide it. I could feel the urgency from him, this must be important.

"In his office. Come" I said as I turned on my heels. I stopped short and turned back around. I ran my eyes over Lunaya and made a snap decision.

"You too" I said pointing at her and Alpha Hina,

"Both of you, come". With that, I turned and headed into the house. I didn't bother to see if they were following me, I just assumed. I got to the closed door of Gunner's office and knocked once, pushing open the heavy door before he had the chance to answer. Gunner was sat at his desk, leaning back in the large chair with his eyes closed. He flew upright and snarled. His angry expression quickly dropped when he saw me walk in,

"Zee?" he said confused, then his eyes turned to the group that was following behind me. I looked over my shoulder to see Tobias right at my back, Daniel right behind him, and Lunaya and Alpha Hina not far behind him. Gunner stood up, placing his hands on his desk and letting a hard expression envelop his face.

"What's the meaning of this?" he asked firmly. Daniel stepped forward, he had snagged a pair of sweatpants from somewhere, thankfully.

"Alpha" Daniel said with a bow of his head,

"Daniel, what are you doing back? You're meant to be scouting for another week" Gunner asked him curiously. His firm voice had dropped, and he took on a more friendly tone.

"Good to see you too man" Daniel chuckled and crossed his arms over his chest. Obviously unimpressed by Daniel's casual display, Gunner frowned and growled lowly,

"What's going on?" he asked, bringing forth a little more Alpha with his question. Daniel straightened and dropped his arms,

"Right, sorry. We were up near Noatak National Preserve in the north of Alaska, looking for the Red Dogs pack, when we ran into some scouts from a pack in Russia" Daniel began,

"Russia?" Alpha Hina piped up,

"What are Russian Weres doing in Alaska?" she asked.

"They were looking for the Triple Goddess" Daniel answered. This brought on a deadly growl from not only Gunner but Tobias and Lunaya as well.

"And what did you tell them?" Gunner growled at his scout,

"I told them we were doing the same thing" he said confidently,

"And?" Gunner pushed for more information,

"And, they said that they heard she was somewhere in Canada, but not sure where exactly. We played dumb, pretended that we didn't know that, and then manipulated them into telling us more" Daniel said smugly.

"And what did they tell you?" I asked him as I moved to perch myself on the edge of Gunner's desk.

"There have been attacks on multiple packs popping up around the central and northern regions of rural Russia. Quiet packs, in the middle of nowhere, keeping to themselves. And then boom, wiped out with no survivors and no idea who is doing it".

"Hunters" Lunaya growled lowly. The disdain in her voice was thick and filled the air of the office. I have obvious reasons not to like hunters, I was tortured by one for eighteen years. But I couldn't help but wonder where Lunaya's deep-seated hatred stemmed from.

"Maybe" Daniel nodded,

"What else do you know?" Gunner demanded gruffly,

"If it is hunters, they must have some sort of new weapon. The Russian scouts said that the Weres had died of suffocation" Daniel answered him without hesitation.

"All of them?" Lunaya questioned,

"All of them" Daniel confirmed with a nod,

"You're sure?" Alpha Hina asked him.

"No, I'm not sure, this is only what the scouts told us. We wanted to bring the news back here, before venturing into Russia" Daniel told her over his shoulder. I looked at Gunner, who was deep in thought, then at Tobias, who was also contemplating the new news. Lunaya's eyes were cast down to the floor, but I could still see the pensive expression on her face. She was worried. As if she felt me watching her, her gaze lifted to meet mine and for the first time, I didn't look away. We stared at each other for a moment, each of us trying to read the other. Her eyes lit up with hope as I stared at her, but the deep worry lines on her forehead told a different story. She knows something, maybe something about these attacks. But why isn't she sharing it? Isn't it in all of our best interests to share the information, to work together to figure it out. Why would she be holding back?

"What do you know?" I asked her firmly. She held my gaze for a moment longer before answering,

"Nothing" she said softly.

"You're lying" I snapped and stood up straight. Gunner made his way around the desk and slipped his arm around my waist.

"I am not lying to you, Sweetheart" she cooed quietly,

"Don't call me that, you haven't earned the right to call me that" I snapped angrily, I fisted my hands and dug my nails into my palms. I could feel my anger rising.

"Zelena" Gunner growled lowly. His grip on my hip tightened and I winced. I looked up to him and saw the black wisps of smoke, swirling around his eyes. Whatever darkness was still left in him, it was feeding on the anger I was exuding. Tobias ripped me from Gunner's arms and a thunderous growl roared from between his sharp teeth.

Lunaya jumped forward and placed herself between Tobias and Gunner.

"Stop! He needs calm, this is only feeding the beast" she pleaded, her voice level and yet still firm. Alpha Hina grabbed hold of one of Tobias's arms and snapped her head to Daniel, "Give us a hand here scout" she growled at him. Daniel was no match for Tobias, and neither was Alpha Hina, but still, they both grabbed hold of him in an attempt to drag him from the office.

Go please, you're not helping!

I flashed as I looked at him with sad eyes. Tobias's glare shifted from Gunner to me, and he softened. Reluctantly, he conceded and let himself be dragged from the office. Once the door was closed behind them, I whirled on Lunaya. I took a deep breath and swallowed down the anger that I so desperately wanted to unleash on my supposed mother. Be calm, I told myself. I forced a smile and glared at the she-wolf. "I'm sorry" I gritted out. I walked past her and curled myself into Gunner's side. His head dipped down, and he brushed his lips to the top of my head. His hand once again found my stomach and he rubbed the area in a slow circle, something I have realised brings him comfort.

"You don't owe me an apology. If anything, I owe you one" she said calmly, offering me a sad smile. I could see that my actions were hurting her. And that's not what I wanted to do, at least I don't think it is. Maybe deep down I want to punish her. I was alone and hurting, even though I knew what happened to me wasn't really her fault. Tobias is right, we need to talk.

"Lunaya, I think it's time you and I have a long talk" I said adamantly.

"Yes, I agree" she answered with a curt nod.

Zelena's story does not end here.

Continue reading for a sneak preview of

Part 3

A Path

Of

Peaceful Destruction

WG-02

A Few Weeks Ago.

I walked through the now empty village. The sun was setting in the distance, painting the clouds in the sky in hues of pink and orange. The warmth that the sun offered was slowly drifting away with its light. I prefer the cold, my body is accustomed to the frigid rattling of my frozen bones. The cold is better suited for my icy heart. I walked up the steps of a small hut and pushed open the door. I stood in the doorway and closed my eyes, letting my other senses take control. I could hear a single heartbeat, thumping erratically from inside the small home. I stepped through the doorway and stood in the middle of the living space. The lounge room, dining room and kitchen were all in the same area. A well-worn brown couch sat against the wall, with a small wooden dining table against the other wall. The kitchen was old and held a small, rusted fridge and a wood fire stove. This is definitely one of the poorer packs I've found. At least this place has power though. Once again, I closed my eyes and listened. The heartbeat was coming from the back area. I lifted my nose and sniffed. A male, only a young one, his wolf hasn't been born yet. I followed the scent and the sound of his fear filled heartbeat to a bedroom. I slowly pushed open the door and filled the doorway. This little cat and mouse game excites me. I love the chase, the hunt. Evoking fear in others is my happy drug. I giggled and stepped into the room.

"I know you're in here, why don't you come out and play" I said with a cheery tone. The sound of his heartbeat accelerated, and I turned my head to the source of the sound. A small wooden wardrobe sat beside a single bed with a blue bedspread. I walked over to the wardrobe and knocked twice.

"Vykhodi, vykhodi, gde by ty ni byl" (Come out, come out, wherever you are) I sang and gripped the cupboard door handle. I pulled the door open and flung back the coats hanging inside.

"Gotcha!" I laughed. The boy was curled into a ball, pressing himself into the back of the cupboard. Whisps of blonde hair poked out from the faded blue beanie on his head. It was summer here, but the air was still cold. The brown knitted jumper the boy wore was littered with holes. I grabbed the boy's shoulder and pulled him out of the cupboard and into the room. He cried out and tried to run past me, but I gripped his arm and knelt down in front of him so that we were at eye level.

"Tsk, tsk, tsk" I clicked my tongue as I waved my finger back and forth in his face. The boy was crying and struggling in my hold, but he was no match for me.

"Gde Troynaya Boginya, malen'kiy mal'chik?" (Where is the Triple Goddess, little boy?)

"Ya ne znayu" (I don't know) he wailed. I huffed and grabbed both of his shoulders. The tips of my nails dug into his skin, and he screamed and struggled even more.

"You wouldn't lie to me, would you?" I asked him sternly. He stared at me blankly with tears streaming down his young face. Judging by the stupid look on his face, the little shit doesn't understand English.

"Ne lgi mne" (Don't lie to me) I growled at him and flashed my sharp teeth.

"Ya ne znayu" (I don't know) the boy cried again and continued to struggle in my grasp. I grow bored of this insolence. I exhaled an exasperated breath and frowned at him. When I ask a simple question, I expect a simple answer.

Am I asking too much of this little stray dog? What a waste of my time this turned out to be.

"Nepravil'nyy otvet" (Wrong answer) I sighed and squeezed his shoulders, pressing my sharpened engineered claws into his flesh. The boy screamed and cried out as he tried to break out of my grip. I sucked in a lung full of air, drawing the air from the boy's lungs. He choked and gasped for air, but there was none left for him to breathe. After a minute of gaging and thrashing, the boy's body fell limp to the floor. I stood up and looked down at the dead boy. I wiped the blood from my hands onto my pants and scoffed. Disgusting maggot.

"Onto the next" I said to myself as I stepped over the boy's lifeless body.

www.ingramcontent.com/pod-product-compliance
Lightning Source LLC
Chambersburg PA
CBHW050601170726
48283CB00001B/57